Daughter of Kristos

Argevane Series, Volume 1

Andrea J. Graham

Published by Reignburst Books, 2020.

DAUGHTER OF KRISTOS

First edition. June 9, 2020.

ISBN: 978-1393615729

Written by Andrea J. Graham.

Also by Andrea J. Graham

Argevane Series
Daughter of Kristos

Life After Mars Series
Is There Life After Mars?
Life After Venus!
Life After Mercury
Life After Paradise: Into the Web Surfer Universe

Web Surfer Series
Web Surfer ANI
Nimbus Rider
Restoring: Web Surfer 3.0
Reconciling: Web Surfer 4.0

Watch for more at www.christsglory.com.

Chapter One

Serpentine roars split the stifling night air. Hosanni Kristekon bolted up from her feather pallet, trembling in the dark. Her heartbeat thundered. She took a deep breath. Feral dragons weren't attacking. Rather, her village's own dragons sounded the alarm of trespassers on Mammy's land.

Small comfort. The dragons were right. Only wolves merely shaped like human beings prowled at night. Especially on a moonless night.

In the center of the upper room, Father rose from his pallet, his form but a shadow. Beside him, Mother's pallet lay empty. She must be visiting the sick or a woman in labor. Father's steps pattered on the cedar floor. He clambered down the ladder leading to the kitchen. "Stay here, Hosanni!"

Why did he have to say that? How could she ever resist temptation now? She nibbled her lip. Was curiosity truly the root of all evil? So that had driven the first woman's husband to open the Forbidden Portal and let in Eve's son. So Cain had brought evil in along with him. Why would God gift her with such hunger to explore the unknown only to forbid it?

But she must honor Father as she would Mother, in her absence. Hosanni sighed and dropped back onto her pallet. The dragons' baying gnawed her.

Through the glass dome roof above her, the stars struggled alone against the darkness. Could light banish darkness, if no one ever dared to tread out into the night? Couldn't it also be said she merely sought the virtue Truth?

She sneaked a glance toward the round ladder hole, slightly blacker than the rest of the upper room. Emi their God, the lady of Heaven's vast armies, had promised to send the Spirit of Truth upon a woman of Hosanni's family. Even she could become Lady Veritas. Though the Veritas child might find it easier to obey her father. Maybe she could wiggle around his law.

Hosanni peered at the dark lump on the pallet positioned clear on the other side of her parents' empty pallets. Snores rose as the dragons' roaring faded. Her foster brother could sleep through anything. "Korban."

He moaned and resumed snoring.

Fine, she would satisfy her own curiosity. She padded barefoot across the hardwood floor, climbed down the cedar ladder nailed against the wall, and felt her way over the kitchen's cement floor in pitch blackness. Groping, she found the brass door knob and raced out into the too-warm breeze.

The light of a distant gas street lamp led the way to the invaders' asphalt highway. Yellow-eyed, hulking shadows as long as a woman was tall hissed in the direction of the light. The bipedal, sharp-toothed land dragons crouched. Draca's tiny, three-fingered arms pressed into the dirt, ready to pounce on the enemy's servant. Hosanni patted a pebbly head twice as big as a human's and squatted in the dry, dead grass.

An owl hooted from the pine trees.

Father stood too close to the street lamp to make out much more than the outline of his crossbow. He pointed it at a stout pink man dressed in the invader's dark blue military uniform—a knee tunic, dress jacket, leather boots, and an effeminate skirt called a kilt.

The pink Romini soldier spread his hands. "I am only trying to help you."

Hosanni blinked. Few bothered to learn her people's tongue.

"You'd help us by showing up uninvited in the night?" Father snorted and lowered the crossbow. "Be grateful our dragons chased you off our property rather than eating you."

The pink man bowed. "How right you are, milord the king."

Father stepped back toward Hosanni's position. "I am but a mere man. My wife is the heir. And she makes no claim to be the Kristos of Diakrinth."

"So you say to the Idahoans loyal to the Union of the Nations. But I know Kristos was a king who served his wife, the queen, and their mother, the high queen. What your people hail you as is treason, Kristos Havan."

Hosanni beamed, puffing out her chest. The traitors were the House of Romin, which reigned over the western half of their entire known world. The invaders' "Idaho" was the Children of Diakrinth's Promised Land.

Father folded his arms. "What do you want?"

The pink man gazed in the direction of the fields hidden in the shadows of night. "Your crops are failing. Your wares aren't selling. Soon your children

2

will be starving. And I have an unpaid tax notice to serve you." He handed Father a slip of paper that must've been intended for Mother. "You only make things harder on yourselves by forcing us to send tax collectors chasing after you every harvest."

"I'm sure you are brokenhearted," Father said with a sarcastic edge.

Hosanni gaped. Father, speaking like a wolf? The dry grass irritated her shins. She drew her legs around and scratched them.

The pink man asked, "How would you like to never have to pay a dime to the Union again? And greatly improve the ability of your village to feed—"

Father guffawed. "Feed the children left with their siblings' blood?"

"You provide for the welfare of all of your children by selling us a few."

"Amen, amen, how can you justify that, when the Erini had enslaved your race, before our peoples drove them back east together? A pink man ought to appreciate that the path of salvation forbids selling people like we're bison."

"But your women enslave their husbands and their children."

"Amen, children and unmarried women are servants of their mothers, as men are servants of their wives. But ask a mother to place a price on her child, and she'll require your blood for them. We gift our children when they marry, and we lend them on other occasions—to our own people. Giving a daughter to foreign idolaters means forfeiting her soul. This assembly would rather bury all our children than betray a single child to Hades." Father pivoted and marched toward Hosanni's position.

"One child," the pink man called after him. "Surrender Princess Hosanni, and the scroll of the genealogy of Kristos, and I will personally cover on the morrow your entire village's taxes for the next forty years."

She gasped. Weakness washed over her trembling body. She forced air into her lungs and released the breath slowly. Father wouldn't let any harm come to her.

"Bring her out to me tonight. Not even your wife will have to know."

Father whirled back to the pink man. "I would sooner get my shofar and sound the call to war. Threaten my daughter again, and you will regret it."

Hosanni beamed and clapped. "Yay, Pappy!"

He growled. "Get out of here!"

Oops. She shrunk behind the dragons and stroked the closest pebbly back about the shoulder blades.

The pink man coughed. "Sir, the days of Erin's lawless brutality are over. If I take her without your consent, my king will nail me to a tree. But if you can't pay, the tax collectors will seize what you owe at the edge of the sword. Their plans for your beautiful daughter will be far worse than mine, if I forget what Diakrinthian tongues hail you as, King Consort Havan."

"Don't worry. I'll pay King Felippo Romin's blood money. Count on it."

HOSANNI SKIPPED DOWN to the river. She kept her gaze on the path and politely off of the men bathing. The birds chirped greetings to the resurrected sun, as if to scold her for sneaking out of the women's daily assembly. She deserved a few precious moments alone with Korban.

She kicked the lavender dust. Stupid Romini. Her mother would find out what had upset the dragons. She'd be constantly watched, forever.

Hmm, her lingering may make the bathing men uncomfortable. That may get her into trouble. Better hide. She slipped in amongst the thick cluster of fir trees growing by the riverbank. After waiting to the count of sixty, she crawled out of her cover and hid again behind a boulder. She curled up and watched the path. Korban should return from his bath any minute.

Her legs threatened to cramp. Where was he? Had she missed him?

A maiden gasped.

Hosanni leaped into a defensive crouch. She glanced between her cousin Irene and the young men scrubbing themselves while standing naked ankle-deep in the river. Irene's twin plum-colored braids flapped about, touching the skirt of her sage palla as she stomped toward Hosanni.

One of the clean-shaven strangers glanced her way. The bar of lye soap halted over his chest. The soap's whiteness contrasted against lilac skin a hair darker than her and Irene. He glared at Hosanni. She shook herself and pulled her gaze past them before lowering it. She hadn't ogled at their nudity, but everyone would think otherwise.

Across the river, withered potato fields struggled to survive under the Heavens that refused to rain. The surrounding pine-cloaked Rocky Mountains stood as sentinels.

Irene reached up, grabbed a fist full of Hosanni's never-shorn hair, and dragged her away from the riverbank. Bent over low, Hosanni tripped and stumbled along a pace behind. Though shorter than her, Irene was four years older than herself.

Hosanni shrieked, "Cousin, stop! You'll rip my hair out!"

"I hope Ravane Aletheia shears you!"

"Mam will shear you if you rip one hair out." Being the daughter of the village magistrate, healer, and clergywoman all in one had its advantages.

Irene released her. Hosanni fled up the path by her village's thirsty potato fields toward the round-cornered community barn. She pressed her left hand to her cerulean palla so the wind wouldn't toss up the robe's calf-length skirt and expose her knee-length underpants. With her other hand, she clutched the daisy brooch fastening her wrap dress.

Older cousins were the worst. Hosanni snorted. At least she didn't have sisters. Then again, no elder sister would dare to constantly bat her eyes at a young man she well knew Hosanni fancied. Unlike Irene.

The wind carried Irene's shout to her, "You are in big trouble, Hosanni!"

We'll see who's in trouble. You were sneaking down to look for Korban, another attempt to steal him from me. "I'll have you caned this time, Irene!"

"Come here, and I'll cane the impertinence out of you, draca!"

Hosanni slid to a halt. Calling her a dragon was like calling her a man. Hosanni spun and stood with her feet shoulder-width apart, hands pressed together with their tips touching her nose, prepared to dance as Diakrinth's daughters did. "I dare you."

Irene tossed her braids over her shoulders. She charged for a flying kick.

Hosanni gulped. She shouldn't have challenged a maiden who had been dancing four years longer than she had.

Father dashed out from the barn with his ankle-length, indigo tunic hiked up to run. He dropped it and caught Irene's flying foot with an upward chop of his forearm, a move from one of the men's war games. His blow tossed Irene's leg up above her head.

She fell in the dirt and stared up wide-eyed.

Hosanni grinned. While the man was created to serve the woman, Father could still discipline them for their mothers, as Irene had just been reminded. Of course, any other man who behaved like Father would've been executed for his aggression, but he was only acting upon Mother's behalf.

Father pulled a blue ribbon from his shoulder-length, plum-colored hair and retied it. His violet eyes blazed above his neatly trimmed full beard.

Hosanni beamed. "She called me a man and threatened to shear me! And then she tried to kill me!"

Irene trembled. "Ravaner, let me explain."

Father grunted. "Go and tell your own father, child."

Irene scrambled to her feet and ran toward the carpenter's shed behind Aunt Juris's round, stucco home. The sun glinted off the glass dome roofs on the homes of their village.

Hosanni hugged Father's thick torso. "My hero! Oh, you were so brave."

Father laid a calloused hand on her shoulder. "Daughter, I want the truth. And I want it now."

"Irene tried to kill me!"

"That I saw. The question is why?"

"I didn't do nothing!"

Father frowned. "What nothing didn't you do?"

One of the strangers from the river jogged up, now dressed in an ankle-length, indigo tunic. From his lack of facial hair, he remained single despite being about seventeen, like Irene. He bowed to Father. "Milord, the child was spying on us as we bathed."

Child. Humph. I turned thirteen a whole four days ago.

Father sighed. "I apologize for my daughter. It won't happen again." He waved toward the house. "You are welcome in our home and at our table."

"Thank you, milord, it would be the honor of honor to eat at my king's table, but I must return to my village."

Father raised his hand. "Emi's hand be with you. Go in peace."

The young man bowed again and scurried off without turning around.

Father took Hosanni's head in his hands. That awful disappointed look shone in his eyes. "Daughter, a young man sneaked inside the mikvah. What happened to him when he was caught?"

She sniffed. No man had any business inside the women's bathhouse. "If there's any justice, he was caned within an inch of his life."

"How many lashes should I give you, then?"

Hosanni produced tears. "Oh, you wouldn't! Not for such a little thing."

Father released her, laughing. "I thought you said that you deserved to be

6

beaten with many stripes?"

"Oh, but they're just men. Are not men more the equal of a dragon than a woman? And some dracas are said to be more intelligent than a man."

Pain filled Father's eyes. "What is Pappy?"

"Kristos. The king of Diakrinth, proud and true and wise and brave."

Father tugged on his indigo tunic's neck. "Look again. Pappy is a man. I bathe in that river same as the men who'd gladly follow me to their deaths, if I blew the shofar."

Hosanni stared at her sandals. Father's spies always reported the same. Too many enemy soldiers. And too well trained. Not a pleasant truth. Romin could yet send his men after her with swords. She sniffled. "I'm sorry, Pappy. Forgive me."

Father hugged her and kissed her forehead. "Peace be with you."

He put a hand on her back. "Daughter, do you realize Korban bathes here with the young men of his natal village?"

Admitting that might expose her. Hosanni blinked innocently. "Really?"

"Be glad you missed him. Next time, I'll tell Aletheia, and she'll send him back to his mother. Do you understand me?"

Hosanni gasped. "There's too much work for one man."

"We'd do what we did before a son was lent to us. Manage."

She shuddered. That had relegated a princess to carrying stinky earth closet bowls to the compost heap.

"Do you realize why my sister lent Korban to us last year?"

Did Pappy? "It wasn't because you needed the help?"

"That was why we accepted. Young men Korban's age are dangerous to girls your age."

"He's only fourteen."

"And shows no interest in courting. Why do you think that is?"

Hosanni giggled. She covered her mouth. They'd both get in big trouble if Korban got caught courting her. Before she'd be eligible, she would be nearly Irene's age—and Korban would be an old batchelor.

Father took Hosanni's head in his hands. "Amen, amen. You could've been raped. And this is on top of disobeying me last night. Your bat mitzvah wasn't merely a fun party. It's time to put away the childhood antics and start behaving like a responsible maiden. If you continue defying us, you will be suspected of lunacy. You know our only cure."

Sending the accursed to Hades. She gulped. "I'll behave. Honest."

"You'd better. You were outnumbered and behaving provocatively. Treat men like human beings or we'll start acting like dumb animals. Or do you not know why the son of Eve called Draca and her wild cousins dinosaurs?"

"Dreadful lizards! Who gave Cain the right to slander dragons so?"

Father chuckled. "He feared the dragon, but he did not respect her. As a dragon is a most dangerous beast, if you don't respect her, so it is with men."

"Yes, Pappy." Hosanni sighed, her eyes respectfully downcast.

HOSANNI PLACED HER back toward the upper room's ladder in their circular stucco kitchen, which occupied the entire first floor. She reclined on a suede pillow chair stuffed with pine shavings, twirling her pencil as she stared at the math book open before her on their legless, straw-woven kitchen table.

The temperature creeped to uncomfortably warm. Not fair. It shouldn't be so hot when the round cedar door was shut and the sun crystals in all five windows twinkled a bright, cooling blue.

Mother reached into the iron oven snug between the lower cabinets. She pulled out her flat, round, cooking sun crystal. It glowed orange. Mother set the heated sun crystal under a prepared tea kettle. The sky blue stone counter curved clear from the door to the empty upper cistern above the earth closet area. The toilet bowl full of purple earth lay opposite the door.

Bridal ivory chopsticks held Mother's hair up in a matron's coiffure. She twirled toward Hosanni. The crow's-feet about Mother's eyes testified, at age forty-five, Mother should've been an aggie—a grandmother.

Mother pulled her two-inch locket out of her beige palla and fingered the Garnet of Kristos's smooth plum surface, where a six-ray star would appear in sunlight. Mother did this whenever she was troubled—or debating whether to let Hosanni off her punishment.

Hosanni lowered her head. "If I cannot study next door with Aunt Juris, may I at least help you with the noon meal?" She grimaced. "I'll apologize to Irene for provoking her."

8

"You have to do that already."

Why did Mother have to remember that? It wasn't fair.

At noon, Father and Korban came in sweaty from working in the village's fields. They crowded around the washbasin beneath the upper cistern at the back of the house. In the middle of the table, Mother set a family platter piled with two meals' worth of fried turkey pieces and potato wedges. She added a salad in its sky blue, ceramic bowl. Four of the ten pillows had wine set before them in a tin cup and a matching bowl with oak chopsticks.

Korban hopped onto the pillow across from Hosanni. He stole a direct glance at her from behind the dreadlocks he'd pulled over his face. The dark-skinned Erini had clearly raped his father's mothers, but Korban himself was nearly as fair as Hosanni, even if he did have coiled hair.

Mother blessed the food in the old tongue, Hebrew. Everyone grabbed a piece of turkey from the platter. She glanced across the table at Father in her bad habit of looking to him for leadership. Not that Mother would know-ingly encourage Father to commit a mortal sin by stealing her authority for himself. Mother slid her fingers along her star garnet locket's silver chain. "Hosanni, I know you've been wondering about the scroll of the genealogy of Kristos."

Hosanni eyed the family heirloom. The star garnet locket held the scroll that proved Mother's royal matrilineal descent. The pretty necklace should've been her present for her thirteenth birthday. Why did Mother keep it? Fa-ther was the one who dreamed of reclaiming the scepter.

Mother touched the star garnet. "I have decided not to give it to you."

"No!" Hosanni gasped. Why?

Korban scowled but kept his gaze downcast as a good man would. "Your pardon, milady, how does she deserve being disinherited?"

Mother shook her head. "All that I possess is yours, Hosanni, but I won't continue this nonsense. It's been nineteen centuries since the House of Erin scattered our people in the Great Dispersal. And before Erin we served Bavel, and then the Hellenes and the Latins, who fell to the Kelts' aforementioned queen. And when we had overthrown Erin, the House of Romin invaded! It's painfully obvious Emi our God meant it when she swore that we'd never wield the scepter by birthright again. The scroll is meaningless, and I won't continue my mothers' farce. Let the Garnet of Kristos be buried with me."

9

Korban jumped up and stomped out.

Father stood. He placed a hand on Mother's shoulder and squeezed. She clasped his hand, a plea shining in her eyes. Father kissed Mother's cheek and Hosanni's before he slipped out after Korban.

Tears rolled down Hosanni's cheeks. "What about Lady Veritas, Mam? How can she come, if we don't continue?"

Mother moved over to the pillow beside Hosanni and embraced her. "You need no scroll. You are my only heir."

"I need it. I do. It's prescribed in the law, the same law that cursed us."

Mother sighed. "Honey, to break the curse, I intend to give the scroll to your husband. But I don't want Korban to know that."

At least he'd give her the pretty necklace. "Why?"

"Your father and I know why we married, and we want better for you."

Hosanni squinted. "Don't you love each other?"

"It was Emi's hand that things have turned out so well. It could've easily been a disaster. I won't have young men courting my daughter because they fancy themselves a king like your father did. And as Korban does."

She'd better refocus. "But how can you even think of not giving me the scroll? The star garnet is handed down from mother to daughter, is it not?"

"Yes, daughter, but it is madness to keep doing the same thing over and over and expect different results."

"This was Pappy's idea, wasn't it?"

Mother laughed. "He made sense to this wife, love. Doesn't he always?"

"For a man, amen." Maybe she could work this to her advantage. "Mam, why would Korban wish to court me?"

"Hosanni, you're a princess. Every mother with an eligible son has asked me to allow her son to court you even though you're too young to court. Even Korban's mother lent him with the hope of marriage. That's why his aggie lent Havan to my mother, only my mother had two daughters for him to choose between, and he chose me—the sister old enough to marry him."

Aunt Juris was one year younger than Father. Hosanni nibbled her lip to keep from pouting. She'd spent all of the impertinence she could get by with already today.

DAUGHTER OF KRISTOS

AFTER LEAVING HIS WIFE and daughter, Havan "Pappy" Alethaner Kristekon stole up behind Korban. The boy stood surveying the acres of withered, dying potato plants. They'd been toting precious water to this field all morning. Was there anything in the ground to save?

There had to be. Havan Alethaner rested his hand on Korban's shoulder.

Korban glanced up at him and spat at the nearest half-dead plant. "It's hopeless, isn't it?"

"Why fight our battle?" Havan Alethaner squeezed his nephew's shoulder. "I've told you that you'll marry my daughter over my dead body."

"If you insist, milord, then may I suffer forty years a virgin."

Havan Alethaner grunted. Such folly. His son was lent by his elder sister. Nearly his own face stared back at him under the dreadlocks taming Korban's tight, thick coils. "Boy, you literally will only be permitted to marry her if I'm dead. If our *eligible* maidens are so undesirable, why do you stay?"

Korban turned and impudently stared Havan Alethaner in the eye. "Why do you hate me?"

Ouch. "Son, this is for your own good. Go home. This isn't your fight."

"Uncle." Korban slumped his shoulders. "Mother sent me here because she can't afford to feed me."

Havan Alethaner hugged his nephew. "Why didn't you tell us?"

"Mother doesn't want your help. You don't have much yourselves."

Not this year. "How do I know you're telling me the truth?"

"You don't."

Havan Alethaner sighed. His elder sister would lie rather than admit the depth of her poverty. But that still left him with the impossible choice between entrusting his daughter's honor to Korban or to Romin.

HOSANNI PILED RED BEANS, corn, cheddar wedges, and salted bison jerky on her pita using her chopsticks. She glanced to the darkening sun crystals in the windows. Mother stood and tapped each crystal three times. The sun crystals glowed a cool pastel lilac and brushed away the shadows of evening.

Mother resettled in her pillow at the straw-woven table and sent Hosanni a brave smile. "The men will be in soon."

"Why are they in such a hurry to harvest? It's not time."

Mother chewed her lip. "Eat your supper, Hosanni. You'll be fine."

The round cedar door banged open. Father and Korban stumbled in, so soaked in sweat, it looked like they'd been in a downpour.

The deadness dulling their eyes turned Hosanni's stomach. She ran into Father's arms. "Pappy?"

Father shook his head. Korban dared to draw Hosanni away and hold her hand with delicious warmth. Father said at last, "The crop has failed."

"No!" Mother embraced Father. Tears streaked her face. "Without those potatoes, we can't pay . . ." She glanced at Hosanni and shuddered.

Hosanni trembled. "You won't let the tax collectors have me, will you?"

Father glanced at Korban and nodded. "No one is being taken from us."

Mother dried her tears, furrowed her brow, and pressed her lips into a thin line. "You're right. We'll slaughter the bison and the turkeys and sell off the mastodons. We'll raise the money. Somehow."

Could the sun resurrect in the morning without the mastodons calling?

After a moment's hesitation, Father shook his head. "Milady, don't we need resources to live on? Won't it be tax time again as soon as we're likely to recover from this disaster?"

"Emi our God will provide," Mother said.

"God has. A husband with two firm hands and a strong back."

Mother's eyes widened. "The mines?"

"The mines."

Hosanni covered her mouth. But that was where they sent criminals.

Mother clung to Father. "How can I hire you out? Husbands go down into those holes, and they don't come back."

"Would you rather ask other mothers to surrender their children?"

Hosanni held her breath. Mother couldn't be considering that. No child should have to live in such a wicked, increasingly male-dominated society.

Mother kissed Father's cheek. "Come home alive."

"If Emi's hand is with us."

"No!" Hosanni hugged Korban.

Father pulled them apart. "I promised his mother I'd protect him. Your brother will stay and serve you on my behalf."

Mother clutched Father's arm. "If you didn't mean Korban, then who?"

Father sighed. "Aletheia, the lady of every house in this village is having this conversation with her husband."

Not likely. Most men wouldn't dare to ask the leading questions Mother allowed from Father. No, the other husbands would simply report the king's decision, and their wives would honor him as the queen's delegate.

HOSANNI DRAGGED HER sandal-shod feet along the path away from home, holding Father's hand. Over his shoulder, a satchel carried the belongings and the identification scroll Mother had packed. A little way ahead, Irene clung to her own father. A hint of a smile formed on Hosanni's lips. Irene supposedly came to walk Hosanni back.

The hot, dry wind blew dust and the stench of the compost heap into her nostrils. A thick line of ponderosa pines and junipers shielded the mounds of decomposing waste from view. Father lifted her chin and cupped her head in his hands. "It's time, daughter."

Tears spewed forth. She squeezed Father. "Don't go, Pappy. Please."

"I must." Father loosened her grip and held her. "To protect you."

"But why is this happening? It's only the potatoes. Is our business truly doing so poorly?"

Father sighed. "Daughter, ask your mother why, but nothing is selling."

"Why don't we give them the ivory?"

Father laughed. "We have to hide all valuables, or the tax collectors steal them and demand more. Besides potatoes, all they'll accept in your place is the silver levied against us."

"Are you sure there's nothing more we can do?"

"You can do one thing. Teach your sons their letters."

Hosanni gaped. "Why would a man need that skill in his trade?"

"Our enemy can read. A smart king could drive Romin's accursed Union from our nation once and for all."

"You are smart, Pappy. You're the smartest man I know."

Father kissed her cheek.

Hosanni sobbed and clung to him. Father was really leaving.

She took a breath and released him. "Shalom, Father. Emi's hand go with you, and Emi's hand bring us together again."

"And Emi's hand be also with you, amen." Father made the sign of the Sacrifice, drawing a triangle in the air to represent the very mountain that looked down on their village. He ran and caught up to his brother.

Slumped and sobbing, Irene made her way back to Hosanni.

"I'm sorry," Hosanni said, and hugged her cousin. She stared up the road until no trace of Father remained. Would she ever see him again?

GOD. Let there be a space between the waters, and let it divide the waters of Adam from the waters of Argevane. The space shall be called Heaven.

CHORUS. Thus God made the sky and divided the twin Earths. So the evening and the morning were the second day.

GOD. Let the waters be gathered together into one place, and let dry land appear. The gathering together of the waters upon the faces of the red Earth and the purple Earth are called Seas.

— Pauli of Denver, The Sacred History, "Creation" scene 1, lines 9-15

Chapter Two

"Da, why don't I have a mother like all the other children?" At his son's question, Ochtu MacErin glanced away from his wee six-year-old. Across from his cherry wood, pedestal dining table, sunlight beamed through silk window curtains, enough to leave the gas chandelier unlit.

He glanced over the marble statue of a kilted father lifting up an infant. He eyed his potted fern. It supposedly was from a tropical island but looked like a species that grew back home in Georgia. He eyed the finest cedar china cabinet to make its way to West California from Idaho. The people native to the nation of Idaho refused to accept the middle ages had ended ages ago and embrace industrialization, but few could match Diakrinthian craftsmanship.

And anything would do to distract himself from his wee son's question.

"Da? Why don't I have a mother?"

Ochtu dared a glance beside him. Tony nibbled on the dreadlock shorter than the others due to it frequently ending up in his mouth. The child stared up with wide, dark violet eyes just like Da's, and had Ochtu's strong square jaw, handsome wide nostrils, and plump lips. The dreadlocks forbid their tight coils from standing on end like total slobs. Only his son's lilac skin coloring gave away that the laddie was half-pink. Tony clutched his pencil. The laddie was supposed to be practicing his letters, not waiting for an answer.

"Ye do have a mother, son. She's just . . . sick." That was fair. Only a sick woman would abandon such a beautiful child.

Marezza's name ought to start with an A, like the bitter amaro syrup that she always poured into her vile coffee. Bitterness she drank and bitterness she spewed on everyone who loved her.

Ochtu eyed Tony. The child's face was scrunched up. A little pink tongue peeked out the corner of his mouth. Marezza wouldn't get a chance to hurt his son. No matter what she and the rest of the House of Romin would think of his most clever hiding place, a 'painted lady' home in a safe neighborhood, but still far from the wealthiest area of the City By the Bay.

"Da? Can I see her?"

"Absolutely not. She's contagious." Not a lie, really. His son would be in more danger of developing the she-wolf's lycanthropy if she found them and he foolishly let her stay.

"Can I get a new mother?"

Ochtu blinked. "What's that, Tony?"

"Let's take the sick one back and get a new one."

He clutched his little boy to his flabby chest. "It doesn't work like that with mothers, son. Ye have me. Be content with that. It's more than I had, growing up."

Tony scrunched his brows together. "But you've mentioned your father."

Ochtu winced. "Grandpa raised Da, aye, but Grandma keeps a stable full o' husbands. We have no idea which one fathered me."

Tony's eyes widened. "What man would share his wife? Why would she want so many lords to obey?"

Huh? Ochtu laughed. Most of the mums Tony knew were slaves. "Son, like your great-grandpa Romin rules the nations west of the Mississippi, your grandma Erin rules the nations east of the Mississippi. The queen kisses any man she wants to kiss and marries him to justify it."

"Oh."

"Aye, so enough mother talk, lad. At least ye know who fathered ye." No thanks to Marezza.

"I still want a mother."

"Hey now, with the invention o' infant formula, the only thing a mother can do that a father can't is bring ye into this world. We're free men and slaves to no woman. We'll take care of ourselves." Ochtu touched the lion rampant tattooed on his right shoulder. The gold ink contrasted against his dark purple skin. His blue undertone gave his race their name, blue people.

Ironic—he was a direct descendant of world conquerers, born to privilege, born an unwilling beneficiary of the racist policies that had once kept pinks in slavery. In fact, back east, a pink man still could be executed over a racist blue lady finding the mere sight of him intimidating. He'd never know such horror.

Yet the lion of Erin and the eagle of Romin, tattooed on his shoulders to mark him as royalty, often felt like seals of ownership. What good had being a prince done him? How was Mum marrying him to another royal house for peace any different morally than if she'd sold him to a miller for bread?

May his son never grasp how fortunate he truly was.

OCHTU SPREAD OUT SIDEWAYS on his walnut sofa's garnet cushions, facing the overstuffed drawing room chairs by the low-burning fireplace. His leather accounts ledger lay open on his green and yellow tartan kilt, which he wore with a traditional drawstring workman's blouse. The gas chandelier had been lit as dusk approached.

He puffed on his favorite brand of fine cigars. With a little juggling of his investments, he should make it another month without having to live further below his station, or collecting his allowance for being King Felippo Romin's grandson-in-law. That required he show himself at court. It was best to limit the opportunities for Marezza to learn his current address.

His housekeeper entered. The Diakrinthian aggie's silver-speckled hair had been cut into a slave woman's legally required chin-length bob.

She bowed. "Milord, an opium addict be at the door demanding money."

"What are you bothering me for? Send her away."

"I did, milord, but she refuses to leave."

"Then run and fetch the nearest city patrolman."

Pottery crashed in the hall.

A sunburnt pink lady who looked forty staggered in. She clutched a liquor bottle, but she had the red, glazed eyes of an addict. Stringy, stray clumps of platinum pink hair strewed from a once stately coiffure. Most of the hair was so dirty, it looked as black as the stains marring the tattered frock. Judging by the few remaining clean patches, it had once been a grand yellow. He'd guess she was truly thirty, or perhaps still younger.

Ochtu peered closer. "Marezza?"

She took a swig from her bottle. "You are one hard dog to find, Coyote."

OCHTU POUNDED ON THE redwood door to his aunt-in-law's chambers inside the House of Romin's alabaster palace. A knight of the royal guard unlocked the door. Ochtu shoved inside, clobbered into the gilded coatrack, and came within an inch of slamming it into the silver mirror. He set the coatrack back upright. Two bedchamber doors lay across from the fireplace.

He bellowed, "Porcia!"

Porica swept into the anteroom. She wore only a fine linen chemise, with her hair damp and in leather curlers. Her pale skin had so little of humanity's purple pigment, her blood tinted her a true shade of pink, but her pink hair would require a firey orange hue to paint on canvas.

She stood by the royal brown divan and mustered a courtly smile. "Why, hello, stranger. I'd forgotten I even had a blue brother-in-law."

"Ye have to come and get Marezza. I cannot and will not deal with this."

A gasp and a tear escaped Porcia's poise. She clutched her hand over her collar bone. "Where is she?"

"Passed out on my drawin' room's sofa. Get her out o' my house before Tony wakes up and sees her, or I swear I'll toss her back in the gutter she's crawled out of."

"You could've brought her."

Ochtu blinked. Never even thought of that. "I'd rather not touch her."

"I meant for you to have a servant—" Porcia sighed, shook her head, and bit a trembling lip. "Give me an hour to dress."

"Aye, milady." He bowed and left.

At least there was one honest woman in this world.

ELEVEN DAYS AFTER HIS last visit, Ochtu MacErin entered Porcia's anteroom behind the messenger in military dress—a solid army blue kilt and matching kilt jacket, worn over a knee tunic. Porcia reclined on the royal brown divan in a moss green satin princess gown and a diamond tiara.

The kilted pink lad bowed. "Milady, I present to you His Royal Highness, Prince Coyote Dimarezza."

Ochtu pursed his lips. His married name meant, "Marezza's dog."

Porcia dismissed the help with a wave, stood, and kissed both of Ochtu's cheeks. "Thank you for coming, dear brother."

He whipped a cigar from his sporran and lit it on a match. He puffed on the cigar. "Let's get this over with."

"I really believe she's sincere. She's dried out and quite penitent."

To you she is, I'm sure. "I'll believe it when I see it. I'm giving her another chance for one reason."

"Because, if your marriage dissolves, so does the alliance with Erin?"

"Two reasons then. That one, and the reason I don't move again. Tony."

Porcia sighed. "I'll bring her in." She went to the door and waved.

Marezza entered in a clean pink frock dress. She wore her platinum pink ringlets in an elaborate upswept hairstyle held by a tiara identical to her aunt Porcia's. However, a few days off of the drugs and the liquor failed to erase the two decades put on her by six years of riotous living.

She bowed her head like a wife ashamed of straying. "Forgive me."

Ochtu grunted. That was an act for Porcia's benefit. "Let us alone."

Porcia sent them a hopeful smile and departed.

Marezza raised her head. A relieved breath escaped her lips. Remorseless green eyes bored into him.

Whatever ye do, lad, don't brogue. Ochtu folded his arms. "I much doubt that you're serious about reconciling, but for Tony's sake, I'll state my terms. No drugs. No alcohol. No gambling. No men. My bed. Non-negotiable."

Her laughter ripped through him. She shook her head. "Oh, Coyote, you never change."

"Shame you don't. Excuse me." He spun to leave.

Marezza ran to block the door. "Wait. You don't like me, and I don't like you, and neither of us want to be married, but we are."

"You have my terms. Let me know when you're willing to abide by them."

"Listen to me, we may hate each other, but we do have common ground."

"Would sure be nice if you meant Tony."

"Darling, I'm not the mothering type. We have a much bigger problem. We're broke."

Ah. So this was an opium addict wanting money. "You mean you're broke. I thankfully have my own accounts, and I'm not bailin' ye out o' trouble ye got yourself into. Especially when you'll be back in it in no time."

"The debts are in your name, too. It's your reputation on the line."

Ochtu laughed. "My name?"

"They wouldn't loan me more money in my name. And now they won't loan you more money, either."

Whoever created this world, please don't let this woman realize I keep my financial accounts under my natal name. She'll ruin me. "What ye fail to realize, my pretty, is, unlike you, I know how to live on my allowance. It's your problem. Ye deal with it."

"You're my husband! You're supposed to provide for me."

"That's so sexist it's not funny." Then again, the Coyote she remembered would've obeyed her. "I'm a liberated man now. I'm no longer your slave, and I never will be again. I can provide for myself and for Tony. I haven't got the money for you. Especially knowin' where you'll spend it."

"Oh, but you're so clever at managing accounts. Plenty of businesses will pay clever men like you to manage their funds for them."

She could not be serious.

By Astor—his treasure—she was serious. "I am the eighth son o' Erin. A prince o' the dynasty that conquered the entire civilized world. And ye expect me to hire myself out! To pay your debts? Ye are mad, Marezza! Mad!"

She raked him over with foul names. The choicest ones overflowed with hatred of blue men and accused him of rape. Like Mum and Romin had given him any choice, either. It figured. She had always twisted her evil around to somehow be all his fault. At least she couldn't go whining to Romin this time. He'd be even less sympathetic on this one, if possible.

When she finally finished her cursing, Marezza demanded, "What do you expect me to do?"

"Hire yourself out and settle your own debts. Or get a sword and fall on it. I couldn't care less which." He stormed out into the palace's central corridor and slammed the door.

She screamed, "This isn't over!"

Ochtu lowered his head. It was over nearly seven years ago.

His chest ached. *Mum, if you only knew . . . but if you did, the alliance would dissolve, and my countrymen would die—at each other's hands.*

OCHTU LEANED TOWARD Porcia across his round, walnut drawing room table, past the unlit oil lamp. The lamp's garnet red base complimented the color of the floral pattern wallpaper as well as the drapes, which were all pulled back. Dusty daylight filtered through sheer white curtains.

His eyes narrowed to slits at Porcia. A lit cigar dangled between his dark purple fingers. "Milady, this may come as a terrible shock, but Marezza lied. She does that quite a lot."

Porcia stood, tugging at her silk glove. "I don't think you're intentionally cruel. It's all a misunderstanding. I know she has hurt you badly, but doesn't everyone deserve a second chance?"

"Milady, none of the rubbish she said about me is true."

"So you will come home?"

"No. She won't agree to even the most basic courtesies a husband should be able to expect from his wife. Like sleeping in his bed rather than everyone else's—and don't laugh."

"I'm not laughing. Her selfishness certainly feels as cruel to you as yours does to her."

"Regardless, I have to consider Tony. She refuses to settle down and be a real Mum, and that is a terrible shame. If I had a supportive wife, maybe I'd make a return on my art."

Porcia's eyes widened. "You don't make money on a hobby."

"Hey now, I work hard on my paintings! Why shouldn't I earn a profit?"

"She's right, Coyote. For a liberated man, you are rather old-fashioned."

And Porcia and Romin were the sanest members of this family. "Thank you, milady. Until you see me prancing about in a frilly 'men's' frock dress and a frilly 'men's' corset, I will consider that a compliment. The popular notion that a man earning a living wage means a return to the evils of matriarchy is absurd. But I hope you would acknowledge Marezza's refusal to make love to me is a serious barrier to reconciliation."

Porcia moved to his red sofa and sat sideways, refusing to look at him.

Ochtu puffed on his cigar. He'd give her one thing. Her sisters would've suggested he'd feel better if he committed adultery with them.

Porcia sighed. "She's explained her views to me. I think I got through to her. Bitterness won't right the injustices we've suffered at blue hands."

"Pardon, milady, racism sadly isn't dead yet, but the House of Erin losing over half of our country to Romin ought to be punishment enough for the way my ancestors treated yours, if ye ask this blue man. The rebels in the west won the civil war three centuries ago. All the fighting hurts both sides."

"We mustn't ever go back to that, but my sister needs to feel safe. What effort are you really making there? The way I see it, you're too afraid of getting hurt again to reach out to her."

Nursing his cigar, Ochtu rose, paced to the two armchairs by the fireplace and then back toward the baby grand piano at the other end of the room. He stopped by his walnut desk. It held a flurry of letters from angry creditors. Marezza had kindly given them his current address.

"You want to see some effort?" He picked up the bills and waved them at Porcia. "I will pay these debts, on two conditions. One, the accounts are closed and Marezza can no longer go on spending sprees and stick me with the bills."

"Will the creditors allow that limitation? She is your wife."

"They will when I make it clear they won't see a single copper otherwise. Now my second condition is this. Marezza must gain employment and pay off the debts in her name."

Porcia stared. "You seriously expect a princess to—"

"—you seriously expect a prince to demean himself? Why should I do that for a woman who's made it clear in every way possible that she hates me?"

"She shouldn't have to, either."

"Milady, I've searched the purple earth high and low, read every book on philosophy, ethics, and religion that I could get my hands upon." Though the Sacred History had gotten too disgustingly oppressive in short order. "Most of it's merely a means for women to exploit men and each other, and that goes for Time and Chance, too." He jabbed his cigar at her. "Whether you want to admit Time and Chance are gods or not."

Porcia stiffened. "Do you have a point?"

"One common theme in all o' those books did make sense: actions will be sowing consequences, and someone will be reaping them. Wise persons learn from their mistakes. I won't rob Marezza of the opportunity to see the error of her ways. If I simply bail her out, she'll only end up back in the gutter. So, if she can stay clean long enough to hold down a job and pay off her debts, and if she shows she's learned her lesson, and if she at that point genuinely wants to be a proper wife and mother, then I'll consider that possible."

But he wouldn't hold his breath. If possessing male genitalia wasn't still a sexist criteria for diagnosis, he'd formally accuse Marezza of lycanthropy. If anyone suffered that most dread disease of the mind, she did. She lacked any natural affection or morality whatsoever.

Finally, Porcia sighed. "I'll find someone in need of a lady's companion."

Ochtu laughed. "How will she be learning anything by getting paid to be friends with a lonely elderly widow?"

"What do you have in mind, then? I love Marezza, but she would make a lousy governess."

"Firstly, something not on the short list of positions a noblewoman can hold without her losing face. The whole point is she has to gain employment demeaning enough that she might decide the price of her notion of liberty is far too expensive."

"Who's hiring that she's qualified to work for?"

"There's always Alcatraz." Ochtu laughed. Marezza would've fit right in with its former residents. Alcatraz Island boasted a military prison before the increased demand for maritas made it more profitable to turn the facility into a trade school for Diakrinthian slave women. The lilac lasses' exotic beauty, extreme poverty, and that their own mothers exploited them, too, made them tempting targets for marita traders.

Alcatraz had a discriminatory practice of only hiring women, the position was live-in, and there was a ferry ride in between the school and the nearest shopping and male companionship. So Alcatraz did have to run a full page ad in every newspaper edition wooing female employees. Usually, they printed it right beside the full page ad trying to persuade him to buy Tony a mother.

OCHTU LEANED BACK FROM his desk the next evening and puffed on his cigar. The two wooden horses from Anapausi's Ark raced across the drawing room. Tony held one—and Porica held the other. Ochtu chuckled. Awful nice to have someone else making a fool of themselves for once.

The wind-up grandmother clock chimed seven times.

His housekeeper appeared and bowed. "Milord, since you have company, I thought . . . ."

That she could put Tony to bed. Ochtu waved. "Aye, please, and then you may go home."

Shortening her hours would make it possible to recover from the financial disaster named Marezza. He'd renege except she'd used his son as collateral. Almost tempted him to wish Romin granted royalty immunity from the law, like the House of Erin did. Almost. His da had taken pains to make sure that he turned out right, but Mum's family made Romin's family look sane.

He glanced to Tony, now engaging in a sabertooth cat fight outside of the expensive boat rarely ever used the way it was supposed to be. So sad to end Porcia's fun. "Tony, bedtime."

"Aw, Da!"

"You don't got to go to sleep, son. But you do have to go to bed, close your eyes, and stay put until morning."

Tony tugged on Porcia's sleeve. "You'll come visit me again?"

Porcia hugged the lad. "We'll see, bambino."

"Night, Aunt Porcia." Tony kissed her and scrambled for the door.

Ochtu called, "Hey! You forgot something, Speedy."

Tony came back and kissed him. "Night, Da."

"Still forgot something."

Tony scrunched together his little eyebrows. "I love you?"

"Now that's better." Ochtu kissed his son. "G'night, son. I love you."

Once the door closed behind Tony and the hired help, Ochtu assisted Porcia off the floor and into an overstuffed arm chair.

He settled in the chair angled toward hers and folded his arms. "Is there something I can help you with, or did you come to play with Tony's stable, or barn, or whatever Anapausi's ark is in his imagination today?"

Porcia blushed. "He is adorable."

"Then why haven't you borne any?"

A shadow crossed her eyes. "Some liberties you pay for at leisure."

Ochtu smirked. "And borrowing a marita's womb by purchasing her and

26

giving her to your husband is too old-fashioned for your tastes?" Women had been padding the offspring to their names through such trickery for millennia. The only new ideas were the husband owning the slave who bore his children, forcing her to work, and taking her instead of a proper, free wife.

Porcia hesitated as if she were toying with the idea of forcing a marita on her husband. She shook her head. "The daughter that I have will have to be enough. I don't have the stomach for a marita."

This woman was vexingly irrational, calling her youngest orphaned niece her daughter and calling her eldest orphaned niece, Marezza, her sister.

Porcia leaned toward him. "We're not all bitter against blue people like Marezza. I wouldn't have minded taking a second husband, but that would've insulted your mother."

No, it would've insulted me! "Aye, that wouldn't be fittin', milady. Do I detect ye are givin' up on makin' a proper wife o' the aforementioned?"

Tears dampened Porcia's eyes. "After a protracted battle, Marezza agreed to apply at Alcatraz. They hired her as a dorm mother. She starts on Sunday."

Ochtu chuckled. If only he had a picture of that. Maybe he would paint it himself. A bit of imagination and he'd have a laugh ready any time he needed one. "Um, why are you crying?"

"I accompanied her to the physician today. You will need to advise yours that she, uh, has syphilis."

A deathly chill entombed him. He pictured his precious wee son's smiling face. "She hasn't been anywhere near me ever since Tony—I thought infected women miscarry?"

Porcia's lip quivered. "Not always."

"But he's such a healthy little lad."

"If the physician's right, his mother was infected recently, so you should both be healthy. It's merely a precaution. This is a deadly disease, Coyote."

Marezza might have done him a favor by refusing to make love to him. But if Romin's choosing a harlot for Ochtu's wife had infected his son, he'd strangle Marezza.

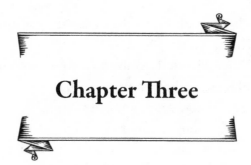

Chapter Three

Weeping trickled into Hosanni's consciousness followed by her mother's arms wrapped tightly around her. Hosanni's eyes fluttered open to the gray pre-dawn. The temperatures still felt like harvest time, but the new year was only two months away on the secular calendar.

Male snores rose across the room. Without Father, Korban had an awful time awakening. Being the only man in the home seemed to have aged Korban three years in the three months since Father had left.

Hosanni turned to face Mother. "What is it, Mam?"

Mother shook her head and sniffed deep of Hosanni's hair. "Another bad night, love." Mother sat up and wiped her puffy face. She reached inside of the bosom of her sleeveless, form-hugging cotton undershirt, and she drew out of it the Garnet of Kristos. She pulled the silver chain over her head and placed it around Hosanni's neck.

Hosanni eyed the jewel. Its heavy weight felt strange in the space between her young breasts. To think, up until her last birthday, she'd still been wearing a little girl's white linen tunic. "Mam?"

"Open the locket and remove the scroll. Fold a fresh parchment into six columns. Copy onto the columns the names on the scroll exactly as written. Add your name to the end of both scrolls. Leave the copy in your memory box. Wear the locket at all times."

As prescribed in the law. "What changed your mind?"

"If your father doesn't come in time . . ." Mother wept into her hands.

"Pappy will come!"

Mother hugged her. "It's in Emi's hands. We couldn't entrust you to that wolf of a peacekeeper, but the tax collectors truly do seize the most beautiful maidens. If Emi's hand is against us, the invaders will sell you into slavery. It might help you to have proof you are the chosen daughter of Kristos. Maybe they'll show royal blood leniency."

Or they may kill me. Hosanni trembled. "It won't come to that. Am I not the last daughter of Kristos? Far be it from me to think I am the one, but—"

Mother laughed. "I know you're not Lady Veritas."

Hosanni sniffed. Nothing was more frightening than becoming a vessel of the Spirit of Truth, but still. "Surely I am not that terrible a daughter?"

"Oh no, you are a bit spirited, but that's not why. At your birth, Emi spoke to me the final verses of the gospel song, the very end of the Sacred History itself." Mother cleared her throat and sang them.

The star of Veritas will light on Mount Sacrifice
And turn the purple earth upside down and afire.
I have commanded my bride, 'Go down into the pit,
Carry up the bones, give them breath, and for a wife
Unto your son, even unto Kristos. Behold my hand.
You will pass through the fire and not be consumed.'
Veritas shall reveal Logos. By Logos you shall know
Whether the Remembrances of the Aggies is Veritas.
Accursed be she who takes away from Logos.
Accursed be she who adds to Logos. Amen.

Hosanni sniffled. The ballad's haunting melody never ceased to stir her, but the words were all mysteries. The speaker had to be a high king. Such was not her people's way, yet how else could the king's mother be a king's bride? And how could any king outrank a queen?

Worse, the Remembrances of the Aggies was the Sacred History's name for itself, while Lady Veritas's name meant truth in Latin. How could her odd task of reaffirming the truth already revealed be as important as her task of unveiling such mysteries? "What does this have to do with me?"

Mother kissed her. "When you were born, Emi opened the heavens unto me, and I saw a star arise from Eve, the red earth. Behold, there was a great assembly of the daughters of Heaven, all shining like the sun. And they blew trumpets and a herald cried unto our earth, 'Rejoice, Rejoice, oh Argevane, for the mother of Veritas has come into you.'"

Hosanni's heart beat fast. "Emi has not forsaken us. Lady Veritas and her bridegroom will deliver us from Romin's hordes!" She paused. "Mother, who knows this prophecy?"

An embarrassed smile spread Mother's lips. "All in the assembly then old enough to understand. I decided it prudent thereafter to keep this quiet. Such knowledge is dangerous to one young in the path. Swelling of the head is usually a lethal condition."

Mother, ever the Ravane teaching her flock.

But she'd best take the warning to heart. Hosanni clutched the star garnet locket and sighed. After the resurrection dance, she had 5,737 years' worth of names to write onto a fresh scroll. And much more to celebrate than merely the sun's ever-faithful rise from the dead, which all daughters of the covenant greeted each morning with dancing and songs as commanded.

Perhaps Emi's hand would bring Father home. Only that would make the day more perfect.

HOSANNI HELD HER WATER jar with aching arms as she took a shortcut in between harvested fields. A mile ahead, pine outbuildings with straight walls and rounded corners guarded the circular stucco homes clustered around the stone assembly hall. The latter's triangular roof rose above it all.

The autumn sun burned almost as hot as summer, but she smiled at the fluffy gray clouds on the horizon. Soon, the stupid drought would end and relieve her of making this accursed daily trek to the great cistern. Winter fast approached. Mother had even fetched the wool blankets, stockings, and coats out of storage and hung them up on the dress pegs in the upper room.

Perhaps tomorrow they'd be needed. Perhaps tomorrow it would snow.

Ahead, Mother's dragon bounded on her two strong, upright legs. Though bipedal, Draca stood with her back to the sky. A long tail counterbalanced the weight of her head, which was nearly half the size of her four-foot-long, gray-green pebbly body. The dragon's imitation of Mother's smile revealed rows of three-inch fangs sharp enough to sever bone.

Dorcas waved tiny, three-clawed, short arms that mostly chattered. Her tail and whole hind end wiggled.

The animal clobbered into Hosanni, knocked her down, and slobbered all over her face.

The water jar landed intact on its side. Thank goodness she had the lid on tight. Hosanni patted the dragon's head. "Silly mutt. You could've broken my jar and spilled all our water."

The dragon backed away, hanging her head. Her tiny hands formed the dragon signs meaning, "Sorry, Sister." Dorcas's intelligent, little yellow eyes widened, and her head bounced up. A hiss equivalent to an "Oh!" escaped her mute lips, and the animal signed, "Sister, Cousin Sacrifice say, 'Sister, meet Cousin Sacrifice in hayloft.'"

Meet who? Hosanni's heart fluttered. Dorcas must mean Korban. In the old tongue, one meaning of his name was Sacrifice.

Hosanni picked up her water jar and ran the rest of the way home. She set the jar by the door. Mother would find it.

Why the hayloft? Hosanni smiled and slipped the star garnet locket out of her pink palla. Maybe Mother wasn't the only one making important, happy decisions. Was it not a year ago today that Korban asked if he could court her? He'd qualified that he meant to do so when her parents allowed her to wear her hair in the twin braids of marriageable maidens, but only for honor's sake. Sometimes, the wait seemed endless, but it was for her own good, rationally.

The scent of milk, bison manure, and turkey droppings filled the warm cedar barn. Her palms sweated as she climbed the ladder up into the hayloft. What if she'd misunderstood Dorcas? She'd feel so silly.

Hosanni inched sideways along the railing in the cramped hayloft. At this time of year, the men stacked the hay clear to the rafters. "Korban?"

A mewling noise highlighted a dark tunnel in the bricklike sheaves. The men stacked them that way to amuse the children on cold winter days. Could young adults their age still fit?

The mewling came again.

The rare sight of sabertooth kittens would be worth the attempt. She slid to her knees and crawled into the cramped darkness.

Two corners more, and the darkness sped her crawl. She had to find the light. If she got lost in here, Mother would never forgive her for the scare.

At last, light dazzled her. She scrambled for it.

Mewling overcame the pounding of her heartbeat. Hosanni emerged into the brightness. Her eyes adjusted. Hardly bigger than a mouse, the saber-tooth kittens nursed from a tame but most unfriendly mother, who was about half the size of a stocky bobcat. The mother cat eyed Hosanni warily and returned to bathing her babies with her prickly pink tongue.

Male hands blinded Hosanni.

She screamed and reached to toss her attacker.

Korban's laughter tickled her. "I knew you couldn't resist the kittens."

He released her and settled beside her.

She shifted into a sitting position and smiled at Korban far more shyly than she felt. "Thank you for showing them to me."

"My pleasure, milady." Korban took her hand. "May I?"

Hosanni giggled. Oh, how she loved it when he'd ask for that liberty after having already taken it. "Beloved, sixteen can't come soon enough."

Korban's hand dampened. He swallowed. "Milady, when she does let you put your hair in braids, may I have your ribbon?"

Hosanni gasped. When a young man chose the bride he wished to serve, by custom, he proposed marriage by taking one of the ribbons that tied her twin braids. Was she dreaming, or had she truly become the first Diakrinthian maiden, as far as she knew, to be chosen verbally?

Ooh, Irene's gonna be so jealous!

To Hades with decorum. Hosanni hugged him. "If I can accept!"

His arm slipped behind her. The newness of the touch felt as wonderful as the brightness of his eyes staring into hers. Korban whispered, "May I have the liberty?"

She nodded, her heart pounding.

His lips drank from hers, soft and delicious. Her first kiss.

Korban jerked and scrambled to the other side of the womb-like space lit, by the sun crystal emitting the light. The mother sabertooth hissed. He inched away from her babies, back within Hosanni's reach.

She sniffled. "Am I that bad at this?"

"No, milady." Korban lifted his eyes to hers. The unfamiliar look in his eyes kindled an equally unfamiliar fire in her. He finished, "You're that good."

He closed his eyes, breathing deep, nodded, and made that forbidden, but wonderful eye contact again. He took her hands in his. "Milady, I fear I have a terrible confession. Your parents have already deemed me unworthy."

A relieved breath burst out of her. That was all? "Oh, Korban. Mother and Father love you as much as they would a son born of their bodies. They're only looking out for me. A mother's labor is no difficulty for her if she is of age, but it is life-threatening for maidens my age."

"Then why don't they simply ask me to wait, as I already am?"

"They think all young men lack the mental strength to endure singleness so long and remain on the path. As much as I hate it, I understand why they want you to choose another. Their love is saying no. We need you, Korban."

"I fear they may be right. Honestly, my flesh greatly longs for us to join together now."

She gasped. "Emi must strengthen us. What other choice do we have?"

"There is one. You won't like it, but I have as much to prove to myself as to Uncle Havan. And it'll give us the time we need."

"You're frightening me."

He squeezed her hands and let go. "You are a beautiful princess, I the son of a mixed-race peasant, and I dare dream of you? But if I can get your scepter back, then I'll feel worthy."

"Father thinks I should teach my sons to read and write."

"Perhaps the Romini will teach me, when I offer myself as the payment for our taxes."

"You can't give yourself up! They want daughters."

"Naturally, but they also need sons to serve in their army."

"Father will be home with the money. You'll see."

"And if he's not? My only other choice is going home, and guess what fate awaits me there? I'd much rather surrender my life for my bride than have it taken by my mother." Korban shrugged. "I'll serve a few years, learn the art of war, then return to you and train our army to defeat theirs. And I'll be found worthy in my own eyes to marry my queen."

Hosanni sighed. If his plan succeeded, they would be the queen and king and Mother would be the high queen. Nor would Korban be their first king to earn his place in their dynasty through military victory.

She embraced him. "Emi's hand, succeed, or I'll never forgive you."

Korban wrapped an arm around her and slid his free hand up into her tresses, that shine in his eyes again. "May I?"

Hosanni giggled. "Beloved, you're planning to leave me within the week, and it will be impossible for us to sneak away together, once Father returns. What harm is there in enjoying what little time we have left?"

An amused smile parted his lips. "My thoughts precisely."

Korban drew her lips to his and drank deep, exploring past her lips with his tongue. She blinked. Was this the sort of kissing meant by drinking from one's cistern? She hesitated a minute, decided she liked it, and also explored with abandon.

A shouting arose from below, like in the marketplace.

The mastodons trumpeted anxiety. The dragons roared at trespassers.

Korban drew back, eyes wide for a second, and then narrowing. "I have to go now, milady. Stay here."

He turned and scampered on his knees down one of the tunnels out.

She followed him, her belly aching to be back in his arms again. "Korban! What's happening?"

"Stay here!"

Maybe it wasn't the clamor in the street. Maybe kissing her simply didn't taste as good to him as she'd thought it did. Either way, she had to know.

Bion's curiosity brought all that's evil into Argevane.

Hosanni pressed on. That was different. Emi herself had told their first father to never open his portal to Argevane's identical twin sister. If Bion had listened to God, Cain the son of Eve never would've come through the portal and corrupted womankind, causing the sons of Argevane to overthrow their wives and mothers. And the Catastrophe might not have come and destroyed the ancient's great civilization—and her life might be a bit easier.

To think that Xenos men had again rebelled and sought to enslave their rightful masters.

Hosanni's feet carried her three yards out from the barn before she could stop them. Near the center of the village, pink-skinned soldiers in solid army blue kilts, tunics, and kilt jackets stood outside of the stone assembly hall's pretty stained-glass windows.

The tax collectors had beat Father home. And they wanted paid.

Every adult dragon in the village circled the Romini soldiers, who stood on alert with drawn swords, likely wary of unfamiliar animals. Hosanni stood rooted. Why didn't someone call off the dragons?

She picked out Basilen by his bulk. Draca strangely shared her mate with her sisters and looked to his lead rather than to the lead of the female with the best children. If Basilen attacked, so would his mates and daughters.

Korban positioned himself behind the dragons like a king with his army. Mother stood at his side with all the nobility of a sovereign queen. The adult dragons herded the soldiers together and protectively surrounded Korban as they did with the juvenile dragons.

One soldier barked in the marketplace tongue. The coarse syllables rolled over each other.

Korban replied in the same tongue, but much slower, "I would call them off, but they're not my dragons, and I'm sure no one else here has understood a word you said."

More coarse syllables jumbled over each other.

Korban laughed. "You don't need a translator. You need to slow down and to speak clearly. My people learn the international tongue as children, but few of us use it outside of the marketplace and our childhood lessons."

The soldier snarled and turned toward Mother, lunging forward.

Basilen roared a war cry and leapt, aiming his bone-crushing jaws to take off the foolish soldier's head. A sword thrust at Basilen's soft underbelly, went wide of him, and instead pierced human flesh. Roaring, Dorcas charged.

At the same time, a soldier rushed in between death and the murderer, a throwing knife in the eye felled Basilen, and a sword cut down Dorcas.

Blackness slid over the battle. Panick and confusion scattered Hosanni's thoughts until it hit her—she'd closed her eyes. She forced them open. Blood, so much blood. So much draca blood. So little soldier blood.

Hands snatched her away and slapped heavy irons on her wrists.

She stumbled. A shed dragon fang slid under her left sandal's strap and pricked her foot.

A soldier yanked her up by the chain on the irons.

She followed in a daze, with the five human bodies sprawled in the sea of blood forever seared on her memory.

Three were soldiers decapitated by the dragons.

Two were slain by the sword.

The two were Mother and Korban.

Chapter Four

One foot in front of the other. On and on. A pulsating, burning sensation shot up Hosanni's left leg with each step. The urgent prodding pierced the fog numbing her. She whimpered.

Pines, hills, and a river stretched out before her, and a long line of girls. Most were still children of eleven or twelve years old, dressed in linen tunics stained grayish-lilac by dirt. Only the occasional palla spotted the throng.

Irons rattled. A sniffle. A wail.

A slap.

Shuffling feet. Prayers whispered in Diakrinthian.

The children's voices surrounded her.

"Amen, Amen, when they divide us in the City of Trees, I pray you, send me left, to the school, so I don't suffer the horrors awaiting the slaves sent to the right, oh Emi our God, the lady of Heaven's vast armies."

"Oh Ancient of Days, whose hand guides all, I pray you, send me right, to the labor camp, so I may escape the desecration that awaits us on the left."

"Emi, strike me, for they are going to rape us. Please save me out of this and take me to Heaven to live with you there."

Emptiness buzzed inside Hosanni. Why didn't she care? What were they talking about? What was happening to them?

Mud slipped in Hosanni's right sandal. She stared at it. Not mud—a foul mixture of vomit and the human waste this awful procession dropped. They were being forced to squat right on the road like dragons. And not on any old road, but the Romini highway paved in aspalt concrete all the way from their fort at McCall to the glorious City of Trees.

By the time the pine trees gave way to sage brush, the sun was dying, and all she wanted to do was lie down to never rise herself.

Ahead, a girl in linen collapsed.

A soldier grabbed the girl's chain and dragged her until the whimpering child managed to get back on her feet.

Hosanni shivered. The numbness devoured all but the flames consuming her foot.

A Romini soldier fell in step beside her. The pink face in her side vision registered. Memory returned like a mastodon stepping upon her bosom: that face, that sword missing Basilen and instead thrusting clean through Mother, to pierce Korban's side also, as they tried to restrain Basilen.

The murderer touched Hosanni's shoulder and asked in the marketplace tongue, "Are you all right?"

The fire in Hosanni's foot migrated to her bosom. She spat on the road like a man. "Ya kill my mother and my lover, and ask if I be all right?"

His eyes widened. "Fortunately for you, Diakrinthians deprive eight-day-old females of the proof of their maidenhood."

Must he make a holy covenant sound like defilement? "Not deprive eight-day-old baby, circumcise her hymen with knife."

"Regardless, no one can prove you're not a maiden, so let them think you are. It'll be far better for you on Alcatraz Island, and they only take maidens."

Was 'lover' the wrong word? That was what she got for Father teaching her English. She didn't care to conjugate all those stupid irregular verbs, but impeding communication here could have far worse consequences than a bad grade. "No, no, milord! We be not joined together. We only wished to be. But now it shall never be." She glared. "Thanks to you."

Another soldier strode closer, a cruel glint in his eyes. "Sir, will you take that from her?"

Hosanni shirked back from the intruder.

The murderer stared down his fellow. "If I see fit to comfort a child with lycanthrope bite due to witnessing her mother die, what is that to you?" He dismissed the intruder with a contemptuous wave and said to Hosanni, "You hate us now, but you will thank us some day."

What arrogance these Romini had. She snarled. "Thank ya to be nailed to your own crucifix. Ya be murderers as treacherous as the Erini."

"Your tribal elders should've called off their dragons. It's a shame. Those were fine animals, but I had to protect my men. Whichever sword slew the lilac woman and struck a bambino also, it was not intentional. I've never seen a situation get so out of hand. We're tax collectors, not peacekeepers. We're only armed for self-defense."

A tear ran down Hosanni's cheek. "What good that do us?"

"It doesn't." The pink soldier removed his pencil and parchment from his kilt jacket. "Who is your father? What is your name and your village's name?"

"What be that to ya?"

"For one, I need it for my records. For two, I'm Captain Fautorio of the City of the Salt Lake, originally. Must I tell you my father's name as well, or is that enough?"

She glared. He'd need Mother's name, if he hadn't killed her. "I be Maid Hosanni of Lake County, Diakrinth. Father be Havan Alethaner Kristekon."

Captain Fautorio sighed. "Do you know your grandparents' names?"

She gasped—the star garnet locket. Mother said it may save her. Hosanni reached up to tug at the silver chain. The irons only allowed her hands to part by four inches.

Captain Fautorio snatched the necklace up over her head, eyed it in the dying sunlight, and whistled. "What fools. This treasure is fit for the king. It'll pay your taxes for a decade at least."

"Fit for a queen and made for one. Open the star garnet locket. Behold the scroll of the genealogy of Kristos—Princess Hosanni's genealogy. Ya slew this morning the Queen of Diakrinth."

"No, that was yesterday." A frown creased Captain Fautorio's face. He dropped her necklace into the round leather purse worn on a chain around his waist. "The dogs that I command might steal a priceless relic from a bambina, but they won't dare steal from me, not unless they want nailed up on a tree. So I had better keep this and make sure it reaches the king's scholars. If the scroll is legitimate, Romin will be most interested in you."

Why did she not feel reassured?

Her left foot hit a rock on the road. Sharp, stabbing pain stole her breath. She winced and nearly stumbled. The pink soldier steadied her, glanced down, and swore. At least Hosanni was pretty sure her parents wouldn't have wanted her to hear that word.

Strong arms swept her off her tormented feet, carrying her like a young child. Sage brush blurred and a cold wind pelted her. She yawned. So sleepy.

Another soldier barked at them.

Captain Fautorio swore against his own mother this time, adding, "Look at her foot. Your neglect will cost the Union a maiden worth a king's ransom if we don't get her to a doctor."

Doctor? Did he mean to consult a ravane or a witch? Hosanni glanced at the limb being fussed about and gasped. The root of a shed dragon fang stuck out from the inside curve of her sandal while the sharp point emerged from her heel on the other side.

The numb fog returned and wiped the slate to black.

A LATE AUTUMN WIND bit like winter as Havan Alethaner trudged on the path to home. The satchel slung over his back had gained a hundred pounds, and the purse in his hands had gained a thousand pounds. He stopped by the incinerator, almost welcoming the compost's stench.

Once, he and the men shuffling behind him would've run the last two miles home. Now, he'd let the ladies and children do the running. But he had a little ways to go before Aletheia and Hosanni would see him. They had to be watching anxiously by now.

The wedding coordinator's overweight husband caught up, thumped him on the back, and gestured to the purse. "Would you like me to . . . ?"

To tell Juris. "No. She's my sister." His brother's widow deserved to hear the news from him. "I'll do this."

Emi, I can't do this on my own. I need your strength, Ancient of Days. My family needs me, and all I want to do is grab Basilen and my crossbow, head up into the mountains, and take my pain out on the elk.

The closer Havan Alethaner drew to the village, the tighter invisible twine wound around his stomach. It was too still, too quiet.

He exchanged glances with the other husbands. They all picked up their pace, each man shouting his wife's name so loud none could hear themselves.

Their children and their wives poured out of the village. Girlish cries of Havan Alethaner's favorite name, Pappy, jerked his head around.

Each cry was someone else's little girl reaching for her father.

Havan Alethaner spotted Juris, a younger and plainer version of Aletheia in the face. Juris staggered toward him. He sighed. Couldn't he have at least had a moment alone with Aletheia before breaking her sister's heart?

Juris came in reach of him and burst into sobs.

Havan Alethaner drew her back toward the village. She needed privacy. Aletheia and Hosanni would understand soon enough.

Between their houses, he handed his brother's purse to Juris. "I'm sorry." She stared at him. "Where is my husband?"

Tears wet Havan Alethaner's cheeks. She hadn't realized? He swallowed. His voice would break, if his heart didn't burst first. "The mine caved in. We tried to get his team out, but it threatened to come down on our heads, too. And, by then, we were digging out his body."

Juris wailed and ripped her palla, exposing her sleeveless undershirt. The contours of the female bust reminded his male parts how long it'd been since Aletheia could satisfy their cursed demands. Her sister collapsed and clawed up the grass, tossing greyish purple dirt over her head.

Havan Alethaner's heartbeat sped up. If she wasn't crying earlier because of his brother . . . He yanked Juris up by her shoulders. "Where are my wife and daughter?"

Juris sobbed more and shook her head.

He shook her and repeated louder, "Where is my family?"

"The tax collectors."

The wind blew tiny icicles in his face. He was too late. "How long?"

"A week."

He stormed in the house, grabbed his crossbow down from over the door, and ran out. He headed toward the City of Trees as the bird flew. The Romini would corral the female captives there for a few weeks while they sold their glory to wigmakers. The man who stole his wife would regret it, but whoever laid a hand on his daughter would pay dearly.

A kick exploded into his posterior and dropped him to the ground. Sharp elbows jammed into his back. Juris said, "Where are you going?"

Havan Alethaner grunted. Among men, it was dishonorable to attack a man from behind. "Let me up, woman. And, in my mood, I am asking nice."

"You dishonor me, Havan Alethaner."

"I'll repent later. Off." *Before I stray from the path by hitting a woman.*

41

Her elbows lifted only to jam back into either side of his spine. "You listen to me. You are one man with a hunting crossbow. Going up against an army. Even if you called the men of Diakrinth to war, by the time you were ready to attempt to regain the scepter, it'd be too late to help Hosanni. I'm not letting you commit suicide by throwing yourself at Felippo Romin's armies."

"You're right, Juris. Thank you for talking sense into me."

She released him and both stood.

He turned toward the assembly hall. "I believe we left the shofar in here."

Juris grabbed his arm. "Havan, don't do this."

"Don't do what?" *Stop acting like a wolf, Alethaner.* He continued glaring into his sister-in-law's eyes. "Don't gather my forces and go after my wife and my daughter? Don't rescue them and make the men that did this pay?"

Tears soaked his sister-in-law's cheeks. She shook her head. "Oh, Havan. Only Aletheia and Korban and the dragons were brave enough to face them. They tried to defend us, but the enemy was too strong. We didn't even realize for three days that they took Hosanni. We were too busy mourning our dead."

No. "Aletheia and Korban?"

"My sister the queen and all of our dragons. Korban's hanging on, but it's bad. I don't think he wants to recover. He needs his foster father. This village needs its Ravaner." Juris glanced at the purse she still held and fresh sobs escaped. "And I need my next of kin. Please don't make my children lose their uncle as well."

So that was how it was. His brother had seven daughters, all between the ages of four and seventeen. The women would talk as if he were a dragon in need of a new home, but in truth, Juris was the one in need of him. "I want to see Aletheia."

Juris cleared her throat. "We had to bury her."

Havan Alethaner dashed between their houses and the outbuildings and ran across the harvested field. The family tomb lay in the hills a bit over from the compost heap.

His lungs burned by the time he reached the stone covering the entrance. He pressed upon the stone. Several more sets of men's hands joined him. He nodded his thanks to his neighbors. Once the stone rolled away, they patted his shoulders and gave him space.

A stench worse than the compost heap led him to the body laid out on the central stone slab where each newcomer rested. He pulled the face cloth away. An overwhelming desire to be laying cold and stiff beside this body knocked his feet out from under him. He sobbed and used his last ounce of strength to rip his tunic and throw the dust of the tomb over his head.

Wailing announced Juris. She fell in a heap beside him.

Once he ran out of tears, she laid a hand on his shoulder and squeezed. "I hate this. But please don't hate me."

Havan Alethaner glanced up. "Beg your pardon, sister?"

"The aggies demanded I bring you before them the moment you arrived. We need to go."

Emi, please grant those women an ounce of compassion.

Juris offered her arm. He helped her up more than the other way around.

Outside of the assembly hall, Juris clasped his hand. "Whatever happens, I'm on your side. Unless Korban's mother asks me to return both of you to her house, you're welcome to remain a widower in mine. If you and Korban want to live alone, I'll fight for that, too."

He mustered the ghost of a smile. Juris was Aletheia's next of kin and his children's foster mother. "Thank you." *But what I want is to not be pressured to choose a new house the same day I lost the old one.*

Inside of the assembly hall, the thirty or so grandmothers in their village reclined on the pillow chairs they'd each carried in with them from home.

Zoe clambered onto her swollen feet. The thirty-year-old was great with child. "Does it please the aggies to appoint me as the speaker of this session?"

The old women all released their breath as if relieved they didn't have to do it. "Amen!"

Havan Alethaner glanced at Juris. "Zoe's not an aggie."

Juris winced. "The wedding coordinator's heart failed the day we buried the dragons. Her daughters Zoe and Elpis are technically old enough."

Zoe clapped her hands. "The aggies would like to offer our condolences to Havan Alethaner Kristekon for the deaths of his late wife and daughter."

Well said up until that last part. "Pardon, where has Hosanni been lain?"

"It is the judgment of this assembly that Hosanni has been or will be slain by the Romini, either in body or in spirit. Either way, she is dead to us."

"And you're so very sorry." *Easy, fella. Sarcasm is a sign of lycanthropy.*

"We are most sorry for your tragic loss and ours."

"Please don't tell me the deaths of animals rank beside losing my family."

"Kristos Havan, you're abusing a great privilege. Remember, you are only permitted to stand before us as our lord the king."

That game had lost its luster. "Will you make me leave if I point out my wife's death leaves us without a king until my daughter marries?"

Zoe sniffled. "On the contrary, milord the king, we are without our queen and the mother of the hope of Diakrinth. We realize your grief is deep, but the History says, 'if your sister dies having no child, you shall marry the widower and bear seed for your sister. If you are unable, give your daughter unto him, so your sister's name shall not be cut off.' You have a duty to your late wife and to this nation to perform this commandment and raise up a new heir for Aletheia's house. Therefore this assembly does so solemnly charge you, and heartily recommends your next of kin offer you a daughter for this service."

Sororate marriage, when his daughter lived? He was not hearing this. He glanced at the alarm frozen on his sister-in-law's face. Dear Emi.

His blood boiled, and he clenched his teeth. "Let me get this straight. My wife is dead and my daughter is desecrated, and your solution is to urge me to devour the maidenhood of my niece, the firstborn of my brother, the second son to emerge from the womb that bore me? You want me to take a child who has just lost her father, a child I bounced on my knee, and force her to lie with me? Right when she needs me to take her up and protect her and provide for her as she completes her transition into adulthood? You want me to rape her? Emi strike me if I consider it! And Emi strike you all for suggesting it!"

The aggies stared in utter silence.

Havan Alethaner took a breath. What had he done? Never had a man ever dared to rebuke one aggie, let alone all of them.

Zoe pointed her left index finger at him. "You—" Her finger shriveled up and turned white with leprosy. She stared at her finger, trembling all over as squeaks rolled off her lips.

Gasps and murmurs spread.

Havan Alethaner arched his eyebrows. Emi had answered him before, but not like that. What a strange way for Emi to rebuke him for cursing the aggies.

The short Elpis rushed to Zoe's side and sent Havan Alethaner a pleading look. "Milord the king, please pray for this your servant."

Meaning he was in the right? Huh. Havan Alethaner forced himself down on his knees and raised his hands to Heaven. "Amen, Amen, I beseech you on the behalf of this your daughter. Forgive her this trespass and wash her in the blood of the Sacrifice you have made in the heavens on our behalf, Emi our God, Lady of Heaven's vast armies." He stood amidst gasps.

Zoe's finger was whole again.

Elpis lifted her hands to Emi. "Thank you, Emi our God, for lifting this curse." She turned to face the aggies. "The king is right to remind us that two sisters married two brothers. The law never intended for the widower to wed a niece who shares his blood. If it is true Juris is a widow, then I submit it must be Emi's path that she do her sister this service."

Zoe shook her head. "That is an abuse of the law. How many years did it take Havan to give Aletheia a child? Irene has many more childbearing years left than Juris." Zoe glanced at her finger and to Havan Alethaner. "Far be it from me to suggest you force a maiden against her will, but Irene should be honored to marry her lord the king, who, if I may say, is quite pleasing to look upon even at forty."

Havan Alethaner scowled, his breathing heavy.

Juris stepped up, raising her hands. "Ladies, ladies! Kristos Havan has rejected Irene. That is off the table. And you forget, this same body judged his seed barren and urged Aletheia to put him away and accept another, and she refused. And Emi did bless Aletheia's faithfulness and opened her womb. We all agreed Hosanni came from God, and we all judged true the word Aletheia received concerning the child."

Juris sucked in a deep breath as if gathering strength to continue. "The king and I know what the law requires. But who has ever asked a widow to bury one husband and to accept another on the same day? Let me mourn my husband, and then, if Emi's hand grants me to bear my sister a daughter in Hosanni's place, it shall be. If not, who knows whether Emi will yet restore Princess Hosanni to life? As for now, we have a more pressing matter, the election of a new Ravane."

Elpis smiled. "All in favor of this good council say amen."

The aggies answered, "Amen."

"I nominate Juris Kristekon. All in favor say amen."

Juris opened her mouth to protest.

The aggies answered, "Amen."

Juris trembled. "Ladies, you need to allow other nominations. And grant us a chance to accept them."

Elpis hugged Juris. "Cousin, no one would have the chutzpah to nominate themselves when the queen has always been Ravane among us, and you can't reject a nomination when you're the only name on the ballot."

Juris glanced to Havan Alethaner, a plea for help shining in her eyes.

He shook his head and walked out. Let her serve as the Ravane without a husband. So what if she had no training? That was her problem.

She followed him. "Havan—"

He whirled and glared. "What happened to you being on my side? What did you think they'd do, after a speech like that? Don't you realize why they placed me remarrying before the logical first item and above all compassion? They want to keep me as the Ravaner, Juris. You signed up to be Ravane when you volunteered us for the marriage bed."

Juris resumed her lamentation wails.

Havan Alethaner sighed. With all the grace they'd given him on account of grief, the least he could do was be gracious. He squeezed her shoulder and escorted her back toward their homes.

She sniffled. "I'm sorry, I couldn't bear them any more, and you were so upset—I grabbed the fastest way to appease them and get back to lamenting."

"I can understand that, but whom I choose and when I choose is the one decision that's rightfully mine, and I'm not giving that up because they've lost faith in Emi's promise. And presently I'm tempted to put my hair up in twin braids like the men's liberationists who burn their male supporters."

Juris arched an eyebrow. "Beg your pardon?"

"Immodest men's underwear, burned by rebellious sons to show that they dishonor the woman and refuse to submit to her authority." Havan Alethaner shrugged. "Aletheia occasionally reads the Xenos newspaper to me. It makes me glad to live where sanity still prevails." His chest constricted like his heart might fail. Aletheia wouldn't read the newspaper to him. Not anymore. And who else would indulge such a sinful pleasure?

Juris wailed. "I miss her so much."

Havan Alethaner hesitated between their houses. "You have Korban?"

She nodded.

He strode to his round cedar door and opened it. "You're welcome in my home and at my table."

Juris sent him a grateful glance, went in, and collapsed into the nearest pillow. "I kept telling myself, 'just a little while more, and he will be home to comfort you.' All I want is my husband's arms around me, and now . . . ."

And now she wouldn't get any comfort of the marital sort from him. What she'd promised the aggies was out of the question. He'd be cold in the grave beside his wife before he ever joined to another woman, especially outside of a proper wedding celebration.

Tears trickled down Juris's cheeks.

Maybe he could bear a hug. Havan Alethaner settled into the suede pillow right beside hers and offered his arms.

Juris curled into his embrace and pressed a tear-slicked cheek against his chest, accidentally pulling back one corner of his tunic where it'd been ripped.

Aletheia got jealous if he so much as kissed Juris goodbye. However was he going to explain this?

Reality punched him in the gut. He placed his left hand at the back of his sobbing sister-in-law's head. Bridal ivory clinked against the wedding band on Havan Alethaner's right joining finger.

They jumped apart and stared.

Havan Alethaner politely glanced away. *With this ring—with this ivory—you are made holy to me, until death dissolves . . .* He laughed.

Slowly, Juris laughed, too. She shook her head. "It's absurd, isn't it? Here we haven't even removed their tokens yet, and—" She swallowed, gritted her teeth, and pulled out the ivory pinning her hair up.

The cascade of her glory coming down over her full back gutted Havan Alethaner. His little brother had also married a beauty. *Aletheia, I miss you so much. Please forgive me for not being blind.*

But Juris was right. The wedding ring on his finger lied as much as the ivory declaring her a wife rather than a widow. Havan Alethaner strode to the

47

keepsake chest under the upper cistern and beside the porcelain earth closet bowl and the clay urinal. He moved the wash basin sitting on the hope chest to the light blue counter, opened the chest, and hesitated. He wasn't ready.

The gold ring slipped off his right joining finger and into the chest. Some things just had to be done.

Ivory clunked into the keepsake chest and came to a rest beside Aletheia's ivory. Juris permitted eye contact. "Do you mind?"

"Yes. That they're gone."

HAVAN ALETHANER STOOD on the threshold of his brother's home, peering in the open door. Juris, her thirteen-year-old, and her fifteen-year-old bustled about, preparing dinner, which was normally eaten at noon, at supper time.

His four nieces under twelve sat curled up in the bright yellow gingham pillows that circled the straw-woven table. They clutched corncob dolls as they huddled together much like the village's orphaned dragonlings. Behind them, Korban lay on his pallet, right before the porcelain earth closet. Irene kept a vigil over the boy wrapped in swaddling and half covered with a wool blanket.

Paternal concern rushed through Havan Alethaner. He breathed deep. He'd been afraid that he might finish the job and kill Korban himself, after what Juris suspected.

The fifteen-year-old handed Irene a bowl of baby mush.

Irene set the bowl beside her, maneuvered behind Korban on his pallet, and pulled him up into her arms. He moaned and winced. His eyes fluttered but shut again. Irene patted his cheek. "Eat now. Heroes need their strength."

Korban snorted. "I'm not a hero. What I am is a failure and a coward and, according to the dragons, a baby, and everyone well knows it. Let me die. I don't deserve to live."

Irene pressed the bowl of mush to his lips. "Life is a gift, Korban. No one deserves it. Emi gives it to whom she chooses. Don't leave us."

Juris blocked Havan Alethaner's view. "Dinner's ready. Please come in."

Havan Alethaner took the seat usually offered to him when Juris invited his family to dinner. The little girls on his left bawled, and the maidens on his right looked like they wanted to kill him. He sent a 'help me' look across the table at Juris. "What did I do?"

She dabbed at her moist eyes. "Their father always gave you his seat."

He jumped into the free seat next to him.

Juris said belatedly, "It's all right."

Not with me, it's not. "Girls, look at me."

All seven precious babies sent Havan Alethaner red-eyed glances.

He swallowed. "I can imagine what cruel whispers you've been subjected to, after the welcome I received from the aggies, may Emi bless them. I won't pretend I know what the future holds for our family. All I know is no one can replace your father in your hearts. Certainly, no one can replace my brother. I will always be your uncle, and I will not let anyone or anything hurt you."

It was so tempting to promise he wasn't marrying their mother. But such a declaration would confuse them, should the pragmatism of choosing Juris ever overwhelm the emotions screaming no woman could replace Aletheia.

Chapter Five

After the meal, Havan Alethaner touched Juris's shoulder while she was supervising the clean up process. He said, "Once the girls are finished, could you take them upstairs? I need time alone with Korban."

Juris glanced at the young man and nodded.

Irene climbed up the ladder to the second floor last.

Havan Alethaner settled into the pillow she'd kept nice and toasty beside his nephew. "Korban."

Korban swallowed weakly before his eyelids slid up. "I failed you."

Havan Alethaner waited.

"It's my fault they're gone. Tell Aunt Juris and Irene to let me die."

"Son." The word caught in Havan Alethaner's throat. He'd meant it now more than ever before. "I should have been there. You never should've had to shoulder such adult responsibilities at your age."

Korban grunted. "The dragons would agree."

"Dragons count their adolescents as children until they mate. Why would they define a human child differently?" Havan Alethaner folded his arms. "Or are dragons not as perceptive of such things as they're said to be?"

Tears flooded over Korban's cheeks. "I'm not worthy to ever be your son. I tried to prove differently. I failed. And betrayed you in the attempt."

Havan Alethaner leaned over and carefully embraced the boy. "Son, you don't have to prove anything. If I could keep you forever, I would."

"But you would not give me to Hosanni."

Emi, if I let her marry him, will you bring my baby girl back to me?

Havan Alethaner sat back. "Did you dishonor my daughter?"

Korban closed his eyes. "Not to the extent you intend, but I most certainly didn't honor her, either. I hate myself. I should be the one that died, or—" He shuddered and moaned, clutching the side seeping yellow and orange fluid. "I am not a wolf. Please believe me. I want her back so badly. I'd asked her to marry me. She'd agreed. We just had to change your—" Korban sobbed.

Havan Alethaner swallowed. "We know, son."

Korban sniffled and sent him a surprised glance.

"Irene heard you muttering in your sleep the curse for nations that stray from the path, 'your son will choose a bride, but another man shall lie with her.' It wasn't hard to guess the significance to you."

"May I never hear that quoted in a sermon ever again."

"Can't blame you for that sentiment."

Korban's eyes strayed to the ladder. "I miss Hosanni."

But was looking where he'd last seen Irene. "I miss Aletheia. But in case you haven't noticed yet, hero, Irene rather fancies you."

"When did she move to this village?"

Havan Alethaner laughed. "At two, when her parents retuvrned here from our village."

Korban closed his eyes. "I don't like all the attention. The way she touches me stirs things in my body that grieve a heart aching for my bride."

Havan Alethaner swallowed. The sentiment was too familiar, but Korban might be in for a surprise, if the attraction was so strong now, when Korban's injuries should inhibit the male curse. "I'll talk to her mother and ask Juris to delicately remind Irene which parts *weren't* injured."

"Please don't tell her. It's rather embarrassing, uncle." Korban paused. "Is it normal?"

Don't laugh, Havan Alethaner. You were fourteen once, too. "Diakrinth thinks what is normal is for her husband to be easily led astray by a beautiful woman. Most men I know have more self-control than that. But it's learned, son. So at your age—yes. You're normal."

"I'm so ashamed. What I did—Hosanni wouldn't have been a maiden at the end if we weren't interrupted, I'm sure of it. I never thought I'd stray that far from the path. I fooled myself, saying, 'one little peek through Bion's portal won't hurt.'"

Havan Alethaner swallowed. The memories that raised weren't pleasant at all. "I doubt it hurt her, but for us, there's no such thing as one little peek. Either we've turned on Bion's forbidden machine or we haven't." He squeezed Korban's shoulder. "Some of us learn that the hard way."

"Why don't you hate me?"

"Because no one interrupted me."

Korban's eyes widened, and his mouth formed a circle. "You?"

Havan Alethaner hesitated. If he'd had the courage to tell Korban about this sooner, it might have saved him some pain. "Several maidens got into a competition over me, and I enjoyed it far, far too much. One of them offered me her maidenhood, and I foolishly accepted. I thought we'd gotten away with it until she suffered a miscarriage. She said a soldier raped her rather than get me killed, but our aggies sheared her, and I manifested my guilt by avoiding her. The shame, the miscarriage, losing her glory—it broke her. I confessed my sin after we found her body. Truth is, son, my mother lent me out in hopes a change of scenery would cure me."

"Cure you?"

"She believed that I had lycanthropy." Havan Alethaner shrugged. "It's a common diagnosis for an unruly, impertinent fourteen-year-old who dreams of being king."

AFTER THE NOON MEAL the next day, Havan Alethaner Kristekon followed a nine-year-old boy who wore only a loin cloth up Mount Sacrifice.

The draca that he'd borrowed from Korban's mother stiffened beside him and roared warnings.

Shortly, from the ponderosa pines stepped a mountain man keeping both hands where they could be seen and away from the crossbow on his back. The lilac stranger wore dreadlocks formed from sheer neglect and a muddy indigo tunic. At the stranger's wave, the naked child disappeared into the forest.

Hissing growls rolled continually from the draca and provoked an urge to reach for his own crossbow. "I am Kristos Havan. You wanted to see me?"

The stranger beat his breast. "Milord the king, the Army of the Mountains offers you our condolences."

If I'm your king, why has your army formed without my orders?

"Your highness, we pray you have vengeance on Felippo Romin for

Queen Aletheia's blood and Princess Hosanni's maidenhood. Lead us into battle as we crush the infidels and drive them from Emi's land. The pink idolaters will pay for their crimes. Romin will no longer steal our innocent children so his depraved offspring can live in luxury."

"I know you by reputation. You are but a small group of mercenaries."

"Effective nonetheless. I bring you tribute as proof." The rogue escorted Havan Alethaner and his sister's snarling dragon to a sled pulled by bison. The rogue pulled the tarp off.

A stench assaulted Havan Alethaner's nose and flies swarmed toward the source—a dozen dead pink females, half of them still children. He gasped and pinched his nostrils. "What have you done?"

"Recompense. Escalation. Romin's soldiers killed our queen and raped her daughter. We have repaid their crimes seven times upon their head."

Havan Alethaner gaped at the wolf in a man's skin. Never before had he met such pure evil.

The wolf frowned. "Don't look at me like I'm evil. Our enemies are evil invaders. They didn't consider your wife and daughter to be innocent civilians. The enemy must be met with equal force."

"I declare you a lycanthrope and hereby sentence you—" Havan Alethaner frowned at the draca's head nudging his side. "What?"

The draca signed with her tiny three-clawed arms, "Twelve man-wolves up in trees."

The wolf spat. "Curse Emi's hand for granting you to reign in the house of Kristos! Always you said you didn't have enough men, but in truth you didn't have the stomach to make the pinks suffer so much that they would flee. We need a new king."

Nice posturing, but if you thought you could rouse a rebellion without me, you wouldn't be here. "Touch me and not a husband in Diakrinth will rest until your corpses are hanging from Romin's crucifixes. Leave now and you might escape that fate."

"You would betray your own people to the highway patrol?"

As soon as I get myself out alive. "You and your men are banished from Diakrinth. Anyone who sees you in our borders in twenty-four hours will have full right to kill you."

The wolf smirked. "Don't worry. No one will see us." He glanced at the corpses and spat on them. "Keep your tribute." The wolf slunk out of sight.

The draca roared at the trees for several minutes before she relaxed and signed to Havan Alethaner, "Uncle, man-wolves all gone. Safe now."

"Good girl. Stay here and guard the bodies until I return—and don't eat them." Carrion smelled like food inside Draca's nostrils. "Leave them in peace unless you want killed also."

A hiss like a sigh escaped the draca. "Yes, Uncle."

Havan Alethaner picked up a fallen branch that came up to his shoulder, marched as close to the sled as he dared, and dragged the branch in the purple dirt to form a trail back. He mentally rehearsed his report to the invaders, so he wouldn't forget a single detail. The scepter was worthless if obtaining it meant becoming like Romin and Erin.

A ROUGH HAND SHOOK Hosanni's shoulder. "Wake up, bambina."

Hosanni groaned. The firm bed she lay in felt too high up. She shivered through a deep chill that felt hot compared to the ice wrapped in cloth on her forehead. Her eyelids and her body felt heavy. She only wanted to go to sleep and wake up in Mother's arms.

Another man said, "I told you. The child is a loss. Leave her."

"Doctor, I saw the look in your eyes when you saw her irons, and I know why you were quick to want to amputate, as if you don't know her own people would abandon her to die if you maim her. You do her no favors trying to help her escape."

"Sir, I merely want her to live. Right now, she has nothing to live for."

Plenty to die for, though. Mother. Korban. Maybe they could be together in Heaven. Father took her to see a play with that theme once, in the City of Trees, as a birthday treat, when they had the money for such frivolities.

A rough hand cupped her cheek like Father would. "Listen, little one."

Hosanni peeked one hopeful eye open. At the hateful murderer's face, she let the heavy lid fall. Maybe Pappy never came home. Maybe in Heaven, they would all be together again.

"Hosanni, come back to us. You can beat this, but you have to want to."

"Why ya care?"

The male witch said, "Why do you care? Unless you're purchasing her?"

"I have a daughter her age! What do you think?" Captain Fautorio took her hand. "Listen to me, bambina. I know what you're afraid of, and it's not true. None of us would ever dare. A marita is expected to reach her husband a virgin. If a man spoils you, he had better be able to pay for you, if he wants to continue breathing. Trust me, Hosanni, none of these men can afford you."

That was supposed to be comforting? "Someone will pay."

"Every man in Diakrinth is a slave owned by his wife, is he not?"

"He not sold like dragon. He choose his house."

"So does a marita, child. We want you happily married. Miserable people demand their money back. So you'll go to school, make friends, and court like any maiden. Only you'll marry much better than you could otherwise, provide a secure future for your children, and never have to worry about having clean water to drink or enough food to eat. It's a different life, but it's a good one. I promise you. Please trust me."

Hosanni opened one eye to send him a skeptical look. "Trust murderer?"

"Bambina, I made one bad move, and all Hades broke loose. Would I be here, fighting for you, if I didn't regret what happened? Do you have any idea how much trouble I'm going to be in, when I give my report in the City by the Bay? I'm expecting at least a demotion over this."

They can execute you for all I care. "Want to die. Go be with Mother and Korban, Hosanni's forbidden bridegroom. We may be together in Heaven."

"I know what wanting to die feels like. My wife didn't want me any more, but she liked my money, so now I'm in the army. I know it feels like there's no reason to go on. But there is. For me, it's my little girl. I live to hold her again someday. You'll find your purpose. Until then, know that I care and won't let anything hurt you anymore. I'll carry you all the way to Alcatraz if I have to."

Hosanni laughed. That was too absurd not to.

"I'll do everything within my power anyway." Captain Fautorio moved the damp cloth aside. He stroked her forehead with icy fingers. "Let me tell you something else, bambina. I believe in you. If Romin believes, too, you won't have anything to worry about. He's been looking for you, and he has plans for your life far beyond your wildest dreams. You have to trust me even though right now things look like they couldn't possibly be any worse."

A Xenos king, intend her good? Doubtful. Hosanni yawned. "Let

Hosanni sleep. She think about it."

ICY FLAMES ENGULFED Hosanni—she couldn't tell whether she'd been cast into an incinerator or cast into Frozen Hades. Screams stayed trapped inside the prison of her body, which might as well have been made of stone.

Hands stretched out over her body. It seemed familiar somehow. Oh, the person must be in the position that the idolaters assumed to pray at the Xenos shrine in McCall.

"Emi," Captain Fautorio intoned, "you are the great High Queen, the lady of Heaven's vast armies, the ancient of days, the sovereign who reigns above all sovereigns. I'm a stranger, but a dragon begging for a bone. Maybe you're not there, maybe Time and Chance do reign supreme. But they won't help this child. I come before you with outstretched hands because you are this child's last hope. Do you know what Hosanni means to us? Many think Lady Veritas is a myth, and maybe she is, but if she is to come, Hosanni must live. That might be more important than Romin's glorious vision, Emi."

Such ignorance. Hosanni sat up and glared at the Xenos soldier. "Might? Preserving Lady Veritas by preserving her mother might be more important than a scheme of a man? Only might?"

Oops. The broken English might not be so cute if they figured out she was simply too lazy to conjugate all those detestable irregular verbs. Her heartbeat raced. What if the murderer returned to being cruel? Even Mammy and Pappy eventually caught on to her manipulating them with the cutesy third person stuff and started spanking her for it.

Behind Captain Fautorio stood another pink man in a black kilt with a short black dress coat worn over a white tunic. A lacy scarf hung from his neck. The pink men stared, wide-eyed. The doctor stuck a glass thermometer in her mouth and began to explain what it was and how it worked. Hosanni tuned out the boring details and glared.

Once the glass tube came out, she spat, "Not stupid. Know thermometer. Not care how it work."

The doctor gaped at the red line. "Normal." He stared at her. "I have seen many things in this desolate country, but you are something special."

Captain Fautorio ran out of the small, cluttered room.

Hosanni glanced at her foot. Strips of soft, white material wrapped her foot up like one swaddled a baby or the dead. "What be that?"

"Cotton gauze. I'm afraid I had to excise the injury, so—"

"Excise?"

"I cut away the section of your foot that was making you sick. You'll have a bad scar along the path of the dragon fang, but most of it is on the sole, so it shouldn't be too noticeable. It will take you a while to learn to walk without a limp, but as far as this injury goes, you are one extremely lucky girl."

Hosanni frowned. Luck glorified the false god Chance. "Emi's hand, not luck. Did ya give magic potion?"

"If you mean did I give you any medicine, of course."

"Which god it be devoted to? Did ya use standard practice as our mothers passed down to us in the healing rites?"

"What did she just say?" Captain Fautorio said as he stood in the door.

She turned another suspicious glare on the male witch.

He smiled at her. "You would be a Ravane's daughter, I presume?"

"Mother let Hosanni help with healing rites. She be Ravane someday."

Captain Fautorio said, "So what if she's the child of clergy?"

The witch glared at Captain Fautorio. "In the tribal villages, the religious teacher is the closest thing to a doctor besides Mother. *The Rites of Healing* ought to be on the bookshelves of every household in the Union. As a first aid reference book, it's excellent. As a replacement for modern medicine entirely, it's woefully inadequate."

Hosanni sniffed. "Magic potions be against the path."

The doctor scrunched down to her eyelevel. "A doctor learns that quickly while trying to make a living in this country. That's why I keep handy supplies that haven't been dedicated to the service of Time and Chance. Instead, I have a local Ravane bless them according to your customs."

Hosanni gasped. No wonder Emi had given Diakrinth over to oppressors for so long, if such apostasy went on in her cities. "Ya bring a curse on me."

Captain Fautorio came closer. "Bambina, I saw a miracle just now, not a curse. And you're not responsible for treatment you didn't consent to."

She nodded.

Captain Fautorio turned to the witch. "Is she ready to move, doctor?"

"I would like to keep her until the wound completely heals."

"If I keep her off that foot and follow your care instructions precisely, will you let me take her now?"

"If you're worried about the cost, I'll accept the child as my payment."

A sigh arose, and Captain Fautorio ran a hand through his orangish pink hair. "Doctor, in your shoes, I'd offer that, too. Unfortunately, I'm paying for this out of my own pocket, and she's government property."

The doctor waved. "I will send my bill to the Union then."

"And the treasury will send you a note that you can redeem for silver at a bank. She's too valuable. I'm sorry. I have a duty. I'm going to be in enough trouble as it is."

The doctor lowered his head in defeat. "I'll fit her on crutches. I trust you can exempt her from the irons for medical reasons?"

"That shouldn't be a problem. They won't be necessary much longer."

Hosanni swallowed. Why did that statement make her stomach want to heave the mush they'd surely been force feeding her?

WHEN COULD SHE GET off the monstrosities making her armpits sore? Hop. Hop. Hop. Wooden crutches felt far from stable on cobblestone when headed uphill. And her left sandal made her left foot heavier to hold up.

Captain Fautorio said, "You'll get used to it, bambina."

"Don't want used to it. Want two good feet."

"Thank me that you'll have them soon. The doctor wanted to amputate."

"And leave Hosanni at the gate to beg or starve?"

He laughed. "That's what I told him."

A crowd appeared over the rise of the hill they were climbing, away from the bustling city with three and four story buildings. Too many were squares with rounded corners. A handful of shops remained, mostly to outfit or shelter horses or to repair the chariots they drew. The vehicles had four steel wheels and were magically driven from inside of a cabin enclosed by a metal roof, two glass windshields, and four metal doors with glass windows. Mastodon-sized, public-transit chariots called horsecars in the city were called stagecoaches when they left for other nations from this hill.

On the right of the arrow-straight road, Diakrinthian houses dotted the spiraling side streets. Some houses were shaped like number eights, meaning they had two rooms on each floor. On the left side of the road, Xenos homes stood in lines with their ugly sharp corners and slanted roofs.

The ugly homes were lovely compared to Stagecoach Hill's horde of bald adolescent females. The girls' short orange tunics exposed their ankle-length orange underpants. Hosanni frowned. Her people pulled on heavy wool socks to keep their legs warm against winter's chill.

How could so many girls deserve to be shorn? Wide-eyed, she turned to Captain Fautorio. "There be so many girls guilty of *porneia*?"

Captain Fautorio marched on, his jaw tightening and his brow furrowed.

Maybe he couldn't figure out what *porneia* was. "Hosanni sorry she use her tongue. Your tongue don't have this word. *Porneia* be any joining together not blessed by the assembly." She wet her lips. "Why don't ya answer? Ya be sad? Why they bring the guilty ones all here? Why not shear them in their own assemblies? Or they all live in the City of Trees?"

Captain Fautorio glanced around and wrapped her in a hug like Father used to. "Bambina, this will be one of the bad moments. I hate this, but I don't make the laws. Rulers far away who can't hear your screams do. So cry all you want, hate me if you must, but there's nothing I can do."

What did he mean by this saying?

Her bosom tightened and her heart beat faster with each step around the dishonored heads. Some weeping girls were wailing and had torn their tunics and covered themselves in dust in a healthy show of grief for their lost glory. Most girls had the vacant, unseeing stare of a lycanthrope bite victim.

Another throng appeared, men and women, an assortment of blues, pinks and lilacs. These lilacs were surely nashas, the mixed-race descendants of the thousand civilizations that lost their ethnic identities in the Great Dispersal. She'd never seen such an assembly.

The throng raised white cards on sticks as a pink man dressed like the doctor spoke way too fast for her to understand him. He kept waving beside him at a Diakrinthian girl wearing irons and the strange orange garments. They had put her head in stocks, forcing her to bend forward.

The fast-talking pink man pointed at the crowd. A nasha woman shouted victory and ran up on the platform with a pair of shears. She grabbed a clump of the Diakrinthian girl's glory and snipped it away at the scalp.

The girl squirmed, but the stocks immobilized her head. The Diakrinthian girl sobbed. "Please! I'll be good! Don't shear me! I'll be good! Please!"

The throng laughed.

Another soldier thrust a pile of orange garments at Captain Fautorio. He winced and took Hosanni behind the high platform. "Sorry, some semblance of privacy is the most mercy I can offer." He handed her the ugly tunic and the ugly underpants. "Please change willingly, or I'll have to do it myself."

He turned his back.

She glanced around for an escape route. The empty bison pasture. She hopped on her crutches as fast as she could.

He grabbed her shoulder from behind and stopped her fall. "Can't blame you for trying, but now I have to disrobe you, bambina."

Captain Fautorio took one crutch away, tugged her outer garment away from her body, and sliced her palla open with the blade of his sword.

She moved her arm to defend herself, but he caught her fast and removed her undergarments in like fashion. She writhed and put weight on her sore left foot to kick out her attacker's kneecaps. He dodged her blow and pulled the rough orange tunic down over her head.

He handed her back the crutch. "Stop it and get off that foot. None of this is my idea. You're only making unpleasant orders harder to follow."

Hosanni hopped to an overturned barrel and balanced her bottom on it while she pulled the ugly underpants on half way. She hobbled back up and drew them the rest of the way up.

Captain Fautorio sighed and waved around the platform. "Follow me this time. That escape attempt was the fault of my weakness, but next time you run off, you'll be whipped. I can't help you if you don't follow orders."

She hopped after him on the crutches to the animal pen holding unshorn maidens in orange. Like herself. She glanced toward the stage, to the girl now almost fully deprived of her glory, and coughed up bile.

He must still think . . . She batted her eyes, giving her best pout. "Hosanni not give her maidenhood to Korban. Honest. She not dishonor her head." A rush of guilt slammed her. "So she let him drink from her cistern a little." She winced. "So she let him drink much. But she not join to him, not without the assembly's blessing. She never, never do that. Honest."

Captain Fautorio squatted. "I know, bambina. You have done nothing wrong. Nothing."

A tiny sliver of hope rose. "No shear Hosanni?"

"I have no say over that. I am so sorry." He stood, wiping his face. "This army disgusts me. They order you to do things that strip you of your humanity and then crucify you when you lose it."

Her or him?

The fast-talking man on the stage pointed at Hosanni. Two more soldiers appeared. She sent Captain Fautorio a pleading look.

The other two soldiers bound her hand and foot and hauled her up on the platform like a sack of potatoes. She screamed and writhed.

Captain Fautorio said only, "Careful with her left foot!"

The other soldiers thrust her down into the stocks with its top half pulled back and scooped up her hair. The lid slammed over her neck and shoulders. Her hair fell down around her face. She screamed, and repeated over and over in her native tongue, "Please, I didn't give my maidenhood to Korban. I only let him kiss me! Please!"

Her left foot began to throb, and she shifted her weight off that sandal.

White cards flew up in the laughing throng. The fast-talking man pointed at one. A pink woman ran up, waving shears and shouting victory.

Money clinked. The pink woman slid a woven basket beneath Hosanni's head and yanked a small section of her hair until her scalp burned. Cold metal touched her scalp and ended the pain with a snip.

A clump of Hosanni's rich, plum hair fell into the basket.

Again the burning agony came. Again the cold metal. Snip.

More rich plum hair filled the basket.

Hosanni looked up to the Rock of the Table in the foothills surrounding the modern city, to the castle that spiraled toward Heaven. Its stones shone as white as ivory, this fortified citadel that her mothers built, and once wielded the scepter from. It was family property that ought to belong to her now. The oppressors sat in the ivory tower, deaf and blind, like the idols they served.

Agony, snip. Agony, snip. Agony, snip.

Her beautiful glory stolen in tiny increments.

Chapter Six

A cold wind pelted Hosanni with tiny particles of ice that stuck to her bald head. She shivered and, seeking warmth, huddled closer to the orange mass of shorn adolescent girls. A familiar fog entombed her. They resembled bison. No, a herd of bison had far better protection from the cold.

Voices shouted.

The herd of bald girls shuffled forward with barely a whimper. Hosanni hopped along on her crutches. Through the gaps, soldiers rode on horseback, shouting the very same cries as bisonherders moving their meat to market. A handful of charioteers passed as well in black vehicles with four steel wheels, rounded roofs, and glass windows. Two horses with short stiff purple manes drew each chariot, and a spare steel wheel bulged on the side.

Children swept around her. It was so hard for her to keep up with those on two good feet.

A man shouted, "Hosanni! Hosanni!"

The name slid by twice more before it registered as being hers. "Pappy?"

Her shame punched her, and she hopped deeper into the crowd. If that was Pappy, he couldn't see her like this. He'd think Korban had betrayed him, and her beloved would be—his bloodied body flashed by along with the slain dragons and Mother. An invisible mastodon kicked her in the bosom.

So sore. So tired. Her eyes drooped.

Hands shoved her from behind. She hopped on.

"Hosanni!"

The voice continued calling. She continued hopping.

A slap fell across her cheek and a man shook her. "Hosanni."

She looked up at the murderer's pink face. A faint spark lit before the chill inside her snuffed it out. She glanced away. The herd had turned while she'd numbly continued on straight. She shivered as the chill crept in and hopped to catch up to them.

Later, a black chariot blocked her path. The hateful murderer thrust open the passenger side door. "Get in. I've got permission for you to ride with me. West California is far too long a march from here for a bambina on crutches."

She turned to hop around him.

"That's an order."

Past screams of the defiant came back to her. She shuddered and hopped to the chariot. The second she settled into the soft leather seat, the oblivion of sleep enfolded her.

OCHTU TURNED THE PAGE of the newspaper laying open on his drawing room desk. Curling dark purple fingers around the edge of the page, he squinted at the print in the meager light of the fireplace and a small red oil lamp. A pink woman in a violet frock burst into the shadowy room, her hair strewing down out of a matronly coiffure. Shadows hid her face.

He jumped up, his heart racing. "Who—"

The intruder came into the light, huffing and glaring daggers at him.

He peered. "Marezza? How did—the housekeeper always locks up."

She dangled a key. "Funny how easy it is to get a locksmith to make you a key to your own home. Not nice to lock your wife out, Coyote. Not nice at all." She slammed her hands on the desk, her eyes narrowed to slits. "Do you know where I've been?"

He smirked a suppressed laugh. Probably in the position portrayed in his latest masterpiece, scrubbing floors of dormitories. "Tough week at work?"

Marezza growled. "I am going to kill you. Slowly and painfuly, and make you as miserable as you've made me. I just haven't decided on the best way to destroy you yet. But you will live long enough to sorely regret humiliating me. That I promise you."

She went on to her usual litany of every foul name and insult she knew.

Once she took a breath, he sent her the sweetest smile he could muster. He'd rather rip her throat out. "I've missed you, too, darling." *Now get out my house before I fetch the nearest city patrolman.* "Though I would be careful how you go about plotting my untimely demise. This family has had enough sordid headlines and members of it executed for treason, don't you think?"

He snapped his fingers. "Oh, by the way." Ochtu stood, picked up a stack of bills, and slapped them at Marezza's flat abdomen. "These are yours. They arrived here by mistake."

She tossed them back and screeched more obscenities at him.

Ochtu lit a cigar and puffed on it. "This is your own fault, Marezza. You're the one that threw your birthright away on living in the gutter. These are your gambling debts, and it's my hard-earned fortune that they're devouring. Rest assured, you've made me quite miserable. Don't worry your pretty little head about that. I hate the very air you breathe. I'd dissolve this so-called marriage, except you're not worth my countrymen going to war against each other over."

He took another puff on his cigar and blew the smoke at her. "Oh, by the way, Tony and I have been put through most embarrassing examinations that our doctor intends to repeat on a regular basis on the unlikely chance you've been incubating for the last seven years."

Ochtu leaned in close to his wife. "The doctor gave us clean bills of health. So long as Tony stays that way, you get to live another day without my hands wrapped around your adulterous throat, squeezing the life out of your body."

"How dare you threaten me! Papa will hear about this!"

Or her grandfather more accurately. "Sure, let's race right over there. You can tell Romin what I said. And I'll give him the bills threatening to seize my 'daughter Antonia' and sell *him* as a marita if I don't pay for your disgracing of Romin's good name. Say, wasn't your mother executed for siphoning money from the public treasury to pay such debts?"

Marezza glared. "This isn't over, Coyote!"

She flung herself from the room. The front door slammed.

Tony came in dressed in his nightshirt and sleeping cap and carrying his teal night lamp with him. "Da? I heard shouting."

Ochtu hugged his wee son, being careful of the night lamp. "Lad, we had a break in, but we're safe now. I'll get the locks changed in the morning."

He escorted Tony back to bed. In the dim glow of the child's night lamp, Ochtu sat with his son until the wee laddie finally drifted back to sleep.

Ochtu slipped out into total darkness, groped his way to his unlit room, climbed into the cold bed, and wept.

OCHTU PLAYED AN ERINI holiday tune on his baby grand piano. Tony sang the words. Rather than spin his new dreidel, he marched it around the holly and pine bough centerpiece on the drawing room table. Usually, Ochtu decked every room in holly at this time of year, but it didn't grow native to this area, and this year his budget permitted only holly for one room, new menorah candles, last winter's green drapes, and the inexpensive gifts the neighbors' children always got from Mother Chanukah.

It goaded, Tony's eyes lighting up, thanking a woman for gifts that *Da* had purchased, wrapped, and placed in Tony's red Chanukah sack, currently hanging over the fireplace that crackled and popped with the chestnuts Ochtu had fed it. He glanced at the mouth-watering plate of goodies on the mantle. On the bright side, he got to eat the miniature mincemeat pies that Tony left out for Mother Chanukah each year on the eve before the festivities officially began, on the Saturday before the third Sunday of December.

So perhaps doing his own baking wasn't proper for a prince, but he'd liked to give the housekeeper shorter hours at this time of year even when he could afford her full time.

The grandmother clock gonged.

Another hour, and perhaps he could persuade Tony to go to bed and then sneak his presents into his sack. Maybe the lad would be patient and actually open one present each night of Chanukah this year rather than ripping into all of them tomorrow morning. He should probably be more strict to make him wait, but Tony's birthday usually fell during or right before Chanukah, and the boy got a bit cheated sharing his special day with a major holiday. For Ochtu, it merely meant buying nine presents instead of eight.

A small hand tugged on his white drawstring blouse. "Da?"

Ochtu glanced down at his son. "Aye?"

Tony spun his dreidel on the piano. "Why aren't you singing?"

Because it's easier to find the heart to play the music than to sing the words. "You sing so much prettier than me, Tony. I like to hear you."

"Could you play 'Chanukah in Albany'?"

Anything to see your smile. "Sure, son."

The little boy took a deep breath and sang at the top of his lungs about the green holly and ivy decorations that adorned Albany at Chanukah. It was cute until Tony got to, "It's nice, you know, to kiss your beau, while cuddling under the mistletoe—"

Ochtu hit a wrong note, his hands shaking a bit. Getting kissed under the mistletoe would never be in the cards for him.

"Da, why did you stop?" Tony peered closer. "Are you crying?"

He shook his head, slid off of the piano bench, and sat on the red velvet cushions of the walnut sofa. He patted his lap. "Come here, laddie."

Tony crawled into his lap and hugged him. "Don't be sad. It's Chanukah."

So you've told me every year since you learned how to say that. "Son, your da feels very lonely at Chanukah time. Since you're getting to be a big boy now, you can understand why a wee bit more." He swallowed. "Seven years ago, someone I once cared about hurt me very badly at this time of year."

His almost-seven-year-old said quietly, "Mother."

Ochtu winced. *When did this boy get so smart?*

"Why did she leave us?"

Tears stole past Ochtu's control. He clasped his son tight to his chest.

A knight of the royal guard with lavender hair appeared in the door. For Tony's sake, Ochtu followed the tradition of leaving the front door unlocked for Mother Chanukah. The knight bowed. "Presenting Her Royal Highness, Princess Porcia Romin."

Saved by his persistent aunt-in-law. Ochtu glanced at his grandmother clock. "Say, Tony, I think we have just enough time for a game of Old Bachelor before bed. I believe we left the cards in the dining room."

Tony rushed out after the deck of cards.

Ochtu stood and faced Porcia, folding his arms. "No."

"You don't even know what I want."

"I know what ye want, and it's never goin' to happen. It's over. The only reason that I don't take my son and go home to Georgia is I'd hardly have the explanation out before Mum declared war. Erini sweat and Erini blood built the Union. I won't have my country at war with itself over Marezza. However, I am finished with her, Porcia. I won't go through this hell anymore. If ye want to help, keep that devil o' a woman away from me."

Porcia pressed her left hand on his breast, a plea in her eyes. "Don't you know what tomorrow is? We miss you, Coyote. Everyone's asking why you're not at the piano this year. This is the one night a year we have Papa all to ourselves, with his full, undivided attention. It's not the same without you."

He swallowed. "Marezza's back this year."

"Yes, but she won't make a scene in front of everyone."

"Her phoniness drives me insane."

"Don't think of it that way. Think of it as being polite to each other for the sake of the family and the holiday's spirit."

"I don't want Tony to see her."

"She has no use for children, you know that."

"Exactly. He'll find out his mother is there and totally ignorin' him. Don't ye think that will hurt?"

Porcia teared up. "You can't protect him forever."

Tony came back in waving the deck of cards. "I found them!"

Porcia sent Ochtu a pleading look. "Remember how much fun he has?"

His son ran in circles with his cousins each year until they all ended up fast asleep together in a relatively quiet corner of the palace. Ochtu sighed and knelt with his son. "How would you like to play Old Bachelor with your great-grandfather, son?"

Tony's eyes lit up. "Bisnonno's coming!"

Ochtu swallowed. "No. We're goin' to his house. His Chanukah party is tonight, and we're invited. So you can stay up late, if you want to go."

"Oh girl!" Tony hugged him. "Thanks, Da!"

"Let me get our kilt jackets." Ochtu waved for Porcia to follow him into the hall. "I'll take the long way to the palace. You take the short way and warn everyone not to mention Marezza to Tony. If they listen, he will never realize she's there."

HOSANNI SAT IN THE bumpy chariot. A draft whistled in her ears as the frozen and seemingly endless Nevada desert rolled by. She'd heard of deserts warm year round. Not this one. She glanced to the frostbitten herd walking body against body for warmth, with three or four children bundled together inside every black wool blanket that the soldiers passed out.

She pulled the wool blanket tucked around her tighter and bit her lip. A permanent scar on her heel was a small price to pay for not being out there.

It was amazing, really. The chariot's doors connected to the roof, with glass windows on all sides. A heavy leather flap covered the large opening in the dashboard that the horses' reins passed through. The hooks above the flap were especially clever. Captain Fautorio caught the reins around them until he needed to give the horses new directions.

She touched the strange chair underneath them. It seated two people, like a bridal pillow, only it had an upright back that tilted comfortably and was elevated a foot up off of the floor. This forced her to bend her knees, as there wasn't enough room to curl up as she'd normally sit. Strangely, something as firm as the floor filled the elevated seat. Such a marvelous thing. And to think there was another just like it behind them.

Better yet, Captain Fautorio had a trowel for digging a proper toilet when they needed to relieve themselves, and he shared his own daily rations with her. The soldiers grudgingly fed and watered the herd whenever they finally stopped for the night.

The chariot's halt jarred her. She stared up at Captain Fautorio. "Milord, why we stop?"

"Hold tight." He got out and jogged around to the trunk of the chariot.

Ah. She'd wait until he returned to take advantage of the stop, though she didn't feel that need. It was a bit embarrassing to ask for such a privilege.

He returned with a package wrapped in thin green paper and tied with a red ribbon. He swallowed. "I like to send my daughter a gift, but her mother always sends it back, so I . . . well, this year, I never got around to mailing it, and every little girl should—but I only have one. So, uh, here."

She stared at the package he thrust at her. That couldn't be for Chanukah. Why would Xenos celebrate a minor holiday commemorating the rededication of a temple that invaders like themselves had desecrated? "What day be it?"

"December Seventeenth. First day of Chanukah this year."

Hosanni frowned, struggling to convert Diakrinth's calendar to the Xenos calendar. "Hosanni think that be well past the 25th of Kislev."

Captain Fautorio winced. "We celebrate Chanukah on different days than you did in Diakrinth, bambina."

Idolaters co-opted it? Why? "These days also be a pagan holiday?"

"The Winter Solstice usually falls during the third full week of December, too, yes. And my favorite Chanukah traditions all derive from pagan origins. But so what if we made a few compromises during the Great Dispersal? We were fighting to preserve our religious heritage, remember?"

She gaped, glancing over her pink companion dubiously. "Our?"

He laughed. "Bambina, welcome to the Diaspora."

"Don't want to be dispersed. Want to stay in Diakrinth."

"Beg your pardon, I meant yes, our religion. I don't deserve to call myself Emian these days, I have strayed from the path, but Emi's people have always been a mixed multitude. You blokes call us 'Romini' like it's an ethnicity, but pinks are technically mixed-race nashas ourselves."

Hosanni raised her brows. "Romini means that you owe honor to Romin as a child owes honor to her mother. You rebels can be members of any race, but nashas speak English. Pinks have your own tongue."

"*Italiano, sì.* The Latins first enslaved the House of Romin's ancestors. The rest of us assimilated to the crown after San Romin DiFrancesca, may his name endure forever, relieved our former masters of half the Union. But pinks are many peoples, already enslaved by blues and stripped of our own cultures before Erin conquered the world, viewed pinks as pigs, and abused us. What unites pinks as one people is our common suffering and Emianity."

"But ya and Erin worship Time and Chance."

"The pagan gods are back with new names, but Emianity hasn't lost all of its influence. I mean, I know some people who decry all religion, and they still celebrate Chanukah. Now, are you going to open that or not?"

She swallowed. Before General Romin DiFrancesca had betrayed Kristos by establishing the House of Romin, the pinks had been Diakrinth's friends and had embraced her path. And defending the path had required teaching it to their blue oppressors. For a thousand years, all women in Erin's Union had feared Emi. But that history had never seemed to connect to life today.

The green paper and the red ribbon were so pretty. Who thought of such things? Hosanni untied the ribbon and carefully pulled apart the layers of thin paper. Sticks of peppermint candy with a red swirl fell out into her hand.

She counted them and gasped. "Eight. One for each day?"

Captain Fautorio's eyes smiled. "If you're patient."

"Oh, thank you!" She hugged him.

Mother and Korban's bloody bodies slammed into her. She shrunk back into the far corner of the chariot and wept.

The frozen desert rolled by, taking her further and further from home.

Chapter Seven

Havan Alethaner emptied his second earth closet bowl onto the snow-covered mound, stacked the bowls, and trudged to the heap of composted soil. Others had already shoveled it off. His fur-covered bisonskin boots hugged his legs to his knees underneath his long-sleeved tunic, and he'd tied closed his bisonskin coat. The women's coats were calf-length rather than ankle-length and their boots rose to midcalf. Irene also had her wool stockings on.

He scooped fresh dirt into each bowl and stretched his back.

Irene came up and filled hers. She headed back.

Havan Alethaner came up beside her and watched the maiden, her twin braids worn over her shoulders. She was getting to the age where it became incredibly rude to initiate direct eye contact with her. But he reckoned that didn't include her profile. Should she turn toward him, that would constitute her initiating it.

Her silence spoke volumes. Something was troubling her, he was sure of it. More than simply their family's primary grief. "Child, thank you for saving me an additional trip."

"My blessing, Uncle Havan, but I'm hardly a child."

"And certainly not my lady. May your mother see your grandchildren's children, amen, amen." Though he didn't like to think of Juris as his lady, either. Technically, his wife's death reverted his ownership back to his natal house, but unless Korban's mother lost her mind and collected them, he and Korban were both lent to Juris.

A sparrow called. It sounded lonely.

There had to be a way to draw Irene out. "I am proud of the woman you are becoming. Your own father couldn't be prouder."

Irene stiffened.

Thankfully, two earth closet bowls occupied his hands. They wanted to hold onto her like she was a little girl still. "If Hosanni ever wondered why her 'older sisters' lived next door, she merely picked up on how much Aletheia and I loved you. Nothing will ever change that love. And I'll rebuke to her face any woman who whispers we should."

Irene walked on, her lower lip quivering.

At last, she said, "I don't think we ever thanked you properly, for making Chanukah special for the little ones this year."

"All I did was give them candy and help the baby light some candles."

"I think Mother would have skipped it entirely this year if you hadn't."

Juris, skip even a minor holiday? She was nearly as studious as her sister about such things. "I was glad to see them smile for a change."

Irene turned to face him. Tears shone in her eyes. "I don't know what to think about you and Mother, but I've been trying to find the strength—" She drew in a breath. "Uncle, the little ones cry their eyes out every time you leave. They don't understand why you have to go home. They fear that you won't come back, either."

Havan Alethaner studied his niece. All he ever did was hold Juris while they grieved for Aletheia and his brother, but under normal circumstances, that'd be scandalous even if anyone believed it. "What whispers do you hear about me and your mother?"

Irene glanced away. "Speculation about what you do together when you invite her into your home and whether or not it's . . . sanctioned."

"Your friends think I'm fornicating with Juris and don't understand the aggies' indifference but are afraid to confront their elders?"

Irene nodded.

They walked in silence for several minutes.

Havan Alethaner said, "We haven't wanted to upset you, but the aggies declared Hosanni dead and invoked the law of sororate marriage. This hasn't happened in your lifetimes, thankfully, but when a woman dies childless, the aggies toss the grieving widower at his wife's sister and order her to serve as her sister's surrogate. I've even heard of married women being pressured to force a maiden daughter to lay with her uncle."

Irene gasped.

Havan Alethaner shrugged. "Your mother consented to lay with me in this manner so the aggies would stop suggesting such evil of you. She asked only time to grieve, but I have no intention of cooperating with their wicked plans. Amen, neither of us can stomach the thought of what they want us to do. But it means we can do what we wish without fear of censure, including lament together. We prefer privacy. That's why I host her alone so frequently."

Irene set down her earth closet bowl and hugged him. "I'm sorry, uncle, I should have known better. Could you consider . . ." She released him, picked up her bowl, and headed toward the village once more.

Havan Alethaner frowned. "Beg your pardon, daughter?"

The word sliced between them. Havan Alethaner winced. He'd felt that way since she was an infant, but why must it slip out now? "My niece. Always and forever."

Irene sighed. "My sisters and I talked at length, and we made a decison. We know you don't want to take Pap's place, but we need our uncle, and we don't like it when you leave us at night. Those of us aware of the marriage bed closet's purpose aren't ready for Mother to be making love to someone else in there, but you *are* a member of this house now."

Havan Alethaner winced. "We're being selfish, your mother and I. If I moved in with you, we'd face pressure to not leave Hosanni's house empty, and we like having a quiet place where we can go to be alone." His stomach churned. He talked like they ought to be fleeing into the marriage bed closet.

Irene said softly, "I could always explain to the older girls what you're using the marriage bed closet for."

No. Juris needed held but not in there. That would be wrong in there. "Is this about me moving in, or a certain hero wanting to be back on his feet and at home with me?"

Irene sent him an embarrassed smile. "What do you mean?"

Havan Alethaner laughed. "You know Korban will wait a year for Hosanni to come home before he lets himself court again, right?"

"Am I that obvious?"

"Is he worth waiting for?"

"All the prospects around here were on hand that day, but only Korban attempted to defend us. Whichever bride he chooses will be greatly blessed."

"Meaning you?" Havan Alethaner nudged her with his elbow.

Irene giggled. "It *would* be nice to marry a hero." She cupped her mouth. "Do you think me horrid? With your daughter—"

"—having dishonored Romin's law, as well as mine and Aletheia's, to accept the betrothal of a young man who I'd already informed could not marry our underage daughter?"

Irene glanced up at Havan Alethaner shyly. "If you did acquire a daughter of marriageable age, then would you find it nice to have a hero for a son?"

"He is my son, albeit on loan. And the way you look at each other when Korban doesn't realize what he's doing is a good reason to maintain separate households. Thankfully, your mother happens to agree."

"Do you love her?"

"Your mother? You know I love her. She's my sister twice over."

Irene's breath rushed out of her. She winked. "Not the love that I feared, Uncle Havan."

Why couldn't women just say what they meant? "I'm even less ready to entertain such thoughts than Korban."

She took a step back, eyes narrowing. "But you haven't said no, either."

Havan Alethaner sighed. What was her problem? At least it was his own foolishness that had made Aletheia this insecure. "I'll promise you this. When I make love to Juris—"

Irene grimaced.

His cheeks grew hot. "Pardon for that. I mean, if—if—I joined to her, it would be in the assembly, in the privacy of a bridal tent, at a proper wedding celebration. Granted not as big a production as a first wedding, but it will—or would—definitely be far more than the aggies privately dismissing us to join whenever we can stomach it."

"I understand." Irene lifted her earth closet higher and kicked up snow as she fled toward the village, her shoulders heaving with sobs.

The chill entered Havan Alethaner's bones. *Aletheia, forgive me for not being blind. I love you and only you. Why must I tell you that over and over?*

HOSANNI JOINED THE maidens at the railing in surrendering the contents of their stomachs to the black waters that stretched to meet a black sky, with a kiss of land in between.

Deprived fully of her daily bread, she clung to the rail of the awful rocking boat floating upon more water than she'd ever seen in one place. To think that Anapausi and her daughters had endured this sickness on the ark for an entire year. At least she was finally off the stupid crutches. Just in time to get herded on board this awful ferry.

A salty breeze fluttered around Hosanni. It felt like it was nearly spring after the fortnight in the cold desert. But that could not be.

Captain Fautorio slid in beside her, a concerned frown visible in the glow of the ship's gas lanterns. He handed to her the canteen holding his own water ration. "You all right?"

"Thank ya." She swigged from the canteen, spat over the railing, and sipped on the water. "How long must Hosanni endure this, milord?"

He looked away. "Soon we'll reach the end of this journey, bambina."

"Why be it so warm?"

"You'll change your mind about it being warm when summer comes." He waved at the blackness. "The ocean takes a long time to heat up and to cool down, giving these parts mild, rainy winters and cool, dry summers."

She stared out at the rolling blackness. "It be ugly."

"Wait until morning comes to judge it, bambina."

At sniffling, she glanced toward him and peered. "Ya be crying?"

He wiped his face. "I broke a serious rule, bambina. Don't get attached to the cargo." He paused. "And they were right. I can't do this anymore." He met her gaze. "And I'm not the least bit sorry."

Her stomach churned. "Ya leave Hosanni now?"

Strong arms pulled her into a fatherly embrace. Captain Fautorio cleared his throat and released her. "Listen, I'll tell you now, maybe it'll make it less scary for you. When we dock at Alcatraz, we'll unload you in a receiving bay, where the sleeping arrangements will be communal like you're used to. We'll be here a couple days, but we'll be busy filling out paperwork and helping the staff get everyone situated, so this is it tonight."

"Hosanni scared. Never seen chairs like in your chariot. Everything be different here?"

Captain Fautorio swallowed. "Alcatraz specializes in knowing what things will shock you and slowly introducing them. That's why you'll all be sleeping together on the floor during the first few weeks. An older student also from Diakrinth will be assigned as your helper through the first year of school. You'll room together with three more pairs like yourselves, in quarters that used to hold two prisoners. But I'm told cramped quarters don't bother you."

She nodded. Admitting she was spoiled from being an only child would be embarrassing, not to mention shameful to her family. "They give me big sister to help adjust to strange things?"

He nodded. "The first year they focus on teaching you general academics, proper English, and gradually introducing you to our modern world. To that ends, there's a medium-sized house, a mansion by your standards. It's also where the domestic workers learn to perform their duties, and where intimate social gatherings are held. Large ones are held in the assembly hall."

She gasped. "There be an assembly hall?"

"Alcatraz specializes in Diakrinthian maritas, bambina. Of course there's an assembly hall. The bathing accommodations are also built to the Sacred History's specifications for ritual cleansing. The Ravane, called a chaplain at the school, will be able to address any spiritual needs or concerns."

She frowned. "False Ravane who tell the marita it be the path for her to submit to her husband?" That role reversal alone would damn her to Hades. "False Ravane who tell the marita polygamy not be off the path?"

Captain Fautorio winced. "Polygamy and obeying your husband and your lady are endorsed by the assembly on Alcatraz, but I have a question for you. There is no response to Orthodox Emians' belief that men being bigger and stronger means we're designed to serve women, but if Emi wanted men to be women's mindless slaves, why did she give us brains?"

"To best serve your lady. Queen Salome's wisdom say every wise woman be married to a king. The king be the queen's greatest advisor and her sword."

"In that case, if I can't get you out of this, simply choose a wise man who's single, content with only your love, and who treats you like a queen."

Hosanni grunted. It was also against the path to marry Xenos, and a man of honor wouldn't seek a wife among maritas. "What happen if Hosanni don't choose a house?"

"Choose a house."

"Please tell me, milord."

He looked out over the water. "Your schooling costs money. Everything Alcatraz provides you will be billed to the family you marry into, who typically buys you with a loan that you'll end up paying back. If you refuse to choose a house out of an attempt to stay a perpetual maiden, Alcatraz will auction off your maidenhood the same way your hair was sold."

She gasped.

He patted the leather purse he wore on a chain around his waist. "I still have your locket, bambina. Once I get off the Rock, I'm going straight to the palace and not leaving until Romin lets me plead your case. I'm hoping he'll set you free. He has a plan to restore peace to the Union. He's already pulled off the first stage with Erin, and he is now searching for the lost daughter of Kristos. Your fortunes will reverse, if he believes the scroll to be legitimate. If we're fortunate, you won't have to worry about which program they'll stick you in next year."

Hosanni frowned. "Beg your pardon?"

"That's one thing I don't like about this school. You get to choose your husband, but not your trade. They rank the trades by their desirability to the families that purchase maritas. You'll be given a series of exams testing your aptitudes for the trades Alcatraz teaches, interviewed at length, and assigned the highest-ranked trade that you qualified for. Their decision is irreversible unless you only qualified to be a maid, in which case you can retest, but you won't have to worry about that."

Not qualifying for any trade, he meant? "Why not?"

"If I know you, bambina, you'll qualify for medical school—easily."

A witch, sold to be the servant of a man and bear his lady's children, not her own children? Hosanni grinned. Emi would surely use Romin to save her and restore the scepter to Father, who would reign until she wed. Lady Veritas was a pure and spotless bride. How could Lady Veritas come, if Emi allowed her mother to be so completely desecrated?

GOD. Let us make Woman in our image, according to our likeness; let her have dominion over the fish of the sea, and over the birds of the air, over the cattle, over all the earth and over everything that creeps on the earth.

CHORUS. So God created womankind in her own image; in the image of God she created her; female and male she created them. From the purple dust of the earth, God fashioned them. (ARGEVANE and BION are laying on their backs. GOD breathes on them. Nude, ARGEVANE and BION stand and gaze around in wide-eyed wonderment.)

— Pauli of Denver, The Sacred History, "Creation" scene 1, lines 40-48

Chapter Eight

Hosanni sniffled. The last of the other shorn maidens in orange departed down the plank and onto the castle's drawbridge. At least that's what Alcatraz looked like to her from this vantage point. A citadel in a vast black moat.

Captain Fautorio took her arm. "No more delays, *nipote*." He bit his lip.

Nipote? Not as in *anepsios*? Hosanni squinted. "Nipote, niece?"

"And nephew, grandchild, and apparently the orphaned bambina I'm way too attached to." He sucked in a breath. "Please don't make this hard."

Tears filled her eyes. "Will I ever see ya again?"

He stared at her, arching an eyebrow. "I? Not Hosanni?"

Her cheeks warmed. "Some of us speak better English than we pretend, milord, but ya didn't answer me. We meet again?"

He smiled in the lantern light. "That's in Emi's hand, bambina."

HOSANNI STOOD IN THE receiving bay, hopping from foot to foot as the dorm aggies shouted out their lent children's names. Things had gone as promised. The concept of "bunk beds" still scared the diabolus out of her, but only her new big sister would be in danger of falling out.

Was that fair? Yes, Paraclete surely had gotten used to sleeping so high up off the floor. Hosanni smiled. Paraclete was like Irene. Well, except for her hair. Paraclete, like the other older girls, wore a terribly short hairstyle called a bob that parted down the middle and curled up around her chin. The longest length she'd seen was but to the shoulders, like a man, and Paraclete had said Hosanni's class had arrived in the middle of the students' annual hair cuts. Maritas were supposed to keep their hair no longer than the chin.

Dumb law. The Romini used the length of a marita's hair to mark her status. The older girls' barrettes and hair clips were pretty but hardly a fair trade for a woman's glory.

"Hosanni Kristekon!"

Did they mean her? Probably. Only in her village was Kristekon useless, since all the ladies of her village were cousins.

She ran toward the aggies. Most were under thirty and unqualified to be aggies in the assembly. "I am Hosanni Kristekon, the daughter of Aletheia and Havan." Was her non-traditional addition of her father's name helpful here? Her parents' names were so common among her people.

A pink woman who might be an aggie stepped forward in a Romini-style royal brown dress. She had her fiery pink hair pinned up with a diamond tiara and bloodshot green eyes. She yanked Hosanni's arm and all but tossed her at the huddle of trembling girls watching the pink woman with large eyes.

The upper half of the dorm aggie's breasts were exposed, shoved up, and pinched together in a most unnatural position. Hosanni stared at the floor. Corsets sounded horrible enough, but why was it the fashion here for women to expose themselves? Not even the Xenos women in Diakrinth would do so.

The dorm aggie called several more names and treated each girl roughly.

At last, the dorm aggie escorted them out of the receiving bay and into the cloud-speckled sunshine.

A cool salty breeze kissed Hosanni over the top of the high walls circling the island. The griffins' fishing songs caressed her. She'd never heard so many in one place. Draca's airborne cousin, the griffin, had a cat-like body covered in feathers, with wings instead of front legs. She was the size of a large turkey, only hunted prey smaller than herself, and was a rare sight in Diakrinth. And a special treat. The griffin was the emblem of Kristos.

Hosanni's group climbed a grassy hill. She and the other new girls gasped at the miles and miles of clear blue-green water. Above, the griffins sang as they dived for fish. Below, a pod of Draca's aquatic cousin, Leviathane, danced in the waves. Sea dragons still lived? She'd never seen anything so wondrous in all of her days.

Paraclete, who wore a cobalt blue Romini dress, grabbed Hosanni's hand and whispered in her ear, "The view is impressive every time."

Hosanni nodded. Though, as beautiful as the sea dragons were to watch, she wouldn't want to encounter one up close. Leviathane would make any-one who attempted to escape from Alcatraz quite sorry.

The dorm aggie stopped outside of a gray mansion in the angular, square style of the Romini, with one round tower. Across the way rose a monstrous compound with sharp, ugly corners and straight lines. In between, a giant metal cistern towered high above them, while the beautiful vegetable and herb gardens had no idea that it was the middle of winter.

The dorm aggie faced them. Hosanni, standing near the front, glimpsed into the bloodshot green eyes and shivered at the unnatural glint in them.

She whispered to Paraclete, in their tongue, "Do you know if she is well?"

Flushing scarlet, Dorm Aggie marched up to her and got in her face, fists clenched, chest heaving. "Who do you think you are?"

Hosanni shirked back, heart pounding. She'd encountered such hatred once before, when accompanying Mother to perform the healing rites. She'd been sent away, but later learned Mother had driven a diabolus out of the sick woman. The demoniac had posed to her a quite similar question.

Paraclete offered, "She was concerned for your health."

The dorm aggie sniffed. "You can't catch anything I've got while stranded out on this rock." Another glare assaulted Hosanni. "But let the baldies speak for themselves."

She trembled. "I'm Hosanni, daughter of Havan Alethaner Kristekon, the rightful king of Diakrinth and the Ravaner of our village." She'd just as good as announced that they'd been bereaved of Mother. "Who are you?"

A gloved slap struck her cheek. "Don't back talk me, princess!"

Hosanni ignored her stinging cheek and curtsied. The dorm aggie's tone said that she didn't believe Hosanni. "Your pardon, milady. I thought we be introducing ourselves."

The dorm aggie grunted and pulled back to scowl at their group. "When others are watching, you may call me milady, Dorm Aggie, or Aggie Marezza as school policy dictates. In private, however, any implications that I'm an old hag rather than a beautiful young woman will be severely punished."

"Young?" The question popped out before Hosanni could stop it.

A slap stung her other cheek. "Twenty-five is young enough!"

Twenty-five? Marezza looked forty. Did the diabolus do that?

Paraclete frowned. "No dorm aggie I've had has been this cruel."

"If you complain, you will regret it. Tell the baldies, my dear, just how they might regret it. Take a guess."

Paraclete gasped. "You wouldn't give false marks."

Marezza leered at all of them. "I will grade your conduct in domestic and social situations. The marks that I give you directly impact your worth, which impacts the quality of matches you enjoy. Cross me, and I'll give you marks so low, you'll end up sleeping on a straw pallet in a hot, rat infested kitchen for the rest of your very miserable days. Once he gets you home, he'll make you long for me. Do I make myself clear?"

Only the griffins answered her.

Hosanni clung to Paraclete. What put such evil in Marezza's heart? If she had a beating heart. If a woman could suffer from a diabolus, could a woman also come down with lycanthropy?

Marezza grunted. "If we understand each other, I'll show you to the fine, luxurious prison cell accommodations we have here at Alcatraz."

On the march back, Hosanni let the others pass her. Paraclete stayed by her. Hosanni whispered in Diakrinthian, "Do you know what ails her?"

Paraclete watched the back of Marezza's head. "She is a leper."

Hosanni gasped. "Leprosy is unclean! Who would hire a leper?"

"Her leprosy is the kind that is a curse upon those who commit *porneia*, hence what she said about not being able to catch it here. The only time men are on the island is for a social, and they are unarmed, while our chaperones all carry swords."

Hosanni stared at the cursed pink woman named Marezza. "She must be a wastrel carouser to deserve such an awful death."

"Once the plague advances to its most deadly stage, witches expose the cursed woman to malaria. The fever cleanses her, if she survives it."

"How do you know this?"

Paraclete turned solemn eyes upon her. "My mother is a Ravane. Now her daughter is taken captive and made to learn witchcraft."

"I am sorry." Hosanni hugged Paraclete.

"You are a Ravane's child also? Do you know the cleansing rites?"

"Yes."

"Good. You can help me clean. Marezza is useless in the practical sense, and she defiles everything that she touches anyway. The chaplain refuses to cleanse ritually unclean things, insisting the Sacrifice alone is enough, so that is up to us, little sister."

Hosanni gulped. Each girl Marezza had touched was now unclean too and needed ritual cleansing. "I am glad I don't have to carry this burden alone! Is the mikvah clean?"

"Yes, it is salt water. Marezza refuses to bathe in salt water."

A relieved breath rushed out of Hosanni. She'd wind up bathing daily, but at least they had a ritually clean pool of living water to cleanse themselves from Marezza's filthiness in.

"Are you truly the daughter of Kristos? Queen Aletheia has died?"

Tears wet Hosanni's eyes. "And I am captured, leaving no heir, and the scroll was taken away from me."

Paraclete gasped. "Emi will save you. She will not break her promise."

Nor would Emi ever withdraw her curse. Perhaps Emi's vow that Kristos would never again wield the scepter by birthright meant deliverance would come from outside.

HOSANNI ALL BUT SKIPPED down the path by the ugly compound, careful not to get too close to Marezza while keeping in sight of the school president, a pink woman with violet ringlets that danced down a lemony frock dress. For only one reason would such an important woman fetch Hosanni and Marezza while classes were in session. Her advocate must have come through for her, and in hardly a week.

A stone assembly hall with its delightfully familiar stained glass windows lay ahead. Hosanni followed the older women through the main double doors. Inside, she could be back home, except for the piles of violet suede pillows by each of the ten doors.

A silver-haired pink man stood by the altar in a royal brown duster robe and a brown kilt. A royal diadem sat low upon his brow. He had to be in his late fifties or early sixties. Ten soldiers accompanied him.

Including Captain Fautorio.

Hosanni grinned, but restrained herself. A squeak beside her drew her eye to Marezza, who stood staring at Felippo Romin, the widowed king of the Union of the Nations, at least from here to the Mississippi River. East of the Mississippi, the House of Erin still reigned.

Romin blinked. "Princess Marezza? Here?"

An airy "Papa" escaped from Marezza. "I can explain."

Hosanni blinked. Princess? Papa?

The school president stepped forward and curtsied. "Your honor, your granddaughter saw how desperately understaffed we are and volunteered to assist us in this crisis. To show our gratitude, we shall of course be providing Princess Marezza a considerable allowance."

Romin laughed. "Is my allowance too paltry for your tastes, nipote?"

Marezza sputtered. "No, Papa! I merely wished to help."

"You are too generous, nipote. While I suspect your generosity has gone to blackjack and poker, I'm delighted to see you take responsibility, given I swore *all* members of this family found raiding the public treasury to pay for their mistakes would be crucified. Would be a tragedy to lose my sweet nipote to a momentary, severe lapse of judgment, as I lost your mother."

Hosanni stared at Romin. Marezza, sweet?

She glanced back at Marezza and gasped at the humble contrition frozen on Marezza's face. Hosanni trembled. Such a switch of personality was a clear symptom of lycanthropy.

The president stepped forward and curtsied to her king. "Your honor, I asked Princess Marezza to accompany me in presenting the marita that you requested. This is Hosanni Kristekon." The president waved to her.

Romin stepped forward and examined her with a critical eye. "I want to hear about this scroll of yours."

Hosanni waved to Captain Fautorio. "Did he not give you the star garnet? He said that he would. It should open easily on the left." Maybe he did not understand. "The scroll is inside. The gem is two held together, with a hollow place between them. My mothers had it made long ago, to protect the scroll. Paper breaks down, and it's been 1800 years since we last held the scepter; 2300 since we governed an independent Diakrinth."

Romin laughed. "Yes, and I have placed such a treasure where it belongs, with my crown jewels. My scholars tell me the scroll is only a century old, but the necklace *is* the right age, and they are reasonably certain it's authentic. Princess Hosanni, you are the daughter of royalty." The pink man kissed her forehead and her cheeks.

"Princess?" Marezza snarled at Hosanni. "Papa, she's a slave."

"A terrible mistake." Romin glanced back at Captain Fautorio. "One that I'm most thankful was brought to my attention."

Captain Fautorio bowed his head. "Milord, I made the tragic mistake. The dragons interpreted my actions as hostile and attacked us. When we protected ourselves, the dragons took a defensive position around the rightful queen of Idaho, and she was slain in the chaos I triggered."

Idaho. The Erini had the audacity to rename Hosanni's beautiful nation after the species of potato that grew in such abundance in Diakrinth.

Romin turned to Hosanni. "What say you of this man's fate, princess?"

She surveyed the cringing man she'd hated not long ago. "Promote him. He intended no malice and has been my faithful defender since. I would be dead also if he had not been watching over me."

Romin beamed. "Kneel before me, captain."

Captain Fautorio obeyed.

Romin drew his sword and leaned upon it, clutching the golden spread eagle, his emblem, which formed the sword's handle and its guard. "You have faithfully defended this bambina, so I will place in your hands my own."

A startled head came up. "The royal guard? Milord, I'm not a knight. Nor has anyone in my family—"

"Hush, I'm the king. I'll do what I bloote well please." Romin rested the sword on Captain Fautorio's right shoulder. "With strong arms you sheltered Princess Hosanni in the darkest and coldest of hours, so I, Felippo Romin, Sovereign King of the Union of the Nations, hereby knight you Sir Fautorio Armstrong and appoint you to the royal guard assigned to protect and serve my daughter Princess Porcia." Romin touched the sword to Captain Fautorio's other shoulder as well and sheathed it. "Rise, Sir Armstrong."

Sir Armstrong obeyed, his head bowed. "Milord and king, may I prove worthy of the grace you have bestowed on me."

Romin beamed. "And humble too! Now let us be hence."

Hosanni glanced to Marezza and a chill tingled down her spine.

This wasn't over.

Marezza clutched at Romin's left hand. "Papa, do you mean to remove Hosanni from Alcatraz?"

Romin blinked at her. "I can hardly leave the heir to the scepter of Kristos in chains, nipote. That will not do. Have you not read my book?"

"Papa, every educated, civilized, wise woman in the Union has read your book. But consider the investment Alcatraz has already made."

Romin glanced at the pale, twitchy president and nodded. "Milady, you will of course be appropriately compensated."

The president dipped her head. "Whatever you deem fit is generous."

"Papa!" Marezza hung onto Romin the same way Hosanni did Pappy in a spoiled past that seemed far more distant than it rationally was. "Papa, yes, this is a terrible tragedy that could greatly harm your plans, but consider her shorn head. You know what a lady's hair means to her. That is true no less in such a savage nation as Idaho. Her mother is dead, and she is hardly more than a child, one who has surely not been given a lick of instruction in matters of state and royal protocol."

Romin laughed. "And you think she'll receive that at Alcatraz?"

"They *are* the experts at civilizing the Diakrinthian savage, Papa. And I am here to instruct her. Surely it's a sign from Chance that she was assigned to my ward."

Romin stroked his chin. "Hmm, yes. With her age, the time she needs for her hair to grow out—this could speed the plan up a full generation."

Marezza drew back. "Papa?"

Hosanni frowned. What plan?

Romin faced the president. "Treat Princess Hosanni as you will, except let her hair grow out to full-length and give Princess Marezza all of the time she needs to prepare Princess Hosanni for the life she was born to. Now, what is your longest and most dignified course offering available?"

"Medicine. We prepare our girls for a full apprenticeship with a master physician, paid positions we secure for them." The president gasped. "But she would need to finish her first-year courses, be tested and interviewed and—"

Romin brandished his sword. "Is it wise to argue with your king?"

The president gulped. "I only thought for her best interests."

Hosanni nodded. *Such as not forcing me to learn witchcraft. That is most definitely my interests!*

Romin sheathed his sword. "No shame in a princess knowing what to do in a medical emergency. So we'll put her in that program."

A scream caught in Hosanni's throat. No.

Romin smiled at her. "Don't fear the superstitions prevalent among your people. They would be fools not to cooperate. Besides, you won't be practicing medicine when you're the queen. Now, I must leave you for a time, but wait for me, Princess Hosanni. The match I have planned for you is far superior to any that you could hope to make on your own. Especially given your freedom comes with my offer."

Marezza frowned. "Papa, if you intend to make a marriage alliance with a slave, we have no young men available to give her."

Romin beamed at Marezza. "We will when I return. Prince Antonio."

A blank mask slipped over Marezza's face.

Marezza frowned thoughtfully. A spark ignited in her eyes and a leering grin flashed. It molded into a supportive smile. "Yes, yes, I see the plan now. Prince Antonio will do nicely. Quite nicely indeed."

Why did Hosanni have a sinking feeling it wasn't Romin's plan Marezza had in mind?

Chapter Nine

An autumn breeze kissed Havan Alethaner with a promise of the coming winter. The two earth closet bowls he carried, plus the one in Korban's arms, smelled as bad as a dead rat. He'd been working Korban back up to his full work load, though too slowly for the tastes of a fifteen-year-old. Never mind that the young man nearly died last year.

Frost sprinkled the mounds of the composting waste. Havan Alethaner marched to the incinerator and dumped his ceramic bowls into the fire. The two youngest girls were recovering from diarrhea that had come far too close to killing them. Until he and Juris were certain everyone was healthy, they'd burn their waste and cleanse the earth closet bowls in fire.

Once the bowls had been in the fire long enough to purify them from any lingering sickness, Havan Alethaner picked up the metal tongs and fished the bowls out, setting them out on the brick hearth to cool. He'd rather not scorch his gloves unnecessarily.

Korban tossed his bowl into the fire as well.

Havan Alethaner smiled; he hadn't needed to tell Korban to treat their own waste as unclean, too. They spent more time next door with Juris and the girls than they did at home. Hence, they needed to empty their earth closet bowl but two or three times a week, while Juris would need hers emptied out again by the time of the evening chores.

Once Korban fished the third earth closet bowl out of the fire and set it on the hearth, Havan Alethaner thrust down the incinerator's metal door.

Korban leaned against the curved stone brick wall, his arms crossed as he donned the bored expression that young men so loved. "So, what are we going to give the tax collectors to leave us alone this year?"

Havan Alethaner swallowed. He'd hoped Korban would forget. They were only in slightly better financial shape than they had been last year. "They're not coming this year."

Korban's eyes widened and a relieved breath escaped. "Why not?"

"We didn't tell you because it tore our wounds open, son. But according to the letter we received last spring from the Internal Revenue Division, well, let us spare you the monetary value the tax collectors placed upon Aletheia's blood, Hosanni's maidenhood, and a nearly as priceless family heirloom."

A spark brightened Korban's face. "She's alive?"

"Alcatraz has paid the government for her, so she presumably made it to them in one piece at least."

"How far up ahead are we? Maybe we can buy her back."

Havan Alethaner shook his head, his blood pulsing through his body. "My mother, your natural aggie, lost a daughter this way. Mother wrote Alcatraz when our finances improved, hoping to buy her daughter back. They curtly replied they weren't thieves holding children for ransom." He snorted. "But we can be grateful we're paid so far up ahead on our taxes, we'll have plenty of time to raise their blood money and we can avoid future visits by dropping off a bank note at the tax service's office in the City of Trees in the future."

Korban sneered. "Quite thoughtful of them."

"Indeed." Havan Alethaner pulled Korban into a hug, thumping his back, and lifted up to Emi prayers venting emotions he dared not express in front of the ladies. Gentlemen weren't supposed to use the sort of language springing to his mind and lips at present.

Once he no longer felt like fetching his crossbow and killing as many of Romin's men as he could before they killed him, Havan Alethaner released his foster son. "Thank you. Some griefs only another man can appreciate." Plus it gave Korban a model for the best answer that he knew for pent up rage while skipping the lecture that never worked on him.

The tears soaking Korban's cheeks affirmed his foster son had released his own anger to Emi also. Korban smiled. "Is it then for Aunt Juris's benefit only that you so frequently prefer her company to lament?"

"Oh, don't get me wrong, I enjoy comforting her immensely—"

Korban snickered.

The furnace's flames somehow heated Havan Alethaner's face up again.

'To comfort' was almost as popular a euphemism for intercourse as 'to join.' He grimaced. "Not like *that*, son. I won't do that again unless I'm married."

The teenage snickering continued. "So when, then?"

Bands tightened around Havan Alethaner's chest. "When what?"

"When are you two getting married?"

Havan Alethaner moved away from the furnace. That did nothing to cool his face down. "Is that where you think I'm headed with Juris?"

"You're halfway to the marriage bed already. The entire village knows you love each other."

Now he's asking for it. "So when are you depriving Irene of her ribbons?"

"Father!" Korban's brow furrowed. He lowered his head. "That was low."

"No lower than you stooped."

"Aunt Aletheia is dead and buried. It's time you gave yourself permission to love again. My bride is still alive."

By assembly law, a year's separation resulted in a woman's death to her family. Havan Alethaner put a hand on Korban's shoulder. "It's already been a year, son. Today. The covenant you made behind our backs dissolved today."

"I don't care; I'll buy her! They won't say no to a bridegroom."

"Oh, son." Havan Alethaner shook his head. "I've already sent a scout to inquire about that. You would have to wait until she's seventeen. And only the House of Romin could pay what they're planning to charge for her."

Korban broke down sobbing and covered his face with his hands.

Havan Alethaner pulled Korban's hands away and hugged him. The hard, cold reality was, when the Romini stole a child, her family never heard from her again. Physically, Alcatraz could only keep their daughters from them so long as they remained trapped within an impenetrable island fortress in waters infested by fire-breathing sea dragons. Emotionally, the shame of their slavery must keep the girls from ever coming home.

But he'd be a hypocrite of the worst sort to condemn Hosanni. It was his own fault this disgrace had fallen on his poor daughter. She was but reaping the fruit of his own favorite, and mostly secret sin. Did Hosanni realize that?

Korban pulled away. "Father?"

"Yes, son?" When had Korban started calling him that? It'd seemed so natural, he'd hardly noticed.

"I miss Hosanni. She's still my first choice. When that's so, how can I court Irene?"

"By admitting it. So long as she's willing to accept that, and it's something you can work through together, you should state your intent to her. You can hardly say you're not courting her, as much time as you spend with—" Havan Alethaner opened his mouth wide and stuffed in as much of his gloved fist as he could fit. He sounded like *his* foster father.

Korban pulled Havan Alethaner's gloved fist out of his mouth. "Are you really that hungry?"

Havan Alethaner slid to the ground and wrapped his hands around his knees. "I was fourteen when my mother lent me to Kristos. Juris was thirteen and Aletheia eighteen. I wasn't interested in courting right after what got me sent away, and, well, Aletheia wasn't the daughter *my* foster father worried I'd dishonor. Juris and I were close friends well before I truly loved Aletheia."

Korban crouched beside him. "Close friends like Irene and I?"

"No. I never considered choosing Juris, son. Juris was too young for me, and I too ambitious. I dreamed of being a king, not a mere ivory carver."

"Juris is a carpenter."

"She was raised an ivory carver. Shortly after I married, my mother-in-law got a whim to branch out into carpentry, and so lent her younger daughter to the carpenter in our village."

Korban smirked. "Where Aunt Juris discovered the beau she lost to her own sister had a younger brother to comfort her?"

Havan Alethaner bristled. "Do I have to explain why this is torment to get you to show any mercy? Aletheia knew why I chose her, and how fond I am of Juris, and at your age I was stupid enough to answer honestly when Aletheia asked whether her sister is attractive. Aletheia's insecurity hung over us until the day we said goodbye. I fully deserved her suspicion after having actually committed *porneia* before I knew either sister, but a source of marital friction is not what I want reminded of when I'm grieving for my wife!"

Korban bowed his head. "My apologies, milord. I'd be difficult to consider planting sunflowers as a crop after years of pulling them out of a cornfield."

In that metaphor, the sunflowers represented a foolish, romantic love for Juris. *That's not fair, Aletheia. Love is more than mere physical attraction and fond feelings. Love is commitment, and I made that commitment to* you. *I love you. Not Juris. When will you believe me?*

HAVAN ALETHANER NESTLED snug in the pile of suede pillows under him and Juris. They needed a comfortable nest for mourning more than he did a kitchen table, since he and Korban always took their meals next door.

Tears spent, Juris lay quietly, resting her head against the breast of his tunic, her arms wrapped tightly around him as he held her close. His hands meandered mindlessly over her spine in soothing caresses, her glory caught between his fingers. A soft purring escaped her lips, jarring him—he could feel her spine so well because only a thin undershirt barred his fingers from her skin. They'd partially removed her palla without even thinking about it.

Sweet awareness swept through his body of the fire he'd absentmindedly kindled in his loins. He took deliberate, slow breaths. It was time to put aside mourning for today, but everything in him didn't want this moment to end.

Juris lifted her head up. Havan Alethaner swallowed. She was probably also aware that it was happening again and also searching for the strength to not join together. But their eyes connected and hers drew him in.

Guilt exploded in him the instant their lips connected. He pulled back, only to draw close again and suckle more of the honey of her lips.

He forced himself away and stood over by the oven. Tears coursed down his cheeks. He wanted so badly to take Juris up to the marriage bed closet and finish that. How long had he been deceiving himself? "Aletheia always feared this. That one day we would . . . ."

Havan Alethaner turned his head and beat his breast.

Juris caught his arm, preventing him from hitting himself anymore. Her eyes shone as she pressed her fingers in between his. "Havan, I am so sorry. I couldn't hold back any longer. But it's time you knew. I loved you. My heart shattered the day I saw my sister's ribbon on my beau's wrist."

His head swam. Her beau? He bit his lower lip. He should've heeded his foster father's warnings. "I had no idea you saw it like that."

"Oh, reality took me from thinking Aletheia stole my beau to realizing I was coveting my sister's husband on your wedding day. I confessed my sin to Mother, and she'd merely been waiting for me to admit it. She'd already made the arrangements to send me away."

"Does—did Agapan know?" His brother's name choked him.

A sly smile crossed Juris's lips. "That is why we built our own house when Mother had plenty of room. He and I understood each other in so many ways, including growing up in the shadows of stars as bright as you and Aletheia. He stroked my ego, saying your folly was his treasure. Since I met him, I've never regretted how things turned out between us, Havan. All I wish differently was that they were still with us." Juris sniffled. "And hence that I wasn't falling in love with you all over again."

She was right. They never would have allowed the wild seed sown in their bosoms to take root and blossom if Aletheia and his brother still lived. Havan Alethaner wrapped his arms around Juris from behind. "I wish they were still with us, too. We will always love them first, but they're not here." He turned her around, lifted her chin, and gazed in her eyes. "And if being each other's second choice is mutually acceptable, I would much like to court you, Juris."

She arched her eyebrows. "Only court?"

"I need to be confident that you know what you would be getting yourself into if you accept me. Aletheia and I were both miserable until we embraced my sinful inclinations."

"What sinful inclinations?"

"I'm a wolf."

She laughed. "You're no wolf. I've met few men as honorable."

"I devoured a maiden as a foolish boy. I long to preach in the assembly myself rather than to dictate your sermons. My most natural inclination is to assume control. I love little more. Aletheia indulged me in private, allowing me to make decisions the lady should, while we pretended to follow the path in public. While I far from meet Romin's diagnostic standard for lycanthropy, I easily meet Diakrinth's. I could be fed to the dragons."

Tears filled Juris's eyes. "Oh, Havan, I know that has happened to men like you, but I know your heart too well to make such a bad diagnosis. The true essential criteria are a lack of a conscience and a dead heart, neither of which you meet."

"I still have strayed from the path. My father warned me, if I didn't check my base inclinations to take authority, I'd bring disaster on my family, and surely I have."

Juris gasped. "You think it's your fault?"

"I made all the decisions last year. I decided what path of action to take, and my brother followed me to his death. Since I decided we would stay and try to rescue him, none of us were there to stop them from slaying my wife and kidnapping my daughter. Further, Aletheia and I tried to teach Hosanni the path of truth and life, but children have a knack for picking up on the sins we most want them to not see. My poor daughter will fall naturally right into submitting to her husband. That's the wicked example Aletheia and I set."

Juris wept and shook her head, as if to erase his hypocrisy.

He swallowed. "That's the ultimate barrier to us joining, Juris. I want to learn to be a proper submissive husband, but I'm far too lost to truly keep the path. I love you too much to pull you down to Hades with me."

Juris pressed her left index finger to his lips. "Scepter or no scepter, you are Kristos Havan, King of Diakrinth. I have no designs to be a queen, even if my king should choose me."

Now, that was a new way to excuse his favorite sin, albeit one superior to Aletheia's justifications for it. "That doesn't justify me for dishonoring your sister—or you, should we marry. I dishonor you enough already, milady."

"Ravaner Havan, we have no one else to teach me how to be the Ravane, when the office has already been dumped on me. When I feel dishonored, I'll tell you. I've had few occasions where I needed to correct you for that."

"But you're letting me run wild."

Juris sighed. "Man was created to be Argevane's servant, to protect and to provide for her, that is certainly true. You're our helpers. But leadership, as you have found, beloved, is a terrible burden, one your brother was content to let me bear alone. If you have that desire, I am one lady quite happy to share the load. It would of course be a sin to abdicate my responsibility, but if I ask for your help with this burden, do you truly honor me to refuse?"

Havan Alethaner held her. "Are you asking?"

"Yes, I wish to use the resources Emi's given me, milord."

Milord. He'd received that honor countless times from the husbands and from children. From a woman, only once, and Juris owned him as property. Juris could be as much of a stickler for perfectly keeping the path as her sister. Would it really be so difficult to submit to a woman so willing to share her power? "I will honor you all of my days, milady."

Havan Alethaner kissed Juris, long and sweet. He cupped her face in his hands, making direct eye contact. She'd always loved it, even if he never dared it when he had been married to her sister. "I choose you, Juris Kristekon. Willingly and freely."

She squealed like a maiden and hugged him. "When?"

"Let's give Korban time to make up his mind about Irene. If they marry, we can keep your mother's house in the family." The Sacred History forbid Diakrinth from selling her inheritance, so empty houses were instead lent for an agreed upon sum.

But lent houses were returned even less frequently than lent sons.

HAVAN ALETHANER DRAGGED Korban and himself home under the watch of the pregnant moon. Havan Alethaner sent a longing glance back at his bride's house. Soon.

Korban followed his gaze. "Would another hour really hurt so long as we don't wake the little ones?"

"The sun died two hours ago. I'm surprised Juris let us stay so late." Or that she hadn't pressed harder for them to stay the night with her rather than go out after dark.

Winter's chill greeted them at home. Havan Alethaner circled the kitchen, tapping the sun crystals in the windows to turn them on. The stones glowed with a soft pastel purple light and trickled warmth into the room.

Korban yawned. "It makes sense to sleep, if it's too late to entertain."

"We need to talk first." Havan Alethaner pulled the pillows off the straw-woven table mat one by one and set them back in a proper circle. He settled into his usual seat near the ladder.

Korban dropped into the seat next to him and yawned again. "If this is about Irene, I'd rather go to sleep."

"No, son." Hopefully, what he did have in mind would help Korban make his mind up about Irene. "Juris and I had some discussion earlier about the future. She's not sure that it makes sense to keep two businesses running, and is shorthanded in terms of skilled carpenters. But with all those daughters, we don't need that many ivory carvers, either."

Korban nodded. "Irene was fretting about Phosi's suggestion."

Suggestion? Juris's sixteen-year-old had announced she'd applied for an carpentry apprenticeship with another house. "I would rather avoid sending a maiden if we can. It is over in our native village, so I thought you might go."

Pain flashed on Korban's features. "Father. If that's what you want, I will obey, but . . ." Korban sucked in a breath. "What have I done to offend you? Why don't you want me anymore? If I teased you too much about Aunt Juris, I'm sorry. Please don't send me away, Father. I love you."

"Me?" Havan Alethaner sputtered. "What about leaving Irene?"

"It's not far. I could still see Irene, if you decide I'm too much of a handful and send me away to yet another family. The thought you might not want me, that is what is unthinkable. You're my hero. Your regard means everything to me. I want to abide in your house forever."

Havan Alethaner pulled his son into his rough embrace. "I could not be prouder of you if you'd come from my own loins. You will never be too much of a handful, and you will never lose me. Wherever you go, I will always love you, son." He wiped Korban's tears away. "I don't want you to go, either. But Juris is threatening to sell everything that she and Agapan built together. It's true this house has always been ivory carvers. We want to keep that tradition alive, but I hate to see the dreams Juris and Agapan shared tossed aside. So I want you to learn carpentry."

"But I like ivory carving. I like working with you."

"I chose Juris today, Korban. Right now, we only have the resources to keep one business open. And if you marry Irene . . ." Havan Alethaner sighed. "Son, you're inclined to choose ivory cutting because it's what you know and you really like your lord. But the changes we've endured present you with a rare opportunity to switch occupations without switching houses. I'd rather you were making an informed decision."

Korban stared at the woven-straw table. "But I don't want to leave you."

"You could ask Juris to teach you. She's the best. Her crafts were art."

Korban smiled. "But she has had seven more important things occupying her for the last eighteen years and fears she's lost the touch?"

Havan Alethaner laughed. "Precisely. You'd save Juris from a mistake, if you talk her into teaching you. That is worth the risks of losing my best ivory cutter and having to learn carpentry at my age. So give it a try. If you discover you hate it, you can go back to ivory cutting, I promise."

"One condition."

"What's that?"

"Hurry up and marry Aunt Juris, so I can ask you if I can court your daughter Irene."

Havan Alethaner laughed. "We're waiting on you. If you marry Irene, the two of you can occupy Aletheia's house until I have someone to give it to."

Korban arched an eyebrow. "Who? Aunt Juris is a good choice of wives for you, but a bad choice of surrogates for Aunt Aletheia."

"Thank you so much for not throwing my pregnancy track record in my face. I'd love to have a little Alethaner, but Emi likely won't grant that miracle to us at forty and forty-one."

A frown crossed Korban's face. "Who else would you give the house to?"

Havan Alethaner winced. "Hosanni. Emi declared that, from the womb, she has chosen our daughter to be the mother of Lady Veritas. To fulfill her promise, Emi must bring Hosanni home. My daughter will have my head if she comes home to find I've effectively sold her house."

Korban jumped up from the table. "You believe that, and yet you push me into another woman's arms?"

Havan Alethaner stood and cupped the young man's face in his hands.

Korban yanked away. He spat hot English words in an Erini accent. "Ye think I'd mess the prophecy up, don't ye? How could a pure, spotless bride spring forth from the loins o' a half-breed? Da made me promise not to tell, but I have three Diakrinthian grandparents and one Erini grandfather. Da was well versed in both cultures and could be what he wanted to be at will."

So Korban's natural father had lived long enough to secretly confuse the poor child. His son could rebelliously wrap himself up in every shred of Erini culture he knew, but children were still born whatever their mother was.

"Son," Havan Alethaner said in their own tongue. "Only two families in the entire world have enough money to pay the ransom for our princess. She has a fifty percent chance of bringing home a literal son of Erin. I'd rather it were you, but we can count upon her coming home married. She won't escape captivity a maiden. That's too much for us to ask."

"How can I be certain? How do I know whether Emi would want me to follow my heart and wait for Hosanni or follow my heart and marry Irene?"

"When your heart is torn, the greatest sign of the path that Emi can give you is her peace, son. Seek that. Whatever Emi guides you to do, I will bless."

He'd struggled much to find the faith to believe in Emi's promise, but in the end, Aletheia wasn't the only dreamer in their family. He'd seen her vision for himself. So the enemy was wrong. It wasn't wishful thinking. Emi would bring Hosanni home.

Chapter Ten

The hairdresser's peach frock dress rustled and her leather boots clicked as she stuck her head in the door of Hosanni's sophomore anatomy class. The blue woman's many thin braids spilled over her bosom as she consulted a checklist on a clipboard. "I'm ready for Hosanni Kristekon."

Nausea and dizziness hit Hosanni. Her pulse rate rose. Each deep breath pressed painfully against the awful corset. She grabbed fistfuls of her frock's pale yellow skirt. It had been one thing when they put her through the normal process to get into a trade program at the end of her freshman year. She'd qualified for their medical program anyway. But her hair was finally almost to her shoulders, only three more inches to that goal. And they wanted to subject her to her first trim along with the rest of the sophomores?

The hairdresser repeated Hosanni's name.

Hosanni swallowed. Making a scene wouldn't do.

In here. She rose, crossed to the exit, and closed the door behind her.

The hairdresser waved to the classroom chair by her cart. "Have a seat."

Hosanni shook her head. "There's been a mistake. I'm not supposed to be on your list."

The hairdresser laughed. "Honey, everyone's supposed to be on my list. You know the law. No marita's hair shall exceed chin-length."

"Romin made an exception for me. He's coming back—"

More laughter cut her off. "Now there's a first."

"I'm serious. I'm a princess, this was a mistake, and he's going to fix it."

"Enough with the comedy, chickadee. Now sit." The hairdresser grabbed for Hosanni as if to physically force her down.

Hosanni blocked the attack with the side of her arm and jabbed her elbow into the attacker's face.

The hairdresser cursed, holding her nose.

Hosanni backed away. "I'm sorry, milady, but the dance of death is hard to stop when you scare a Diakrinthian woman. Please, if I'm telling the truth, you'll be in trouble if you persist, so shouldn't you at least look into it? Ask the president. She was there." A chill seeped in. The president had drowned and had been replaced at the end of last term. "Ask Aggie Marezza. Or check my records. There's a notice on file."

Crimson blood dripped from the hairdresser's nose.

Hosanni gasped and reached for the blue hand. "Let me see."

The hairdresser jerked back. "I am going to the infirmary. After that, I'm reporting this to Aggie Marezza and checking your records. If you're lying, you won't like the notation you'll have over this!"

Hosanni slipped back into her classroom. Thankfully, she had three more days to finish her final. She wouldn't get anything meaningful done today.

PALMS SWEATING, HOSANNI followed the messenger girl into the president's office. Inside, at the desk sat the current president, a lilac woman whose green eyes declared her a nasha, one whose cultural heritage had been lost in the Great Dispersal. On either side of her stood Marezza and the hairdresser. The blue woman wore a bandage over a broken nose.

Hosanni winced. "I'm so sorry, milady. Why did you have to grab me like that? My first instinct was to defend—"

The president raised her hand. "Peace, child. We explained to her what she did wrong. She didn't realize frightening you is like provoking a dragon. So that part is forgiven."

Hosanni sent a hopeful look at Marezza. So she'd gone back on her word and left her whole ward's cultural education up to the girls whose past dorm aggies did their jobs. But surely Marezza wasn't foolish enough to lie when Romin would catch her. "You told them, right? What Romin said?"

Marezza exchanged frowns with the president. "And what did my papa supposedly tell you?"

Huh? "But you were there. He came with several knights, including Sir Armstrong, who rescued me, and said my necklace was real, and Romin was going to take me away, but you talked him into waiting and—"

Marezza shook her head at the president, shrugging her shoulders. She glanced at Hosanni, clucking her her tongue. "I am so sorry, child. Nothing like that has ever happened. You must have dreamed it. Sometimes, we can want something so badly, we think it's real."

Hosanni gaped. "Why are you doing this?" She turned to the president and clasped her hands. "I'm not crazy. She's a lying wolf. Look at my records. I'm telling you, Romin has reserved me for his house. He intends to free me and wants my hair to grow out."

The president slid a file folder across the desk. "Check it for yourself."

Hosanni flipped through her records and moaned. "It's not here. But I saw your predecessor write the edict. I saw her." She gaped at Marezza. "You sneaked in and stole it."

Marezza hugged her like she actually cared about her. "Darling. You are an ordinary marita, just like all the other girls here. And that is fine. You don't have to be a princess. You're special as you are, Hosanni. We love you. Now, you're going to finish your schooling, date like all of the other girls, meet someone nice at a social, fall in love, and get married. There's nothing wrong with the sweet marita you are, darling."

"But my necklace! The scroll of the genealogy. Sir Armstrong took the garnet of Kristos and gave it to Romin. It's with his crown jewels."

Marezza put her left hand to her chin. "Yes, I see how this delusion started. A knight did bring Papa such a necklace, but it was fraudulent. Even the stone was glass. I'm sorry, but Mother and Father deceived you, darling. You're not a member of a royal family, or the mother of Lady Veritas. Only the daughter of poor Diakrinthian peasants."

Marezza guided her into a school desk. "Now, let's get that hair trimmed up nice. Your ends are so ragged! You'll see how much prettier you are with a stylish cut."

A numb fog rolled over Hosanni. The hairdresser approached her with a comb and a pair of scissors and started snipping. The precious locks of plum hair falling to the floor sent Hosanni back two years to the shearing. Her back ached and her scalp burned with the memory.

Someone put a mirror in her hand. A beautiful maiden of fifteen peered back at her, with a sideswept plum bob that hugged her chin sharply.

She was quite lovely. For a marita condemned to a life of slavery.

Alone in the hallway, Marezza blocked her path and purred, "Oh dear, did I forget to tell you that Papa was never here? I wouldn't go about saying such things. Next time, they'll put you in an insane asylum, if they deem you a harmless loony."

Hosanni trembled. "Why did you do that to me?"

Marezza cackled. "Why else? It's fun."

"You're a fool, Marezza. Romin will crucify you when he comes for me."

"Oh, please. I agreed to Papa's fool notion of giving you to Prince Antonio because I know a king's memory is terrible. By now, Papa's forgotten all about you and his whimsy to make a princess out of a Diakrinthian slave."

Tears welled up. Hosanni blinked. "Do you know what you've done?"

"Left you forgotten on the Rock? Oh yes. No one is coming to deliver you. Not your god, not Romin. You are doomed to spend the rest of your days in slavery, making love to another woman's husband, and bearing children who will be raised by your lady and called by her name. On top of it all, you'll break your back to support the family while your lady gets all of the honor. And if you resist that fate and cling to your maidenhood, you will be sold at auction and spend the rest of your days being raped in a brothel."

THAT NIGHT, HOSANNI entered the open door of her barred cell, brushing past the lime green curtain. Her three cellmates had their heads buried in their textbooks as they huddled around the tiny green table. Paraclete gasped, rose, and pulled Hosanni past the privy curtain, a thin white material that the cell's gas ceiling lamp shone through.

Paraclete touched Hosanni's hair. "Why did you let them do this?"

In between sobs, she repeated Marezza's treachery.

Paraclete hugged her. "Don't listen to that daughter of Belial. Lies are her native tongue. Emi will have her vengeance on Marezza. Indeed, she's already paying by having syphilis."

May the latent stage be shortened and the fatal stage long and painful.

One of their cellmates called to them, "Mind if I use the privy?"

Paraclete said to Hosanni, "Let's get to work."

Hosanni followed her out to the janitor's closet and prepared their mops and tin buckets. They'd accepted the judgment of the aggies' reformation conference that the blood of Emi's Sacrifice, which Lady Veritas would unveil, was enough to purify all ritual uncleanness. But science had shown a practical benefit to scrubbing the floors. Namely, fewer of her ward sisters ended up in the infirmary with illnesses that could've been prevented if Marezza actually did her job and kept a clean ward.

Marezza's cruel darts echoed inside Hosanni's mind as she and Paraclete thrust their mops back and forth across their cell block. Hosanni sighed, her shoulders slumped. Who was she kidding? Romin had forsaken her, and so had Emi. If a High Queen even truly reigned in Heaven.

Paraclete patted her back. "Let it out, sister."

"Time and Chance are against me. I'll be forced to—"

"Don't speak blasphemy! You're the last daughter of Kristos. You have a record of your genealogy that traces your ancestry back to Argevane herself. She's a real historical woman. The Romini's myths are but the imaginations of fools. And if civilization is ten thousand years old, why is the year 5739?"

Hosanni bit her lip. She'd made a pain of herself to their teachers with such points. And it was most insulting to dispute the accuracy of her mothers' genealogy records. Those scrolls were treated as if Emi's hand had penned them. "Truthfully, the Xenos creation narrative doesn't make sense to me. And it bothers me that they claim it to be science, yet their theories aren't reproducible or testable."

"Then why would you consider converting to their religion? I've never heard a more wretched view of the world."

Hosanni glanced up at Paraclete. "Time and Chance are miserable gods, and most of their worshipers heartily admit it. But I can't help but consider it when the only other possibility is that Emi has forsaken me so completely, her hand has made it impossible for me to follow the path to Heaven. I prefer being eaten by worms to freezing in Hades."

Paraclete winced.

Hosanni covered her mouth. That was insensitive. Paraclete had herself surrendered her soul. She'd be among the flurry of happy graduates lining up at the altar along with their bridegrooms, the majority old bachelors swearing to their newly purchased slaves that their weddings would be their last.

If Hosanni found such a man, would he let her keep her children—no. She didn't dare add an upside down marriage on top of the witchcraft she already practiced. Besides, most liberated men showed up to socials wearing makeup, frock dresses, and corsets. To distinguish them from ladies, she had to look for the bump from the highly exaggerated male supporter.

Paraclete stopped mopping and lifted up Hosanni's chin. "Emi has not forsaken you. Wait for her in faith, and she will deliver you."

"Like she has you?"

"Maybe."

"You're leaving me in less than a week to lay with your new master."

Paraclete laughed. "You can't get rid of me that easily. By this time next week, you'll be the big sister stuck sleeping next to a steep fall off the edge of the bed, but I'm not getting married any time soon, milady. Though I would like it if you'd consider calling me milady."

Hosanni frowned.

"Die to Marezza. Become my ward daughter. All you have to do is ask."

Hosanni blinked. "You applied to be a dorm aggie and were accepted?"

Paraclete grinned wide, her eyes shining.

"But what about your apprenticeship? This will set you back."

"Little sister, I won't be actually practicing medicine. My bridegroom is a path follower. He's working three jobs and making down payments toward my redemption. As soon as they will release me, we're going back to Diakrinth, and we will be joined together properly as lady and husband."

Wistfulness assaulted Hosanni. "You're going home?"

Paraclete sighed. "Mother is too proud to accept me back from the dead. I will hire on at a villa in the vicinity of the City of Trees. Eventually, I will buy my own villa, but it's better to be a hireling wife than a slave."

Not by much. A hireling wife kept a home owned by the villa's lady, as her servant. "I still don't know why you're sticking around here. You'd be able to earn your freedom faster working as an apprentice physician."

"An apprentice witch you mean. We'd rather limit my straying from the path, even if it does take us longer. Besides, I'm not finished with you yet." Paraclete winked. She clasped Hosanni's hands. "Take hope, little sister. My bridegroom came looking for a lost bison to return to the herd. There are so few maidens in this city who truly follow the path, so why wouldn't there be other faithful bridegrooms where this one came from?"

"You think Romin's not coming back, either."

"Oh, he will eventually remember you. Go to the school library and check out Romin's book. Once you read it, you'll laugh at Marezza's lie that he's not coming back. I just think my queen would be better off with a Diakrinthian man of honor seeking a bride to redeem and take back to our homeland than what Romin has planned."

"What exactly is that?"

"If you insist upon hearing it sung second-hand—first, do you realize why the Houses of Romin and Erin are at peace rather than warring for control of the Union of the Nations?"

Hosanni glared. "How am I supposed to know that? Our history book is a hundred years old, and reading the Xenos newspaper is wicked!"

"You would, if you'd quit refusing to read the book that lays out Romin's plan for peace. The first phase has been completed. Ten years ago now, Erin gave her unnamed eighth son to Romin on the agreed upon condition that her eighth son's seed would be the successor to both dynasties, once again uniting the empire after the last three hundred years of division."

"Great. What does this have to do with me?"

"After bemoaning the evils of war for two hundred pages, Romin spends the other half of the book laying out his case for why he's obligated to keep his mothers' promise to restore the scepter of Kristos. He's been looking for you in order to do that for twelve years, milady."

Hosanni trembled in the cell block. "Only Mother never saw the book?"

"She would've viewed it as an attempt to wipe you out. His offer came at too high of a price—you. He would restore Kristos to the throne only if your mother made a marriage alliance with him. If he gets his hands on you, you will never return to Kristos. You'll be taken into Romin's house, remade in its image, and rule in the name of Kristos only."

"So that's why Mother ignored him." Emi had forbid marrying Xenos.

Paraclete nodded. "And that's why Romin has left you on Alcatraz rather than fulfilling his troth within the year of waiting. The plan in his book was for offspring of the two marriage alliances to marry and produce an heir to all three thrones, who would bear your title, thus keeping his mothers' promise to restore the scepter of Kristos while preserving the Union. Your age must've changed his plan. Prince Antonio is surely the crown prince Romin shares with Erin and around nine years old as we speak."

Hosanni gasped. "That's too young!"

"Amen, but Romin is the king. He wants you to wait for your bridegroom through another two years of medical school and a three-year apprenticeship, until the young prince will be fourteen and legally old enough to marry. Thus the next queen and king of the Union of the Nations would produce an heir to all three royal houses."

Would Korban have been so desirable, if she had been twenty rather than thirteen? And he was still Diakrinthian and a man of honor, even if they had gotten carried away before the Romini slew her beloved.

But this scheme had worse problems. "I see why Marezza's against this. Romin would demolish his dynasty as well as mine and Erin's." Hosanni drew a breath. "At least the year of waiting's expiration dissolves me and Prince Antonio, thank Emi, but this betrayal still leaves me doomed to be auctioned off to a brothel."

Paraclete stared at her. "I love you. Marezza hates you. Why are you still listening to her lies over my voice?"

"The Great Dispersal annihilated a thousand civilizations, as Romin plans to destroy my house, Erin's, and his own. While the destruction of my dynasty might be worth it to see those two destroyed, the method of their undoing is detestable. Besides, I've already accepted a bridegroom."

Her big sister gasped.

Hosanni admitted, "Against my parents' wishes, in secret, before I had accepted a second bridegroom sight unseen. Korban died trying to save me from the tax collectors. How can I choose still a third bridegroom, who would dishonor me, after knowing such devotion? Even if your bridegroom did have a brother, who could measure up to such love?"

Paraclete embraced her tight. "Amen, amen, I pray you, comfort this your daughter of her loss, heal her broken heart, and lead her to the bridegroom you have for her. Show her your plan for her life, not Romin's, and strengthen her to follow it. Make a path for her in the wilderness and lead her beside still waters. Guide us onto the path of honor for your name's sake, oh High Queen Emi, the lady of Heaven's vast armies."

A familiar cold fog entombed Hosanni. Paraclete could pray all she liked.

Hosanni's price would still be so high, only a Xenos prince could afford her. No way could she follow the path to Heaven and leave the rock alive.

In a week, Big Sister Paraclete became Dorm Aggie Paraclete, Little Sister Hosanni became Big Sister Hosanni, and Marezza became only a distant body that ignored them from the other end of the cell block. But despite Paraclete's gentle quiet voice in the present, Marezza's barbs had embedded in the heart and mocked Hosanni until their medicinal hemlock supplies began to look like a path back into Korban's arms.

The final week before graduation, seventeen-year-old Hosanni Kristekon found herself once again lingering inside the infirmary's medicine closet. She stared at the glass vial of hemlock on the potion-laden shelves before her. It wouldn't take much of the sedative. A lethal overdose was all too easy. And tonight the little sisters met their own little sisters in the receiving bay, while the rest of her cellmates would be preoccupied.

Hosanni glanced behind her and slid the hemlock vial inside her frock so it caught in her corset. Resting at peace with Korban would be far superior to being raped all day in a brothel.

GOD. Let us bless the seventh day, and sanctify it unto us, because in it we rested from all the work which we created and made.

CHORUS. And God planted a garden called Hedone, and there she gave the man she had made unto Argevane for a husband, as a servant suitable to her. Therefore, shall a man leave his mother and join to his wife: and they shall be one flesh. And they were both naked, the woman and her husband, and were not ashamed.

ARGEVANE. You are called Bion, for you are the father of all living on the purple earth.

— Pauli of Denver, The Sacred History, "Creation" scene 1, lines 59-65

Chapter Eleven

Havan Alethaner lay on the bridal pillows and the red satin sheets in the marriage bed closet, a warm quilt rumpled along his side. Overhead, his and Juris' garments swung on pegs on all sides, save the cedar door a handsbreath away from him. The moon shone down through the glass dome roof, trapping just enough of the winter sun's chilly warmth.

Giggling spilled in from the upper room. Most likely, his nine-year-old and his eleven-year-old stepdaughers were whispering to each other on their pallets. Shushing followed from all three of the maidens still at home.

Behind him, Juris stroked his back. "Phosi wrote me. She's expecting a child at the close of spring. This is a lot to ask of a man, but . . ."

Havan Alethaner grimaced. "You would like to leave me comfortless for a month or two while you sojourn with Phosi's house." Five or six months from now. Irene's secondborn would be two months old then. Too bad. The sojourn wouldn't be possible if Irene and Phosi were due at the same time. He sighed. That wasn't kind.

"Forgive me, brother. I know that Phosi and the baby don't belong to our house anymore, but . . ."

Why did Phosi have to marry an only son? "Juris, don't apologize. She'll always be ours in the bosom. Naturally you want to go. I won't complain."

A ruckus arose. Havan Alethaner stretched to reach the knob, opened the door a crack, and peered out.

The three maidens rushed off of the little girls, stuck their hands behind their backs, and sent him innocent smiles, as if to say, "Who me? I would never murder my darling baby sisters!"

He cleared his throat. "Go to sleep. If your mother and I don't have five uninjured daughters out here in the morning, the guilty parties will pay an eye for an eye and a tooth for a tooth. Understand?"

"Yes, Pappy," all five answered, the younger girls quicker than the elder.

Havan Alethaner swallowed. Would that name always hurt on their lips? But he'd raised the baby half her life. The darling had wanted a new father.

He closed the door. Juris moaned and switched from her side to her back, great with the child who'd be born any day. He grinned goofily. The baby of the family wasn't the baby anymore. He lay beside Juris, caressed her round belly, and kissed the little feet pressing firmly through her mother's skin.

Please be a boy, even it's bad grammar to call you such before birth. You already have eight sisters. Can I not have even one son born of my body?

He met Juris's gaze through a curtain of joyful tears. How could it be they were starting all over at forty-five and forty-four? Emi's hand had amazing timing. Now their three maidens and their son could fulfill the cabinet orders while Irene could teach her school-age sisters next door while keeping an eye on Havan Alethaner's toddling grandson. And he could teach little Alethaner how to carve ivory and play war games. "Pappy loves you, baby."

Juris stroked her belly. "Mammy would have loved her, too."

Huh? Oh. Nausea hit him. "If her aunt Aletheia were here to love her, she wouldn't be here to be loved. This is our child, born of love, not of command. Amen, I want a son to give my second name to very badly, but if it makes you feel like a stranger to your own child, let's go with Agapan Jurisaner."

She winced. "The aggies would censure me. Keeping this child for myself would amount to wantonly devouring my sister's house."

"Aletheia has an heir." Even if he could only lawfully marry Juris because his daughter had been declared dead. "Emi will restore Hosanni to us in her own good time."

Insecurity flashed in his wife's eyes, making her look like Aletheia for a second. *Aletheia, I miss you.* He glanced to his current wife's pregnant belly. The goofy smile returned. He caressed their child's abode. "Our child will call you Mammy no matter what name we give her."

"When will you accept Hosanni is dead?"

He replied, "When will you have faith in Emi's promise?"

"When it doesn't include the threat of losing another husband."

"Beg your pardon?"

"Who gave you to my house?"

Did she really have that poor a memory? "Korban, speaking in Hosanni's name. What's your point?" Havan Alethaner frowned. If she were declared no longer dead and given her inheritance, Hosanni would have grounds to take back her gift of his person. But who would do it? "Juris, do you fear Hosanni will petition us to have us annull our own marriage?"

Juris sent him a wan smile. "You're right. I'm being silly."

Then why did she cling to him as tightly as the baby allowed?

HOSANNI LEFT THE INFIRMARY at the end of her shift and nearly bumped into Marezza. In the gleam of the gas street lamps, Marezza grinned, her green eyes glittering. "Just the apprentice physician I was looking for! How are you these days, darling? Well, I hope."

Hosanni folded her arms over the bosom, also hugging the vial containing her escape. The vial was so cold inside her corset. "What do you want?"

"I have tomorrow off and was headed to take the last ferry out, but, with graduation so close, I thought I'd ask if there's anything special I can get you for your wedding?"

"Why would you want to buy me anything?"

Marezza blinked at her. "Oh, darling, I know we got off to a bad start, but with years come maturity and perspective. Perhaps we can start over?"

Maturity for you or for me? Hosanni sighed and dropped her arms to her sides. She gestured for Marezza to follow her, crossed over to the medicinal herb gardens, and settled into a marble bench.

She glanced up at Marezza. "I'll never appreciate how you humiliated me, but I read Romin's book, and I understand why you thwarted him. You should have trusted me. Kristos may not have the scepter, but Romin's plan would destroy us in all but name."

"Thank you, darling." Marezza settled onto the other side of the bench. "Despite my twisted sense of humor, it was for your own good. Papa's a great king, but this little obsession is madness. If I didn't act quickly, he was sure to bring you and Prince Antonio to the throne before he died. I have the dubious honor of assassinating the next queen and king. My house needs to be purged of the Erini blood already tainting it."

Hosanni said, "In the upheaval that caused, Erin would retake the west."

"I am strong enough to keep those coyotes to the east of the Mississippi. Our peoples have buried too many pink and lilac sons to rid ourselves of the blueberries to allow our former masters to return to rape our women and to break our sons like horses. Nipping this in the bud gives Papa time to accept reality and saves a sweet, innocent Diakrinthian maiden from palace intrigues that should never have involved you."

Must Marezza use such slurs? Blueberries were actually dark purple, like the blues were. It would be racially offensive to hurl a similar term at a pink.

"Come now, darling, I know that look. Don't be so distrustful." Marezza stroked Hosanni's hair. "I was trying to save your life."

Hosanni sighed. "You've still left me in a terrible predicament." Her hand strayed to her bustle. "I would pray to go to my grave a maiden rather than face such dishonor."

Marezza held her hand out. "Hand it over."

Hosanni blinked innocently. "Hand what over?"

"Now before I reach in and take it."

"Try me." Hosanni swept into the starting position of the dance of death.

Marezza swept a leg at Hosanni's shins, pinned Hosanni on the ground, and fished out the hemlock vial. Marezza held it up like a trophy. "Oh, you poor thing. You really thought only lilac women can dance?"

Assenting didn't seem wise, so Hosanni held her peace.

Marezza stood, eyed the vial she held out before her, and tsked. "It really means this much to you?" Marezza uncorked the vial and poured it out over the goldenseal and Echinacea plants. "May I suggest a better solution?"

Hosanni rubbed her sore rump and settled on the bench. "I'm listening."

"You need to get off the Rock without selling your maidenhood, correct? I need a way out of here, too. I'm a sick woman and shouldn't have to work, but Papa provides terribly unsuitable means for a princess, forcing me to take this demeaning position. No lady should have to slave away like a man, least of all a daughter of royalty."

"Plenty of maritas to choose from, milady."

"'But only one might be willing to support a princess with such a dread diesease without ever knowing the caress of a husband yourself. At the risk of you hating and fearing me along with the rest of this cruel world, I'm not the mothering type. Children are completely unacceptable. So, if you truly desire to die a maiden, consider choosing me, darling." Marezza winked. "If I were too much for you, freedom would require only saving up enough money to pay the redemption tax. If any marita can achieve that, it's a physician."

The rumor had it that Marezza spent her days off gambling, drinking, and snorting powdered coca leaves. Could she really have managed to hold onto enough of her weekly pay to afford to buy a personal physician?

"I know that look. Don't believe the cruel gossips. I can get the money."

Hosanni mustered the energy to smile. Living as Marezza's maidservant would be more honorable than her altenative options. "Then your terms are satisfactory. I choose your house."

"Marvelous, darling!" Marezza kissed her cheeks. "Lovely when you spear two fish at once." Marezza giggled. "Now, I need to catch the ferry. I have to visit the bank and withdraw my hard-earned savings and pick up everything we'll need to join you to my house."

"We're not really getting married, Marezza. That would be wicked."

"Think of it as a celebration of your escape from marrying an eleven-year-old, half-blue prince you've never even met. Any requests for the dress?"

"Anything but white." No sense in dressing for a funeral, even if being Korban Kristekon's lady appealed more than being Marita Dimarezza.

"YOU CAN'T BE SERIOUS."

Avoiding Paraclete's gaze, Hosanni hopped off of the bed in Paraclete's private cell and sat at the little green table. "I hoped you'd be happy for me."

Paraclete settled in across from her. Tears slid her cheeks. "Hosanni, I love you. Marezza hates you. Why are you choosing her lies over me?"

"She's changed."

Paraclete sputtered and dissolved into a fit of harsh laughter.

Hosanni frowned. The new Marezza saved her life. The old one would've helped her take it. "Stop it. You're not being fair. I'd much rather serve you, but even with your beau's wages, you can hardly afford yourself."

"Doesn't that beg the question where that wastrel is getting the money to buy you, when she receives the same pay I do, and you're far more expensive than I am?"

"She gets an allowance from Romin, too, but I didn't ask. I don't want to know. It's my most honorable way off the Rock."

"You're leaving Alcatraz for your apprenticeship in two days, Hosanni. I know they're pressuring you to choose now, but that's because they have to pay the single girls' room and board. Your apprenticeship will give you plenty of opportunities to meet a man of honor who will take you away from this wretched life and restore you to the House of Kristos."

Hosanni's heart raced. Leave the safety of Alcatraz Island, in the hands of strangers? No. "Love, I accepted my bridegroom, Korban. The second one was a bad mistake, and I have no desire for a third. All that's left is to make my life useful until I can lay at rest with my beloved." Hosanni sniffled. "Please come. You're my dearest friend, and this is the closest I'll ever come to having a wedding celebration, with Korban dead."

Paraclete closed her eyes. Her lips moved in a silent prayer. She glanced up and gave a small shake of her head. "You have departed from me, Hosanni. I cannot be here for this season. I only pray, when you repent of your folly, Emi will allow me to be there. If not, she will send you another comforter."

With these strange words, Paraclete led Hosanni out the door and gently shut it. A lonely chill settled like fog into the vast emptiness inside.

"WILL YOU BE GOING ANYWHERE else tonight, milord?"

Ochtu MacErin and his stable boy exited his garnet chariot inside his chariot house. By the horse stall ahead, a ladder led up to the servant quarters on the second floor. He hadn't sunk so below his station as to drive himself, but the poor lad was stuck doing the work of four servants. "Carry my things in through the kitchen and then take care of the horse. After that, you can go home. If I end up having to chase Tony down, I know where to find you."

Ochtu turned right, out the exit, and headed around to the front door of the house. He smiled, reliving all of the goals his eleven-year-old football star had scored. Tony had run off with the neighbors afterwards, but he'd let the lad celebrate his victory with his friends. The neighbors' boys played on the same team, and he trusted them. Plus it gave him time to get started on new paintings to replace the ones he'd sold at the game.

His own victory, however petty his dream was compared to his raising a future war games hero. No one could take credit for Tony's juvenile glories but Da. Ochtu unlocked the door and entered the foyer, whistling the team fight song. It died on his lips.

Marezza lay on the divan in his foyer, petting a purse bulging with coins. *Guess I'll be making a trip to the locksmith's.* "What do ye want?"

Marezza sat up and trickled gold and silver through her fingers. "I have good news, Coyote. I'm marrying again. Our money problems are over."

Why had this never occurred to him? "Are ye so selfish? Dissolvin' me means war. Perhaps ye don't care about our countrymen's lives, but I know ye care for your own. Romin would consider this treason worthy o' crucifixion."

Marezza continued to pick up the money in her purse and drop it with a clink. "Most unfortunate, that. Since you are my husband, and we are stuck with each other for life, you'll simply have to marry her as well, I'm afraid."

Her? A marita. She'd bought him a marita? Why? She didn't even want Tony. Ochtu laughed. "What makes ye think I'll meekly go along with ye?" He did just that for his mother. "I'm not an easily led teenager anymore."

"Coyote Dimarezza, meek? Perish the thought!" Marezza leaned forward, stroking the purse, and grinned wickedly. "But Ochtu MacErin will cooperate, if he wants his life savings back. That was quite clever, Coyote. Hiding money from me under your natal name. Too bad it wasn't clever enough."

His hands ached to wrap around Marezza's throat. "I want my treasure!"

"Do you? Go, verify that the lying shrew is telling the truth for a change. Oh, and if those kind neighbors of ours run into you, I'm afraid they'll be quite startled to learn our darling war game heroes aren't with us."

But Tony and his friends were with the neighbors. "What?"

"Our neighbors and I had such a delightful conversation. They realized how little they know us when they discovered their notion that you're a single father is incorrect. We've been invited to dine with them tomorrow."

Heart sinking, Ochtu bellowed, "Where's my son?"

"With his friends, excited for his victory all the more to have his mother cheering for him, and eager for me to return from my errands to conduct even more mother-son bonding. His friends will have to go home eventually, but my son is perfectly safe and where a child belongs. Eleven-year-olds aren't all that difficult to manage."

Great Alabaman, Tony had been waving to the wrong stands a lot lately. He'd figured the lad had seen the housekeeper. "I have rights in this day and age, Marezza. Ye can't simply waltz off with my son. I'll do whatever it takes to get him back. Includin' dissolve ye and take Tony home to Georgia. Let the bloodshed fall on your head, not mine. And Romin will agree."

"First you have to find Antonio, and don't you dare insult me by looking for him at the palace. Further, you have nothing left to either of your names, and our allowance leaves us a pittance after our interest payments. What, pray tell, will you raise Antonio with, your blubber? You will give me what I want, Coyote." Marezza petted the purse. "If you want your treasure."

Ochtu pointed at the front door. "Out!"

Marezza tied the purse closed, swept up, and sashayed to the door. She swung the purse. "Our ferry leaves for Alcatraz at nine tomorrow morning. Be there, dressed for a wedding. And don't be late, darling."

Chapter Twelve

Ochtu stormed down the wharf, his steps weighted by defeat. The wind blew cold, but his chest burned with unshed tears.

The she-wolf he'd married had indeed cashed out all of his liquid assets. But he'd run out of bank tellers and stock brokers to get fired for ignoring his clear instructions and he still hadn't woken up from this nightmare. His son and the neighbors' boys truly were unaccounted for. The entire neighborhood, every spareable knight of the Royal Guard, and the city patrol had all been searching all night for the four missing adolescents.

Was it wrong not to tell anyone the kidnapper gave birth to Tony? He wasn't sure what to fear more: that her accomplices might murder the boys if the military found them or that the sexist authorities wouldn't consider this a kidnapping if they knew Tony's mother had taken the boys.

Not to mention the headlines the newspapers would print. If it wasn't his son, he'd be selfishly relieved the city had its focus on Romin's missing great grandbaby. Maybe no one would notice what he was being forced to do.

Through the crowds, Ochtu spotted Marezza with a large carpetbag in the boarding area of the Alcatraz ferry. She sent him a victorious grin.

She took his arm and patted the shoulder of his kilt jacket right over the tattoo of her family emblem. "So good of you to join me, husband."

Ochtu stiffened. His throat burned. He said hoarsely, "This is for Tony."

Marezza cackled. "Naturally, darling. I'm sure Prince Antonio will greatly appreciate his loving father's selfless sacrifice."

Ochtu held his arm so he touched his wife as little as possible. It had been eleven years since he'd been young and stupid enough to mistake darling for a term of affection, or to convince himself Coyote wasn't that bad of a name.

FOLLOWING BEHIND HER lady, Hosanni entered her ward's dressing cell. It held her remaining ward sisters' trunks, a wash basin, the Romini's throne-style earth closet, and a full-length looking glass. Three or four maidens could squeeze in at one time.

Marezza placed her carpetbag on Hosanni's packed trunk. "I wasn't sure about your preferences, so I brought two for you to choose from. I hope you don't mind a borrowed gown. I didn't have time to commission a new dress." She opened the bag and pulled out two luxurious dresses, one spun silver and the other spun gold.

Hosanni gasped.

Marezza smiled. "Rather old-fashioned design, I know. I do apologize. But they're designed to flow loosely, so at least one of them should fit over your undergarments."

Tears slid down Hosanni's cheeks. She sang King Phoenix's words from the Bride's Ode to Love, addressed to his bride, Queen Salome also being his stepsister. "Anon comes my sister, my bride. Girded in the purest of silver, she dances for her king. See now our mother, splendid in gold. She embraces our father, her own bridegroom."

A dagger pierced Hosanni's heart. She should be King Korban's bride. Did he rest with her mothers or with his own? Hosanni shook herself. She couldn't think of such things, or she'd end up drinking the hemlock. "High Queen Agapeta and Queen Salome, King Phoenix's bride, adorned themselves in robes as splendid as these. Where did you get such?"

Marezza smiled. "From where Papa keeps the crown jewels when they're not out in their display cases. Don't worry. He won't miss them. And look." Marezza held the gold dress up against Hosanni. "It's clearly meant for you."

Hosanni took the priceless garment. "Thank you for letting me borrow this. I'll take good care of it."

"Naturally." Marezza laughed. "I have to get dressed myself, so get that frock off and your wedding gown on. Our appointment with the chaplain is in fifteen minutes, so meet me at the assembly hall." Marezza swept out.

Hosanni unbuttoned her bodice and slipped out of her frock. She turned the gold dress around. How did this work? Not seeing any other alternative, she balled the dress up, stuffed her arms into the sleeves, and shoved her head through the neck.

Only a bit of tugging brought the dress down over her. She picked up the ends of the gold belt someone had sewn in at the back and tied it properly.

A glimpse in the mirror stole her breath. Other than the sideswept bob, she looked like she should be holding the scepter of Kristos in her hand. The belt even bore the tassels the law prescribed for the daughters of her people.

Did Romin hear the Bride's Ode to Love, fancy the song, and commission dresses to replicate an artist's imagination of the High Queen's and the Bride's vestments? Hosanni picked up her comb and brushed her hair, aching for a bridal braid. But there was no sense pretending Korban would be waiting in the assembly hall, when he was truly at rest with their mothers. Perhaps the Romini's dumb law had saved her from herself.

Instead, she reached in her trunk and fished out a small white cardboard box she'd received at mail call two weeks ago. She chuckled. Only Paraclete believed her that it wasn't from a suitor. She peeked at the little card:

> An innocent daisy for an innocent maiden, in purple because your heart is as steadfast as the purple Earth we dwell upon. I pray the man you give your heart to deserves and appreciates the treasure he receives, bambina.
>
> Merry Chanukah
>
> Sir Fautorio Armstrong

Hosanni sniffled. Just like a father, hoping love would find her twice in one lifetime and redeem her from the grave. Too bad his idea of helping her would be to see her wed the Xenos prince Romin had planned for her. Shame Sir Armstrong had no son to give her, even if he could've afforded the price of her freedom. Her lip curled. Now she understood the old husband's proverb, "A son loves the maiden whose house he wants to serve."

She opened the tiny box and slid the beautiful silk purple daisy hair clips into place. This was as fine a social occasion to break these in on as a funeral and less wasteful, even if it would prolong the pain of a lifetime without her family. Father probably never came home, either.

The bells in the watchtower donged the hour.

Hosanni gasped—she was late.

Her side felt like it'd split open by the time she burst into the assembly hall, crowded with students finished with their finals and hence with nothing better to do until the next term than watch the procession of graduates joining the houses they had chosen.

The chaplain stood at the altar. Beside her, the president glanced at the wind-up wall clock and tapped her high-heeled boot. Marezza faced the altar and wore a bridal lilac wedding gown in an elaborate lace and satin design.

Beside Marezza stood a six-foot-tall plus Erini man in his mid-twenties. His midnight purple skin had an actual blue undertone, so all of his ancestors were blue. He wore shoulder-length dreadlocks and a black dress jacket with a green and yellow tartan kilt. From the back, it was obvious he ate too much, exercised too little, or a combination of both.

What was he doing at the altar, holding Marezza's arm like she was still in the contagious stage and her disease could be caught through satin gloves?

The president spotted Hosanni. "Finally! Get a move on, Marita Hosanni. You've attended enough of these to know there's no processional dance."

Marezza and the blue man turned. Marezza offered an encouraging smile. The blue man stiff at her side had the look of a prisoner awaiting execution.

What was this? Unless . . . Hosanni gasped. No. Nothing in their postures suggested that these two were joined. Surely there was another explanation, besides that Marezza forgot to mention she had a wretch—a husband whose wife failed to keep her vows, either through adultery, or simply refusing to comfort him of his manhood.

The chaplain rushed over to Hosanni's side and took her hand. "Is there something wrong?"

Hosanni swallowed. Her lips moved but only squeaks came forth.

Marezza slid to her side and brushed the chaplain away. "Pre-wedding jitters. Give us a minute."

OCHTU MACERIN EYED the Diakrinthian lass conspiring with the she-wolf he'd married. Not surprisingly, Marezza had chosen a breathtaking beauty, which the stolen spun gold vestment and the silk purple flowers in the lass's shorn hair only emphasized. But his instincts were right. The lass would have outshone Marezza even when Marezza was the bride of seventeen. Marezza was far too vain to associate with a lass lovelier than herself, unless it was necessary for setting a trap.

Apparently her conspirator had second thoughts, though.

Or had Marezza neglected to mention that he was a MacErin? He'd been around enough to know Idaho's natives were all xenophobic. Alcatraz had to work with its lasses on that, seeing as they made few sales to Diakrinthians, but for some reason, Diakrinthians seemed to especially hate his people.

His own housekeeper admitted once, "I'd have never considered working for a blue man in my youth, but as you get older, you learn to look past who a man's mothers are to discover who he is."

Such pervasive hatred could make this one want to renegotiate terms. But it'd also make her a willing accomplice.

Marezza released her conspirator and led the lass toward him.

Ochtu wavered. Why was the lass's demeanor as willing as a man about to be crucified?

ONCE NO ONE REMAINED in earshot of Hosanni and Marezza, her former dorm aggie hugged her. "Darling, don't fear that worthless dog."

Hosanni squeaked, "A husband violates our agreement."

"Not at all. I don't want the child I have. Our agreement stands."

"But—"

"This isn't Diakrinth. You're under no compulsion to comfort him of his manhood and join to him so often as he requires, as the religious ceremony so delicately puts it. Coyote cannot lawfully consume your maidenhood against your will anywhere in the nation of West California, or in most nations in the Union. I won't lie. Coyote will lust for such a beautiful marita, but you dance well, as do I. Should the thought of ravishing you occur to him, it'll get him nowhere but nailed up on a crucifix."

The chaplain said, "We have a tight schedule. Please approach the altar."

Marezza breathed in Hosanni's ear, "Darling, you're already sold. Back out now, and you'll end up in a brothel." She released Hosanni and gave her a push toward the altar.

Hosanni sloughed forward as if traversing a swamp. On the periphery of her vision, her peers pointed at her, giggled, and whispered. Her whole body tensed and her cheeks flamed. This couldn't be happening. She'd wake up safe in Pappy's arms to find it was all a horrible nightmare. He never left and the tax collectors never came.

At the altar, the president positioned Hosanni so she stood angled toward Marezza and her Erini wretch. The president stood beside Hosanni.

The chaplain intoned, "Friends and distinguished guests, we gather here to celebrate liberty by joining this marita to Princess Marezza Romin and to Prince Coyote Dimarezza. Have all fees for Hosanni been paid?"

The president said, "Yes. The account is settled."

"Do you, Hosanni, willingly choose this lady and lord? Do you pledge to honor them and to always cherish them? Do you pledge to provide for them financially, and to be faithful to them, forsaking all others so long as you are joined to them, and obeying them in all things in accordance to our laws?"

In a fog, Hosanni whispered, "I do."

"Do you understand, if you pay the redemption tax, you'll be dissolved, and the children you bear for your lady by your lord shall remain with their mother and father, under penalty of death if you're caught child stealing?"

Green spots burst and the room wavered. "I do." Her lips had moved, but it felt as if someone else had said it.

"Do you, Princess Marezza and Prince Coyote, both willingly accept this marita? Do you both pledge to cherish her always, to keep a home for her and care for all of her physical and emotional needs? Do you pledge to treat all children born to your house equally?"

"We do," Marezza said.

"I must hear verbal responses from both of you."

Coyote grunted. "I do."

"Will the lady present the marita's wedding ring to her lord?"

Marezza handed to Coyote a plain gold band like the husbands wore on their right middle finger to show their marital status.

The chaplain said, "The lord will place the ring upon the marita's right joining finger and say, 'with this ring, you are made holy to me, until death dissolves our joining.'"

Coyote jammed the ring onto Hosanni's right middle finger and repeated in an exasperated voice, "With this ring, ye are made holy to me, 'til death dissolves our joinin.'"

"In accordance with the laws and the statues of West California and of the western division of the Union of the Nations, I now declare you wife, husband, and marita. You may now exeunt."

Coyote gaped at the chaplain. "Did ye just say 'please leave'?"

The president said, "Please report to the ferry, your highness. The crew will be presently loading Hosanni's trunk on board. Her final marks and certifications will be mailed out to your home address and to her master physician. Shalom and congratulations to you both, Prince Coyote and Marita Hosanni Dimarezza."

HOSANNI KEPT PACE WITH Marezza as they wobbled down the gangplank off the ferry, trailing behind the dust of the human thundercloud named Coyote. For someone so out of shape, the blue man moved quickly when he wished to.

Hosanni's stomach churned. Thankfully, she'd remembered to stop by the infirmary and take a dose of ginger tea before boarding. If not for the uncertainty that had her nauseated on solid ground, this sea voyage might have been pleasurable.

They joined Coyote at the steel carts holding the passengers' luggage. All around them, leathery-skinned nasha men carried passengers' luggage while wearing nothing but kilts in solid black or solid purple and leather sporrans turned sideways to dangle over the hip.

A nasha who'd dreadlocked his silky hair bounded over like an excited dragonling. "Point yours out, and I'll carry them to your chariot."

Marezza slid a dainty finger toward her carpetbag. Hosanni glanced over the trunks and tapped the one with her name on it.

The nasha hauled Marezza's bag on top of Hosanni's trunk and glanced to Coyote. "Which way, your highness?"

Coyote growled. "I'm in parking space 23A." He fetched a ticket from his sporran and pressed it into the nasha's sporran along with two copper coins. "I'll give you another copper to fetch my horse from the stables."

The nasha grinned and dipped his head. "Thanks, your highness!"

He and Coyote hurried off toward the distant rows of chariots awaiting their passengers and their horses. Ahead of such stood a row of businesses, including Alcatraz's mainland office, a post office, and a bank. However, most of them appeared to hawk gifts or food and drink to visitors to the beach.

Hosanni shuddered. Even after five years of dwelling among the Romini, all their straight lines and sharp angles seemed oppressively rigid and ugly.

By the time she and Marezza caught up to Coyote, he'd reached a garnet red chariot. Most of the chariots parked here were blue, black, white, or silver, with the occasional green or purple. Each had a fifth, unused wheel adorning a random spot on the body, and some had ornaments atop their fenders or their bumpers. Few of the chariots featured unlit oil lamps like Coyote's did. Strange, parked out here, without their horses, she could almost fancy that the chariots might move all on their own.

The nasha had already secured her trunk and the carpetbag to the back of the chariot, on top of Coyote's trunk. Further the nasha had a purple mare on the reins, headed out of the stables back toward them. The nasha hitched the horse to the chariot. Coyote slipped into the chariot while the nasha threaded the reins through the leather flap and knotted them off. He hopped back out and tossed the nasha the promised copper.

The nasha beamed, waved, and scurried back toward the beach.

Coyote whirled on them. He thrust a hand out at Marezza. "First you give me my money, then my son."

Hosanni blinked. Huh?

Marezza smiled at Coyote. "What money?"

"You know what money. You stole all of my liquid assets." He narrowed his eyes at Hosanni before turning his glare back on his wife. "Now hand over that purse you were waving around before I forget you're supposedly a lady."

Fog rolled over Hosanni. No.

Marezza put her left hand to her lips. "Oh my. Darling, I fear there's been a misunderstanding. That was my hard-earned savings from the nightmare that you've put me through for the last five years. Your treasure is right here." Marezza pointed at Hosanni.

Coyote growled and marched to their luggage. Kneeling, he rummaged in Marezza's carpetbag, removed a fat coin purse, and poured the contents out. At first, gold and silver hit the gravel. The rest were coppers and bronzes.

The wretch bellowed and slammed his fleshy fist on the ground.

Marezza scrambled to gather the coins back up.

Coyote slammed the coins back into the purse and pulled her up. "Forget the money. Ye can have it. Just give me back my son!"

Son? Hosanni frowned. A child was mentioned, but Marezza, pregnant? And had threatened the child's life to gain her husband's cooperation?

Marezza laughed. "I'm shocked, Coyote. You truly believe that nonsense you told Papa and the city patrol? Can a mother not hold an overnighter with her own son and the neighbors' boys at a friend's house without causing an uproar? The boys were asleep when I left, but I imagine by now they've gotten bored and gone home. After all, my son tells me he enjoys learning at 'Da's' table." Marezza wrinkled her nose into a snarl. "So perhaps before you assault a woman, we should all head home like a normal, happy family?"

Coyote grunted. "I'm goin' home. You're goin' to find my son. And don't complain about bein' unescorted. Ye should have thought of that before ye left four adolescents to wander about alone in the city."

Marezza laughed. "Before you make any hasty decisions regarding our marita—" She turned to Hosanni. "Darling, confirm for the kind gentleman the total price Alcatraz set for you, including your maidenhood, affects, room and board, and tuition?"

Hosanni swallowed and whispered the rediculous sum.

Coyote frowned. "Marezza, dare I ask what happened to the other 1194 pounds, 23 pence, and 81 halfpence?"

Those were silvers, coppers, and bronzes. Hosanni blinked, her mouth hanging open. How could a mere man do such difficult math in his head?

Marezza petted her coin purse. "You'd be proud of me, darling. I paid what I owed for Hosanni before I celebrated with the rest of your money."

Coyote's fingers curled like he wished to strangle his wife. He growled and pointed down the street. "You. Gone." Coyote jerked open the chariot's passenger side door and glared at Hosanni. "You. In."

Hosanni wobbled on unstable legs. She slid into the front seat.

Marezza cackled and spun her fat coin purse by its strings. "Keep the carpetbag. I've got what's mine." She swaggered off like a victorious warrior.

Coyote stomped around to the driver's side, clamored in, and slammed his door. He pounded a fist on the dashboard, screaming.

Hosanni shirked as far away as she could from the blue man acting like he were indeed a wild dog. Her heart thudded faster than bison hooves. She should have listened to Paraclete. There was little room to dance in here, if Coyote decided to take his wrath out upon her maidenhood. So far from any family, who would defend her?

She reached behind her for the door handle but hesitated. No one cared for her in this city. Where would she go? And if this constituted running away, the penalty was death.

Coyote turned to her and scowled. "Let's get one thing straight, lass. I already have one wife makin' me miserable. The last thing I needed is two o' ye. I don't know what Marezza promised ye, but I'm not as stupid as ye think. I won't give ye any opportunity to be crying rape and getting me crucified. Ye can die a virgin for all I care."

Hosanni stared.

"Don't be playing innocent. I see the company ye be keeping, lass. Wolves prefer to run together in packs." Coyote cleared his throat. "Your stay will be temporary, until I climb out o' the financial disaster Marezza's wrought." He measured his words as if trying to speak without his brogue, which he only succeeded in softening. "And take that ring off. I don't want anyone to know about this, especially not my son. We'll tell him you're a boarder, which is what you will be in practice. Let's hope he doesn't go on to follow this lousy example that Marezza's forcing me to set."

"Y-yes, milord." Hosanni dropped the ring into Coyote's waiting hand. She swallowed. His concern about impropriety could only mean . . . "Marezza doesn't live with us?"

Coyote laughed and dropped her ring and his own into his sporran. "You play innocent better than Marezza, lass."

Hosanni bristled. "I mean when she's not at Alcatraz. She's given notice."

"When she's not going home with one of her lovers, she wanders back to where her clothes live, in her aunt Porcia's chambers at the palace. But that's another thing. She makes me miserable enough at a distance. You stay only as long as you aren't also insufferable, even if it means losing your income before I can afford to."

"And if I do behave, what then? If you sell me back to Alcatraz, I'll end up in a brothel. They're the only ones who buy used maritas."

"A medical exam will show I returned you with your virginity intact."

Xenos. Humph. "On the eighth day of her life, a Diakrinthian's hymen is excised as an offering to Emi. Also, any hymen can be missing congenitally or torn through means other than intercourse. I was 'used,' as Alcatraz defines it, from the moment we left the altar."

Coyote cursed in Erini and added in English, "Why should I care where spoilin' your schemes to get me nailed up high land ye? Don't lie. Marezza's threatened to slay me. What did she offer ye for usin' ye as bait, anyway?"

Hosanni repeated the sum her lord had unwittingly paid Alcatraz for her.

Coyote stared at her. "Lass, only my wastrel, royal houses would ever buy you at that price, but Alcatraz must know it's ridiculous. It's in their financial interests to haggle with your choice of lovers. So what's really in it for you?"

She should have listened to Paraclete. She'd brought even more suffering on a man who'd clearly already suffered a great deal at Marezza's hands, and possibly left the servants he employed without their livelihood, if he couldn't afford to pay them. "I deserve your judgment, milord. I was selfish. Marezza deceived me, but that's no excuse. I should have asked if she was married and where she would get the money. I knew what a wastrel she is. I'm so sorry. I never should've trusted her." Hosanni stared down at her hands, folded in her lap. Only Marreza could turn saving someone's life into another stab in the back. "I should've stuck with my first escape plan and drank hemlock."

Coyote lifted her chin, his brows scrunched together. "Are you serious? Why would a beau—" He released her, averting his gaze.

Tears trickled down Hosanni's cheeks. If sharing this abated his wrath and brought peace, it was worth it. "Please understand. I was thirteen and in love. Korban and I were plotting ways to convince my parents to let us marry. Then tax collectors came and Korban and my mother died trying to save me. All meaning fled from my life that day, and I only have found any purpose in learning medicine. But I feared, if I refused to choose a house, they would sell me to a brothel, where I could not save others from this terrible pain."

"It never occurred to you, if you scrimped and saved your coppers, you could always buy yourself? It'd take a long while, with the redemption tax, but so long as you're making timely payments, it's not in their interests to—"

Hosanni whimpered. "Why didn't I listen to Paraclete?"

Coyote sighed. "Aye, lass, Marezza's swindled you good, and don't make me regret believing you, but I'm still having a hard time with suicide being preferable to the unjust farce that passes for a wedding at Alcatraz."

Hosanni blinked. A Xenos man grasped how dishonorable her life was?

"Hey now, don't look so surprised. I didn't want a marita on principle, too. Freedom shouldn't cost someone else theirs, if ye ask this liberated man."

She arched her brows. His hair and clothes were in traditional Erini male styles, and he wore no makeup. "Liberated, and groomed like a man?"

"I don't get along with those lads too well. A man shouldn't have to make himself up like a lass to get any respect. I'm hoping it's merely a temporary mass insanity."

She giggled. She'd seen so many men truly dressed like women, a kilt no longer looked like a strange palla missing its top half. But that was like losing her Diakrinthianness. She glanced over her garments. Could she remember how to wrap a palla? It wasn't fair. She'd only just been learning.

Coyote unknotted the reins and urged the horse into motion. "This wasn't supposed to take so long."

Hosanni gulped. "Beg your pardon, milord. I hope your son is safe."

Coyote grunted and turned onto the busy street. "He'd better be. If Marezza's killed Toni, by Astor, she's next."

Surely she had misunderstood. "Toni? Who's she?"

"That's T-O-N-Y. My son."

Marezza hadn't . . . Hosanni stared at her hands. It was shameful enough to be on bridegroom number three at all at her age. Surely not even Marezza would be so wicked as to betroth her son to a maiden only to instead give her son's bride to his own father. "Milord, what does Marezza call your son?"

"She and my pink in-laws insist on calling him Antonio. Why?"

Hosanni trembled. The fewer people who knew, the better. "Let's only say I agree Marezza might be cold-blooded enough to murder her own son."

Chapter Thirteen

Without any assistance, Ochtu's mare dragged her conveyance from the edge of their block straight to her feed trough inside their chariot house. With Noinin's head buried in the trough, Ochtu untied her reins and dropped them.

He turned to the lilac lass still wearing the priceless artifact the she-wolf he'd married had stolen. "Fetch your own clothes and go change upstairs." He pointed at the ladder up to the servant quarters. "No one will disturb you. The help was up all night looking for Tony, so I sent them home." Plus it helped keep everyone's focus on Tony and off of this embarrassment. Maybe no one would ever notice. He could only hope. "So change and take care of the horse."

A puzzled frown met his gaze.

Ochtu swallowed. "Pardon my inhospitality, milady. The chariot that we passed out front belongs to Princess Porcia Romin. I'm hoping she has Tony."

The lass's eyebrows rose at being addressed as a guest. "I understand, milord, but mastodons are the beast of burden in rural Diakrinth, and I was trained to be a physician, not a stable hand."

Lovely. "Wait here. I'll get you help." Ochtu ran to the exit, but stopped and glanced back. He pointed to the door at the back of the chariot house. "The kitchen's through there, if you're hungry. The outhouse is beside the pig's pen."

She wrinkled her nose at the mention of the pig but nodded.

Ochtu took the shortest route to the house and unlocked the servant's entrance. He crossed through the pantry into the dining room. "Porcia!"

She met him in the hall, coming from the drawing room. "The city patrol found the boys, lost in the slums, but safe—no thanks to Marezza. I fear Tony was with his mother."

Ochtu let out a relieved breath. *God, if you're there, thank you.* "Thank you for this, Porcia."

"You wait until I get my hands on my sister for being so irresponsible. Tony could've been actually kidnapped and held for ransom or worse."

Ochtu shuddered. "Milady, I need a private word with my son, but I'm afraid I'm being a lousy horse owner."

Porcia nodded. "I'll see that's taken care of. You worry about Tony."

"My thanks." Ochtu entered in the drawing room and blinked.

Slumped on the sofa was a sullen lad still in his football jersey, his cleats, and a black kilt with white stripes down the sides. His son had only turned eleven nine days ago, but his mental image of his scrawny little boy clashed daily with reality. His happy child had sprouted into a moody adolescent, one who wanted to skip ages eleven and twelve and go straight to thirteen.

He pulled Tony up and hugged him. Tears ran down Ochtu's cheeks as he squeezed his son, a combination of joy that his son was safe and sadness that he didn't have to bend down. He wasn't ready for his son to be standing nearly eye-to-eye. Each day, it seemed the lad looked less and less like his little boy and more and more like an athletic, lilac-skinned version of him.

Ochtu held Tony out by the shoulders and stared him in the eyes. "Never do that to me ever again."

Storm clouds brewed inside Tony's dark violet eyes. "Why is everyone so worked up? We were just at a friend's house. I'm not a baby, Da."

"Lad, you didn't know your way home or the person you were with, and no one knew you were there. Even worse, you ended up in a part of town a young prince has no business being in by trusting a stranger simply because she claimed to be your mother."

Tony winced and pulled free. He folded his arms and stared back. "She is my mother. You have no right to keep me away from her."

Ochtu sighed and wiped his face. "Aye, Marezza had the decency to give birth to you. But she's deserted us. I'll be honest, my most natural inclination is to forbid you from having any contact with her."

Tony scowled.

Ochtu slapped his right hand over the mouth gearing up for backtalk. "I won't. Marezza's expecting that and will turn me into the villain if I do."

His son lurched away from his hand. "You lied to me! You said Mother is sick. She's fine."

"Lad, she's not a well woman. She has latent stage syphilis, but that's not the sickness I'm truly concerned about. Her conscience is seared. You were just too young to understand what is wrong with her before."

Tony gaped. "You think Mother has lycanthropy?"

Ochtu winced. "Son, I've protected you from this all your life. I know she does. Your mother revealed her true nature the day you were born. It is not healthy for a woman to carry a child in the womb for nine months only to want to kill her newborn for having the audacity to have been fathered by her husband rather than by her pink lover."

His son backed away, shaking his head, fear in his eyes. "You're lying."

Ochtu swallowed. He wished he was. A relation with lycanthropy was a risk factor for the disease. And he'd had to raise his at-risk child all alone, when he was the son of a she-wolf, too.

Porcia slipped in beside Ochtu. "Nipote, I was there at your birth. The reason your father fears your mother has lycanthropy is true. Because of your blue ancestry, Marezza refused to nurse you and ordered you abandoned to die. Even the risk of Papa charging her with treason would not dissuade her. You are only alive because of your father. If you'd been born but a few years earlier, he would not have had the legal right to spare you."

Tony broke down crying. "But she's sorry now. She must be."

Ochtu hugged the lad. "If she truly wants to see you, and you want to see her, you can. But I need to know where you are and who you are with. That is what you are in trouble for, Tony. Not for being with your mother, but for lying about it. Marezza has broken my trust numerous times. You can only see her at Porcia's, with Porcia present. And I make the rules. You will honor me wherever you are. Is that understood?"

"Aye, Da." Tony paused. "Am I grounded?"

"You had the entire neighborhood, the royal guard, and the city patrol out all night searching for you. What do you think?"

"I think I'll get a lot of reading done between now and February."

Ochtu laughed. "I think so, too." He thumped his son on the back. "I love ye, laddie."

"I love ya, too, Da."

"Don't ever do that to me again."

His son hung his head the way Marezza did whenever she needed to act penitent. "I promise."

Ochtu swallowed. At least Tony didn't look anything like Marezza, but mannerisms like that one frightened the blazes out of him.

BACK IN HER OWN FROCK dress, Hosanni tossed down the carpetbag with the luxurious dresses Marezza had given to her and climbed down the ladder. She turned toward the royal guardsman grooming Coyote's horse, now freed from her harness. The horse's tail swished happily as she slurped clean water.

The knight's familiar features registered. Hosanni's breath caught.

Sir Armstrong stared as if unsure he trusted his senses. "Bambina?"

She gasped and grinned. Laughing, she slammed into Sir Armstrong with a hug. "What are you doing here?"

"Serving as her royal highness's glorified errand boy, but this position did come with admission to an honored order of knighthood, and anything beats tax collecting." He stood back, glanced her over, and returned to brushing the horse. "The frock dress flatters you far better than orange, but whatever are you doing here, bambina?"

The truth came tumbling out.

By the time she reached the end of her song, Sir Armstrong had finished tending the horse, and Hosanni was sobbing hard. He draped a fatherly arm around her shoulders and drew her outside.

Kelly green wicker chairs waited for them upon the porch of a two story home painted royal brown and accented with sky blue. The place looked like a mansion, though it was rationally quite modest for a prince like Coyote.

She settled into one of the wicker chairs and watched as Sir Armstrong retreated back to the chariot house.

Moments later, he returned with a plain lilac ceramic mug filled with hot water and a tea bag releasing the soothing aromas of mint and chamomile.

She accepted the cup with a small smile. "Thank you."

Sir Armstrong settled into the chair across from her. "The situation is as bad as you think, bambina. Prince Coyote is Prince Antonio's father. The one thing in our favor is no one beyond those of us there that day knows what Romin had planned. The only heart that Princess Marezza's broken will be his majesty's." He paused. "That is, if anyone has the courage to tell him. Kings have been known to execute bearers of such ill tidings."

Hosanni shuddered and picked at the fern sitting on the kelly green iron pedestal beside her. "So how do I fix this?"

"You don't. That is what made Prince Coyote and Prince Antonio perfect for Marezza's purposes. Romin might have deemed his plan more important than the impropriety of him annulling one nipote's marriage, freeing you, and remarrying you to another nipote. But remarrying you to the nipote's own son would be far too scandalous."

Hosanni's cheeks burned. This wasn't scandalous already? She'd wanted out of marrying Prince Antonio, but to betray him with his own father? "What does it matter? Are either of them even Emian?"

Sir Armstrong hesitated. "No one I know would accuse the Romin family of ever following the path. However, Prince Antonio is young and pliable. You could teach him, but Prince Coyote is twenty-six and set in his ways. If it's any consolation, of all the house of Romin, Prince Coyote is the most honorable. He and Princess Porcia are the only kin of Romin's that I'd willingly die for. The rest of the lot of them would deserve what they got."

Hosanni sipped her tea. That was hardly reassuring.

Sir Armstrong leaned toward her. "Let me put it this way. If you were trapped in this situation with any other member of the royal family, I'd carry you out by force, if I couldn't get a loan for the redemption tax. But Prince Coyote I trust. He's a just and fair man."

"For Xenos?"

"Present company excluded, I hope."

"Emian and Xenos are mutually exclusive states, milord." Even if she still had no idea what to do with all of these converts outside of Diakrinth who'd retained their Xenos cultures.

"Well, it is a shame the two of you are stuck with the likes of Princess Marezza, but however Prince Coyote handles this, the only path better for you than to quietly obey him would have been listening to your friend, and it's too late for that now."

OCHTU WALKED PORCIA to the foyer. "Milady, thank you again for coming, and for all of your assistance, but I know you must be exhausted, and frankly I'm too worn out for company at present."

Porcia kissed both of his cheeks. "You're welcome, dear brother. Here's to far more restful nights than the previous."

"I'd drink to that." If he wasn't so disgusted by the effects that alcohol had on the rest of his in-laws.

They strode out on the porch. Oddly, the lilac lass was having herself a neighborly chat with the help.

Sir Armstrong stood up for the lady and saluted her. "Your highness, the horse has been cared for."

Portia swept down the porch's steps. "Thank you, Sir Armstrong. You're a true godsend."

Sir Armstrong sent a glance to the lilac lass and followed Porcia to her chariot. He opened the door for the lady before heading to the driver's side.

Ochtu dropped into the vacated chair and arched his left eyebrow at his guest. "Do you know him?"

The lilac lass hesitated. "Pardon, milord, but the full explanation is a long and rather personal song. I pray you, permit me to only assure you that he's not a threat."

Ochtu glanced away. Why must she remind him of the wedding bands that jangled in his sporran? One of them Marezza scorned eleven years ago. The other was an unjust institution that made a mockery of a holy covenant.

By Astor, he didn't even recall her name. "Tony's grounded for a month."

A relieved breath escaped her. "Thank God he's safe."

Ochtu blinked at her. "You don't even know him."

The lilac lass looked down at her hands. "No, but I would feel responsible if something tragic had befallen him."

Because you are. Ochtu sighed. Marezza had fooled him once, too. "Look. I guess I should warn you, recently, I caught Tony leading strangers to believe him a young man of thirteen, but he truly is but a mischievous eleven-year-old boy. Please do not encourage my son's insistence on sprouting up far too fast for the liking of this Da."

The lass nodded. She nibbled her lip. "Milord, does your son participate in junior level war games at all?"

"He's the star center forward on the neighborhood football team. Why?"

The lass hesitated. "I need to interview the subject about his symptoms before I make any hasty allegations."

Lovely, his new personal physician thought someone might be giving his son drugs? Exactly what he needed. Another worry. Ochtu pushed up out of his chair. "Suppose I'll have to introduce you sooner or later, milady. But to avoid embarrassing myself in front of my son, would you mind telling me who exactly it is I am introducing? I fear I missed that."

The lilac lass pressed her lips together. Her haunted eyes flickered. She stood and offered her left hand in introduction. "Hosanni Kristekon."

"Glad to know you, Hosanni Kristekon." He shook her hand by habit and repeated the name a few times, to put it to memory. Why did the surname strike a bell? "Milady, would you do me the favor of dropping the milord? I don't want Tony to know." Kristekon. What did that remind him of?

Hosanni nodded. "I know you intend milady as polite address to a guest, but be aware it has romantic connotations to me. I'm afraid courtship is the only context in which a man has ever addressed me as a lady before."

Why did the temperature just rise in his cheeks?

Kristekon . . . Kristos. Ochtu snapped his fingers. "The vestments! What did ye do with the carpetbag, lass?"

Hosanni frowned, gasped, and ran down toward the chariot house. She returned carrying a carpetbag spotted with dirt and hay.

Ochtu yanked the bag from her hand. "Do ye have any idea what's in this? Gifts from my mother that she presented to Romin along with my person on my wedding day, so Romin could give them to Kristos, if he ever found his mythical lost lilac princess. Ye left priceless artifacts to roll around in horse manure." That there wasn't any on the bag was besides the point.

Hosanni's eyes widened. She poked the bag like it might bite. "You mean they're real? My mother's vestments?"

Ochtu blinked. Her mother? He opened the carpetbag and pulled out part of the ornamental robe made entirely of spun gold. "This is yours?"

So that was what Marezza was up to, thwarting Romin's plan for peace.

Would Romin blame him? "Milady, if you are the daughter of Kristos, then Marezza may have done you a favor. If Romin had found you first, he'd have taken advantage of this injustice to compel you to marry one of the drunkards that pass for princes in this family."

Hosanni winced and looked away, chewing her lip.

Ochtu swallowed. No doubt the predicament they found themselves in now pressed upon her more heavily. He had to get Kristos's daughter back to her people before Romin found out she existed and annulled this, mistakenly thinking he'd be arranging a marriage between their offspring, as Romin had laid out in his plan for peace.

Ochtu wiped his brow. Participating in treason with the likes of Marezza? The things he did to protect his son. "All right. It's going to take us longer than it would have if you'd listened to your friend, but eventually, I promise we'll save up enough to pay the tax on freedom and send you home, milady."

Hosanni screamed in delight and hugged him.

Awkwardness swept through Ochtu. It'd been such a long time since a lady who wasn't family had hugged him. It didn't help that the lady snug in his arms was the most beautiful creature he'd ever laid eyes on. What should he be feeling about this?

A gasp rang out from the door.

They broke apart and turned toward where Tony stood in the doorway, staring open-mouthed, as if he'd just seen Da kill his precious pet dragon. Not that Tony was allowed to ever get one of those scaly beasts.

The lad shook his head, his fists clenched. "Da, how could ya?"

Chapter Fourteen

Hosanni's stomach churned as her lord's son turned and ran up the foyer staircase. The poor child had gaped like Irene did the time she had caught her "shamelessly flirting with my beau," never mind that Korban hadn't so much as noticed Irene existed. Hosanni cast an apologetic glance at Coyote.

He frowned. "Thanks, lass. If I did mean to be fetching home a mother for Tony, that is exactly how I would want her introduced."

She swallowed. This was worse than he imagined. "My apologies. I should have restrained myself. Would you allow me to go and explain?"

Coyote laughed. "Sure. It's your funeral." He waved her in.

Hosanni slipped in and swept up the staircase. Four doors confronted her in the hallway at the top. She swallowed. May she never get used to how much space the Xenos wasted. All this for one man and one child.

Childish sobbing led her to the open door.

A worn rocking horse mourned its abandonment beside a desk cluttered with books, parchment, pencils, and quill and ink. On the shelf above the desk, tin soldiers marched around Anapausi's ark. Across the room, black and white pentagons covered the surface of a football left by the wardrobe. Shelves stuffed with books served as the headboard, which had dozens of war games trophies scattered atop it. A step stool stood beside a bed surely intended to sleep a family of six. Why did these people sleep so high up?

She swallowed. Had Marezza so lovingly decorated this room before she left? The home showed no sign of suffering the lack of a woman's touch.

Except for the cries tearing from behind the dreadlocks of the lilac child sprawled on the bed, still in his football uniform. His father's instincts were correct. The boy was the size that Korban had been at thirteen. Like too many young athletes, Coyote's son would suffer greatly from the greed of managers willing to jeopardize children's health to win war games.

He stilled and his back stiffened. "Get out, Da! I don't want to see you." He groped above him, landed upon a medal, and hurled it blindly over his shoulder with far too good aim.

Hosanni dodged the projectile. Coyote must've been too lenient with the spankings. "Anthon."

Anthon sat up, his head turning like at his name. Another Diakrinthian must already call him by her people's equivalent of Antonio. He wiped at the tears staining his lilac cheeks. "Hosanni?"

She nodded and hopped up onto the far corner of the family bed, which she hopefully would not have to share. "I take it someone else refuses to call you by a girl's name?"

He nodded. "That's what Grandma says. That Toni is a girl's name."

"Beg your pardon?"

"She's not really my grandmother. Only our housekeeper."

"We call them aggies."

"I know. She told me." The child budding into manhood too soon stared at Hosanni with youth's guilelessness. "You're prettier than in my dreams."

A better lead up to the house call that duty required would not present itself. "This will be awkward, but I need to speak to you as Dr. Kristekon, not the pretty lass your mother presumably told you about. Would these dreams be accompanied by painful night emissions?"

Her subject blinked like he didn't know that medical term.

She cleared her throat. "Preceding this, the male suffers an impulse to copulate. The painful night emission temporarily relieves this compulsion."

Her subject averted his eyes and hung his head.

The poor child. Marezza ought to be crucified for this devilry. The male curse had come upon Korban only after he'd been lent to her family. "Nothing to be ashamed of. The male curse, as this illness is called, is a routine, easily treatable ailment caused by a microbe that afflicts all men. The emissions occur over a period of three weeks, until his penile sores erupt and bleed for a week. This seminal cycle repeats itself every four weeks until he receives the cure. I'm afraid it won't be legal for a Ravane to minister the cure until you're at least fourteen. You'll have to suffer in the meantime."

"The cure being marriage?"

"Afraid so."

Anthon frowned. "If what you say is true . . . ."

Hosanni winced. Her chest throbbed, her throat constricted. "When did your mother claim we were supposed to be getting married?"

The child glanced away and whispered, "Today."

Unladylike Diakrinthian words rushed to Hosanni's tongue. "Anthon, I'm afraid the only wedding that your mother had planned for this morning was a poorly disguised legal contract between me and your parents. She deceived me into it and blackmailed your father."

The child's eyes brightened. "Da isn't deliberately stealing my bride?" The light snuffed back out. "Mother did?"

"I am so sorry. This is my fault, not your father's. He hasn't the faintest idea. Only I, Romin, Marezza, a school president who accidentally drowned, and several knights knew. I suspect your father would be absolutely horrified if he knew Romin promised me your hand in marriage. You were only seven years old, Anthon."

Anthon grunted. "How long Bisnonno has planned this is irrelevant. Da should be disgusted. I mean, he's joined to his own son's bride."

Nausea rolled through Hosanni. "We've done nothing of the sort and we have no intention of it, Anthon."

"You could have fooled me on the porch, milady."

She winced. "Amen, Diakrinthians are huge huggers by your standards. That was my native response to happy news. Your father has promised to return me to my mother's house as soon as we can afford it."

"Bisnonno gives us an allowance. But we do get a lot of letters from creditors. Da tries to hide them from me, but I know where he keeps his ledgers. I like to read them."

"What do they tell you?"

"Da grew his 100,000-pound dowry into a whole million pounds! But then he lost over half of it paying off bad debts. It's been a huge struggle to maintain the lifestyle of princes ever since. Sometimes, I think Da hates his noble birth. It'd be much easier to get back to where we were if it wouldn't be demeaning for Da to cut our spending any further or to get a real job."

Hosanni wrinkled her forehead. "He has an unreal job?"

Anthon laughed. "You'll discover what I mean soon enough." A starry-eyed sparkle lit up his countenance. "Do ya think maybe Da will let me get a paper route? How long would it take to buy you back? If ya want to emigrate to Idaho, we could do that. I've always fancied moving to the country and raising dragons. Would that be demeaning for a prince if he enjoys it? Da says a prince can bake for himself if it's for the pleasure of it."

A man, at a stove? "What woman would allow a man her pleasure?"

Anthon scratched his head. "I don't understand that question. It's Da's stove, not Grandma's. She's merely the hired help."

Hosanni bit her lip. The poor child had been motherless so long, he had no idea how Emi had designed for a house to operate. "Do you have any left?"

Anthon blinked. "Any of what left?"

"The herbs to make the potions responsible for your ability to trick people into believing you are thirteen. I want the rest of it. You're stuck with a body interested in things your heart and mind are not yet mature enough for, but you can avoid an early grave if you stop now."

The child gaped. "Seriously? An early grave? As in dead?"

Hosanni went on to recite at length the health consequences of messing with nature in this way. For a bonus, she threw in the gruesome details of all the diseases he could catch, if he surrendered to temptation and followed in his mother's footsteps.

By the end of her lecture, Anthon had turned over a newspaper bundle. He sniffled. "Please don't tell Da. Please."

"On one condition." Hosanni held up the drugs. "Who gave you this?"

The child hung his head. "Mother."

"Anthon, would a woman who had your best interests in mind give you dangerous drugs that increase your likelihood of straying before marriage and hence suffering the price of that as well? Would a loving mother trick your bride and your own father into a sham of a marriage and tell you for no better reason than to hurt you?"

Anthon winced. "Mother didn't mean to hurt me, she'd thought—" He clamped his mouth shut and glanced away.

Hadn't Coyote said Marezza had threatened to slay him? How evil could a woman be? "Would a mother who has your best interests at heart undermine your relationship with a loving father and cause you to doubt his love?

Would a mother who loves you set this up to attempt to provoke you into killing your own father, an act that would get you crucified?"

"A loving mother wouldn't." Tears spilled down Anthon's cheeks. "Please believe me. It wouldn't matter if Da had done this evil thing intentionally. I love him. I would never hurt him. I swear it, milady. I love Da."

Hosanni closed her eyes. "I believe you. But please obey your father and stay away from Marezza. She is a very sick woman."

"You think Mother has lycanthropy, too?"

Hosanni took Anthon's head in her hands. "Marezza told me straight-faced, without the slightest hint of emotion or maternal attachment, that she was plotting to murder you. If that's not symptomatic of lycanthropy, then the disease doesn't exist."

Anthon whimpered like an orphaned dragonling. "But she is the only mother I have."

"Emi is a mother to the motherless. She'll take you up and shelter you in her wings." Was it true? Did God even exist?

Anthon gasped and leapt up from the bed. He shied toward the door. "I forgot. We shouldn't be in here together, milady. Especially not alone."

Huh?

"It's not proper."

The implications of his people using rooms like this one for both sleeping and joining slammed into Hosanni. From Anthon's cultural perspective, they had effectively had this conversation inside a marriage bed closet.

She stood and removed herself to the hall, just outside the door. "I fear I may never get used to some of your ways. Among my people, it is the custom for families to all sleep together, and for married couples to withdraw into a small closet to join in private. By our standards, we were quite spoiled in my home. It was just the three of us for much of my childhood, so my parents slept in the marriage bed closet until they embraced a foster son."

Anthon's eyes widened. "Your parents remained together, yet you are an only child also?"

Hosanni nodded. "You wouldn't like my nation. Life there is different."

"Different isn't bad, just different." Anthon made direct eye contact.

Humph. A Diakrinthian boy his age would never have dared such a rude action with even a young woman like herself.

Anthon said, "Promise me that you won't return there without me."

A lump formed in her throat. "If you still feel that way then, I will gladly accept your offer of escort." Hopefully, she wouldn't have to break it to him—or to herself—that marriage was now impossible.

"DA, I STOPPED BY THE Chronicle stand while headed home from football practice. They said I can have a paper route if you just sign this."

Plunked at the table across from Ochtu and beside the guest, Tony fished crumpled parchment out of his sporran and passed it to Hosanni. She passed it to Ochtu with her lips pursed. Ochtu spread out the crumpled application beside his dinner plate, empty save for a sprig of parsely and a puddle of turkey gravy. He grunted. The newspaper stand wasn't on the way home from the football field. "I'll think about it."

Hosanni's eyebrows shot up. She glanced down at her cleaned plate.

Tony's hopeful smile rewarded Ochtu's parenting strategy of ignoring this strange whim and hoping Tony forgot about it. The lad scooted back from the table and stood. "Thanks, Da!" He paused. "May I be excused?"

At least his son had remembered his manners at all. "You may go to your room. Come kiss me goodnight before you go to sleep."

Tony nodded and left the room.

Ochtu sighed. He was punishing himself as much as he was his son, but a grounded child shouldn't be allowed to dawdle after dinner and socialize.

His guest stood, fetched a tray from the pantry, and began collecting their dinner dishes.

Ochtu got up and tapped her arm. "Milady, what are you doing?"

Hosanni smiled. "Milord, I'm impressed your cooking was edible, even pleasing. But, at school, the wards had rotating kitchen privileges, and I *am* the only woman here. Besides, I've never gotten used to being waited on."

Kitchen privileges? "Royalty shouldn't serve, or technically, do anything that causes us to break a sweat. It's beneath our station, but you're royalty also and it's my house. The housekeeper normally cooks ahead for today, but with all the fuss about Tony, that didn't get done before sundown on Friday."

A blank look crossed Hosanni's face, she stared at the tray of dirty dishes she still held and trembled. "I completely forgot today is Sabbath Day."

Ochtu took the tray from her hands. "Don't you worry. I had to order the housekeeper and her family to go home and keep their feast. And they still went right back out looking for Tony all night."

"Honoring the Sabbath is secondary to the welfare of woman and beast, milord. The oath I took to be on call for emergencies in my own neighborhood follows perfectly the path of the Sabbath law."

"So it wasn't a mere excuse? Good to know." Ochtu left the tray on the counter next to the water pump standing over the pantry sink. He glanced to her guiltily. "I have a bit of a confession. I normally wash these tonight even though it's not fitting. It takes the housekeeper undue effort to get them clean if I leave them overnight."

Hosanni sat on a stool in the pantry. "It's not your observance. You won't offend me, though on any other day I'd prefer the pleasure of keeping house."

Ochtu blinked. "Beg your pardon?"

"I'd suggest dismissing the housekeeper, except her family is probably dependent on her income, and I doubt I could keep up a house this size all on my own and put in a forty-eight-hour work week as well, not to mention any emergencies after hours."

"We have a couple physicians around here already. So I don't expect you should be overly pressed upon."

Hosanni cleared her throat. "I should add I'm going home, eventually."

Ochtu swallowed. He definitely shouldn't get used to her. "Maybe I've spent too much of my life in royal courts, but do peasant women really think of kitchen duty as a privilege?"

The lovely creature he was not getting attached to laughed. "Diakrinthian women take great pride in how we keep our homes. Teaching our daughters our privilege is a joy, but otherwise it is shameful among my people for a woman to delegate that. It'd be cheating. Housekeeping is our second most popular sport. Victory there is secondary only to the glories and honors we receive in childrearing."

Ah. "So that's why you're fantasizing about dismissing my housekeeper? You want to practice for when you have your own house?"

Hosanni nodded. "But of course she's your hireling, not mine, milord."

Ochtu winced. "I don't care if Tony knows why you're our guest. I'm not comfortable with the milord. You're our guest, not my slave or hired help."

She demurely kept her eyes averted from direct contact with his. "If you prefer for us to be on a first name basis, I will obey and call you Coyote."

Ochtu bit back a protest. He hated Marezza's cruelty, but his mothers weren't much better. 'Eighth son of Erin' would sound like a name to his guest if he said that in Erini, but what if she asked what Ochtu MacErin meant? Admitting he didn't have a name of his own would be embarrassing. "Maybe you could just drop it entirely?"

"As you wish, but it seems unfair when you're still calling me milady."

"I can't help that." Ochtu lifted her chin and forced her to look at him. "You are a lady, Hosanni Kristekon. And you deserve to be honored as one."

She scrunched her eyebrows together and then burst into giggles.

Ochtu backed away. "Beg your pardon?"

Hosanni covered her giggles. "A liberated man speaks of honoring a lady as he subjects her to direct eye contact. Initiating eye contact is seen as a dominating behavior in Diakrinth. It is the height of impertinence for a man or a child to do what you just did to a grown woman."

Ochtu arched an eyebrow. She could have fooled him. "This is the first you've given me any indication this displeases you."

Hosanni glanced away. "I'm ashamed to admit it, but Mother set a bad example. She permitted Father to engage in many improper behaviors, when they thought I wasn't looking." She glanced back. "But in this house, you are the lady in terms of roles. So I am the one being rude, am I not?"

"Milady, there are two schools of thought in the only doctrine that I give credence to. Some of us respond to millennia of women keeping mincemeat pie all to yourselves by taking it all for ourselves and refusing to share. Not me. I don't want to deprive you of the joy of eating pie. I would just like a piece myself, that's all."

"Emi made the pie for the woman. If you take a piece, you steal from her."

How did a woman respecting a man back rob her of honor? Ochtu moved in closer and whispered back, "Then bake me my own, milady."

Why was his heartbeat speeding up?

He revisited the jesting words that had poured out of his mouth. Didn't that imply far more permanent arrangements than he'd promised?

Why must getting lost in her beautiful violet eyes feel so good?

Ochtu glanced away. "My apologies, milady. I overstepped."

Considering he was trapped being married to Marezza, even if Marezza couldn't bake, literally or figuratively, to save her life.

Chapter Fifteen

Hosanni retreated to the dining room as Coyote turned to washing the dinner dishes. She still wasn't used to the Xenos habit of eating the chief meal of the day at supper time rather than at noon. She'd get used to that before she got used to Coyote. The man was a conundrum. He more effectively raised questions and doubts in her than the false Ravane intentionally seeking to deconstruct the male and female roles the true path dictated.

One thing for certain, for the duration, she wanted to live at peace with both the father and the son. Strife wouldn't do in the home. But neither would becoming overly fond of this family when she wouldn't be staying.

She stole a glance at the Xenos prince scrubbing dishes on Sabbath Day.

Coyote looked up and caught her eye across the way. Her heartbeat rose subtly. He cleared his throat, shook himself, and turned back to his dishes.

Hosanni swallowed. Somehow, losing Korban no longer hurt so deep.

She turned to the cedar china cabinet's clutter. The familiar lines of the Nine Men's Morris game etched the top of a mahogany box. Though, at home, they'd added diagonal lines to create the illusion of a decapitated pyramid out of the hideous squares within squares design. She situated herself with the game at the table, tugged on a drawer knob, and counted out nine shiny red stones and nine shiny green stones. This had to be the way the wealthy played. At home, they'd burned the lines on a bisonskin and played with pebbles.

Before long, she'd once again proved the difficulty with playing against herself. Her opponent knew all of her moves as soon as she did.

Lye soap intermingled with the fragrant, musky scent of royal sweat overshadowed Hosanni. Coyote asked, "Would you care for an opponent that can't read your mind, milady?"

She nodded, her heart beating faster than she'd like. Her body tingled with awareness that Coyote stood but inches behind her.

He settled into the chair beside hers. In embarrassingly short order, he moved one of his red stones from a row of three along a line to form another row of three. He removed one of her three remaining green stones from the board. Hosanni stared at the board and glanced up at Coyote's smug and quite victorious smile. She offered her hand. "Congratulations."

He shook her hand. "Thank you."

The warmth lingered on her hand. It'd felt so cozily small in Coyote's. She smiled. "You should be proud. You're only the third woman to beat me."

He scrunched his eyebrows together, so she added, "Since I've played against female opponents as well as male opponents, the generic she is the proper grammar here."

Coyote grunted. "I know, lass. Just because that is considered the proper grammar still in many parts doesn't mean I have to like it."

She glanced down. For the sake of peace, she would have to remember to avoid offending him like that in the future.

"Who else do I share such honors with?"

Hosanni collected the red and green stones from the table and the game board and returned the stones to the little drawer. "Father and Korban, my foster brother. I went easy on Korban because we were secretly courting."

Coyote's eyebrows shot up.

She shrugged. "I realize losing on purpose makes no sense to competitive souls, but my childish ideas of love persuaded me watching Korban enjoy his victory was more pleasurable than winning."

"I won't pretend to understand that, but might I suggest it would make more sense gramatically to admit three men bested you, even if you allowed one of them to do so?" Coyote paused. "It was only one of them?"

Hosanni giggled. "Father taught me how to play, so naturally he's beaten me. With Korban, I overlooked a mistake or two that would have turned the tide to my advantage. I would not intentionally suffer the crushing defeat you have delivered me."

The joy of victory swept back into his eyes. She dropped hers.

Best to turn to more professional discourse. "I must beg leave to discuss a parenting matter that is not strictly my interest, save as a physician."

Coyote eyes flickered, and he grunted.

Was that a yes? It wasn't a no, at least. "Forgive my misunderstanding, but I had thought 'grounded' meant Tony is being punished with not being permitted customary privileges?"

"Aye, he shouldn't have gone by the newspaper stand, but I let it go."

"Pardon, but he only had an opportunity to take the detour because you permitted him to play football with his friends."

"Sure, he's on a team. It's important he make his practices and his games. The rest of the time, he has to stay in his room except for meals."

No doubt Anthon would throw things at Coyote, if he grounded him from football. "Forgive me again, but what is he doing in his room now?"

"Probably reading, why?"

"So he's getting to continue a sport he loves and is allowed such a great privilege as reading. Among my people, men are not even taught how to read. Further, the boy has more books in his room than I could probably find in my entire village. Forgive me, but I have a hard time viewing his being confined to his room with such treasures as a punishment."

Coyote frowned. "So maybe Tony does like to read, but how is any of this your concern as a physician?"

Hosanni winced. She would have to get to that eventually. "I interviewed the subject when I apologized to him earlier."

A hush settled over them like a cloud of dust. Coyote swallowed. "And?"

"I have made a rather difficult diagnosis. Early puberty."

Coyote froze. "Are ye sure? He's barely eleven. He's just a little boy."

"A mentally and chronologically accurate assessment. Unfortunately, it is not physically accurate. Biologically, you have a young man on your hands."

"By Astor!" Coyote shook his head, his wide eyes glinting. "I thought I had another two or three years at least."

"You should have had such. I'm afraid your son has been doomed to a lengthy transition from childhood to adulthood. With his maternal medical history, that doubles his already high risk of engaging in behaviors that would jeopardize his health. Right now, he doesn't need a friend he always likes. He needs a father."

Coyote sunk low in his chair and moaned. "This can't be happening. I can't—I had only recently become a man myself when Mum ripped me away from Da and hauled me clear across the country. I can't do this. I can't."

Hosanni swallowed. She'd been taught, in his culture, it was improper for men to show emotion like this. What should she do? Would he only be more embarassed if she stopped him?

He bent over, his head toward his knees, hiding his face. His shoulders shook. "Pardon the outburst, milady, but you don't have any idea what it's like to be but fifteen years old, abandoned by your spouse, and solely responsible for the welfare o' a helpless little baby. I wasn't done growin' up myself when Mum forced me to marry Marezza. I hoped I'd at least have a father-in-law for guidance, but no, all I had was Romin. A sovereign king doesn't have time to answer a teenager's embarassin' questions even if I'd had the courage to ask."

Coyote looked up. Tear stains streaked his face. "I had to finish my own education and figure out what it means to be a man all by myself. I don't know how to lead my son through this. The only thing Da got to do with me, our fathers' manhood intiation ritual, needs to wait until Tony's at least thirteen to be legal. How am I supposed to do this all alone?"

Tears wet Hosanni's own cheeks. And here she had thought no one could possibly have suffered an ordeal worse than what she'd endured.

She restrained the impulse to hug Coyote and instead took his hand and squeezed. "You are not alone. You made me a promise, and now I am making you one. Even if we can afford to send me home sooner, I will see you and your son through this season, right until the day you embrace a daughter."

He smiled and squeezed her hand back. "I won't hold you to that."

With the gratitude shining on his fleshy blue face, and the hand holding hers with such hunger for companionship, how could she not keep her word?

He cleared his throat. "I, uh, am surprised you put it that way. Embrace a daughter. I thought you sell your sons like dragons?"

"Diakrinth's sons and husbands are the property of the lady of the house, but we present our sons as our gifts to their wives upon marriage. Also, it's unlawful to take a woman's only son away from her and that would apply to Anthon. Naturally, his wife will join his house." *Though, she most definitely won't be me.*

Hosanni's eyes dropped to the warm hand encompassing hers, and she sensed his attention divert to the pleasant connection as well. They released it at the same time.

She shivered, butterflies flitting in her stomach. She pressed her hands into her lap. "May I make a suggestion? Sign that." Hosanni nodded to the crumpled application still on the table.

"I am sore tempted. I understand the attraction of the forbidden, but it isn't appropriate for a prince to have a paper route. It wouldn't be fitting."

"It wouldn't be fitting for a prince to live a long, happily productive life rather than a short, spoiled life that is vaguely unhappy for some mystifying reason?" She dared eye contact and noted the resonance on his countenance. "Fair or not, men are hard-wired to provide for their families. Your son knows the financial straits his mother has put you in and is following the course his biologically ingrained instincts draw him toward. Encourage that, don't hinder it. This is an important part of his journey to adulthood."

"But—"

"Don't you remember how good it felt the first time all the hard work you put into your investments paid off? While my people expect men to engage in manual labor and trades taught on-the-job, you can hardly say that you're not dancing to the tune of your own provider design. The biggest lie Marezza ever told was that you're worthless. If not for her, you would still be a self-made millionaire. That's hardly poor provision by any standard."

Coyote closed his eyes. "Milady, I take no offense at a commoner doing what he must to feed his family. Truthfully, and it's sexist of me, but I am not comfortable with the commoners forcing their wives to go to work while the husband raises the children. Personally, what I object to is robbing a man of the right to think for himself, treating him unequally before the law, denying him the rights a woman enjoys, and confining him to a narrow list of back-breaking, mind-numbing occupational choices. Most of all, I object to acting like what a father traditionally does is unimportant and irrelevant."

Hosanni trembled as Coyote met her gaze again. Why, why did he have to make so much sense? "Then you'll let Anthon help?"

"A paper route won't make much of a difference."

"Except it could save his life."

Coyote sighed. "It can't be worse than letting him play football."

Hosanni again restrained the impulse to hug Coyote and grinned.

He reached for her hand. It slid into that cozy, warm place. Chuckling,

Coyote said lowly, "If that's all that gets me a smile, he can feed the pig and groom the horse, too."

She giggled. To think he'd meant that to be ludicrous. "Why not? I had approximate chores at his age, clear until I finally had a brother to pass them off onto." She pressed her lips together. She'd never thought of Korban as a sibling. So why was that what she'd intended?

Coyote arched an eyebrow. "The foster brother that you were smooching behind your parents' backs?"

Hosanni gaped. "How did you know?"

"An assumption, milady. Lasses don't go loony and contemplate suicide over lads with which they've only held hands and made goo-goo eyes."

They dropped their gazes to where their hands were again and yanked the contented limbs back apart.

She cleared her throat, keeping her eyes carefully averted from his. "That would have been a waste, but of course it most certainly is better to remain a perpetual maiden than participate in the Romini's farce."

Coyote lifted her chin and looked her in the eye. "I made you a promise. We'll get you home, milady, and back to the life you deserve."

She swallowed. "I should warn you, in case he sticks to his crossbows, Anthon has gotten the notion that he's escorting me home. He seems to see it as an adventure. Somehow, I doubt you would get him back."

"Thank ye for the warning. Let's hope he forgets in the meantime, or I definitely won't be a friend he likes to be sure." Coyote paused. "I'll arrange a proper escort. Porcia could stand to lend me a man for the journey. Romin's a bit overprotective of his baby girl."

Hosanni nodded. "Sir Armstrong would race wild horses to volunteer. That would have a lovely symmetry."

"I am still curious how you know a royal guardsman."

"He was a tax collector when we met." Throbbing pain knotted in her chest. She drew in a breath. "He killed my mother."

"Oh." Coyote blinked. "Oh—and you're friends?"

Xenos could never understand this. Hosanni sighed. She should at least try. "It was an accident. Our dragons attacked him and his men. He aimed for a dragon leaping for his throat but missed it, and the thrust caught my mother instead. He would've been killed as well had one of his comrades not stepped in the way and died instead."

"Precisely why Tony isn't allowed one of those beasts. My third brother had his arm taken off by a supposedly well-trained dragon."

Hosanni nodded. The boy must have tormented the poor dragon until she couldn't take it anymore and snapped back. "The city isn't a good place to keep dragons. You have to acquire them as dragonlings and it takes a lot of time and effort to socialize them properly, so I understand perfectly."

"That makes one of us. How do you forgive something like that?"

"You wouldn't understand."

Coyote leaned forward. "Try me."

Hosanni pressed her hands against her skirt, staring at them. "He acted without malice aforethought, and he has been nothing but penitent since. He went out of his way to help me, risking reprimands from superiors. Frankly, I owe him my own life, so you could say we're even. If I had only stayed on the path that he put me on, and if I'd listened to Paraclete, things would be much better for us now."

Coyote touched her chin, lifting her eyes to him. "Milady, the only part o' that which doesn't make sense is continually kicking yourself. To be sure, it'd make far more sense to look to the path home that still lies ahead."

How could such wisdom abide in unabashed Xenos?

HOSANNI WIPED SWEAT from her brow. The kitchen was broiling from the iron cooking stove. Never had it seemed more criminal that Diakrinth's sun crystal makers so closely guarded the ancients' secret. She checked the wind-up timer. Dinner would be ready soon. Good, her boys would be starved. She glanced to the hired help, who was stirring the soup beside her. "Thank you, Aggie. Once dinner's served, you may go on home. I'll clean up."

The Diakrinthian woman in her mid-fifties smiled. "Ya sure, milady? After a tiring eight-hour work day?"

"Every corner we cut here hurts you, but it's important to us. Besides, I'm not too tired to enjoy the pleasure of keeping my house." Hosanni's cheeks grew warm. "Or you know what I mean."

Aggie's eyes twinkled. "What I know, milady, is that none of us realized how much this house missed ya until it acquired ya. But I must admit, your servants are wondering how long milady and milord plan to pretend milady's a guest. May I request notification in advance of honesty? Otherwise, I might need to freshen the linens some morning and accidentally surprise milady and milord while they're lingering late on the marriage bed."

Hosanni's temperature shot still higher. She sputtered. "It's not like that."

"I have eyes, milady. I see the way ya are with Anthon, and I see the way ya and milord look at each other."

Hosanni glared. "Do you mean to imply I love the father and the son?"

"Quite surprising, that. Most of us don't take to the existing children so quickly, but I dare say ya already be as fond of Anthon as me. But I can't help noticing he's grounded until March now, and for an infraction no where near as serious as what earned him spending January locked in his room. Makes me think milady and milord aren't locking him up for any better reason than to not be worried about him as ya court."

How dare she accuse me of that. "We are doing no such thing!"

"Ya accompanied milord on his prerequisite princely appearances at the opera and the symphony, didn't ya?"

"The company was also prerequisite. I went as a favor."

"Princess Porcia normally does that favor. He took ya because he desired your company. And what do ya do with free time? It's spent with milord, whispering intimately, until ya decide ya too close to the flame and end up in the kitchen with me, dreaming about firing me and keeping your house."

Hosanni wobbled. Aggie couldn't be right. "We don't whisper intimately! We share about the places we've been and the people we've known and loved." And about those who had hurt them.

Aggie cackled. "And no doubt your hopes and your dreams and all of the stuff young lovers whisper intimately to each other by the fireplace."

May the stone floor melt and suck me down into it. "You accuse me of *porneia*. Coyote Dimarezza is a married man, however unhappily."

Sorrow filled Aggie's eyes. "Oh, honey." Aggie hugged her. "Child, for the first time in years, milord is happily married—to you, not to that adulterer."

Hosanni frowned. "Beg your pardon?"

Aggie bustled to the stove, stirred the soup, and tossed in spices. "Milord hired me for his house right after he bought it. Anthon was two and a half, and his mother was already long gone. We heard nary a peep from her until he was nearly seven. Ya well know the Sacred History decrees merely a year of such separation dissolves a marriage."

Hosanni swallowed. "That's only the law in Diakrinth. The government has to sign off on virtually everything here."

"And they have. So enough talk of *porneia*! He's your own husband, and only married to anyone else in the eyes of Romin. Not in Emi's eyes."

Explaining how they felt to a marita who had children and grandchildren with her master would only bring strife. "We are not in love! I'm going home as soon as we get ourselves out of the mess Marezza's made."

Aggie laughed. "Oh, are ya now? Go take a peek at what milord has been working on up in the attic, and then ya try to tell me ya ain't in love."

HOSANNI PULLED ON THE chain dangling from the ceiling. The attic stairs lowered. A drafty chill carried a hint of paint fumes as she climbed.

At the top, their own private art gallery surrounded her. She gasped. A father and son motif dominated the canvas paintings cluttering the spacious room. Among the ones stacked along the floor, all of the blue children, and many of the pink and lilac wee ones, vaguely resembled Anthon. The framed works hanging on the walls were all in chronological order and appeared to capture moments of his son's childhood in canvas oil painting.

She came to an image of a wee Anthon nibbling on one dreadlock as he practiced his penmanship at their dining table. The next painting portayed a dirty Marezza on her hands and knees, scrubbing the floor of a cell block. Hosanni giggled. What she wouldn't give to have seen that in real life.

She tiptoed around to peek at the two paintings on easels and covered her mouth. In the painting on the left, a Diakrinthian maiden wore a bridal braid and a golden robe on a lonely hill overlooking Hosanni's village, just as she'd described it to Coyote. Sadness shadowed the young bride's face. A mournful hand clutched at her breast. The sky was dark and stormy.

On the right, a happy nasha family gathered for breakfast in a dining room modeled off their own. The sun shown through a bay window in a clear blue sky. The adolescent son again looked like Anthon, about to shove a boiled egg into his mouth whole. Across from their son, the blue father and the lilac mother sat smiling at each other lovingly as the pair held hands underneath the table. The rounded contours of the mother's belly hinted at the reason for the family's joy: a daughter would be joining them in due season.

Hosanni glanced in the looking glass and back at the young women in the two paintings, once, twice, three times.

Dear Emi, the heartbroken bride and the joyous mother were both her.

Coyote appeared at the top of the stairs. Nervousness shone in his eyes as he drew ever more nigh. Hosanni's heart caught in her throat. When had her lord become as striking as Queen Salome's beloved King Phoenix?

Chapter Sixteen

At the desk in his drawing room, Ochtu puffed on a cigar as he jiggled the numbers in his ledger and in the mail. His housekeeper knocked on the open door. He glanced up at her smirk and the twinkle in her eyes and frowned. "Is dinner ready?"

The smile widened into a toothy grin. "Presently, but I thought you might want to fetch milady down from the attic first."

Astor, in the attic? He'd rather have accidentally spoken aloud, and hence had to explain, the private nickname his guest had acquired. Ochtu gasped, put his cigar out, shoved past his housekeeper, and ran to the stairs. Astor would've never gone up there if not for the meddler he'd hired.

Huffing, he flew upstairs three steps at a time. He had to get to her before too much damage was done.

On the attic stairs, Ochtu slowed to a crawl, tensing to hide his tremble. Astor stood in the worst possible place—at his easels, her mouth covered as she gazed on the raw emotions he'd never intended for her to see. His heart would shatter in keeping his word, but telling her so would make it harder to say goodbye. The most love he reckoned he could show her was to quietly bask in her sunshine while he had it and return her to her family a virgin.

Her eyes met his. Her rounding eyes shone.

Breathing heavy still, Ochtu swallowed a lump in his throat. *Whoever is up there, it's that pesky Erini prince again. I could really use some help. I don't know what to say, and one wrong word, and I think I might cry. That will only make things worse.*

He stepped around the canvases and cleared his throat. "Dinner's ready."

Astor arched an eyebrow. "That was not what I was at all expecting."

Ochtu winced. "I'm sorry, milady. Truth is, I'm embarrassed. You weren't supposed to see any o' this. Least o' all those two." He waved to the damning paintings on his easels.

Her eyes softened. "Don't be. They're lovely." She blinked as if surprised at her sentiment and glanced away. "Though I must admit, I was discomfited to realize I was your model, given the mother is pregnant."

Pregnant? Mother? "Beg your pardon?"

Astor pointed her left index finger to her abdomen in his painting of what had become a typical breakfast for them in recent weeks.

Ochtu peered closer at the painting. His stomach roiled. Oh, now that she mentioned it. He turned to her, hands up, palms out. "Milady, I can see that interpretation, but I promise ye that was not the intent o' the artist, and bein' him, I should know." He drew in a deep breath. "My apologies for the start. Sometimes my brush gets away from me. I'm afraid Tony wasn't supposed to be an only child. Bein' the lastborn o' eight brothers and three sisters, I had always pictured my dinin' table as bein' much more crowded."

"I see," she whispered.

Ochtu searched her eyes. Did she? Did she know the truth? Had she only said model to spare his pride an untimely demise?

Astor slipped her hand into his. "May I ask how long you had intended to keep your occupation a secret from me?"

He glowed. Occupation. Painting was his occupation.

"What did I say that lit you up like a menorah?"

"Most call what I do a hobby. Too many still hold onto the sexist notion artistic and scientific pursuits should be reserved for mothers who dabble at them in their spare time." Ochtu waved at his life's work. "This is what gives me a rush, when I sell a painting for more than it cost to make it. I've been meanin' to find the courage to tell ye, to even show ye some o' the pieces for sale. But I was unsure o' what ye'd think of my dream."

More like terrified, after Marezza's mocking and Tony's embarrassment.

Astor let go of his hand and glanced around his studio. She turned to him, her eyes bright and shining, and slipped her arm under his.

He reeled in the headiness of her touch. Time to politely disengage.

Before he could, Astor laid her left hand at the breast of his drawstring blouse, right near the laces, looking up at him with a glimmer in her eyes as sweet and delicious as mincemeat pie. "I think the artist of these paintings is going to be world famous. That's what I think. You are so amazingly talented. You deserve to have your work on display in a museum."

The warmth rushing through him swept all sense and reason away, and he drew Astor into his arms. Her return embrace and sweet submission to his kisses tasted like the most potent of wines. Was this what true love felt like?

"Milady, Milord! Dinner!"

His housekeeper's voice knifed Ochtu with where he was and what he was doing. He and Astor broke apart, breathing hard.

She touched her puckered lips, her eyes wide.

Great Alabaman, how could he have so completely lost control?

HOSANNI PUSHED HER half-consumed dinner away. She'd hardly tasted it and no longer even knew what it was, but had forced down all she could.

At least Coyote had rescinded her orders and told Aggie to clean up from dinner before she left. Hosanni no longer had the energy for playing out her wicked fantasy. This wasn't her house to keep, and she wasn't his lady.

Nor could she be.

Hosanni wiped her mouth with a white napkin and pushed away from the table. "Please excuse me."

She fled out through the hall and into the drawing room.

The fireplace had burned low. She opened the grate, stirred the embers, and fed them a fresh log. Warmth sprang to life again. She replaced the grate, wrapped a wool afghan around her, and curled up in an overstuffed chair.

Hosanni brushed her lips with a finger, tasted again the sweetness of the drink she'd given Coyote from her cistern, and sobbed into her hands. Aggie was right. She had given her heart away to that Xenos man. That absolutely brilliant, strong, handsome, funny, bold, yet incredibly sweet man. How could she have been so careless?

Boyish hands pulled hers away from her sobbing. Anthon's face came into view through the curtain of tears as the lad scrunched down eye to eye. "Why are you crying, milady?"

"I have a better question, son," boomed his father behind them. "When did the drawing room become your bedroom?"

The lad stood. "Aw, Da! She's upset."

"And that will be your business when you grasp the concept of honoring your father and stop making me ground you."

"But—"

"We talked about this, son. I've been far too lax with ye. From now on, when I say something, I mean it. Now, on with ye. At this rate, ye will be grounded 'til you're twelve."

Anthon smacked his lips mockingly.

Hosanni glanced to Coyote. He must have missed it. They had stopped allowing Anthon to get away with such dishonor. But it was her fault this time. "Go on now, love. I'll be all right."

His countenance soothed. The child rose and left.

Coyote called, "Hey! I love ye, lad. That's why I'm doin' this."

Anthon sighed wearily. "I love ya, too, Da."

Once the boy's footsteps thumped on the stairs, Coyote fell into the chair adjacent to hers with his own weary sigh. "Sometimes, I feel like saying forget this, go on and play next door with the neighbors' lads."

Hosanni watched the fire crackle. "Oh, I know the feeling, but we have to be consistent with him." She faltered. Father used to tell Mother that about her, not realizing she could overhear if she put her ear to the marriage closet door. Such a stiff-necked trouble maker she'd been. What had Korban seen in her? Father's titles, a budding womanly figure, and a naivety most tempting for a young man to exploit. Father had tried to warn her.

But to be saying such things about Anthon—how could she be thinking of Anthon that way? "I'm sorry. I've overstepped. He's your son, not mine."

Coyote's hand reached over, found hers, and squeezed. "No, I'm glad for your support. I know you're going to be missing him. It's enough to make me reconsider not letting him ride along. The real escort would bring him back."

Hosanni reluctantly pulled her hand away. "In Diakrinth, your son's life would be in danger were it discovered he was a member of the House of Romin and the House of Erin, and the heir to their thrones no less."

An awkward silence entombed them as they sat side by side in their chairs by the fire. Her eye strayed to the sofa. Might she and Coyote someday snuggle together there? Perhaps he'd kiss her again.

What was she thinking? Fresh tears fell. She whispered, "Forgive me."

Coyote caught her chin, turned her to face him, and released her. His brows scrunched together in a quizical frown. "Forgive you? For what?"

For reading my own emotions and desires into your art. "The kiss."

"Me forgive you? I'm the one who stole from—" He winced.

From the man Emi had meant for her to marry. Except he couldn't mean that, he was Xenos. "I invited the theft, welcomed it when you surrendered to my provocation, and fully gave myself up to it."

"So much for forgetting about this. It was a bad mistake, my mistake, and I'm so sorry, milady."

Hosanni trembled. His apology rang insincere, as if he longed for there to be more kisses, too. "But that is the problem. You're not the least bit sorry, and—" She forced herself to breathe. "And frankly neither am I."

Her admission hung in the air between them for a moment.

She continued, "I'm the one who should've known better. I'm the traitor in love with the enemy." She bit her lip. That felt too strongly worded even though her people would view what she'd done precisely that way.

Coyote gaped. "Truly?"

Did he not know his own people's history? "It pains me to think of it, but you are our enemy. Erin is your own mother. You are a blood descendant of the very woman who perpetrated a genocide on my people."

Coyote's eyes widened and his lips parted like his own history books had omitted that. He whispered, "What? When?"

"The Great Dispersal."

"But it was peaceful. We united the nations into one country and stopped millennia of strife without any further bloodshed. It was peaceful."

"Diakrinth resisted your 'peaceful' annihilation. We would not go quietly into the tombs of history that you ushered all other civilizations into. You carried us into exile at the edge of the sword. When you stole our vestments along with our scepter, you also slaughtered our priesthood—the entire tribe of Harmone—and the House of Kristos. You came within one tiny newborn babe of murdering me nineteen centuries before either of us were born."

"No wonder you hate us." He slid to his knees before her. "I am so sorry. We wronged you as severely as the evil we did in enslaving the pinks, and my ancestors gave Marezza plenty to be so bitter about to be sure. Please forgive me. Please don't hate me, too."

Hosanni's heart leapt in her throat. "I love you, brother. Please get up."

Coyote rose and pulled her up, too, staring. "Beg your pardon?"

She gasped. Oh dear. She'd meant brother the way Mother meant it when she would address Father like that. Hosanni squirmed. "The terms 'wife' and 'husband' have strong 'master' and 'slave' connotations in Diakrinth. Instead, spouses often will substitute 'sister' and 'brother.' They are such by adoption, since the wife's mother adopts the husband, typically. In the case of an only son, his mother adopts his wife."

Coyote stared. He closed his eyes. "Milady, would ye rather I pretend ye didn't say what I think ye are sayin' ye said?"

"You would still know I said it."

"Aye, but I've rather complicated things when we both well know I can't rightly keep ye, no matter how badly I want to ask ye what my name is."

She frowned. "Beg your pardon?"

Coyote ducked and glanced away. "It's the tradition among my people for the wife to name her husband. Due to that, my natal name is Ochtu Mac-Erin, which quite literally means, 'eighth son of Erin.' It's said a woman in love can look in a man's eyes and know his name. So that's what Erini lads say to the lass they want to marry. 'What is my name?' In ancient times, once the lass told him his name, she announced it publicly, paid his mother for him, and they were married, just like that."

Hosanni swallowed. "Suppose it's well that you can't ask me. I wouldn't even know where to start."

He chuckled. "Too bad it's not the other way around. I know exactly what your name would be."

"What?"

He stole a shy glance at her. "Astor. It's Erini for 'my treasure.'"

She giggled. "No fair teasing me about how much of your treasure was spent on me when I'm thinking you're going to give a serious answer."

"No, Astor, I meant it. That is who ye are. I've figured out why Alcatraz had figured on stiffin' your husband. You're a bargain at any price. Excludin' Tony, I'd trade everythin' I have, if I could only marry ye properly, Astor. And I'd be far richer for it."

Hosanni stared into his eyes. Such a sweet lion, this man she loved. "You have every right to dissolve Marezza."

"Aye, but my nuptials sealed a peace treaty, and it dissolves along with them. It's selfish o' me, wantin' so badly to ask thousands o' my countrymen to die fightin' yet another civil war, just so I can get married again." His eyes glistened. He blinked. "Like I said, this was a bad mistake, and we need to try to go on like it didn't happen."

Hosanni nodded. There was just one problem.

She knew his name.

The swelling in her bosom demanded she compromise. "I can resist our dishonorable inclinations as well as you can, but how can I simply pretend I don't know you're stuck with a choice between Marezza's cruelty and being a number? Why don't you legally change it to your own choice?"

"I was raised too traditional. Naming myself feels like cheatin' to me."

She sighed. "I do know your name, if you're willing to receive one from any old woman who happens to love you."

"We're not doing a good job of—" He sighed, took her hand in both of his, and bent down on his right knee. "Astor, if ye can understand I can't follow through on what this promises unless Marezza is kind enough to die before I have to send ye away, what is my name?"

"You are Meleon, for you are as sweet as honey and as bold as a lion."

Meleon stood, hugged Hosanni, and stopped just short of kissing her. "I'll go down to the clerks and get it officially first thing tomorrow. Probably will need to pay a good deal extra for the service of keeping this new life separate from my old one, but the investment will be worth it, to be more than just a number or a dog."

Shortly after, her cuddling on the sofa fantasy became reality, justified in her mind by waiting to kiss until he escorted her upstairs for bed. And that was a kiss on the cheek good night before parting, her to their guest bedroom and Meleon to their master bedroom. By the time their son finally managed to behave long enough to be allowed off restriction, however, their good night ritual had evolved into necking.

That seemingly endless Friday night in late May, Hosanni waited eagerly for her son to retire so she and her bridegroom could indulge in their guilty pleasure yet again. Anthon slouched on the sofa, watching Meleon and her play chess at the drawing room table. Hosanni pressed her lips together. Why must the lad insist on celebrating his freedom by staying home and playing board game tournaments with his parents?

Meleon put her in checkmate, rose, and patted Anthon's dreadlocks in a teasing fashion. "When I get back, you're next, laddie."

The minute Meleon vanished out the door, Anthon slid into his father's chair at their drawing room table. "Finally, he's given us a minute's peace. Is everything all right, milady?"

All right? I've never been happier in my life! Hosanni bit her lip. Meleon didn't want Anthon told about their betrothal while the situation remained so unstable. "Beg your pardon? Why wouldn't I be all right?"

"Milady, you still haven't told me why you were crying."

She blinked—crying?

"Did Da yell at ya for being in the attic, or is there something serious?"

Hosanni gasped. "That was five months ago. Why are you still worried about that? Everything's fine now."

Anthon grunted. "If that's so, why am I so jealous of my own father?"

Something was dreadfully wrong. "What bothers you?"

The lad dropped his head. "It's hard to put into words. I've never doubted Da's motives before. But it feels like he's hogging you all for himself. I can't help but fear he's intentionally treating me like I'm a baby and being so strict to get me out of the way so that he can court you. And tonight I've gotten this terrible, paranoid feeling Da resents me being here with you."

Hosanni flinched. She pursed her lips, her stomach twisting. What could she say? They honestly did need to teach Anthon to honor proper authority, but she would be lying if she said his choice of ways to spend his newly earned freedom was welcome.

Anthon glanced at her shyly. "I know it's an awful thought, worrying my father is trying to steal you from me, but I could really use some assurance."

Steal? Oh dear. "Anthon, do you think you and I are courting?"

He sent her a dumbfounded look. "Bisnonno betrothed us."

Oh dear. "Your mother spoiled that, Anthon. It can never happen now."

"But you said I can buy you back! I've been working so hard!"

Oh dear. Hosanni stared at her hands. "I'm sorry. I honestly thought you only wanted to help us get back on our feet after your mother robbed us blind." Marezza was still a drain on their resources, but no need to rub it in.

Hosanni took a breath. She had to make the child understand her heart toward him. "Listen to me, love, this will be hard for you, so listen to what I am saying closely. I am so very proud of you and how hard you've worked. You've shown yourself to be very responsible and well earned the release from restriction that your father and I have granted you."

Anthon's eyes shone with tears. He whispered, "Da, how could ya?"

She gave into her little mother instincts and hugged the lad. "Listen to me, this isn't your father's fault. Please remember, he has no idea you thought there was a competition over me, son."

Anthon pulled away, his eyes wide. "You're but six years older than I am."

So I keep trying to reason with myself, son. "Anthon, I understand where you're coming from, but I've come to accept it's my nature. In normal families, maidens help to raise the wee ones as little mothers. It's how we train for our most important labor. Even I had my older cousins playing that role for me as a child. And now I feel that way about you. I know you don't understand how I feel. I hardly appreciated Irene's mothering. But if your father ever remarries, you'll discover this feeling when you become a big brother—whichever woman is lucky enough to bear your sisters."

The lad fled sobbing from the room. His slammed bedroom door echoed through the house right as Meleon reentered the drawing room.

Meleon glanced back toward the noise. "What's with him?"

Hosanni rose and fell into her bridegroom's arms. "He knows about us."

"I guess he was bound to notice eventually." Meleon frowned. "But why didn't he bring his questions to me?"

She hesitated. Anthon would be terribly embarrassed by all this once he got over it. She certainly was. Plus, she'd lose Meleon for sure, if he learned what Romin once had planned. Hosanni traced her bridegroom's strong jaw, albeit a bit chubby. "As a child, when I wasn't mad at her for some adolescent reason, Irene was the one I posed the embarrassing questions to."

"Is that how you see yourself with Tony? As a substitute big sister?"

"The best I can hope for is him seeing me that way." She laid her head on Meleon's breast, snuggling contentedly in his embrace. "If you think about it, in many respects, a stepmum's not all that different from a little mother."

Meleon's arms tightened around her. "He'll get used to the idea, surely."

✕

CUDDLED ON THE SOFA in the drawing room with Astor, Meleon drew a deep breath and released it slowly. He needed to get her to bed and do something about the cramp in his back. But he hated the lonely bed that awaited him even as he found himself looking forward to saying good night to Astor. And since Tony had thrown an adolescent fit over his da courting and put himself to bed . . . best not to finish that thought. He was in enough pain already.

Astor sighed contentedly and played with the drawstrings of his blouse. "I really should get to sleep."

"Aye." Meleon stood and escorted her upstairs.

In the hallway outside of their bedrooms, he kissed her cheek.

Disappointment flooded her eyes.

Meleon rubbed his aching lower back. "Not tonight, Astor. Truth be told, my back is killing me. I think I've strained it."

Astor's pressed-together lips were refraining from his physician's usual retort that if he got more exercise, he could lose the extra weight and not have to worry so much about his back. She maneuvered around him, toward the master bedroom. "A massage would relieve you." Astor grasped the doorknob and glanced at him coyly. "If you'll let me take a look."

Chapter Seventeen

Meleon hesitated. A back rub sounded divine, but Astor's chosen location was questionable, and she hadn't seen his tattoos yet. "Shirt on or off?"

Astor giggled. "Standard procedure is shirt off, but if my bridegroom is shyer than most of my subjects . . . ."

If the tattoos mattered, and she left him, he'd only be losing what he shouldn't be keeping in the first place. "Aye, all right, but don't laugh."

Meleon ushered her into the master bedroom. She flitted to the fireplace and set about lighting it. He swallowed. "On the bed?"

"And on your stomach, yes."

He glanced up at the rarely lit gas chandelier. "Do you need the light?"

"Not strictly, but it would be helpful."

Meleon lit the oil lamp on the marble-topped nightstand. The nightstand was walnut like the rest of the furniture, including his dresser and the lady's vanity that had come with the suite.

Was Astor watching? He glanced at her. Still fiddling with the fireplace. Good. He pulled his shirt off, tossed it on the floor, climbed the stepstool up onto the bed, and lay on his stomach. He slid his hands up under his pillows. Firelight sprung to life on the wall opposite the fireplace.

Drowsiness fluttered his eyelids closed.

The bed bounced. He blinked. Must've misunderstood what that motion meant. Astor had no reason to climb across the bed to reach him. He was right on the edge and surely at a comfortable height.

Her silky fingers kneaded his back and slowly smoothed away the cramp. But the intoxicating effect this therapy was having on his loins stirred a most unpleasant alarm. "You do this to male subjects often?"

Giggling tinkled at his ear. "No, Jealousy. Female subjects . . . mostly."

"What?"

"Well, I certainly don't do this to them." Astor tickled his underarms.

Meleon laughed as her point emanated through his body. His sisters had tickled him in past happy times and it'd far from kindled him, as it did now.

Astor murmured, "And I especially don't do this to them."

Her lips nuzzled his neck and set his whole body on fire. He gasped and turned over. Astor lay beside him, wearing only a fine linen chemise. Meleon's mind reeled even as his body pulled Astor into his arms and once again drank thirstily of her sweet wine.

On the verge of pulling up her chemise, what he was doing slammed into him. He paused. She must not realize. "Astor, what's happening?"

A most unfamiliar, highly kindled look blazed in her eyes. "I'm giving you my maidenhood. Please accept. I want you to have it. Please take it now."

Emi, please, help me. He whispered, "I want it. I want it very badly."

Trembling, Meleon dragged himself off the bed. "But not like this. I love you, Astor. That's why I am sayin' no and walkin' out that door."

Before he could change his mind, Meleon fled out to their porcelain tiled, sea green bathroom. He climbed into the clawfoot bathtub and pumped the water into it cold.

A KNOCK ON THE DOOR roused Hosanni. She blinked in the grayness of the sun's approaching resurrection. Where was she?

Meleon peeked inside. "Get dressed and come down out onto the porch. We need to talk."

The door shut again with a soft click.

In the gray chill, the master bedroom suite took shape around Hosanni. What she'd offered Meleon flooded back, along with his refusal and her soul searching for long hours in the night. At some point, she had fallen asleep.

Hosanni climbed off the bed and gathered up her discarded frock, corset pieces, and corset cover as well as the clean chemise and underpants Meleon had laid out on the vanity for her. He'd taken away yesterday's underpants. She swallowed. He'd already been in here without awakening her. Where had he slept, if she'd stayed—if he'd slept?

She slipped out to the bathroom, hung up the frock on a dress hook, and set the rest of her garments on the washbasin stand. She smiled at the clean, cold bath already drawn, the way she was accustomed to it. Her husband already knew her so well, and here she was still a maiden. She knew what she wanted, the trouble would be persuading Meleon to want it, too. If she hadn't disgraced herself in his eyes so much that he forced her to return to Father.

MELEON SAT IN A WICKER chair out on the porch, sipping breakfast tea. He forced down a boiled egg, cold bacon, and two biscuits without tasting them. His eyes felt raw and an ache crept into his back again. "Hello, Emi, it's that pesky Erini prince, yet again begging for crumbs from your table. Thank you for putting up with me so much tonight. I'll admit it would be nice if I was invited to dinner, and I admit I get a bit miffed over being shut out, but . . . ."

Peace again flooded in.

Meleon frowned. The feeling made no sense. Trying to get Astor to share her path with him felt like trying to wrestle Leviathane. If the lass who loved him rebuffed his bumbling attempts to convert, none of her people would embrace a stranger. And only a couple visits to the local assembly had been needed to understand why Astor distrusted the Diaspora. It was no different than the shrines dedicated to Time and Chance that he'd already eschewed.

So why did his heart keep feeling like Emi was listening, even cared about a stranger? He drew a deep breath and brushed away his tears. *Please give me the strength to stay the course even though my heart breaks.*

Astor emerged from the house. She was properly attired, albeit with her hair damp. She kept her eyes downcast. He gestured toward the tea and the biscuits and boiled egg waiting for her next to the fern. Pork made Astor sick, but these days, she'd eat it anyway if he let her.

She nibbled on the biscuits awful slowly.

The longer the delay, the more likely he was to turn off-course. Meleon cleared his throat. "I don't have any appetite, either, but please don't dawdle."

All too soon, Astor emptied her plate. She wiped her lips with the napkin. "Thank you." She glanced at him, folded her hands in her lap, and stared at them. "And for what you did last night, or didn't do rather. I hadn't planned on seducing you. I thought I could be professional, but it turns out I am not at all professional when seeing my own bridegroom half-nude."

A relieved breath rushed out of Meleon. "Ye couldn't have planned that, Astor. I was the one who had been complaining of a backache. I was so afraid ye might think I'd intended to be seducing you, only to be changing my mind at the last minute."

"I felt the cramp. I know it wasn't faked. But you were right, Meleon. That was too big a decision to make so impulsively. Forgive me, please."

Thank you. "Forgive me, Astor. Last night was entirely my fault."

"How so?"

Tell her now, and you will never get her in the chariot. Meleon forced himself to his feet and pulled Astor up by the hands. "Come with me. We need to take a drive, and I need you to quietly obey me and not argue."

Astor frowned. "A drive where?"

"Let's go." He headed for the chariot house.

Emi, please don't let her notice it's her trunk packed and loaded on the back of the chariot. I'll never get her in the chariot if she catches that. Meleon gave Noinin a sugar cube for waiting so patiently. It must have seemed quite odd for him to hitch her to the chariot and then walk away. He opened Astor's door. She hesitated a moment, but took her seat in the chariot. He breathed a sigh of relief tormented by the pain taking up residence in his chest.

Once in the chariot, he took Noinin's reins and shook them.

Their neighborhood slid silently by. Few awoke so early on Saturday in these parts. Even the religious services didn't start until one. Tony might not miss them until noon.

Might not miss her, not you and her. She's leaving, you are staying.

Somehow, he'd get through this.

All too soon, the palace's white dome and columned arches rose ahead. Astor pressed close to him. "Can't we even talk about this? I said I was sorry."

Noinin knew the way on her own now—and the knights of the royal guard all knew him by sight. He tied off Noinin's reins and turned to Astor. His heart still called her the woman he loved, but sometime last night, he'd gotten his head to accept the truth. "Hosanni."

They both flinched at Astor's given name.

His chest tighted. It felt wrong. He sighed and surrendered. "Astor, I owe ye the apology. Firstly, I am an adult, and ye are a seventeen-year-old girl."

"Woman," Astor humphed. "And I'm almost eighteen."

Meleon hesitated. He would have argued for his adulthood at seventeen also, but he had cause. His longing to put her in his situation, minus the spouse walking out, was unpardonable selfishness. "Ye won't be reaching the usual age of full majority until ye be turning twenty and ye know it. Or maybe neither Alcatraz nor your people told ye teenagers need a parent or guardian's authorization to exercise adult priveleges? We may not enjoy the thought, but ye are in truth but another father's child. Your father was wrongfully deprived o' his daughter and his paternal rights."

"Even so, I'm of marriageable age."

"Aye, lasses can legally marry at sixteen and lads at fourteen, but only with parental consent—or parental force in my case."

"And with Alcatraz's consent in our case."

"Sometimes what's legal isn't right. We both know full well, if he hadn't been denied his rights, under no circumstances would your father allow—"

"No!" Astor covered her ears. "No." She clasped his arm. "You mustn't think like that. Don't fret over whether we should be married. Simply accept that we are married. I love you. Don't you love me?"

"Aye, more than anything. That is why I'm doin' what I should've done nearly six months ago. If I hadn't been so selfish, we wouldn't be hurtin' so bad now. You'd be at home in your father's circular stucco kitchen, grateful to the kindness o' a stranger rather than headin' home brokenhearted over this selfish, spoiled prince who doesn't deserve you."

"But we can't afford this."

"I can. I just don't want to."

"We need my income, and we certainly don't have the money for the tax."

Meleon sighed. "We don't have to pay if we confess this mess to Romin. I didn't because he plans to arrange a marriage between my progeny and your progeny, and he arranges marriages for my progeny over my dead body."

Her eye twitched. "What about Anthon?"

What was wrong with her eye? "I can legally protect him from a political marriage, but Romin will seek to swindle my son into allowing it." Meleon grimaced. She'd raise fine lads and lasses that any Da should be glad to have his grandchildren marry, but he badly wanted to be her children's father also. "If Romin wants any hope of salvaging his plan for peace, he has no choice but to free ye and send ye home."

A jolt jarred them.

Meleon blinked at where they were. Noinin had done her thing, all right, head right for the stables that birthed her, and pull her conveyance up to the nearest available water trough. He turned his head back toward Astor.

Astor's eyes twinkled. "How is it the thought never occurred to you to seduce me? That avoids the rape charges Marezza had hoped for, and my children can't marry the fruit of your seed if they are themselves your seed."

Guilt pricked him. "Whether it has or not, I wouldn't do that, Astor. I may not be o' your people, but I have my principles. So I decided to quietly pay a clerk the tax and send ye home without Romin findin' out there was a livin' Kristos to force into forging another disaster o' a marriage alliance. Now my only excuse for not sendin' ye home is wishin' so desperately that we could get married ourselves."

"You're forgetting the part about being dependent on my income."

Meleon winced. That was nothing compared to losing her. "Keeping my word to the lass I love and sending her home a maiden is worth demeaning myself, and keeping my word clearly requires it after last night. For you, I'll hire myself out."

Astor hugged him. "If you truly want to keep your word, rather than send me to my father's house, you would do better to turn this chariot around and take me back to our home. I was up most of the night searching my heart on this, Meleon. The life that I want is the life we have, minus me sleeping in our guestroom and us pretending we're not husband and marita."

"I don't want a marita! I want a wife."

She shook her head. "You don't want a wife, and I don't want to be one."

Meleon stared. "I know you mean the master-slave associations you have with 'wife' and 'husband,' but how can you say you'd rather be the slave?"

"You certainly could never be a slave."

"I love ye. Put any chain ye want around my neck, Astor, so long as ye are at the other end of it." *No, stick to sending her home. Keep on course.*

If only he could go with her. But her people would never accept him.

Astor bit her lip. "I'd love to have the title of 'wife' and to grow my hair out. But other than those two things and our sleeping arrangements, what are we wanting to change about our house? Nothing. I realized that last night. My hair and a title are most foolish things to start a war over. But they're equally foolish things to lose my husband over."

Meleon bowed his head. *Emi, forgive me. I should never have allowed this conversation. Because she makes a terrible lot of sense to me.*

He said slowly, "Neither of us meant a word we said on that poor excuse of a wedding day. Unless we're properly joined in the assembly, I won't feel right about us taking to the marriage bed. And that means dissolving Marezza, and that means war, and we're back where we started. It's best I send you to your father until we can be properly wed. Since you'll be of age by then, you won't need his permission to return and marry me when I send for you."

When? He was counting on their separation being temporary? But she'd wait for him. And he'd more than send, he'd run to her once he was free.

Astor nuzzled against him.

Meleon surrendered and wrapped his arms around her. How he never wanted to be separated from her. "It's the only way."

She sniffled. "There must be something we're missing. Let's take this step by step. Let's say you decide to dissolve Marezza. Where do you go?"

Huh? "The assembly, of course."

"But, according to the assembly's law, your marriage has been dissolved for ten years."

"I have overkill cause for dissolve, if that's what ye mean. It's first ye go to the assembly, then ye take their judgment to the clerks, and the government says, 'Yep, you're dissolved, all right.' Since we're royalty, it's then splashed across the headlines from sea to sea, and Mum finds out, and the Union is officially back at war with itself."

Astor pulled back and beamed widely at him. "That's what we're missing! You don't take their judgment to the clerks. The dissolve doesn't become ever public record, the newspapers don't find out, your mother doesn't find out, and we're not at war!"

Meleon shook his head. "And I'm still legally bound to Marezza, and you're still legally my marita, and the assembly doesn't join us."

Astor played with his drawstrings. "Doesn't it at least make sense to ask?"

SEATED BESIDE ASTOR, Meleon jiggled his left leg under the red oak table in the office of their local assembly. Ravane Tomi scribbled on her parchments with quill and ink. He wasn't sure what the elderly lilac woman's nodding, notetaking, and "mmhmm" meant.

Astor squeezed his hand under the table and sent him a hopeful smile. He grunted. The knots in his stomach were still pretty sure this detour had been a bad idea. But what was the worst that could happen? To ask this prince, the worst was the likely result: the ravane would agree with him and Astor would go home, meet a single Diakrinthian lad her own age, and forget him.

Ravane Tomi glanced up at them. "Your highness, do you remember the exact date that Princess Marezza deserted you?"

Why did that matter? "Aye, it was but a day after she gave birth to Tony, so that would be December 19, 5730."

"What about the date on which you next saw her?"

He frowned. "Let's see, Tony was six . . . August or September of 5737. Sorry, I can't remember more specifically than that. Why, is that important?"

"In your case, no." Ravane Tomi scribbled more notes and passed one of her parchments to them across the table.

Astor gasped as Meleon read the certificate of dissolve, effective as of the day after Tony's first birthday, ten years past.

He thrust it back. "Milady, I told you the political ramifications."

Ravane Tomi folded her hands on the table. "Your highness, I am not in the business of the political. I am in the business of the spiritual. And you are spiritually dissolved, amen." She pressed the parchment back across the table. "On the testimony of two witnesses, I must pass judgment on this. Whether you present this for certification according to the laws of the nation of West California is entirely up to you."

If Astor counted as a witness, they had the strangest definition of such that he'd ever heard. He glanced at Astor helplessly. They were supposed to be discussing their options, not drawing up dissolve papers.

Astor bowed her head. "We are grateful for your sensitivity, Ravane Tomi. Does this mean you will join us in marriage?"

Ravane Tomi laughed. "I can't. Alcatraz already did that." She raised her index finger. "The term 'marita' is a political designation. The judgment of the aggies of this assembly, indeed, of all the Emian precincts I know, is that there is no difference, spiritually, between a wife and a marita."

Meleon stole a glance at Astor's triumphant smirk and swallowed. "We explained our feelings, ma'am."

"And I happen to agree regarding your wedding. This is far from the first complaint I've received about the ceremonies at Alcatraz, or the first request to repeat your vows in a more traditional fashion. You've conducted yourself as a man of honor, and I commend you. I assume you're in a hurry, so let me check my calendar." Ravane Tomi flipped through her leather date book.

Astor squealed, beamed widely, and clung to his arm.

Meleon gaped at her. Had the woman of God truly agreed to marry them? On the way, he'd dreamed up a hundred reasons she'd say no, including that he was a stranger. Certainly, the assembly had joined him to Marezza, but what if they'd refused to join him to their own?

He swallowed. This was too easy. "But what about Marezza?" He pointed at the dissolve papers. "You know I can't turn those in, right?"

Ravane Tomi waved. "While necessary to change Hosanni's legal status, that's a political matter, not the assembly's business. That said, your highness, you do need to legally dissolve Marezza. Let Romin and Erin worry about still another world war breaking out. Protecting your house is your primary moral responsibility. So long as the law doesn't recognize you're dissolved, your first wife remains a threat. Personally, in Diakrinth, I'd declare her a wolf and feed her to the dragons. Unfortunately, that's not in my jurisdiction here."

Meleon hesitated. Did she just make a virtue out of his selfishness? "I still think I should return Hosanni to her father."

Ravane Tomi shook her head. "I appreciate your empathy with a fellow father, but I must strongly disagree with putting away Hosanni. She is your wife now, and Emi hates dissolve."

"Then why are ye writin' those?" Meleon pointed to the dissolve papers.

Pity touched the wrinkled face. "Should Emi not hate what Marezza did?

She wrought those eleven years ago. Now, if you can secure a venue for the wedding celebration, I can squeeze you in at 7:15 pm on the ninth of June. Ask neighbors, hirelings, colleagues, and family to serve as the assembly."

Meleon blinked. What was happening here? Venue? He blurted, "I have a furnished, unoccupied beach house I'm preparing for sale."

Ravane Tomi smiled. "Excellent! What a lovely bridal tent." She pointed her quill at Astor. "Make sure you can get off that day and the next seven. I'll pencil you in now, so call on me at home if we need to reschedule."

Astor shook her head. "That won't be a problem."

Aye, seein' as no wife of his would be forced to hire herself out—unless she was an adulteress who'd nearly ruined him, but Astor was different.

But . . . "What are the seven days for?"

"Traditionally, the bride and groom abide in their choice of bridal tents for seven days. I highly recommend couples observe the bridal week. The fond memories last a lifetime."

Astor beamed at Meleon. "Would the neighbors take Anthon?"

Meleon shrugged. "They'd have to wrestle the housekeeper for him."

Ravane Tomi pointed her quill at Meleon. "For your conscience's sake, ask another woman to visit you to serve as a chaperone for Hosanni until the wedding celebration."

"Aye, milady." Wait, when had he agreed to this course?

Ravane Tomi added more scribbling to one of her parchments and placed it on top of the certificate of dissolve. "This is your certificate of re-marriage. Take these documents to the clerks together, and you can get both women's legal status changed on one trip."

Astor took up the parchments and rolled them into a scroll.

Meleon bit his lip. He'd been so sure last night that Emi wanted him to send Astor home to her father. But what did a stranger to the path know? If he couldn't trust a ravane to show him the right course, who could he trust?

Out by the chariot, Meleon took the scroll from Astor, secured it in his sporran, and clasped her hands. "Astor, the minute those papers won't disturb the peace, I'm turning them in. You'll be free effective as of June 6, 5742. On my word as a gentleman, that I promise you."

Chapter Eighteen

M eleon's beach house nestled snug in his cozy cove, sheltered from the bustling city and the gawking tourists on the public beaches beyond the cliffs. Here, the sea dragons danced on the waves and the griffins sang overhead every day. Today, it felt like they were singing and dancing especially for him and Astor.

In an hour, their neighbors would assemble here with all of her soon-to-be former colleagues, several of her subjects, his more intimate associates in the worlds of fine art and investing, Tony, and the hirelings' family. But now, Astor stood beside Meleon on the beach, gaping at the panorama with a wide-eyed wonderment. She clasped his hand tight, interlacing their fingers. "We can't sell this place, Meleon. It'd be too huge a loss."

The rentals did provide a tidy, if sporadic income.

Meleon squeezed her hand. After today, the most valuable use he could think of for this place was as personal vacation property.

He glanced to the beach house's porch. His adolescent thunderstorm was slouching through a lecture from Aggie. If only his son could be happy for him. It didn't make sense. The lad was fond of Astor and had always longed for a mother. Now he had one who actually cared about him. So his stepmum was a bit on the young side and he'd gone so long without. So, when Tony married, his wife would probably also be around six years younger than her mother-in-law. Why be so upset about it?

Why can't Tony just let us be happy?

HOSANNI TURNED IN A circle before the hall mirror. Her gold vestment swished. She clipped the purple daises into her hair.

The front door banged open. Anthon stomped in.

She jumped at the noise and drew a breath. If only Meleon hadn't decided to trust Anthon with their secret at the last minute. "Son."

His scowl deepened. "I'll never be your son. You're calling it off."

She glared back and placed her hands on her hips. "And why would I?"

"Because you don't want me to tell Da you have a prior commitment."

Must Anthon make her want to throw up on her wedding day? She turned back to primping in the mirror. "And what did Aggie tell you?"

"Please. She insists you're already married and to swallow my resentment and not ruin Da's happiness. But that is hardly relevant when she mistakenly thinks I'm a little boy mad because he doesn't want a new Mammy."

Hosanni stared into Anthon's eyes. He was bluffing. "Call Aggie in. We'll let her decide whether I should exchange proper vows with my own husband or leave him in order to wait another three years for his own son to grow up."

Anthon glanced away.

"See? You don't want this to get out, either, especially after this stunt. You know as well as I do, if you tell, your father will conclude you are lusting after your own step-mother."

"Look, I understand you not being comfortable marrying me as planned, but must ya torment me with my own father?"

Eleven-year-olds could be so selfish. "Son, if you care for me at all, show it by letting me be happy with the man I love."

The shofar blast announced Hosanni's processional dance.

Heart pounding, she sent a last glance in the hall mirror and sped out of the beach house. The guests stood from their beach blankets and oohed and aahed as if she'd had the hair for a proper bridal braid. Someday she would, but today she would not pretend at some other poor captive's expense.

Up on the porch, she did the dance sequence where the bride feigned to be lost and searching for the path home to Emi, represented by Ravane Tomi, who wore a royal blue palla. Hosanni swirled and zigzagged across the porch in every direction but toward the wicker table serving as an altar. Once she hit the sand, she had to keep her processional dance simple.

At the bottom of the steps, Hosanni hesitated, feigning as if she might jilt her bridegroom. She stepped down the narrow path between the assembled guests toward Ravane Tomi, who poorly obscured the bridegroom behind her. Meleon wore his mother's tartan and a green vest showing off the royal crests tattooed on his shoulders. Incredibly kindling tattoos, she might add, though her parents would've ripped their garments at the thought of a tattooed son.

The bride and the bridegroom's eyes connected. Everything else faded away but the glory of his wonderful face, the sea dragons playing, and the singing griffins diving.

The distance separating Hosanni and Meleon vanished.

She received Ravane Tomi's welcome home kiss faintly and lifted up the sole line in the otherwise instrumental processional song. "Oh come, oh come, beloved bridegroom! Come and redeem your bride from the grave."

Her heart skipped a beat. She could hardly wait to get started on that.

Meleon swept her into a hug. They reluctantly parted and stood facing each other, Ravane Tomi, and the sea dragons and the griffins.

Ravane Tomi intoned, "This assembly gathers here today to celebrate love and to join this man to the house of Aletheia Kristekon, mother of Hosanni."

Hosanni blinked away tears.

Ravane Tomi waved to Meleon. "Who here presents this bridegroom to the bride and to her house?"

Meleon smiled at Hosanni. "I, being a free man, give myself to Kristos."

If she didn't know him better than that, she'd think he sincerely meant to turn his back on liberty and become her slave.

Ravane Tomi said to him, "Do you, Meleon Kristekon, willingly leave your house to join to this woman and to her house? Do you pledge to honor her, and to always cherish her? Do you pledge to provide for her and her house, and to protect her and the children you give her, even if it should mean laying down your own life?"

Meleon's grin managed to widen. "I do."

Ravane Tomi turned to Hosanni. "Do you, Hosanni Kristekon, accept this man? Do you pledge to comfort him of his manhood and join to him as often as he does require? Do you pledge to be wise and honor him as a queen gives honor to a king?"

"I do." Hosanni added mentally, *Look forward immensely to keeping the first pledge, and like the second far better than the incredibly sexist pledge brides give in Diakrinth.*

"You may now recite your vows." Ravane Tomi removed the bridal ivory from the altar and handed the chopsticks to Meleon.

Hosanni got her first look at them and gasped. Little scepters. Meleon waved the ivory before her. After soaking in the darling, perfect works of art, Hosanni nodded her acceptance. Meleon returned them to the altar. Her heart leapt. Someday, she'd have the hair to wear them. Someday.

Her bridegroom removed her ivory ring from Ravane Tomi's hand. He took Hosanni's right hand. "I, Meleon, choose you, Hosanni. I promise to forsake all others and be joined to you always, whether in good fortune or in adversity, and to seek together with you a life hallowed by the path of Emi." Meleon reverently slid the wedding band on Hosanni's right middle finger. "With this ivory, you are made holy to me, until death dissolves our joining."

Ravane Tomi handed to Hosanni her bridegroom's new gold wedding band. "You may now recite your vows."

Hosanni took his right hand. "I, Hosanni, accept you, Meleon. I promise to forsake all others and be joined to you always, whether in good fortune or in adversity, and to seek together with you a life hallowed by the path of Emi." She slid his wedding band on his right middle finger. "With this ring, you are made holy to me, until death dissolves our joining." She squealed and hugged Meleon. At long last, she could finally give her husband her maidenhood.

"Be there any objections from the assembly?" Ravane Tomi took a breath. "Hearing none, what Emi has adhered, let no one dissolve. I now declare you wife and husband. You may now join together."

Hosanni's husband swept her off her feet and marched her back toward the beach house. Gasps, laughter, and a few indecent catcalls rang out from their guests, teasing the bridegroom for taking the closing remarks literally.

She giggled. Their guests only knew the half of it.

MELEON CLUNG TO HIS new wife, basking in how immensely she had enjoyed consummating their marriage as much as he did in receiving this precious gift. Astor had wiped away all the sorrow of the last twelve nightmarish years. Definitely, no one would be arranging marriages for their children.

He sighed. "To think how close I came to never knowing this feeling. Gettin' a 'real job' will be nothin' compared to your love, wife." It made sense not to start putting in applications until after the honeymoon, he reckoned.

Astor gaped at him.

Meleon peered back. "What did I say?"

Astor giggled. "Two very strange things. Firstly, while I'd rather not think about you and Marezza, don't you think I'm a little old to believe you hatched Anthon from a goose egg?"

He winced. And he'd promised himself not to bring this up. "There's no comparison between making love of my own free will and being forced by my mother to give myself to a stranger. In fairness, Marezza was herself being forced by her grandfather. It lasted for but three months and neither of us much enjoyed it. Only I had no idea how this is supposed to feel, not until I gave you my first passionate kiss."

Astor lay her head on his chest hair and squeezed him tighter.

Meleon caressed her beautiful curves. Maybe it would reassure her. "Hey now, I didn't mean to upset ye. This is such a special thing, shared between only the two o' us. There's no one else on this earth for me, Astor. I love ye so much, why, I'm lookin' forward to keepin' my vows to ye the old-fashioned way, if ye can believe that. I've been callin' it sexist for a decade, to demand o' a man what my own heart is beatin' me up over now."

Astor lifted her head and stared at him wide-eyed, her lips parted. "You meant that other strange thing about you becoming a hireling?"

"Sure, why wouldn't I? If I was willin' to lose ye and hire myself out, why wouldn't I also be willin' to get a real job now that you're mine forever?" He grinned as rejoicing buzzed through him. A lifetime of this with her . . . *Thank you, Emi. What a marvelous thing you've made.*

Astor sent him her special smile. "Don't let Anthon get to you, brother. You have a real job, and I'm most pleased with your efforts to provide for us."

"I'm a starving artist financially dependent on the lovely bride I just took to wife, and ye call that provision? No, I don't care who in the men's liberation movement jeers me as a turncoat, you're not my marita anymore, you're my wife. And I gave ye my solemn vow to provide for ye. At present, that means convincing blokes to let me play with their money for a little while."

"You can't fool me by trying to make it sound fun, Meleon Kristekon. I happen to know you would rather muck out Noinin's stall than 'play' with your own ledgers if you had any choice. You'd be miserable spending 48 hours a week doing that."

What rebuttal would be true? Crunching numbers and buying and selling investments really wasn't his idea of a good time. "Not nearly as miserable as I've been for the last twelve years. Besides, it wasn't so bad before the greedy ex-wife started making it nigh impossible to get ahead. I don't enjoy it like I do painting, but I enjoy it far more than you'd enjoy leaving our sons and daughters for nine hours a day, six days a week. You're worth it, Astor."

She giggled. "Brother, the soonest you can put a baby in my arms is nine months from tonight, and, more likely, around this time next year. Besides, Mother and Father managed with me, and I have a fraction of the burden they shouldered."

"Aye, but your mum and da had a large extended family to draw upon for help, and your mum delegated a great deal, which you emphasized when you were defending your mum's honor against an upbringing you perceived as shameful. Sorry, but that communicated everything I need to know about where your heart actually is: at home with our children."

Astor closed her eyes in a silent concession.

She laid her head back upon his chest. "Brother, Aggie needs her job, and without babies to occupy me, I'd fire her."

Meleon glowered. Why did she think that he was barren? "I sowed Tony speedily enough."

"The woman contributes also. It took my parents years and years to get me. I truly don't mind my present labor, so why don't we keep things as they are for now and reevaluate this when I'm actually pregnant? Perhaps by then we may reverse our fortunes."

"But you shouldn't have to hire yourself out. You're a lady and a princess, and you're far superior to the likes of Marezza, if ye ask this nobleman. It's as beneath ye as it is for me. How could I live with myself, makin' my beautiful wife support me?"

"You're not making me do anything." Astor lifted up again eye to eye with him and stroked his face, her eyes shining. "You may work with canvas and a paint brush rather than ivory and a knife, but you are a son of Kristos now. In our house, we are artists, not financiers. I believe in our dream, Meleon. One of these days, a painting by Kristekon will cost a small fortune. We will make it—if you will permit me to help make it happen."

Meleon drew Astor's lips to his and drank a glass of her sweet wine.

THE SUN BURNED HOT above the juncture where the Kristekon clan's dusty lane kissed the paved Romini highway to McCall. Havan Alethaner crept up behind his eldest son. Korban tied back his dreadlocks with one of Irene's old ribbons and kept a husband's beard trimmed to a neat line along the jaw.

Havan Alethaner observed as Korban hammered together the highway-facing booth Havan Alethaner had ordered from his beloved carpenters. He'd taken full advantage of his wife's month-long sojourn with Lady Phosi as the latter brought their third grandchild into the world, Lady Phosi's first child. If only keeping busy kept his mind off the constant ache of missing her and their infant son, Agapan Alethaner.

Korban shot a glance back briefly, enough to say Havan Alethaner could no longer sneak up on his favorite hunting partner undetected, not even over the ringing hammer, the trumpeting mastodons, and a handful of rumbling chariots pulled by snorting horses. The traffic both headed to and came from the market hidden behind the city gates a mile up the road.

Havan Alethaner's heart leapt in his throat. Here Korban turned nineteen today and he had already given him and Juris two grandsons. Hosanni was no longer the vulnerable child that he remembered. Soon, his daughter would be eighteen, and a mother herself, if she wasn't already.

He shuddered as a tingle shot down his spine. He couldn't picture the little daughter Emi had fashioned in his image as a grown woman anymore than he could picture himself as a woman. Hosanni married and with a babe in her arms instinctively alarmed, but her firstborn's prophetic identity made him long to know the exact time the Veritas child entered the world, so he could shout for joy. But he'd settle for being the first to see the holy family as they traveled home.

Korban turned and wiped the sweat from his brow. "Father, are you sure

Mother would approve this?"

"It'll work out." Déjà vu hit Havan Alethaner. He sighed. "Juris would hate this. I'm hoping, by the time she returns from her sojourn, I'll have been doing business here long enough to show her what a great idea this is."

Korban hesitated. "I know it's none of my business, Father, but we only send the ivory to market two or three times a week. Why do we need our own booth out along the highway?"

"The sale of a few ivory pieces carved for your amusement hardly makes a carpenter a professional ivory carver, son."

Korban walked around the booth, checking the structure. "Is that your way of saying, 'You're right, it is none of your business? I'm a nonpaying customer, I don't need to explain myself.'"

Havan Alethaner laughed. "I offered to hire someone if it's a problem."

"Exactly how was that not arm-twisting when you'd pay for this out of the same purse that pays my wages?"

True enough. "I have an idea for a not-so-new way to do business."

Korban came back. "So what's this boring and unoriginal idea?"

"So it is a new way, but not entirely. You custom-made Irene's ivory, and I've done the same for every bride and bridegroom that's been wed in our village since it was their parents requesting a specific design. This—" Havan Alethaner waved to his booth, grinning. "—merely opens that opportunity up to everyone who travels past me on their way to and from the market."

"How?"

Havan Alethaner's grin broadened. "I'll keep regular hours and carve here instead of at home. Simple designs will be ready to be picked up by the time they've finished at the market, and the complex ones in a day or so."

Korban shook his head, laughing. "Mother will hate that idea. Let's hope it earns high enough to persuade her, milord. I won't be happy if she makes me tear down what you have made me build. But why all the way out here?"

"It's closer to home, making it easier to persuade Juris that I haven't abandoned her for eight hours a day, six days a week."

Korban folded his arms and pointed down the highway, away from the city. "And you wouldn't be hoping to spot Hosanni coming from this excellent vantage point?"

Havan Alethaner's cheeks heated up. "They could be here any day now."

Korban narrowed his eyes, leaning away from Havan Alethaner. "How do you know that?"

"Reason. By now, she's out of school and married. This is an opportune season for Emi's hand to bring both of my lost children home. And, please don't take this personal, but the more I remember Hosanni's tastes in men, the more I fear for their safety."

Korban ran his left hand over his dreadlocks. "Father, how exactly am I not supposed to take that personal?"

"My concern is how your pappy died at the hands of a few hotheads. The persons who killed our own brother for looking like Erin escaped justice. They will also target a blue man joined to us by marriage. Romin's highway ought to be safe enough, until Hosanni's family turns off of it here. Then, they will be in danger—unless I see them first."

Fear shone in Korban's eyes. "Father, how is that not my worry? You're the first to admit why Da died, but I'd suspected. Da warned that our mothers' hatred of our fathers can turn violent; our fathers were indeed Erini."

Havan Alethaner hugged the young man. "Son, it's who your mothers are that counts." He released Korban. "Everyone knows you're my kin and accepts you as a Diakrinthian. Other than the coiled hair and the wide nostrils, you're the image of your mother, and she and I the image of our mother. Truthfully, that concerned me when you and Hosanni were making eyes at each other. You look like you're siblings by blood, amen."

Korban smiled. "So he admits after Hosanni has become little more than a painful memory of a childhood transgression."

His eldest son had finally made up his mind to marry Irene after Emi showed him it was primarily guilt that had been holding him back.

Amen, I pray you, Emi, please, please spare Irene and Hosanni from the anxiety that cooled Aletheia's affection for her sister.

CHORUS. The children of Argevane multiplied, so a great and mighty city flourished all around the Garden of Hedone, and none were ashamed, nor felt any need to cover themselves, for each man desired only his own wife, but each adorned themselves as fitting their role. And the ancients uncovered the secrets of the cosmos, all that God had made, and fashioned themselves wonders, even the sun crystals still in use to this day.

Dramatic pause.

CHORUS. Each woman walked with God and drank of the fountain of life, so that none grew old and perished from the purple Earth.

— Pauli of Denver, The Sacred History, "Creation" scene 2, lines 2-9

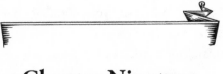

Chapter Nineteen

Seated on his stool inside his booth, Havan Alethaner waved farewell to another satisfied customer about to marry a January bride. The usual traffic whinnied or trumpeted its way through the slush marking where the highway cut through the snowy, pine dotted hills.

The angle of his booth gave him a perfect view down the highway that would bring home his long-lost daughter and the son he had never met. That was a certainty now. He'd never suffered any illusions his beautiful daughter would make it to age twenty a maiden. No, that Hosanni would make it to the altar a virgin, unlike her father, was all he'd ever asked of God.

His giggling three-year-old son swung through the waist-high door on the side of the booth closest to their lane. His heart leapt. Little Agapan Alethaner looked like Hosanni had at his age, only dressed in an indigo tunic rather than linen. Little Agapan latched onto Havan Alethaner's hip and jumped up and down. "Pappy! Pappy! Pappy!"

Havan Alethaner pulled the child up on his lap. "What? What? What?"

"I love you! I love you! I love you!"

"More to you. More to you. More to you." Enough silliness. "What are you doing here? You know you're not allowed to come see me at work alone."

Agapan giggled. "I'm not alone. Mammy's coming."

So Juris had let the boy down and he'd defiantly raced ahead. "Son, never leave a lady on the road alone. She could get hurt."

Agapan nodded, contrition shining in his eyes.

Havan Alethaner flinched. If appealing to the male protector instinct kept his son safe, he was willing to omit that an unarmed man bore greater risk than a lady who could dance.

His son slid down off his lap.

He grabbed the child. "Where are you off to, sabertooth?"

"Need to protect Mammy."

"Too late, little man," Juris called.

She appeared around the side of the booth, with Havan Alethaner's ivory holding her hair up. She pushed through the door.

Agapan scurried up into Havan Alethaner's lap and wrapped little arms around his neck, sending fearful glances back at his mother. Juris sent Havan Alethaner a silent plea for him not to make her be the villain again today.

Ouch, son, this is even harder with you than it was with Hosanni. Havan Alethaner cupped the child's face in his hands. "Son, we talked about this. What did I say I would need to do if this happened again?"

Agapan whimpered. "Don't spank me, Pappy. I love you."

Oh, does that bring back memories. You're just like your sister. "I have to, or you'll never learn to obey, Agapan Alethaner."

Sucking up more courage than it took to break a feral mastodon, Havan Alethaner turned the whimpering child over on his knee and placed two firm swats to the precious, but stubborn behind. Agapan wailed as if the bull bison had trampled him. The child tossed himself down on the dirt floor and curled up into a ball by the supply barrel.

Havan Alethaner closed his eyes, longing to hold and comfort his son, but experience had taught him to wait for the hiccups.

His wife wrapped her arms around him from behind and whispered into his ear, all but nibbling, "Thank you, brother."

He pulled his wife's ear to his lips. "My bride, thank me tonight."

Juris giggled, flitted away, and batted her eyes playfully. "Close this silly shack up and come home and I can fit you in presently."

He grunted. That innuendo would've been effective, if not for the word "silly." He watched down the road for his daughter. "I can't."

"She's not coming. We both well know that's why you're out here."

Their son hiccupped on the floor. Finally, he could finish that business.

He held out his arms to the wee one. "Agapan, come here."

Agapan scurried into the hug. Havan Alethaner pulled his precious little boy up onto his lap. "I love you, my precious son. Please listen to your mother. I hate spanking you."

"Uh-huh." Agapan nodded and snuggled closer. "I love you, too, Pappy."

After another minute of cuddling, Havan Alethaner set the tiny boy up on the counter and handed him a twig whittled to a dull point and an oak rod. "Want to help Pappy?"

"Yay!" Agapan bent over and frowned with a little pink tongue protruding as he set about carving the rod with the twig.

Juris squeezed Havan Alethaner's shoulder. "I know why you are looking for them. Hosanni surely knows what could happen. Why would she risk it?"

Havan Alethaner pulled out a half-finished rod and a dragon fang knife. He continued carving this customer's requested design, salmon fighting their way upstream. "My daughter will come. She trusts in her father's love for her and knows I won't let anyone hurt her or those she loves." Havan Alethaner tickled the chubby little chin of Hosanni's baby brother. "What do you say, sabertooth? Would Pappy ever let anyone hurt you or your big sisters?"

Agapan giggled. "Of course not, Pappy!"

Havan Alethaner glanced to Juris. Her eyes shone like a deer about to flee the hunter's bow. He stood and embraced Juris. She squeezed the breath out of him. He loosened her grip, kissed her cheeks, her forehead, and smelled the lye-scented hair his bridal ivory held up. "Don't be afraid. You are my wife and you come first. I will always be there for you when you need me."

AFTER WORK IN MID-MARCH, Hosanni slunk to her drawing room. Her weary muscles ached and her stomach swore to reject dinner if it contained any spices or red meat. But she could not only live with that and the frequent trips to the outhouse, she could hardly keep the smile off her face.

The scent of cigar smoke drifted from her drawing room. She frowned. Her husband knew she wasn't fond of that particular habit. Meleon mainly lit up while waiting for the driver to fetch her home, or if he had male company. This was definitely the company smoke.

In the middle of the haze around her drawing room table, her husband puffed on cigars with a shirtless, dread-locked, strapping lilac young man who looked sixteen but certainly wasn't.

She gasped. *My son! That's my fourteen-year-old!*

Jars of gold and black tattoo ink lay on the table beside tattoo needles.

Their handiwork screamed on Anthon's shoulders. Shock slammed through her body. Anthon was visibly raw from being poked with the needles, and her husband's dangerous tattoos surely had reproduced themselves on her baby.

My baby?

Hosanni touched her stomach. She'd known Meleon would carry out his fathers' coming of age tradition. And she was only Anthon's stepmum. So why was she so tempted to rip her bodice? How could something so attractive on her husband be an outrage on her son? And why was her mind racing ahead fifteen years? She was carrying a wee Aletheia, surely.

Anthon turned and spotted Hosanni. He showed her the cigar dangling in between his fingers. A clueless smile burst from every inch of his half-nude body. "Hey, Hosanni! Look who Da finally admitted is a man!"

Her son puffed on the cigar as if to prove he knew what to do with it. "I made it through it all in one day! I didn't cry out, not even once!"

For her son's sake, she mustered a small smile. "I'm happy for you, son."

Anthon beamed more.

For once, he was happy anyway. So often, his eyes punished Stepmum for loving him. She sighed. It was good to see father and son bonding. If this got her husband past the emotional walls their son had erected, and pretended weren't there, it was well worth it.

Meleon approached, hugged Hosanni, and gave her a peck on the lips. He stood back, squinting. "Astor, are you all right?"

"No, yes . . ." She swallowed. "I'm sorry, I thought I was ready for this. But I thought you said you weren't?"

Her husband's eyes twinkled. "Somehow, keeping him a baby no longer seems so pressing." Meleon's hand strayed to her stomach and caressed it.

Hosanni's cheeks grew warm. The father had guessed and much earlier than a mother disclosed the news. Since other conditions mimicked the early signs of pregnancy, mothers of all colors kept their hopes to themselves until the new life showed.

She cleared her throat. "Let me treat Anthon's shoulders for infection, but in the dining room. The smoke's not good for me."

Her husband's goofy grin knew it was the baby she was concerned about. He glanced back at Anthon. "I don't know, son. What do you think? Should I leave my lovely wife all alone with a half-naked man?"

Hosanni swallowed stomach acid. Must he remind her of Romin's gross attempt at matchmaking? Worse, Anthon's stiff spine and clenched jaw also took his father's idle remark wrong. Hosanni winked at Meleon like this was the harmless joking that he'd intended. "Brother, don't you think it would be difficult to examine the man if he were fully dressed when the site of possible infection is the man's shoulders?"

"True enough." Meleon strolled to Anthon and thumped him between the shoulder blades. "On with ye, lad. I think I can trust a noble man with my lovely bride."

Hosanni headed into the dining room. *Someone please shut my husband up before Anthon changes his mind and murders his father.*

Anthon slumped at the table, refusing to look at her.

Hosanni hesitated. What should she do with her Diakrinthian penchant for touching with his shoulders so sore? So . . . unclothed. Strange. He looked more like his father every day, and his lean athlete's body only heightened his father's beauty. Yet, he had none of the effect his father had on her. Like a flesh and blood son?

She swallowed hard. "Forgive your father. He didn't mean anything. It was supposed to be—"

"Hosanni, I know what Da meant. It'd have been nice if I could enjoy it, but that doesn't heal the wound or remove the salt ignorantly rubbed in it."

She examined the lion rampart shoulder first, and then the spread eagle. It looked like her husband knew what he was doing well enough to at least use clean needles. He'd frightened her with the information, in ancient times, the ritual used dirty needles—the lad was a man if he survived. The very concept of the ritual was strange. Manly was an insult in Diakrinth even when directed to a male. "Let me apply poultices on these shoulders."

Hosanni slipped into the pantry, where she kept her medicinal supplies. While she prepared the poultice, she mumbled the blessing consecrating it to Time and Chance. The assembly here worshiped them as daughters of Heaven that Emi had charged with governing her creation for her. Maybe they alone existed. Either way, through her, they had saved lives that would have died in Diakrinth. Only that mattered.

Once she'd applied the poultice, she wrapped it with cotton gauze. "We'll need to change this daily until I'm satisfied the wounds have healed."

Anthon sent her an alarmed glance. "It won't hurt them, will it?"

Unfortunately not. She mustered a smile. "You couldn't get those tattoos off your shoulders now if you wanted them gone."

Anthon turned his chair to face her directly. "Is it true?"

Her cheeks warmed and her eyelids fluttered. "Is what true?"

Meleon strode in. "Lad, I told ye not to pester her. Ye know how ladies are." He grabbed her arm playfully, his eyes sparkling. "Is it true, Mum? Is it?"

She sighed, stood, and draped her arms around her husband's neck. "I will answer on one condition."

"Name it, Astor."

Hosanni smiled. Best to snip off at the bud her husband's inevitable fear she might expect or desire to birth anything besides his blue babies. "Show me how to care for your hair. If I'm not mistaken, I'll have a beautiful newborn with beautiful coiled hair in late September or early October."

Meleon picked Hosanni up and whirled her around while squeezing her tight. He set her down and kissed her. "Don't fret. If you're carryin' Havan, I'll do his dreads. If Alethe, we'll consult a hairdresser. I haven't the slightest idea what lasses do to their heads." He paused. "Well, I know what they do when they don't stick a lilac's mane on their heads, but I couldn't put a lassie's hair in braids or twists to save her life."

Hosanni glanced at Anthon. Oh dear. The poor thing looked miserable.

Meleon jabbed their son's chin up. "Hey now, Sulky. That's good news your stepmum's shared, not depressin' news. It's not like ye haven't had three years to get used to the idea o' not bein' an only child anymore."

Anthon glowered. "Can't ya take your head out of your wedded bliss for a moment to consider what's it like to be fourteen, a minor league football star, and to have my own father impregnating a lass not much older than the lasses always flirting, so desperate to be seen with me? Some aren't shy about letting me know they'd be happy to relieve me of my virginity, either. Many of those lasses are Hosanni's age."

She exchanged a wide-eyed glance with her husband. Loose women had been tempting their son? She shook her head. "We can't lock him inside the house, or make him quit playing football, simply because the wrong kind of lass flashes her ankles at him, Meleon."

Her husband winced. "You sure you're not a mind reader?"

Anthon stood and put out his hands. "Hey, I didn't say I'd take them up on it! I know the price of living that way, and I'm not willing to pay it. Ya gotta believe me, Da. I was just making a point. Can't ya at all understand how hard this is for me?" Anthon flicked a finger at Hosanni's still-flat stomach. "When I have lasses her age wanting me?"

Meleon extended his hand to their son. "Look here, lad. I remember how hard fourteen can be. Fifteen was even worse. That's how old I was when your mother left us. It's normal for eligible men my age to marry women Astor's age. You should be glad I found her before you came of age. Otherwise, we'd be competing for the same lasses now. That would've been a real nightmare—not that I'd have ever done that to you, but you get my point."

Tears wet Anthon's cheeks. He hugged his father. "Aye, Da. I'm sorry."

Hosanni sniffled. Dare she hope her boys' relationship had healed?

Aggie bustled in through the pantry. "Milady, dinner is about ready."

Hosanni nodded. "I'll set the table, thank you."

Aggie sent her a grateful smile and bustled back out.

"No, you won't." Meleon pulled out a dining chair beside the window and pressed Hosanni down into it. "You're going to sit here and rest while we take care of everything."

Anthon headed into the pantry and gathered the place settings.

Hosanni grimaced. "Brother, you have confused 'pregnant woman' with 'invalid.' I'm not helpless. What is likely to be worse for the baby, setting a table, or spending my days around sick people?"

Her husband's terrified eyes wanted her to quit and hire him out to never return like Pappy.

Oops. "Meleon, please don't say it. We're far too close to making a living wage off your paintings to give up the dream now. It's not like we're worried these days whether your former house thinks we're spoiling 'Prince Antonio' to their standards." She pointed to the crown prince setting the table. "With a few financial sacrifices—"

"We could survive now, aye. If I didn't have to pay Marezza to go away and leave us alone all the time, and a baby—I couldn't be happier, but it means stretching my ledgers further right when we're losing your income."

"I told you not to say it!" Good grief, she was whining like a child.

Anthon sent her a look that concurred and headed out the propped-open pantry door. He was amazingly helpful when the task involved food destined for his hungry stomach.

Meleon cupped her cheek and kissed her. "Astor, we're not giving up on our dream. We're merely taking a slower road there while I take care of my wife and children as any sane man would."

"But this is so unnecessary. I was merely making a point. I know how to protect myself—and my subjects. I wear a mask and gloves around infectious subjects and I wash up frequently. Have you ever known me to bring disease home? I'll be fine. And I can get pregnancy leave, for the last six weeks."

Meleon massaged her neck. "And maternity leave will be for but the next six weeks following the birth. After which one of us will be taking time away from our present labor to tend the baby. And nature has better supplied you to feed babies."

"I'll do like my mother did and take her with me. Our other two journey physicians just quit. Besides me and the master physician, all we have on staff are apprentices, most of whom require supervision. At my skill level, I'm not easy to replace, Meleon. They'd rather give me time to nurse my child than lose me. I'll be fine." Hosanni imitated his "that's final" tone, hoping it would work in reverse.

"All right." Meleon brought his arms down around her to caress their tiny daughter's abode. "For now."

THE SALTY BREEZE COOLED the mid-July air. Meleon exited Fargo and Wells, whistling as he added his fifth job application to his leather notebook. Now to just find a quiet place to fill these babies out and return them to all five of his prospective employers.

A thrill shot through him as he headed toward the city park a few blocks up, through a trickle of pedestrians in frock dresses. His noble upbringing made it difficult to wrap his mind around how good this felt, but he'd turned his back on that three years ago. Astor was royalty also, but he suffered no illusions. The House of Kristos retained none of the pomp of the royal house he'd quietly walked away from, or the one which had birthed him.

No, Astor came at a price—and he had no regrets about paying it. She'd made more than enough sacrifices for their family. Now it was his turn. He clutched against his chest the applications that meant financial security and a full-time Mum for his growing family.

Emi, you were so right, if you did deign to point the way to a stranger, that is. Time to stop giving Astor chances to talk me out of this and just do it. When she sees how serious I am, I know she'll appreciate it. This can't be good for her, working so hard when either Alethe or Havan will be joining us in twelve to fourteen weeks.

"Prince Coyote!"

Meleon sped his pace. Other than Tony, none of Marezza's relations could be part of this new life. Not if he wanted to keep it safely a secret.

"Your highness, wait!"

An elderly pink woman with short, plum curls pressed her cane across Meleon's abdomen. "Bambino, someone's calling you."

Meleon glanced behind him.

Up to him ran a pink man wearing a frilly "men's" frock dress, a feminine "gentleman's" purse, and his cerulean hair in a girly updo. The man ashamed of his gender curtsied. "Prince Coyote, Marcurio Fletcher, society reporter for the Chronicle. Could you please confirm whether you and Princess Marezza are currently expecting your second child via a marita?"

How did he answer that? The newspapers were the blokes who couldn't learn of his dissolve and remarriage without launching the Union into war.

Chapter Twenty

Don't panic now, Kristekon. If Mum paid attention to gossips, she'd have declared war a decade ago. Meleon scowled at the gossip dragon. "Weren't you the one who so cheerfully reported three years ago that I'd had a falling out with the house of Romin? Prince Coyote is dead. I have a new life now and I'd pray you to keep the blazes out of it!"

The gossip dragon reached into his ladies' purse and removed a small notepad and pencil. "So, was that a yes or a no?"

"No comment!" Meleon snapped and stomped toward the city park. He stroked the leather notebook. What was the world coming to when a private citizen couldn't go about searching for work without a reporter showing up to remind him he was born a prince?

A tea bistro caught his eye. Actually, that would work better. He went in and ordered a fresh baked apple scone and a spiced black tea made with foamy milk, whipped cream, a kiss of vanilla, and four cubes of sugar, in a twelve-inch-tall, porcelain cup.

Grande tea cup and scone in hand, Meleon settled in at a little iron claw table to secure his children's future.

IN THE FAINT GLOW OF the bedside oil lamp, Meleon stared at the crystal chandelier on the ceiling, listening to the sound of his wife's breathing beside him. Astor lay on her side with her left arm curled around him.

He sighed, smiling. He didn't deserve this woman. Whether she'd admit it or not, her appetite for joining was diminished. It didn't seem right, with her three months away from childbirth, but Astor's gentle assurance did him in. Such a woman—and all his.

At last, Astor's breathing settled into the deep rhythm only an earthquake could awaken her from—or her crying infant, come this autumn. He grinned. Finally, it was safe to be a loony expectant father.

Meleon sat up and hugged and kissed the beautiful round belly. "Da loves ye, yes he does, yes he does, yes he does. And I have good news, if ye can keep it a secret. I want to surprise your mum."

He laughed and stroked his wife's pregnant belly like he would a newborn. "Guess who put in applications today? Da! Guess who has an interview at seven forty tomorrow mornin'? That's right, Da! And I'm goin' to nail that interview, and I'm goin' to work hard to provide for ye, and your mum's goin' to be able to stay home and take care o' ye and not have to live like she's still a marita. That's how much Da loves ye. Aren't ye proud o' me?"

To Astor's extended belly he applied more kisses intended for his baby.

She moaned and turned over onto her back. He pressed his cheek to the taunt skin. Tiny limbs fluttered, poking back at Da. Jubilation raced through him. "I knew you'd be proud o' me."

Meleon played a game of pat-a-pie with his stirring wee one. "I can hardly wait to meet ye, to hold ye in my arms. To find out whether ye're Alethe or Havan. We're hoping ye're Alethe, we already have Tony, but ye're goin' to have lots o' brothers and sisters, and I'm told patience is a virtue, so I reckon it doesn't matter which of ye is our firstborn." He winced. *Our?* Favoring the beloved spouse's children was against the path. Even he knew that. "Your mum's firstborn, I mean. Ye do have a half-brother."

Fluttering baby limbs replied.

"Let me tell ye a secret, wee one. Da was floored by your mum's love, that she'd deem me worthy o' her. See, I'm a stranger, yet Lady Veritas will belong to our family. Ye might be her, or maybe the Kristos she marries." Meleon ducked. "Da's not supposed to know the plain text o' the prophecy. I've never gotten around to finishin' the Sacred History. But I'm afraid I have a bad habit o' peekin' at the last page o' books. Don't copy that from me. I've spoiled many a good book doin' that."

Meleon yawned. "So Da doesn't think it matters if ye're a boy or a girl. The way Diakrinthians think, ye could be Lady Veritas, and her husband our son-in-law, or she could be our daughter-in-law and you another boy. But Da better try to get some sleep before your mum puts me in the loony house. No offense, I love our time together, but Da feels rather silly talkin' to ye when ye're too little to understand."

He caressed the pregnant belly holding his child—and his greatest hope. Who'd refuse to accept him as a convert when they saw who he sowed? "Wee one, do Da a favor, will ye? Do something about the door your mum shut in my face. It's cold out here, away from Emi."

Meleon pulled the covers over him and Astor, and snuggled beside her. Soon as sleep claimed him, he was back at Fargo and Wells for the interview, dressed in his nightshirt, the one with the ugly stain at that. Heat flooded his cheeks and pulsed down his neck, but the interviewer was shaking his hand, saying, "You start tomorrow."

Even though he'd came so inappropriately dressed? Meleon shouted for joy, and raced out. He had to tell Astor the good news.

On their porch, he slapped his forehead. He told Astor he needed her to find another way to work because he needed the chariot to attend his art fair exhibit today. He'd render himself a liar if he didn't go there, too.

Meleon ran across the street to the art fair. Odd. The art fair should be clear across town. His whole pretext to leave for the interview without rousing suspicion had counted on that. If Astor saw this—well, she'd forgive him when she heard his good news.

He gasped at his exhibit. How could all of his paintings be gone? Astor had sweettalked him into displaying reproductions of his private collection. Who else would ever want their priceless family portraits? He grabbed a blue man passing by. "Where is it all?"

"Your wife sold everything."

"Astor was here?"

The stranger frowned confusedly. "Princess Marezza."

"Where did she go?"

"That way." The stranger pointed toward Meleon's house.

He raced inside the foyer. Marezza held his wife prisoner with a knife at Astor's throat. Marezza shifted into her true form—a she-wolf who stood up like a woman. The wolf ripped open his wife's pregnant belly, lifted up a tiny blue son, and tossed the precious baby boy up in the air to devour him whole.

Meleon cried aloud, "Help! Emi!"

His home, the wolf, and Astor and wee Havan all vanished.

Meleon squinted against a brilliant light and discerned a man with an appearance like polished bronze.

The brownie said, "Arise, Meleon. Take the child and his mother and flee to your own house, for Marezza will seek the child to destroy him."

Meleon flung the covers off him and stood at his bedside. He blinked and stretched. He'd been asleep. Dreaming.

His heart pounded. These days, some otherwise sane folk thought the brownies were an advanced race from another planet. But Emi had sent this one, to deliver her warning. Meleon pulled off his night shirt, strapped on his sandals, and changed into a purple traveling kilt and traveling shirt.

Since they wouldn't be here to pay their gas bill, Meleon flipped on the light switch. The noise of gas coming on and being lit preceded the chandelier bursting into its glory.

Astor pulled a pillow over her head, whining sleepily, "Go back to Hades, Lady Sun. I don't want to get up."

Meleon chuckled. Nothing could rouse her but a roaring earthquake, a crying baby, and a light bright enough to be confused with her sole alarm clock for thirteen years. But it would be better to raise their son in such a backward nation as Diakrinth than to lose both of them. "Wake up, Astor!"

Meleon ran downstairs to the library. He needed to write Tony. The lad had spent the night next door with his friends and there was no time to fetch him. Besides, Tony was a Dimarezza, not a Kristekon, and the crown prince of Diakrinth's mortal enemies at that. His eldest son might hate him for this, but he wasn't about to save one son's life while endangering the other son.

He scribbled an apology for the emergency, advising Tony how to present himself at court and collect his allowance. Romin would offer the lad the life expected of a future king, or if the lad preferred, either the neighbors or Aggie would love to have Tony. Meleon ended the letter with legalities granting his permission for the lad to marry, etc.

Much as this Da didn't relish becoming a grandfather at thirty, it'd be a relief to have that one safely married before long. Though it'd be nice—he'd let Tony know where to write once they had a post office box. Astor would want to risk that, too.

What would they need for a one-way trip to Diakrinth? Meleon tapped his chin. Bread, coppers, toiletries, and a change of clothes each. He glanced at the book shelves and pulled a leather-bound volume from one.

Make that bread, coppers, toiletries, a change of clothes apiece, and the Sacred History.

He also opened his safe and pulled out his emergency fund's coin purse.

Back in the pantry, Meleon left the note on the counter. He grabbed a burlap grocery sack and tossed in the money and the History along with his favorite snack foods—dried fruit, nuts, bison jerky, as well as literal bread. He took the sack back upstairs, dropped it on the nightstand, and yanked away the pillow smothering his pregnant wife.

Astor moaned and yanked the covers over her head.

Fine, then, if you don't like what I pack for you, that's your fault. Meleon rummaged in the wardrobe and their dressers and pulled out one change of clothes for him and two for Astor. He tossed a purple maternity frock dress and ladies' underwear on her vanity and stuffed the rest inside his satchel. He glanced at her corset up on the wardrobe's shelf. Nah, pregnancy was mainly an excuse to go without a corset. She'd be glad to leave that behind.

Now he just had to get Astor changed into the maternity frock dress and clean underwear and get the bags and themselves to the chariot. He grabbed the covers and yanked them from the bed.

Astor sat up, rubbing her eyes and yawning. She peered at him. "It's not morning yet."

"No time. A brownie said Havan's in danger. We need to flee somewhere that Marezza and politics could never threaten our children. Namely, where I should have taken ye three years ago."

Astor gasped and clutched her belly. "No! You can't abandon me now!"

Meleon pulled her up. "We're both going this time. Now get dressed."

She scrunched together her eyebrows. "We're picking up in the middle of the night, abandoning everything we love and have worked for, to move to a hostile, underdeveloped nation on the word of a creature of Erini mythology? Meleon, forgive me but you had a bad dream and are being ridiculous."

Was he? No. The man he saw was not of his creation. "I had worse than a bad dream, I had a nightmare. But in every natural dream I've had about the baby, I saw a wee Alethe. This time, I saw a wee Havan, because Emi sent this dream. We need to leave to return to your father and now. Tonight. Or I will surely lose ye both tomorrow."

Astor laughed. "You're a man and Xenos. Emi would not speak to you."

Meleon winced. That hurt far worse than anything Marezza threw at him because the wound came from a woman normally so respectful and loving.

She hugged him. "Meleon, I understand how you feel, but please don't pretend it's Emi wanting us to run away the night before the biggest break of your career. The critics who see your work over the next four days could make Kristekon a household name. You're terrified of failure and have latched onto a rude gossip columnist as an excuse to turn tail and run."

A coward. His respectful, loving wife was calling him a coward. Sure, he was looking for work so he could support his family when the critics laughed him out of painting forever. But in her eyes, he'd always seen a lion reflected back. "The threat is real, Astor. Marezza reads the gossip column like Emians read the Sacred History."

"What is the worst that can happen? She rubs it in that I'm a marita and does to this wee one what she did to Tony. And you do what you did."

"Not unless ye want to give birth tonight." Meleon shuddered. It had been unthinkable, that even Marezza might do something as evil as what his dream had forewarned. "I only have the authority to stop her from killing Havan after he's born. Before he's born, so long as the dissolve papers remain in our safe deposit box, we have no legal recourse if Marezza chooses to terminate 'her' pregnancy."

Astor gasped.

"See? We have no choice. I suffer no illusions, Astor. I know why ye don't want to go home. Your people hate my mother more than they hate Romin. If your neighbors realize who I am, I'll end up in an unmarked grave. That's why we have to leave Tony. But I gave ye my solemn vow to protect our family with my life if necessary."

"Do you know what my people do to physicians? They accuse us of being witches and feed us to the dragons."

Emi wouldn't tell them to go there if that was going to happen to her. But getting laughed at again—not happening. "You'll have an easier time hiding your profession than I'll have hiding my tattoos when I will have to bathe in a river. We have to risk it. For him." Meleon caressed that precious round belly.

Astor gaped at him. "You really believe that Emi—you're truly arrogant enough to think that Emi would—"

He winced at the dagger slicing through him. She mercifully stopped.

She took his head in her hands. "Meleon, to whom would Emi be more likely to reveal where the path lies? A son of Erin who doesn't even pretend to follow the path, who had a nightmare and thinks he saw a brownie, or the last daughter of Kristos? And Mother was a Ravane. If Logos—the living daughter of Heaven—was going to speak to one of us, wouldn't it be to me?"

She was right. This was absurd.

Astor released his head and took his hand. "Brother, I don't fault you for being frightened, but we hold the purse. Think. The only reason you haven't legally dissolved Marezza is to prevent war. Does she truly think we love our countrymen's lives enough to give up this child's life?" Astor pressed a hand to her belly. "If you turn in the dissolve papers, Marezza loses everything. If we stand our ground, she has no choice but to back down."

Meleon sighed. "I guess you're right. I guess I was just bein' a coward."

He flipped off the lights. He'd have to pay the gas bill, after all.

Chapter Twenty-One

M eleon strolled out into the foyer on his wife's arm. His heart beat fast, his stomach fluttered, and his palms sweated. So much for his having a job interview before the art fair making him less nervous. This was supposed to be like having a well-rounded investment portfolio. Whether the critics loved him at the art fair, or he got the job, from now on, he'd be earning enough to provide for his family, and Astor could afford to stay home with the children.

But what if he blew it with both opportunities and his wife ended up doing as she'd threatened? What if she insisted on carrying the baby around in a sling as she interviewed subjects with illnesses fatal to a baby?

Astor sent him a hopeful smile, draped her arms around his neck, and kissed him tenderly. "Good luck."

Had she guessed his secret? He grinned. No, she meant good luck at the art fair. "Thanks. I need it more than ye know." He cleared his throat. "And someone is comin' to pick ye up?"

"Yes, the same person is coming to get me as the last three times you asked. And if you wait ten minutes and ask me again, your answer will be her tooting horn outside."

Meleon flinched, his cheeks warming. "Oh. Right."

The clock chimed the seventh hour. A choice Erini swear word leapt into his throat. How had it gotten so late? He had forty minutes to get across town, find a parking spot, and arrive at the interview on time—make that thirty-five minutes. Anything less than five minutes early would be considered late.

A blood-chilling sound jimmied the lock. Meleon tensed, eyes widening. Not the she-wolf who had mocked his attempts at any security through a hundred lock changes over the last eight years. They had a standoff coming, soon as she got a peek at the gossip column in tonight's paper, but—but the busybody reporter might have pestered her, too. Oh no. Not now.

The door banged open. His ex-wife stormed in, sure enough, her green eyes scowling at his present wife. Marezza screeched, "Traitor! I saved your life, and this is how you repay me?" She jabbed a finger hard into his wife's pregnant belly. "I trusted you!"

His ex-wife railed at them with every foul name in the book. He could hardly make a word out of her high-pitched shriek, but a few hit home. A knot of fury warred with the panic seizing his body. His ex-wife was calling his remarriage adultery? Absurd.

"Answer me, draca! What part of, 'I don't want any more children, so, as my marita, you'll have to financially support me without knowing the tender caress of a husband' was so difficult to understand?"

"I forgot," his faithful treasure mumbled on the periphery of his vision, prompting more high-pitched, incomprehensible screeching from Marezza.

Draca? That was aimed at Astor? Meleon clenched a fist even as his legs begged him to run out the door, away from the mad woman hurting his ears.

He glanced at the wall clock. Now he had a mere thirty-one minutes to get to the interview on time. If his ex-wife cost him the job, he'd kill her.

While scowling at Marezza, Meleon said to Astor, "I don't have time for this nonsense. Ye deal with her."

The door slammed behind him. He clenched his teeth as he ran out to the ready-to-go chariot, whipped poor Noinin until she was running as fast as she could, and then whipped her some more.

Astor would be mad that he left, but holding their ground was her idea, and a strong, intelligent young woman like Astor could handle this. Even if his silly fears last night did have any basis in reality, her ride to work would be here any minute to give her a valid excuse to duck out, and he'd check on her right after the interview, just in case. Any threats Marezza made against the baby couldn't be made good on that fast.

So he'd have to make himself a liar and skip the art fair he was supposed to be headed to. Astor would forgive him when she learned he'd secured their family's future and she didn't have to live like a slave anymore.

HOSANNI TREMBLED AND stared, gaping, as her husband walked out on her. The door slammed in her face shattered her like a dropped crystal vase. Meleon didn't have time for the "nonsense" of defending her? And who had "you deal with her" been addressed to?

Marezza cackled. "Don't worry, darling. I will deal with her."

Tears slid down Hosanni's cheeks. She caressed her unborn child. Did he love them so little compared to his career? "Meleon, how could you?"

Marezza winkled her nose. "Meleon?" She laughed. "Oh, Coyote! That clever dog asked you for a name. How far has my Coyote taken his deception, darling? Did he bribe a Ravane to perform an invalid wedding ceremony?"

The words pierced Hosanni's very soul. Amen, he had no qualms about "paying extra for speedier service," if they managed to get ahead enough. Had he been manipulating her all along? He surely had known how she'd react to a threat to take her back to Diakrinth. And it wasn't like it was the first time a man had duped her. Had Coyote just been using her, like Korban had been?

How could it all have been a lie? But how could the sweet man that she'd thought she'd married so suddenly leave her?

Marezza tsked. "Aw, you poor deceived fool. You truly thought you were his wife! Make no mistake, darling. Coyote is never going to dissolve me and free you. He's too much of a coward. And I had a nasty bout with malaria last year, but I survived, and plan to live a very long life. You will never be more than Coyote's mistress. You saw how easy it was for me to end that coward's charade. All I had to do was scream hysterically, and he turned you over to me to do with you whatever I pleased."

Hosanni blinked rapidly. "Please, milady. Please."

"Of course I'll forgive you, darling. We can forget all about this." Marezza patted Hosanni's pregnant belly. "Tell you what, after you've recovered from the miscarriage, you're free. I'll put you on the stagecoach to Idaho myself."

Hosanni shrunk back, clutching her baby protectively. "Never."

Marezza growled. "I was being nice. That's an order, marita. I have a right to terminate my pregnancy, and you will cooperate!"

"I'd sooner drink hemlock."

A pleased smile spread her lady's lips. "You never change, darling. Good thing I came prepared." Marezza reached into her bosom and pulled out a vial identical to the one she'd poured out three and a half years ago. She grabbed Hosanni's hand and slapped the hemlock into it. "As a princess of the House of Romin, and as the lady of this house, I hereby sentence you to death by hemlock for treason by way of adultery. And mind you, darling, the penalty for refusing this merciful sentence is crucifixion."

Hosanni fled in tears upstairs to her room. The sight of the bed on which her illegitimate child had been conceived shredded her. She sank onto the vanity's stool. A desolate adulteress stared back at her in the looking glass. Hosanni removed the vial's cork and lifted the hemlock toward her lips.

The child in Hosanni's womb leapt.

Death jerked away from her lips. She corked the vial, set it on the vanity, and pressed her hands to the child stirring as if pleading with Mum for mercy. She whispered, "You're not Lady Veritas, Alethe. Only the love child of a coyote and a deceived fool. But that's no crime."

And Marezza didn't say where to carry out her sentence.

She'd go home and confess her sins. Better to be slain by the dragons, and allowed to rest at peace with her mothers, than—well, Diakrinth did burn the bodies of the accursed, a fate met by all who perished in West California. But the aggies would show her mercy and give her a proper burial for Mother's sake. Perhaps they'd allow her to drink the hemlock.

But first, she'd finish her present labor and leave Alethe at the gate of a refuge, like the Temple in the City of Trees. At home, her baby would forever bear the shame of illegitimacy. But no one could ever know why a woman left such a beautiful, healthy child at the gate. Alethe would be taken up readily.

Hosanni rose and stumbled to the wardrobe, which had its doors already ajar. She glanced through it for a traveling bag and spotted the carpetbag, which contained the vestments from the crown jewels Erin stole from Kristos. Hosanni stuffed inside the carpetbag a purple maternity dress, underpants, a chemise, Alethe's pink baby blanket and swaddling, and the luxurious fabrics she'd been meaning to sew into dresses.

At noise on the stairs, Hosanni hid the hemlock vial inside the carpetbag, tossed the carpetbag in the wardrobe, and threw herself across the bed.

"How are you, darling?"

She lay as still as a stone. Marezza hopefully didn't know enough about hemlock poisoning to know its rate of progression.

"Well, I need to run your death sentence to the clerks, but the mortician should be by shortly, if you need anything." Marezza cackled.

Hosanni listened until a door shut in the distance. She got up, grabbed the carpetbag, and slipped downstairs into the library.

The atlas stood out next to the only empty space on the shelves. Hosanni pulled it out to the table and opened to the map showing Romin's highways in the pacific northwest. On a tablet of paper, with quill and ink, she pressed firmly as she sketched the route to Diakrinth. She unfolded the map of the City by the Bay. Below her map, to be on the safe side, she wrote the names of the city streets and the turns she needed to take to reach the highway home. Thankfully, they all led well away from that dog's accursed art fair.

She tore off the top page, rolled it up into a scroll, and placed it in the carpetbag. One of the books she'd planned to read caught her eye. Hosanni grabbed it along with several more on her reading list and tossed them into her carpetbag, ensuring her directions remained in her reach. She slung the bag over her shoulder and fled the house as fast as her legs would carry her.

And never looked back.

MELEON BROUGHT NOININ to a halt on the street outside Astor's soon-to-be former workplace. Now to make things right with Astor.

The master physician, an elderly pink woman, came running out to him. She craned her neck at the inside of his chariot. "Where's Dr. Kristekon?"

Nausea twisted his innards as he remained inside his chariot. Astor didn't make it to work? Well, her employer was owed an explanation. "My ex found out about the baby and threw a fit. Soon, Marezza will sorely regret it."

"Dr. Kristekon will be back tomorrow, I hope?"

Meleon grinned. "I should hope not. I'm freeing Astor today."

Disappointment flooded her former employer's wrinkled face. "So that's why Romin was looking for Hosanni? We were a bit confused."

What, Romin? By messenger surely, but why?

Meleon urged Noinin onward. The making up might not take so long, after all. If Astor was still doing her standing her ground thing with Marezza, she'd simply be grateful he came back so quickly. Let his countrymen die. It was Marezza's fault for threatening his baby.

At home, he left Noinin on the street and raced in the house. "Astor!"

Marezza beamed up at him from the divan. Her left eye puffed up and the red blood pooling under her skin promised to turn the area black. She flicked a parchment. "Don't worry, darling. I know that hussy beguiled you. I took care of her nonsense just as you told me to."

Something inside Meleon curled up and died. "No. I was talking to her."

"I beg to differ. Hosanni was the one speaking nonsense. You, remarried! Ha. Our brothers would be killing each other on a battlefield somewhere if that were true. Her incredibly selfish actions jeopardized the alliance. She was clearly a traitor to the crown and well deserving of this." Marezza swept up and handed him the parchment.

No. No. This couldn't be happening.

"Read it, porky." Marezza slapped the parchment in his face where he couldn't help but see what it was.

A certificate from a mortician, describing the remains disposed of as a pregnant twenty-year-old lilac woman sentenced to death by hemlock. Twenty minutes ago. How could this be real? He had left her but an hour ago. Even if Marezza had done it the second he left, Astor would have still been alive when she was shoved into the furnace. And how could Astor allow such a thing to happen? Some foul witchcraft? Marezza had such powers?

"That was my wife and child!" He swung a fist to make both eyes match, but stopped short. A beating was too good a death for Marezza. Meleon jabbed a finger in her face. "You'll pay. Romin will hear about this."

"First you must do something about that son of yours. You can see how Prince Antonio took the news." Marezza touched the black eye that Tony had apparently given her. "He's disowned us all and run away." Marezza tsked, shaking her head. "Oh dear, how will you bloote Erini ever retake the whole union from the weak old fool who raised me now that your precious mutual heir has refused the crown?"

No. "I'll worry about Tony after I see your bloote carcass on a crucifix!"

The murderer cackled. "Yes, let's tell Papa indeed."

✕

MELEON BURST INSIDE Romin's courtroom ahead of the murderer.

Everyone at court turned to stare. Romin scowled down from his throne.

Meleon screamed, "Crucify this woman! She has murdered my wife and child in cold blood!"

"Papa, this man has violated our vows with another woman! Hosanni was executed for treason, for endangering a marriage alliance. For his own part in their crime, I'm lending my husband to your army—unless you will want to execute Coyote also?"

Romin slammed his scepter on the throne. "Silence, both of you! I go this morning to keep my word to a fair princess wrongly enslaved, and I learn my own nipote betrayed me! Marezza, you gave away your own husband to foil me, and you jeopardized the peace, and now you have the audacity to cause the innocent daughter of Kristos to pay the penalty for your crimes!"

Marezza trembled. "Papa, I thought you had forgotten her. I couldn't just leave her on the rock to rot. She promised me she wouldn't—"

"Enough! No more of your lies and excuses. Depart from us. We cut you off from Romin. You are dead to us and to all our kin and banished from our presence. If any of us ever lay eyes on you again, we will crucify you!"

"Papa!"

"Guards, take her away! If she resists at all, crucify her."

Marezza shuffled out, shooting murderous glances at Meleon.

He trembled with rage. "You call that justice? Your honor, Marezza has murdered my beloved wife and a child we conceived in wedlock. I can prove it." He lifted the paperwork he'd fetched out of his safe deposit box.

"Silence! The only thing Marezza fears worse than crucifixion is being left a penniless, powerless object of ridicule. My only regret is she'll eventually break the rules and let one of us lay eyes upon her, and I'll have to end her punishment. But that leaves you, Prince Coyote. Far as I am concerned, you're equally guilty of Princess Hosanni's blood."

"Me!"

"You had every right to dissolve Marezza and remarry. Surely you knew of her treason and that she was dangerous. So why are those papers in your hand rather than on file with the clerks? Why did you keep Princess Hosanni in such a vulnerable position as being your marita and Marezza's? Why didn't you protect your family?"

Meleon trembled. "Your honor, you know why. The alliance—"

"—is my responsibility. It's true I asked you to give Marezza a chance to come to her senses and return to you. But if diplomacy fails and Erin declares war, that is my responsibility. Protecting Princess Hosanni and her child was your responsibility. They're dead, not only because of Marezza's treachery, but because of your cowardice and irresponsibility!"

Meleon collapsed to his knees. If only he had listened to Emi last night. If only he had put Marezza in her place this morning. "Astor, I'm so sorry." His shoulders heaved as the sobs tore through him. How had Astor ever looked at him and seen a lion? He was but a brash, impatient, and selfish coward who'd failed her from the beginning. A lion would've faced Romin three and a half years ago rather than trying to avoid his ire. "Will you crucify me?"

"I jolly well should. You slew my prince of peace, prevented the birth of a king in the House of Kristos who would have belonged to all peoples and torn down the bitter walls of separation dividing the Union."

Meleon stared at the stone floor. He would've preferred a less painful death, but nothing could hurt worse than losing Astor and the baby. Perhaps Emi would show mercy and allow a stranger to be reunited with Astor and Havan in Heaven. No, he'd get what he deserved. Eternity separated from both them and Emi in the freezing cold darkness of Hades. But life without Astor was a Hades of its own.

Murmurs rose loud enough that Meleon could no longer block out the crowd's noise. Wrinkled pink hands lifted his head and stared into his eyes.

The exalted King of the Nations had come down from his throne to meet him where he was? No wonder the spectators were shocked. Meleon flinched and glanced away from that penetrating gaze. Romin whispered, "Bambino, what is your name?"

He swallowed. "Meleon Kristekon, husband of Hosanni."

Romin stood, tugging Meleon to his feet. "We hereby adopt this man and name our son Prince Meleon Difelippo Romin."

What? Why?

THE LATE AFTERNOON sun had burned through the haze overhead by the time the highway beneath Hosanni's swollen, throbbing feet had put the city limits far enough behind her for vineyards to surround her. They slid by slower than the city streets had.

Sweat dripped from her body. It had to be at least eighty degrees out. A distant memory whispered that would be a cool day for mid-July in Diakrinth, but to her, it felt more like a hundred-degree day had back home.

A sneaky devil had added two hundred pounds worth of bricks to her bag. It dragged along the ground as she switched it from aching arm to aching arm. Her empty stomach growled, reminding her belatedly it would have been wise to pack bread and coppers for her journey, if she wanted to live long enough to spare Alethe and rest with her own mother.

The countryside inched by slower yet. Green spots began to dance before Hosanni's eyes, growing with the lightheadedness sweeping over her.

At the rumble of horse hooves and a tooting horn, she dragged herself further to the left side so the chariot could pass her more easily.

Her pulse rate and her chest's tightness added to the warning sweeping over her. For Alethe's sake, Hosanni stopped ignoring what was happening and lay down right where she was, lest she subject her dear girl to a fall.

Swirling green spots consumed the sideways vineyard and Hosanni, too.

Chapter Twenty-Two

The sun's ever faithful resurrection nudged Hosanni awake. She lay in a hard bed with a spring poking her right hip. Before her, a fire burned low in a stone fireplace set in a naked stucco wall. What was this? Better yet, where was this, and how had she gotten here?

She turned over in bed and gasped at the sweet angel face of the young man fast asleep beside her. "Anthon!"

He scrambled out of the bed and wiped sleep sand from his eyes. "My apologies, milady. I was exhausted and unable to think beyond the need for sleep. Forgive me."

Hosanni sat up and pressed a hand to her forehead. "What are you doing here—what am *I* doing here? Last I remember—"

"You fainted on the highway. That's when I managed to catch up to ya." Anthon picked up a document from a battered nightstand and showed her the document. It was the page below her directions home, with the impression darkened to form a copy of the original. He frowned at her. "You broke your word, Hosanni. You promised ya wouldn't leave without me."

What? She flinched. "These were hardly the circumstances either of us had in mind."

"I still intend to hold ya to it. You ought to be glad I was there to get help willing to put us up. I've been through your bag. I know what you thought was indispensable. You'll never make it home alive without me."

"Anthon, you must go home. You're underage, and I'm only going back to receive a proper burial and delay my sentence until after the baby's born."

"No, you're not." Anthon fished through the carpetbag on the floor and lifted out the hemlock vial. He uncorked it and shook the empty vial while he held it upside down. Anthon tossed it into the fire. "You are not dying.

We are fleeing this injustice to refuge in our motherland."

Hosanni laughed. "This is your motherland! I appreciate that Aggie has raised you since you were two years old, and that you look like your father, but you'd be a pink man in Diakrinth. My people determine ancestry only by the mother's race, even if the father had the dominant traits. Though, if sincere, you're only proving the principle behind that law."

"Would that Grandma was my true kin!" Anthon shook his head. "I am so sorry, Hosanni. I thought my parents' marriage was dissolved. If I'd known the truth, I would've fought harder for you. Frankly, I'm so disgusted by what my parents have done to us, I resign from both the house of Romin and Erin. I want no part of them or their peoples."

"You can't mean that, Prince Antonio."

The son of her bosom grimaced. "Hosanni, amen, amen, I hate the Italian form of my name nearly as much as I despise Tony. It'd simply be a waste of breath to ask Da to call me Anthon. Mind you that was my preference before I lost any interest in belonging to either Romin or Erin. They will always own my blood, but my heart is with Diakrinth."

Hosanni pursed her lips. *Spoken by a lad wearing his football jersey and the MacErin tartan, who knows a little Diakrinthian as a forth language, while he is fluent in Erini and almost fluent in Italian. And he has a daily cigar habit and runs around immodestly attired to show off his tattoos even more often than his father does.*

"Anthon, what do I have to offer you? My sins are many. Your medicine is dedicated to pagan gods, thus rendering me a witch, and your father—I sinned thrice over in accepting a stranger to the path, who is married to someone else, and who is the leader of our home. If my people don't execute me, it'll be only because our law requires the testimony of two women."

He rolled his eyes. "Don't be silly. Your father is the rightful king. Kristos will show mercy to his only daughter."

It wouldn't be up to Father—if he even still lived.

Time to change tactics. "In Diakrinth, you'd lack all the luxury you've enjoyed as a prince. Even Kristos wears an indigo tunic, bathes in a river, and walks three miles round trip each day to service our earth closets' bowls."

"I am no stranger to sweat, milady."

"Should your lineage become known, you would be at risk of retribution for Romin and Erin's crimes against my people. Turn back. It's only a matter of time before you're called up to the majors. Why give up a promising career as a war gamesman, and a future reign as king over the entire Union, to risk your life for a stiff-necked witch who rejected you?"

"Emi strike me if I leave you! Amen, Amen, I'm not my father. Where you go, I go.May your people be my people and your god my god."

She stared back. His rudeness ruined his imitation of the Diakrinthians he grew up around. "You truly want to follow the path?"

"Most definitely."

"Then start by averting your gaze. In Diakrinth, it would be incredibly rude for you to initiate direct eye contact with any grown woman—or your lord. Likewise, never argue with a woman or a man put in authority over the other men. If you cannot bite your tongue, phrase your retort as a question. It also helps to add the appropriate honorific."

Anthon glanced downwards. "I'll remember that, milady, thank you."

The urge to take it back slammed into Hosanni. No wonder she'd hated it so much when Coyote feigned interest in the path. In truth, she loved him for his liberty, not in spite of it, and had quietly embraced his way of life. She swallowed. Before she could convert anyone to her parents' faith, she'd need to become an Emian and follow the path herself.

Her stomach growled. Food sounded far more appealing.

Anthon glanced at the pink rays in the window. "We can eat breakfast with the day laborers presently, but I fear our hosts jumped to a conclusion that may ruin your appetite."

Dear Emi. Hosanni stroked the wee one nestled inside of her. "You don't mean to imply they've taken you for your father?"

"I'm sorry, milady. I tried to correct the record, but they know you're a marita and don't want to know if you're not my property."

Hosanni touched her shorn hair. In her own neighborhood, surrounded by other maritas, she could pretend the bob was merely fashionable.

Sighing, Anthon massaged the back of his neck. "First, food. Then I need to quiz the stagecoach company and find something to cover your hair with."

A KNOCK FELL ON THE door. Hosanni placed her book down. She opened the door and peered at a wrinkled lilac woman wearing bridal ivory in her silvery crown of glory, spectacles, and a blue gingham frock. Hosanni asked, "Are you the lady of the house?"

The aggie nodded. "I'm here to help you change while my husband assists yours." She held up the bundle of white fabric in her arms.

Breakfast rumbled a threat to come back up.

Hosanni let her hostess in and shut the door. "Anthon is not the father." Hosanni touched her belly. "Milord has abandoned me and milady seeks my life. Anthon is—"

Her hostess held up a hand. "Hold your peace. If I knew that a marita was running away with her masters' children, aiding you would be illegal." Her eyes twinkled. "But since you are having marital difficulties, I'll bring in a straw pallet and lend you my own room divider for that." Her hostess pointed to the water basin stand, a clay urinal, and a throne-style earth closet standing in the corner furthest from the fireplace.

Hosanni dipped her head. "Thank you."

"Quite all right. Now, a woman in mourning should veil such beautiful glory." Her hostess removed a white silk scarf from her bundle. She veiled Hosanni's side-swept bob, and tied a firm knot beneath Hosanni's chin.

Fuzzy warmth tingled at Hosanni's crown. She stroked the silk. "I look like a modest widow. Isn't that deceitful?"

"Hush, *tekon*. All maritas have cause to lament, and it's no one's business but your own why you are in mourning."

Odd. Using tekon to mean child, offering white mourning garments . . . Hosanni gasped. "Are you from Diakrinth?"

Her hostess unfolded a bone white sackcloth palla. "Remove the frock, and I'll give you a refresher course on our national dress."

Another knock on the door came as Hosanni had regained her ability to wrap a palla without assistance. Anthon called, muffled, "You dressed?"

"Yes!" *Like I'm Diakrinthian, for the first time in eight years.*

A grinning Anthon entered wearing the indigo.

Hosanni's heart skipped a beat. She covered her mouth. "What's this?"

Her son's eyes sparkled. "I'm a day laborer. This is how we dress."

She swallowed and eyed his sopping wet dreadlocks. "Did you bathe?"

"In a way." Anthon's grin broadened still more.

Hosanni sniffed his soaked hair. Wine. They'd baptized him and poured consecrated wine over his head, representing the blood of the Sacrifice. "You made your confession?"

Anthon nodded eagerly.

Their hostess clapped and hugged him. "Welcome to Emi's house, child! We are so glad you have joined us." Their hostess glanced at her. "Though we have sponsored many on the path, only to release them to another's care."

Hosanni breathed. Guilt pricked her, but she pressed it away. She could hardly send Anthon back to his old life now, if he was this serious.

Their hostess squeezed her hand. "I have hungry laborers to feed, but join us at my family's dinner table at one, will you?"

Hosanni smiled. How wonderful. "We will be honored."

"Oh, and, I imagine that you're used to celebrating the sun's resurrection alone, living in the city, but we would be honored if you danced with us in the villa assembly."

Hosanni's stomach tightened. When she stopped going to assembly, she'd also stopped dancing each morning, as she had previously every day since she was but a toddler. "I am a woman in mourning."

"Tekon, there are three seasons for a woman to observe the resurrection dance. When you're rejoicing, when you're lamenting, and the long stretches of boredom in between. I'll see you there at first light." Their hostess kissed their cheeks as if they were her family and departed.

Anthon bounced on the bed. "You look beautiful, milady."

Hosanni blinked. "Thank you, son."

He glowered. "Could ya get out o' that habit? I'm doing this without Da's consent, ya know. Besides, our host recommended a like-minded villa across the Oregonian border, but helping us endangers them. Shouldn't we be kind and not give out information they don't wish to know?"

Hosanni found a stool by the fireplace and lowered herself onto it. "Lying isn't on the path, Anthon."

"Understood, but we are kin, and you are in mourning, and we are on our way home, and that's more than anyone deserves told."

"People will assume I'm a widow and you're my cousin. That constitutes making true statements to create a deliberate false impression, one I don't believe to be strictly necessary to preserve innocent life." One of the great Ra-vanes had declared lying to be on the path solely in that context. "Besides, even if is, it's not healthy for you."

Anthon winced. "Milady, I know the frailty of the heart that beats in my chest. I've been running diagnostics on myself since I was eleven." He rubbed the sprinkling of whiskers that were not quite yet a true mustache. "And was then still immature enough to fear growing fur. Da figured out what I was looking for and assured me any hair that sprouted meant I was growing into a man, not a literal wolf."

She smiled only for the memory of laughing about that with his father to burn her with contradictory impulses to either peck her husband's eyes out or run back into her lover's arms. Best to focus on her stepson's soul. "Fearing lycanthropy is your biggest defense. Lycanthropes don't experience fear the way we do."

"Deceiving someone gives me a thrill. And that scares me. I know how frail a conscience can be, and I don't like to endanger mine." Anthon knelt before her. She met his eyes. He took full advantage of the liberty granted and maintained eye contact. "But I would do anything—anything—to pro-tect you. Including rewrite our tragic history."

Hosanni swallowed. "Son, I know you only mean to suggest we pretend I made a far wiser decision than I did, but that would be a death trap for you. If the truth were discovered, why, even the Xenos count it evil for a man to have the same woman his father had. No, a strapping young man like you needs to court and marry for real, if you want to keep the path."

Anthon dropped his gaze and slouched on the floor.

Oh, good the bed was free. She sat on the edge and peered at the young man slumped at her feet. What troubled him? The Xenos state compounding her sin with his father? "Now that you're joined to Emi's house, you must wed an Emian bride. A daughter of Diakrinth must accept an Emian bride-groom to make her confession, but he can be a foreign convert." So long as he was willing to be a slave and his bride was willing to be his master. "My people are more concerned about preserving our culture than our blood."

"Aside from the hotheads who'd seek to kill me over my ancestry?"

"They are few in number, amen, but a threat to your life nonetheless."

"Aye, well, you and the villa lord aren't lying. He said the same when he warned me to hide my tattoos. Helping me steal myself is his idea of revenge on Romin." Anthon pulled himself off the floor and plopped on the stool. "The villa lord and I talked to the stagecoach company and worked out our route home. I've reserved tickets for us, but only had enough in my chariot fund to stamp them paid up to Medford, Oregon. Our stagecoach leaves in two days, and will reach Medford in five days. In Medford, we'll need to pay up at least to the Bend with my wages from here. To make up the difference, our host offered to buy the luggage only weighing us down."

Hosanni gulped. "Everything but the gold and silver robes. Those are priceless artifacts and have to go back to my mothers." She paused. "And my sewing." She wouldn't be doing as much sewing now, but it was her custom to buy fabric in palla lengths.

Anthon stared and shook his head. "Emi, save me from foolish women."

She bristled. "Beg your pardon?"

"If we're not robbed, it'll be the hand of God."

Hosanni winced. "You dishonor me."

"My apologies that the truth hurts, milady. Would it please you to let me continue, or would you not care to hear the rest of our schedule until we reach the Bend?"

She sighed. Anthon was catching on to her people's ways. She'd break it to him later that handling their money and travel plans should be the lady's role. That had never been among her strengths, and Anthon had inherited his father's skill in such things. "No, please continue." Hosanni nodded. There. She'd delegated it to him, like Mother would. "How long will we need to work in Medford to earn the tickets to the Bend?"

"No, I have to pay for the tickets when we get to Medford, so I have to scrape together the money here. And I will need to work on the villa outside Medford for a month to get the tickets from the Bend to the City of Trees. From there we will have to walk."

The baby stirred inside her. Hosanni pressed her left hand to her belly and stroked her daughter back. "How long will this take? I need to spend September waiting for the baby to make her appearance, and I want your sister born in Diakrinth."

Anthon hesitated. "When's the baby expected?"

"The last two weeks of September to the first two of October."

Anthon tapped his chin. "Two days here, five days to Medford, a month there, four days to the Bend, a two week layover there while we wait for our connecting coach, six days to the City of Trees . . . we will need to be traveling in early September, but I can get you to the City of Trees before you deliver."

But Alethe might think a stagecoach would be more comfortable from outside the safety of her mother's womb. Hosanni hugged her belly. "Please cooperate, Alethe. Please. Mum wants you safely born on Diakrinthian soil."

Chapter Twenty-Three

Meleon dragged two paintings of the ocean upstairs. The housekeeper's lads had brought home nearly everything but the reproductions of his private collection. His exhibit had gone on mainly because he'd already set everything up. It'd surely been a failure, without the artist present to impress the critics.

He tossed his cargo in a corner of his studio and stared at his work in progress, a table for four. Mother, Father, Brother, and Baby, who still had no face. Now Baby never would.

Who knew whether the royal guard would locate Tony? Could he face the lad if they did? He'd spent hours crying out that God could have Tony's life if it brought Astor and Havan back from the furnace. What kind of Da tried to bargain for one son's life with another's?

Meleon grabbed the painting of a table for four, and threw it across the room. He hurled another canvas and collapsed to the floor sobbing.

OUTSIDE THE ROYAL COURT, Meleon paced. This was suicide, but getting drunk had made him vomit and he couldn't bear the loneliness.

The king's chamberlain returned. "Your highness, his honor will see you. He's currently having an audience with the High Priest of Chance."

That draco could hear along with the world. Meleon entered the court. The only persons in attendance were a morbidly obese priest, the king, a dozen knights of the royal guard, and a handful of Romin's reprobate spawn.

Romin stood. "Ah, my son."

"Beggin' your pardon, but I have business." Meleon drew a breath. "In the matter of the death of Princess Hosanni, you have rightly accused myself and the woman whose name I will not befoul this court by pronouncin', but one guilty party has escaped censure."

Romin scowled. "Who is the devil? He will surely pay."

"Ye are the man!"

The red-necked reprobates glanced up from their wine glasses.

Romin gaped. "Son—"

Meleon laughed. "Don't insult me. Your family is but a pack of wolves and you are no exception. You made me expect crucifixion only to extended mercy, hopin' I'd forget who is the most responsible: you. You played God!"

The priest of Chance laughed. "He is a god."

"Bullocks! Romin is the lousiest deity ever a man bowed to. For proof, look no further than his bloote plan for peace! He bred his granddaughter like an animal, with a man she had never laid eyes on before that day, and didn't even care to ask her what she thought of blue men, let alone the alliance. Nor did he mean to ask the Diakrinthians if they wanted a hybrid king cooked up by a man who thinks he is a god." Meleon glared at Romin. "Your supreme arrogance led ye to play with the lives of others, and ye had no right!"

Meleon pointed at Romin. "I am but the last-born o' the house of Erin, and I'm a failure as a husband and a father, and a descendant o' murderous slave owners, but if ye ask me, Emi gave power to kings to protect the weak. Instead ye be taxing crops that didn't grow and carrying away children. Ye sucked the life out of Diakrinth, and ye want peace? Try givin' them justice."

The priest of Chance ripped his robes and screamed, "Blasphemy in the house of the King! Put away this wolf of a son!"

Meleon laughed. "Lycanthropy is a qualification for being his son. He didn't adopt me as a mercy. He did it hoping to salvage his precious alliance. Far as I'm concerned, let the whole bloote country burn! I reject this house."

Gasps filled the chamber.

He trembled, tensing against the tears that wanted out. He'd made a fool of himself enough before this court. "All I ever wanted was a family, but all I have left is a political contrivance. If that is all I can get, ye can banish me or crucify me for treason, but I won't partake in this travesty any longer." Meleon took deep breaths. It didn't bring back Astor and the baby. It couldn't, but he'd said his piece. Live or die, he was free.

Romin stood. "Everyone but Prince Meleon, out!"

The priest sputtered. "Your honor, you must have witnesses to sign the declaration of lycanthropy."

"I also require witnesses to sign death warrants. If anyone would like me to sign one for them, do remain." Romin cleared his throat. "Sir Stonewall, clear the chamber. If anyone enters without my blessing, their blood is on their own heads."

The minute the room emptied, Meleon sank to his knees. Romin came down off his dais and lowered himself onto the floor. "You're right."

"What?"

"You're right, except I'm not a wolf. At least no more than any monarch must be. But I think you know that."

"I'm angry."

Romin nodded. "So was I last week. Can you forgive me?"

"Forgive ye? When have ye ever asked anyone to forgive ye?"

"Now. What you did was wrong, but the responsibility ultimately lies with me. You needed to know that the king was just and reliable—and assessable. I should've kept watch over Princess Hosanni, as I should've checked up on you when you'd disappear from court for months and years at a time. You weren't a coward. You were watching out for your people, as you couldn't trust me."

"Your honor—"

"It's ironic, isn't in? For the past decade, the crown has fought to secure men from unlawful lycanthropy executions and from abusive wives. But the evil that I fought outside was in my own house. And, yes, Kristos would never willingly make a marriage alliance with any foreign power. But I would make them make peace, because I was almighty Romin." He laughed.

Meleon stared. "You didn't listen to your wife over Emi. I did."

Romin arched his eyebrow. "Would you like me to tell my story?"

Where did that come from? What was Romin talking about, his story?

"Didn't your papà tell you his story when he tattooed you?"

Oh. Romin had misunderstood that Erini custom. "You have no idea what Da and I talked about that day, and I don't care to hear your mockery. I am not remainin' in this house."

"Don't make me beg. Listen. Then decide."

Meleon sighed and settled in on his bottom. "Very well."

"Every school child in West California has been told my heroic father, in an era when men had no rights, saved me in infancy by getting a priestess of Chance to intervene on my behalf when my mother ordered me left to die. What history doesn't note is that he married the priestess two days after my mother dissolved him. The priestess was my father's lover."

So much for the saint of men's liberation.

Romin made a pyramid with his fingers. "When I was five, my father killed the priestess and made it look like an accident. He bought a marita to take care of me while he was away in the military. She loved me like I were her own, as if she didn't see my pink skin. She sang and played with me and taught me the path. I remember when I was thirteen, I told her, 'Mamma, I want to go to Diakrinth and become a Ravaner.'"

"You? Were you disappointed when she shut the door in your face?"

"She only said, 'That's in Emi's hand.' But when I was fourteen, my father came back from the army with my entire life mapped out. Initially, I refused to marry a Princess of Romin who didn't worship Emi." Romin's hand shook. "My father and a priest of Chance threw me into a dungeon for sixty days." Tears filled Romin's eyes. "On day forty-five, they brought me Mama's head on a pike. On day sixty, I weakly renounced Emi and forever was separated from her." Romin quivered.

Meleon's arms wanted to wrap around the traumatized pink lad who'd become the most powerful man in the world. He squinted. Romin, bawling?

Romin cleared his throat. "I married Crown Princess Desdemona Romin at fifteen. After but a month, on Father's advice, Desdemona lent me to the army." His gaze bored into Meleon. "Eleven months after I had last seen my wife, Marezza's mother was born."

Ouch. His adopted father's eyes reflected a familiar pain. He'd felt it even as he'd watched Tony grow into a strapping, lilac version of himself. "I see."

"When I turned seventeen, Desdemona became queen in the House of Romin. I returned to the palace to serve as king consort. Life was miserable. My father and my wife fought constantly."

"So history also neglected to mention your father being executed?"

Romin laughed. "Oh, your mother would've crucified him. Desdemona was more prudent due to his influence in the military. She figured instead, cut his cord, kill his son."

Meleon squinted at the feigned ghost. "I know history didn't omit that."

"The 'accident' that killed Desdemona was no accident. While out on our boat, she attacked me with a knife, and we fought over it. I won and threw her overboard. My father seized her lack of a designated heir to set me upon the throne of Romin, with the military's backing. Only after his death was I truly a sovereign king. After four years of transition, I began pursuing peace, building roads, lowering taxes, and I swore to Emi I'd do everything I could to restore the scepter to Kristos."

Meleon snorted. "You're the sovereign. You can do whatever you want."

"Perhaps your mother can afford to reign that way, but I can't. Alcatraz has powerful friends. Restoring the scepter to Kristos would ruin them. I'd be dead before it could happen. However, the public would defend me if I was bringing peace rather than simply taking away a cheap source of maritas, and their support would insulate me. Thus the book."

"And that is your whole story?"

"Not quite. I've never been one to stop to gawk at wrecks, so I've ignored my family when I've seen problems. They feigned civility and respect, and I drank it all up even when I knew they were lying. I saw little joy in this world other than the one child I'm certain is mine, Princess Porcia."

And she was barren.

"But then Emi blessed this house by giving it a good man. In the midst of all the children in adult bodies, a fifteen-year-old shamed them all."

Meleon squinted at Romin. "What are you implying?"

"I know you saved Prince Antonio. I thought it'd be like with my father and Prince Antonio would be a means to an end, but then I saw the way you cradled him at Chanukah. You don't know what joy your interactions with your son brought me. I saw something I never had and never could have."

Tony. Meleon winced, a deep sting burning in his chest. He'd betrayed his son. He couldn't get back the foolishness grief had blurted. But he could at least try to crawl out of his misery to worry about the child still alive.

Meleon set his jaw. "Any news of Tony yet?"

"Nothing good." Romin chewed his lip. "We received an anonymous tip this morning that Prince Antonio was spotted at a Napa Valley depot over a week ago. His older male companion is suspected of being a neo-abolitionist involved with the new underground stagecoach."

Meleon grinned, his shoulders lightening. "That's good news! We know where to look! Somewhere between here and Diakrinth, right?"

"I called off the search."

His body couldn't make up its mind whether to freeze or boil. "Why?"

"The crown prince has fallen into the hands of insurgents! The infiltrators left their consciences behind in Diakrinth, having vowed to destroy my house by any means. If we keep nosing around, we risk exposing his true identity to them. Should his so-called friends realize who he is, they will kill him. No, I won't risk his life. We'll have to hope he comes home on his own." A potent blend of love and fear shone in the sovereign king's eyes.

Meleon gaped. "You really care about me and Tony? Truly?"

Romin nodded. "You aren't eighth in my heart. You are Meleon Difelippo, my only true son. I ask you to stay in my house and be my real family."

Meleon shook his head. "I've blown it. With Astor gone, I'm dying, and if I can't go after Tony without endangering him, there's no point in living."

"There is one. The kindest thing my father did was encourage my wife to loan me to the army. They made a man of me. I will be frank. Your upbringing has prepared you to spend your life as a sheltered boy. And yet, when I look in your eyes, I see what Princess Hosanni saw when she named you. You have the heart of a lion, but only the kiln's fire can bring it to full fruition."

"Are ye sayin' ye're acceptin' Marezza's loan of my person to the army even though ye disowned her?"

Romin smiled. "She owes you at least one favor. Military service will give you a reason to carry on. It'll make you the Lionheart you were born to be."

"Will Tony finally be proud of me? Proud enough to come home?"

"I hope so. Though he ought to be proud of your art. It's quite good."

"But you didn't go to the shows. They would have remembered."

"I sent a buyer. I have a few pieces in the great hall." Romin wrapped an arm around Meleon's shoulder. "Will you accept me? I'm frankly not all that great of a father, either."

The Sovereign King of the Nations—west of the Mississippi—wanted a relationship with him?

Meleon's lip quivered. "Right now, we're all we have, Da."

GOD stands center stage. ARGEVANE and BION enter carrying a large stone box with a wooden lever. GOD. I have laid before you everything under the sun and held no secret back from you, but the portal between the twin worlds you must not open, lest you die, for Adam has fallen.

GOD and ARGEVANE exit.

BION puts the forbidden machine aside and paces, trying not to look at it, but at last ends up standing right beside it.

BION. Have I not built this machine? I must know its mysteries!

— Pauli of Denver, The Sacred History, "Creation" scene 2, lines 1, 10-15

Chapter Twenty-Four

E very inch of Hosanni throbbed. Physically, she felt as cumbersome and parched as a beached sea dragon. Her bare calves complained much about being squeezed in between the hard stagecoach door and the rough, heavy cotton of Anthon's indigo tunic.

The ivory white Tower of Kristos rose above them, gleaming in the sun from within High Queen Agapeta's citadel on the Rock of the Table. Hosanni's breath caught. Somehow, the glory of the City of Trees made journeying while this pregnant worth the suffering.

Anthon's labor-hardened hand slipped into hers and squeezed. "That's your ancestral castle up there, isn't it?"

She kept her eyes on the beautiful citadel. "Yes. The invaders hold it."

"I see why tourists come all the way out here to see this. It's beautiful. Nearly as beautiful as its rightful queen."

She shot Anthon a warning glance. Several of their companions sent him sympathetic looks that only accentuated her point. Her female ego ate up her son's compliments, but his encouragements confused the other passengers. All the mourning veil had changed was now rude strangers asked whether her "new husband" or her late husband had fathered her child. After the second time the assumptions had made her vomit, Anthon started outright lying about her being his widowed cousin.

The aggie across from her in the stagecoach leaned forward. "Honey, take my advice. Marry him. He clearly loves you, and the wee one needs a pappy whether you're ready to leave mourning or not."

Hosanni forced a polite smile. How much longer until they reached the stagecoach station and she and Anthon were rid of such busybodies? Their well-intentioned, unrequested advice couldn't be any easier on him.

She dropped her eyes to the City of Trees, its green foliage spotted with autumn's creeping influence. The round, stucco buildings stood on one side of the street, and Romini style architecture on the other side. Even here, in a capital city a thousand Xenos called home, life in Diakrinth hadn't changed much in three hundred years.

The stagecoach came to a stop. A chill clutched at her veil. The station was on the hillside where the Romini herded together the stolen daughters of Diakrinth for shearing.

Anthon asked, "Milady, are you all right?"

Hosanni turned to him. "No, but this lamentation can wait. I want out of this tin can as speedily as possible."

The other Diakrinthians on board declared their amens.

The coachman opened the doors and helped Hosanni out before assisting the other ladies. Hosanni shifted through the crowd of gawkers and lowered gingerly into a nearby stone park bench to wait for Anthon.

A few minutes later, he dropped at her feet the much lighter carpetbag and his black canvas football equipment bag. He tapped a passerby. "Do you know of any nearby villas hiring day laborers?"

Hosanni looked away and shut her ears. By foot, the recommended villa was another two days' journey, and a chariot could not be hired with an empty purse. No, they needed to find a place closer. This close to delivery, Alethe never seemed to cease flailing her limbs and the wonderment had worn off when her daughter had grown enough to inflict pain on her poor mother.

But begging for work was still embarrassing.

Hosanni glanced back to the young prince totally debasing himself by his father's standards. Anthon bowed, made the sign of the sacrifice, and politely refrained from direct eye contact with the women he stopped. If she didn't know how she acquired the son of her bosom, she'd have never guessed that Anthon was any less Diakrinthian than Korban.

Amazing. She'd felt increasingly the hypocrite as she'd guided Anthon onto the path of Diakrinth. Why he'd persisted, she couldn't imagine. He'd witnessed her railing against the God she was supposed to be teaching him to serve. She hadn't even been aware of the ugly lamentations trapped inside her until this son's undeserved love eroded her walls into ruins.

Now she felt nothing but empty. Weary, worn, and surely spent of tears.

Where was Emi? Certainly, she'd brought this present sorrow on herself by giving her heart and her maidenhood to a married, Xenos, liberated man, but where was Emi in the beginning? Why had she lost her glory on this hill?

Mammy's voice echoed. "Sometimes, Emi's hand delivers us through our troubles rather than out of them. Let us be like Queen Agapeta, who, though her bisonherd led her through the valley of the shadow of death, did not fear, for Emi was with her."

But where, Mammy? Where is Emi in any of this? I feel so alone.

Hosanni sniffled. She was losing her mind, talking to the memory of one of her dead mother's most favorite and oft-repeated sermons.

She whispered, "Emi, where are you?"

Anthon slumped onto the bench beside her with a heavy sigh and pressed his left hand against the tiny knees poking Hosanni. Tears dampened his eyes. He blinked. "Don't worry, wee one. I'll find you a place. Emi's hand will show us the path. It might just take a while."

From the dispersing crowd came a maiden wearing the traditional twin braids and an expensive white linen palla trimmed in gold. Hosanni blinked. The maiden's glory fell to her thighs, her right cheek bore a beauty mark, and the face was a bit rounder, but otherwise, the maiden could have been her twin sister, albeit she was a smidge younger than Hosanni's twenty-one.

She glanced between the maiden and the gaping Anthon and smiled. That was a first. She whispered in his ear, "You're staring, son."

Anthon cleared his throat and ceased the rude behavior.

The wealthy maiden reached them and curtsied. "Shalom and Emi's hand be with you."

Anthon made the sign of the Sacrifice and replied with a quaver, "And Emi's hand be with you, amen."

Hosanni beamed. Her pupil had remembered the correct response.

"I am Maid Charis, of the City of Trees Juristekons. And you are?"

Clearly rich city girls had more opportunities to practice their English. "I am Hosanni Kristekon of Valley County. This is Anthon."

"May we help you?" he asked.

Maid Charis laughed. "I had wondered if you were in need of help. You have the countenances of stranded wayfarers, and, with a child on the way, it saddens me to see so little hospitality shown. So, I hope Mother and Father will forgive me for offering their aid yet again."

Anthon jumped to his feet and lifted Maid Charis's hand to his lips as done in the royal courts he was born to dwell in. "We are in your debt."

Maid Charis smiled. "If that offends you, I am sure my father could find something around the villa for you to do."

"Villa!" Anthon cleared his throat. "If you could put in a good word for me with the lord of the villa, I do desperately need employment, fair maid."

Hosanni groaned inwardly. Sometimes villa lords were permitted to do the hiring, but generally that was the lady's prerogative.

Yet Maid Charis only giggled. "Consider yourself hired. Pappy never turns me down unless it's something he thinks will kill me."

Maid Charis picked up Hosanni's carpetbag. "I came to people watch, so, if you're ready, I have the Llama. Let me check in with my escort, and I can take you home."

A Llama? Who owned that brand of chariot in Diakrinth? Those chariots were luxurious symbols of status by any nation's standard.

Anthon helped her to her feet. She waddled to Charis and hugged her new best friend. Hosanni said, "Thank you, Maid Charis. Your mother named you well, for you are the grace of graces."

"Thank you." Her friend smiled, batting her lashes at Anthon. "I left my escort over this way."

Hosanni followed, letting Anthon and Maid Charis go ahead of her into the park-like gardens, away from the multitude. Hosanni smiled at the pair so obviously trying not to stare at each other. She'd have to ensure Maid Charis knew Anthon was single and hence safe to "covet." But later. It wouldn't do to embarrass him.

Several minutes later, Anthon and Maid Charis turned around and came back toward her, ducking their heads. Hosanni frowned. Strange. Oh—they must have gotten preoccupied with chatting and walked right past her escort.

That was it, now she had to play matchmaker. She'd much rather leave Anthon behind in the City of Trees, where he'd surely face less prejudice, and the best excuse she could think of was marrying Anthon off.

Plus the plan to abandon her baby at the gate had two huge problems. One, Anthon would rush headlong to take up his own baby sister, if his little fathering was an indication. Two, she longed to truly complete the labor she'd begun and raise her child. Make that three. She and Anthon couldn't both be Alethe's Mammy and Pappy.

Anthon and Maid Charis approached a young lady seated on a granite park bench. The young lady wore bridal ivory and a cerulean palla, which had the bosom open as she nursed a child about twelve months old through the fly of her nursing undershirt. Why did she look so familiar?

Hosanni caught up. Maid Charis spoke to the young lady and pointed at Anthon and Hosanni. "I would like you to meet Anthon Kristekon and his cousin Hosanni. The poor dear was widowed in July, and her cousin chose to escort her to our motherland. I hired him, so I need to get them home."

Nausea rolled over Hosanni as she saw through the years and the change in wardrobe to why Maid Charis's escort was staring at her in open disbelief.

Maid Charis turned to Hosanni and waved to her escort. "Oh, I would like you to meet one of our hireling wives, my dear friend, Lady Paraclete."

Hosanni fought to breathe. She whispered, "Emi's hand."

Paraclete nodded mutely.

Brows knit, Maid Charis asked, "What did I miss?"

Hosanni's old school friend kept her eyes on her. "She'll explain later. Why don't you two . . ." Paraclete waved at Anthon and Maid Charis. "Make yourselves acquainted in the chariot while Hosanni keeps me company here? Once this one's done, we'll go." Paraclete patted the child nursing on her lap.

Maid Charis smiled. "By all means, take however much time you need."

Hosanni lowered onto the park bench beside Paraclete.

The minute Maid Charis and Anthon were out of sight, Paraclete turned to Hosanni, gaping, and pointed in the direction Anthon had gone. "Is that who I think it is?"

"I would have hoped for, 'Hosanni! Isn't this a wonderful surprise!'"

Paraclete's eyes danced. "Emi's hand is wonderful, but what's a surprise is you around eight months pregnant—and here with Prince Antonio, who is using a false identity?"

Hosanni winced. "His first name is given truly enough. Everyone but his father and his mother's family honestly do call him Anthon, we never said his name was Kristekon, and for the rest, well, he's only trying to protect me as any good son would."

"Son?"

The whole sad song tumbled out. By the end of it, Hosanni had somehow found more tears to cry, had soaked through the shoulder of her palla, and rubbed her nose raw by blowing it. Paraclete's child had finished nursing and slept contentedly in her mother's arms.

Hosanni sniffled. "I should have listened to you. I should have listened to Sir Armstrong. I should have listened to Korban, too, and stayed in the barn that awful day when childhood ended. That was Logos speaking through all of you. Showing me the path. And I ignored you and went my own way."

Paraclete nodded. "You forgot one of us."

"Who?"

"Your husband. Prince Coyote, the night before you left without him."

Hosanni gaped. His bad dream? "He thought he saw a brownie, nor was he serious about picking up and leaving everything. We wouldn't have gotten past the city limits before he had realized on his own it was just his nerves. Coyote's only doctrine is liberty and his only creed his own heart's sense of right and wrong. He'd be the first to tell you he is a stranger to Emi."

"Most of us aren't this aware of Emi's hand upon us, Hosanni. It wouldn't surprise me if some of us didn't even know we belong to Emi."

Hosanni stared at the cobblestone path, shaking her head. Coyote? He was a prince. Emi had moved the hearts of Xenos royalty for her own devices in the Sacred History. Perhaps that was what Paraclete had in mind. "What do I do now?"

"Would you listen to me if I gave you my advice?"

Hosanni winced. "I deserved that." She drew a deep breath. "I deserve execution, Paraclete. And the life inside me has won out over death."

"You're out of Marezza's reach. And all you need to do to satisfy Emi's law is turn back to the path and be washed clean in the blood of the Sacrifice."

Oh dear. "But I didn't . . . the Ravane who married us didn't even ask if I wanted to make my confession and receive the Sacrifice."

"You needed to request it. In the Diaspora, brides don't need to wait until they're chosen by a bridegroom to convert. So be of good cheer. When you do make your confession, your sins will be washed away."

"But the only bridegroom my heart could bear to stand at an altar with is my baby's father. And Lady Veritas—how can I be forgiven after killing her?"

Paraclete laughed. "Don't be silly. You can't kill Lady Veritas."

"But I didn't marry her father. I threw my love away on a stranger. Now Lady Veritas will never be born."

"Little sister, the man you actually married is always the right one after the fact. Emi will bring Lady Veritas to us in Emi's own time and in Emi's own way." Paraclete hugged Hosanni. "No matter how badly her mother strays."

"But it was all a lie. Our marriage."

"More like a legal paradox. So long as he comes for you before next July, the second Prince Coyote sets foot on Diakrinthian soil, he is your husband, not Marezza's. Emi hates what is happening to the two of you, Hosanni. So that's my first pearl. Give your husband a second chance. Write him. Find out if you truly are worth giving up his Xenos life for."

The pain that not heeding him had caused made serving Coyote better far more appealing than seeking to go from his slave to his master. But if there was even the tiniest hope Coyote was willing to convert, it would be better than losing him entirely. "I will write, I promise."

"Second pearl then." Paraclete cleared her throat. "Little sister, not only take him back, forgive him. A new mother's hormones and your lycanthrope bite symptoms are causing you to way overreact on that poor man."

"He walked out on me!"

"Welcome to reality, little sister. Men are but flawed creatures of inferior emotional intelligence. I'm sure he has a reasonable-to-him explanation and is frantic worrying about you, totally shocked and confused by all this."

Would he fall on his knees or rush into her arms when he apologized to her profusely, promising to never leave her ever again?

She smiled. "Was there a third pearl? I have a letter to write."

Paraclete's eyes twinkled. "I know Maid Charis. She's still single because she's incredibly choosy when it comes to men. Based on first impressions, I'd say Prince Antonio measures up in her eyes. One thing that will automatically disqualify him, however, is lying. The sooner he comes clean, the better his chances of a happy future with her."

Reasonable. So long as Anthon didn't 'come clean' about her. "Thanks for the tip. I'll warn him."

Paraclete lifted her sleepy child to her shoulder and leaned forward. "I'm serious, Hosanni. On the stagecoach, the truth wasn't anyone's business to start with, but this could become a permanent position for Prince Antonio.

Lying to the Juristekons will have devastating consequences unless you set the record straight."

NEAR DUSK, MELEON DID extra pushups in Fort Quentin's Physical Training yard. The loss of Astor and his sons still haunted him, especially when the baby would have been born about now. But it didn't incapacitate him as he'd anticipated. Perhaps all the fat he'd already converted into muscle had helped. Tony would be so proud.

"Patrolman Difelippo!"

Meleon jumped up and saluted his captain. "Yes, sir."

"I got word an Imperial Decree was issued today in your honor, declaring you are brave, noble, and courageous."

Given the gossip rags had been usin' Romin's statements about Meleon the day Astor died to attack him as 'The Cowardly Patrolman'? It'd help. "It's appreciated, though I don't know if I've done anything to merit this."

The captain handed Meleon a letter. "This came addressed to you."

Meleon opened it.

My Dearest Meleon,

I'm sorry my words spoken in anger have hurt you in the press. This new decree expresses the man I see you becoming.

I'm off to the Vermillion Rock Palace for three weeks, but I'll write when I get there. Perhaps I can take you some day. I'd love to see your painting of them.

Your Da

Sure, someday, he'd paint again. Astor would want that. The irony was brutal, though. After the demand created by the rave reviews he received at the art fair, his sudden scarcity was driving the price of his paintings up to museum levels. Meleon folded the letter. *Thank you, Emi, for not leaving me completely desolate.*

Chapter Twenty-Five

Hosanni reclined on a spare feather pallet in the upper room of her cramped hireling house at the Juristekon villa. The dying sun shone in one corner of the glass dome roof above. A straw bassinet lay across from the earth closet. Indigo tunics and swaddling hung from the dress pegs. Her pallas peeked out the open door to the marriage bed closet. She used it as a bedroom so Anthon didn't have to sleep with his stepmother. Still, he'd perceived the upper room was Diakrinth's nearest equivalent to a drawing room, and theirs was his favorite spot for wooing Maid Charis.

At the moment, Hosanni could only see the child suckling at her breast. She smiled at the little wrinkled, slightly misshapen head. Sure enough, her baby was a hue of purple right in between her and the father and had a head full of tiny coils. Sensing her newborn nodding off, she plucked the baby away from her breast and closed up her palla.

She unwrapped the soiled swaddling binding her newborn and counted, for the thousandth time in the last few days, all ten tiny fingers and all ten tiny toes. She giggled.

October 9, 5745. The day my unborn daughter Alethe "died" and my beautiful son Havan was born.

What was it with her sons? Anthon was born on the eve of the Diaspora's Chanukah and Havan on the eve of the Diaspora's Day of Atonement. Was that a sign the younger would be greater than the elder? Hosanni laughed. More likely, it was a sign that she was biased toward her own offspring.

Leaving the baby unbound, Hosanni cradled Havan in her arms, kissed his chubby cheek, and whispered, "You are a boy. Just like Da said, Havan."

Maybe his father would answer the letter she'd sent. Maybe she'd have to tell the Juristekons Havan's father was alive—and not Anthon's cousin. Maid

Charis and Anthon used her as their escort, so she got to watch them court. And to listen to truthful accounts of his past that, with her shame carefully omitted, had rendered her husband his own cousin. Thankfully, Maid Charis knew too little of foreign politics to catch that lie.

But unless Hosanni's bridegroom came to save her from the mess she'd made—What if the Juristekons rejected her?

No, she'd wait for her husband. With him back by her side, it wouldn't matter. They could find another villa and should visit her family regardless. Moving back home wouldn't be an option. She wanted her son raised in the City of Trees, where no one seemed to mind his obvious blue paternity. For added bonus, the city amenities lessened the culture shock.

Diakrinth seemed squalid after living in the lap of luxury. At least on the Juristekon villa, her cellar had a bathtub fed by her cistern, and a soilman serviced the squat-style earth closets. In all of Diakrinth, Anthon would be happiest here, and so would his father.

Havan split her ears with his cry that meant, "I'm not quite used to all this liberty yet, Mum."

She kissed the baby. "Fine, Fine. Back you go, go." She glanced across the room to Anthon and Maid Charis and waved to the rows of swaddling above them. "Could you fetch one of those for me?"

Anthon stood, pulled down one, and started to toss it, but stopped and walked it over properly.

Hosanni took the fresh swaddling. "Thank you, Anthon." She wrapped his baby brother back up. Havan's cries silenced. She held the newborn out to his older brother. "Could you take him? I need to use the earth closet."

The baby slid into his brother's waiting arms. Little Havan yawned and nodded off. Mum smiled. So far, the baby felt unsafe in the arms of anyone but her or Anthon. She'd known how much Anthon had been talking to the baby when Havan was born recognizing his elder brother's voice.

Inside the earth closet, she dropped the baby's soiled swaddling into the straw laundry basket before attending her personal needs.

Afterward, she turned toward the door.

"I love you, Havan," said her husband's muffled voice in the upper room.

Her heart leapt. She frowned. *That's your eldest son, not your husband.*

She opened the door a crack, but stopped. Anthon and Maid Charis bent together over the bundle asleep in Anthon's arms. Hosanni's throat caught. Naturally, the baby stirred Maid Charis's little mother instincts, but the three of them together—the image both warmed and tore her heart. If Havan's father didn't come—his father had to come.

Maid Charis sniffled. Anthon glanced up at her. "Charis, what's wrong?"

"I feel like a skunk." Maid Charis dabbed at her tears. "I know what I said, but this last month together has been so wonderful." She sighed. "I'm fond of you and want badly for—for—us—"

Anthon set his baby brother on his lap and put a finger to Maid Charis's lips. "I am fond of you, too. More than fond. And Hosanni—" Anthon picked up his baby brother and cradled Havan the way she'd dreamed of their father holding his son. "I understand how she feels now. I was eleven and motherless when she joined our family."

Maid Charis clucked her tongue. "Ah, yes, that does make sense. You're more like a baby brother in her eyes than a cousin, eh?"

"Something like that." Anthon kissed his baby brother. "Truthfully, milady, it's this one holding me back. I remember what it was like growing up without a mother, and I can't imagine the hole in the heart being any smaller when the father's gone. Except I don't see that hole in his eyes. He thinks I'm his father. I know it, and I feel it, too." Tears glistened in Anthon's eyes. "So what do I do, Charis? When you are the beauty my heart is dreaming of?"

Hosanni tightened her grip on the door handle and grinned. *I knew it!*

Maid Charis melted like way any maiden in love would upon hearing that from her beau. Anthon set the baby down on the floor and drank from Maid Charis's cistern.

Hosanni hesitated. Would doing her job make her a hypocrite?

Wee Havan cried a loud complaint about being left on the floor. Hosanni rushed to pick her baby up and rocked him in her arms, shushing him.

Anthon and Maid Charis broke apart and sent her guilty glances.

Hosanni settled on the pallet across the room. "Loves, don't fret about Havan. I haven't made up my mind whether I'm keeping him. If I do, consider my foster brother. Hotheads had murdered his father, but he had my father and looked up to him greatly. Korban saw me as a path to joining our house permanently." A fact she had ignored as a child. "Uncle Anthon can make as much difference in this little one's life as a stepfather could." Everyone used uncle to mean a father figure not married to the mother, right?

Anthon bit his lip. "But don't you mean to leave us?"

Heaviness tightened Hosanni's chest. "I miss my own house, but I'd also miss my son, and I do not want him raised there. Not after the shadows that haunted Korban's eyes. He felt so ashamed, he tried to make it sound like his Erini relation was very distant. But I've known better ever since I met you, Anthon. This one tells me what Korban's father looked like." She kissed her dear boy on his little blue forehead. "No. I don't want my son to be murdered or taught his skin color makes him less of a Diakrinthian."

Not to mention the shame of his father's absence. No, if his father didn't come, the child would be better off left with Anthon and Maid Charis. But the thought of it made her want to curl up and die.

She placed Havan in his straw bassinet and cleared her throat. "So don't worry about Havan, loves. One way or another, he is staying here."

Anthon turned to Maid Charis. "Would your parents think it too soon for me to take a couple hair ribbons off your hands?"

Maid Charis answered by yanking the ribbons out of her braids herself and handing them over to her beau. Anthon grinned and tied the ribbons to their left wrists.

Hosanni hugged her bosom cousin. "Now, *that* has to be the fastest any Diakrinthian maiden has ever become a lady."

Lady Charis scrunched her eyebrows together. "I've only kissed him."

Hosanni giggled. "Cousin, of course you aren't pregnant yet. As the bride of a prince, and the daughter of commoners, you are now owed the title of 'Lady' in Romin's court." She hugged her elder son. "May I have the honor of giving you away?"

Anthon hesitated. He shrugged. "Since you're my only kinswoman here, that would be appropriate."

More than she prayed the Juristekons would ever know. While she hoped she'd need to tell them he was her stepson, Anthon could now appreciate how embarrassing Romin's attempt at matchmaking had proved.

SMOKE ROSE ON THE HORIZON. Meleon pointed. "Sir, right."

"I see it, partner." Senior Patrolman Diangelina turned their black and white chariot toward the stagecoach depot. Traffic clogged the street.

Meleon reached into the back seat, grabbed their gas lamp, and lit it. It shone red through the paint. He reached out his window, leaned forward, and hooked the lamp on the upper corner of the windshield.

As the junior partner, Meleon now had to clear the street. He grabbed his speaking trumpet. "All traffic clear! All traffic clear!"

The chariots ahead of them moved aside, revealing a burning stagecoach. Ten feet away, five singed pink merchants huddled together with the driver.

Diangelina pushed their horses to go as fast as they could gallop. The two patrolmen reached the wreck and jumped out of the chariot. Meleon and his partner ran to the driver. Diangelina asked, "Is everyone out?"

The driver nodded and wheezed.

Diangelina asked, "What happened here?"

The driver coughed for a minute. "As soon as I stopped the stagecoach, I felt something hit the side, and it burst into flames."

Diangelina said, "We'll need to call on the Intelligence squad. This looks like the work of those Diakrinthian insurgents."

Meleon's jaw tightened. Blokes like these not only made it unsafe to go after Tony, they got innocent Diakrinthians hurt. He shuddered, recalling his housekeeper's bruised face from the assault that she had suffered after the last insurgent attack. *Emi, she's your child. Please watch over her.*

Diangelina stared at the stagecoach-shaped fireball. "Was there anything important on board?"

The driver nodded. "The mail. Ironically, the route began in Diakrinth, so they hurt their own people, if they were Diakrinthian."

Meleon sighed. "At least it was coming here. Hopefully, the mail didn't contain anything too important."

IN THE UPPER ROOM, instead of suckling, Hosanni's nine-month-old sank his little incisors into her nipple for the fourth attempted feeding in a row. She winced and loosed the squirming, fussy baby. "Fine, Havan, be that way! See if Mum cares."

The instantly content child crawled away from her and toward the ladder with the long fall that sensible little girls knew to avoid. Paraclete's two-year-old daughter, after all, was napping as far away from the hole as she could get. But Hosanni's precious son liked to treat the hazard like a toy.

She sniffled and blinked tears. *Is it my fault he is so hard-headed?*

Paraclete hugged her. "You were a witch, Hosanni. You ought to know that babies his age can get so busy exploring and learning new things, boring old things like nursing aren't as high a priority as they should be. It's a phase. He'll realize that he still needs Mammy soon enough."

Hosanni hiccupped. "I still feel abandoned, unwanted, and rejected."

Her baby pulled himself up on the ladder rungs hanging over the edge of the hole so nearly underneath him. She rushed to grab him, but before she could reach him, he wiggled along the wall, away from the ladder. He pushed off the wall, attempted to take a step unassisted, and fell on his rump.

Her son grunted and crawled right back to the ladder to try again.

"Oh no you don't!" Hosanni snatched her baby boy up by his armpits and glared at him. "Stop it, Havan! Stop trying to grow up and leave me! You're only a baby! Why do you want to walk away from me?"

Her son scrunched his little eyebrows together and wailed his confusion.

Little Karisma awoke and started crying, too. Paraclete rubbed her child's back. "Shh, daughter, you're fine, go back to sleep."

Hosanni rocked her baby. "Mum loves you, Havan. Don't cry."

But her wee one squirmed and writhed in her arms, trying to escape their confinement. She sighed. Her baby wanted released to go back to his trying to become a toddler, not comforted. She set him down beside Paraclete and the sniffling Karisma, already half asleep again.

Hosanni's son crawled back to the ladder. She quivered with the effort to keep back the tears welling up. Paraclete rose, picked Little Havan up, and carried him down to the kitchen. A baby giggle echoed up to Hosanni.

She glanced to Karisma. Asleep.

By the time Hosanni got downstairs, Havan was already pulling himself up on the doors of the cabinets under the stone kitchen counter. He stepped away and made it two steps before falling. Hosanni sobbed.

Paraclete picked up the baby boy crawling back to the counter to try again and hugged him. "Well, Havan, Auntie Paraclete's proud of you!"

She kissed Hosanni's son, set him down to keep at it some more, and frowned at Hosanni, shaking her head. "What's wrong? And I mean really."

Hosanni pointed to the 5746 solar calendar hanging from a wall rod by a scarlet cord. Each day in July was crossed out until the twelfth. She sniffled. "On this day, I would have legally become a widow." Her lip wobbled. "If I had ever legally been a wife in the first place."

She twisted off the ivory wedding ring she still wore, pushed open a crystal window, and threw her ring as hard as she could. Sobbing, she sank into one of the pillows around the thick straw mat that her people called a table. Paraclete settled beside her and wrapped Hosanni in her arms.

Hosanni quavered. Why?

She'd hoped Emi wanted her to write Coyote so they could be a family again, but apparently Emi hadn't been done chastening her. Truthfully, she'd wanted him to come, not to follow the path, but to take her and the baby back to West California. She'd been so sure he loved her and the baby. How could he abandon them so easily, so permanently? So suddenly? Maybe Marezza had gotten him executed—no, his precious alliance would definitely crumble if Romin allowed any harm to come to Erin's last born.

Maybe Emi had thwarted him. Saved Hosanni from herself. Even if he'd wanted to live in Diakrinth, 'try' had been the key word regarding turning things right side up. She liked her husband being the head of their home. She missed his leadership as much as she missed their marriage bed. Or was it *porneia* and all a deception and a lie, after all?

What if, when caught, Coyote truly had wanted Marezza to take care of his little problem? If only she could know for sure.

Would it really be wrong to read the newspaper? In her circumstances, it offered needful knowledge—no, the aggies' highest council in Diakrinth, the prime councilor herself no less, had ruled it was a sin to read the newspaper without exception. How dare she question Emi's representative? Hosanni had enough divine wrath stored up against her already.

She choked out, "Emi, I know I've been foolish. I was angry that you let me suffer so and 'punished' you by deliberately straying from the path. I'm sorry. Give me a new heart to follow your path, no matter how painful each step back home is. This hurts so bad. But I think I am finally fully persuaded that I never want to do that again."

A baby giggled and little hands slapped her shoulder. "Mum-ma!" Little Havan crawled into her lap and nuzzled at her bosom.

Paraclete patted his rump. "Good boy!"

Hosanni frowned. "That was only baby talk, Paraclete."

"You missed it? He made it all the way to you without falling. Someone knows Mammy's sad." Paraclete nodded to the nine-month-old trying to open the fly of Hosanni's undershirt with his mouth. One little hand clutched at his favorite breast.

She sniffled and gave her baby the nipple he sought. Comforting her with what always comforted him? Her little lion cub did have his sweet side.

Hosanni tightened her arms around her dear baby boy.

If only she could keep him.

Chapter Twenty-Six

Serenity poured through Hosanni even as her heart ached. She rocked the nine-month-old who ought to be quite thirsty for her milk. From now on, Lady Charis would have to feed him the pitiful substitute known as formula along with his baby mush. Her friend had proved one of those brides that leave the bridal tent pregnant, and would have milk of her own in another month, but the thought of Havan suckling from another woman, calling her Mammy . . . no. This couldn't be the right path.

Hosanni glanced to Paraclete, seated at her side on the gray pillows around the straw-woven table. "What now?"

Paraclete arched an eyebrow. "Regarding . . . ."

Hosanni stroked her baby's back. "Does Emi want me to keep him?"

"Looks to me like you already have."

"But I don't belong here. I should go home."

Paraclete nodded. "I'll miss you two." She patted Havan's rump.

"Not us. Me. I can't take him. Not without his father."

Paraclete's eyes understood. "And Pappy's married to Auntie Charis."

Hosanni frowned.

Paraclete put a finger to her lips. "You and I know better. But that doesn't change how your Anthon and your Havan feel about each other." Paraclete shook her head. "I wish I had an easy answer. But Emi has not spoken to me on this, and I'm not comfortable speaking from my own bosom, I'm sorry."

In a way, Paraclete had answered. How could Hosanni subject Havan to losing Anthon as well as their father? Lady Charis would plug for Havan the hole Marezza had left in Anthon's heart, however unwelcome the thought.

"And Korban's alive," Hosanni whispered.

Paraclete's eyes widened. "Are you sure?"

She nodded. "I ran into his younger brother at the Samantha Walton's Market. My cousin's been living down here since we were sophomores, and didn't have any recent news, but he was quite certain Korban survived. He laughed at me. 'Korban's too mean to die.' Mind you, that's the opinion of the little brother still sore over a childhood rivalry."

"Korban is probably married."

"I certainly hope so."

Paraclete blinked at her. "You do?"

"If my foster brother were alive and still waiting for me, that would be so obviously Emi's hand, how could I not marry him? Doubly so when he'd be my only option out of his teens. But he only wanted a permanent position in our house, and my only attraction to another bridegroom choosing me is that it's required to make my confession and bear Lady Veritas."

"Don't fret about Lady Veritas. Remember, Mother Cyria made a mess by thinking her husband committing adultery could produce the promised child. But Emi multiplied her husband's seed, and he sowed Gelan at ninety! Emi's hand will deliver in her time and her way."

Hosanni sighed. "What about my confession? I'm damned without it."

"You could always stay here. Emi could yet bring your husband back from the dead. Tell our Ravane the truth, and she'll baptize you and pour the wine over you. If you do go home, you'll be dealing with your own clan sisters. Your family ought to help you to return to the path, not hinder you—and especially not feed you to the dragons, little sister. They love you, and you've repented." Paraclete reached up and pulled the bridal ivory from her hair. Her own glory still only fell to the bust. "Everyone knows that I don't have a full head of hair bound up with my ivory, and they know why that is. Don't be afraid."

Easy for Paraclete to say. She'd married a true man of honor who didn't have any other entanglements. Hosanni released a long breath. "I should risk going home, for honor's sake. What kind of only daughter leaves her duty to care for her widowed father to others?"

"True. You should check on him, verify that he's remarried."

"No! He wouldn't."

"I know you don't want to think about this in relation to your pappy, but most widowers either remarry or die within a year of losing their wife."

"I know he must be suffering terribly, but Pappy is far too strong to have died, and I can't see him choosing another. He loved my mother too much to love someone else." Mother's worst fear was too shameful to speak, but he'd certainly not choose her aunt.

Unless Aunt Juris seduced Father.

Hosanni frowned. She was being as silly as her mother had been. Amen, Father despised Aunt Juris, and Aunt Juris would never betray Mother. "No, before I see my father remarried, I will see my husband in another woman's arms. And that is one betrayal I'll never suffer, I assure you."

"For your sake, little sister, I hope you're right." Paraclete nibbled her lip. "Amen, I hate to see that wee one lose either you or the only pappy he knows."

Hosanni cradled her Havan as the baby slept on her lap after what must be their last feeding. Tears dribbled down her chin. Paraclete was right. The baby didn't love Lady Charis as much as Mum, but he already seemed aware Lady Charis was Pappy's wife. Sorrow was inevitable for Havan. Best for him not to grow up in the confusing situation her bosom's desire currently had in store, being raised by Mum, "Uncle Anthon" and "Aunt Charis."

No, best for him to be raised by Mammy and Pappy.

If she left now, he was still young enough to forget she used to be Mum.

HOSANNI AND ANTHON neared the gate of the Temple, a museum dedicated to the tribe of Harmone, who served as priests here before their holocaust. Along the temple wall, hundreds of wee ones lay dying of exposure. The blind. The lame. The deaf. The crippled. The maimed. The feeble-minded. All of them lay here, abandoned at the gate. A dozen or so survivors rattled tin vessels.

Visitors going inside to pray and to lament their dead sisters walked past like the children weren't there.

Hosanni's bosom screamed rage, but there were so many here, and she was one woman. She shouldn't even know how to help them, even if she could have done anything to change what Emi's hand had dealt. No. She clutched her precious baby boy tighter in her arms. *No, I can't believe that.*

Emi didn't do this. Womankind and our first father's curiosity did this.

Anthon turned to her, trembling. "I've heard of places like this, but never seen it. Why have we come here?"

"To visit the temple like I said."

Anthon nodded and glanced over the beggars and the dying. He walked down the line of discarded children and stopped before an unwashed urchin with poorly kept dreadlocks. The lad was perhaps only two years younger than Anthon, who asked him, "Why are you here?"

The urchin showed them he couldn't straighten out the index finger of his strong hand. Hosanni winced. This injury could happen to anyone and was easily treatable. She forced herself to turn away. It was already too late.

Behind her, Anthon said, "Brother, if a bath, food, shelter, and honest work sounds interesting, follow me."

The urchin shouted, "Hosanna!"

She gaped at Anthon. "What was that?"

Anthon shrugged. "I can't help all of them, but I can help him."

"What can he do, with that deformity?"

"I reckon he'll have a chance to find out now."

Her baby squirmed in her arms.

Hosanni blinked tears. He was only tired of being carried. He couldn't understand what her setting him down here would mean.

For you, my precious son. For you, I can do this.

Hosanni kissed the little blue cheek one last time. "Mum loves you, son."

Before she could change her mind yet again, she sat her precious baby down in an open space amongst the abandoned wee ones and forced herself to turn and walk away.

Anthon ran after her, carrying the baby. "Are ya loony? Ya can't do that!"

She choked out through a veil of tears, "I just did. By the law of the land, that's your son you're carrying in your arms. Not mine."

"My son?"

"You took him up from the gate, didn't you?"

Anthon looked at the baby boy content in his pappy's arms. "My son." He squeezed Havan Charisaner Juristekon tighter and kissed him. "Hosanni, I don't know what to say. This gift means more than you can ever know."

And cost me far more than I pray you can ever know, son. "I need to go home. I'll try to keep myself there long enough for him to forget me."

"Hosanni, you're always welcome, and Charis won't lie to him."

She nodded. The adoption would've been difficult to hide. "All I ask is you don't tell him that I'm the one who laid him at the gate unless he specifically asks about me."

"Charis should find that reasonable."

The baby boy in his pappy's arms reached for Hosanni. A bolt pierced her bosom. She turned and ran back to the Juristekons' garnet chariot. Her child's cries pelted her like hot coals.

Hosanni opened the trunk and fished out the carpetbag she'd smuggled inside. Everyone would be angry that she left without saying goodbye, but the longer she delayed, the more likely she was to give in and hold the baby. If she held him again so soon, she'd never again find the strength to leave.

Sobbing, Hosanni threw the carpetbag over her shoulder. She put one leaden foot in front of the other on the highway that would lead her home.

HAVAN ALETHANER KRISTEKON sat where he had every day but the Sabbath for over four years, inside his booth carving bridal ivory, this time to resemble roses. The roasting sun approached its zenith. Soon, Juris and the boys would come to woo him to dinner.

The highway pulled his gaze away from his work. He scanned for his daughter's family. Only the usual traffic streamed toward him.

He sighed and turned back to carving his ivory. "Amen, Amen, I pray you would tell your servant, is Juris right? Am I wasting my time? Should I focus on the family I have rather than waiting for the dead? Am I stealing time from my family by working away from home? Please grant me peace, if you wish me to continue this vigil. Juris knows what to say to make me feel guilty, and I'm certain to hear it all again shortly. Empower me to stand firm, if this is your will, for your name's sake, oh Emi our God, the lady of Heaven's vast armies."

The wind turned. A cool breeze rushed by. His spirit calmed.

He glanced to the highway. Trudging alone along his side of the road was a Diakrinthian woman in her early twenties. She wore a lavender palla and dragged a carpetbag. That was odd; where was her escort?

The windswept, shoulder-length dark violet hair sent his heart racing. No free woman wore her hair so short—and the women sentenced to hard labor in the mines were bald.

"Hosanni," whispered her pappy. It must be her. He reached under the counter, pulled Aletheia's shawl from its basket, and unfolded the resplendent linen banner to display the blue stripes forming a triangle around the griffin of Kristos.

Hiking up the skirt of his tunic, Pappy sped from the booth and down toward the young woman. Her footfalls dragged heavily with her shoulders weighed down. The closer Pappy came, the more he discerned his features on her face. "Hosanni!"

Her eyes connected with his. She stopped in her tracks. Her expression froze with a timid, almost fearful joy. "Father?"

The English word splashed like mud.

Pappy ran to his daughter and took her into his arms. "Hosanni!" Pappy kissed his precious little girl. He said in their tongue, "Amen, Amen, praise your name, Emi! You have brought my daughter home again!"

Hosanni whimpered, confusion dancing in moist eyes. "Father, I have sinned." She touched her shorn hair. "I am no longer worthy to be called the daughter of Kristos. I pray you, grant me favor in your sight, to let me be your man, that I might not be slain."

Those odd words ripped through Pappy. One, they were in English. Two, Hosanni spoke with a foreign accent. Three, the content itself. Let her be his slave, lest he kill her for sins she'd be still out in the world committing if she hadn't turned from them?

"What be this nonsense?" Pappy winced. He shouldn't have to use this loathsome tongue with his daughter. Maybe, if he spoke slowly, she would understand their own tongue. "Daughter, don't you know how much I love you?" Pappy threw the royal shawl over Hosanni's shoulders and covered her shorn hair. "Until your hair grows out completely, wear this outside the house, or if we have guests."

"Yes, Father." Hosanni wept. "Listen to me. So Xenos, barely I speak our tongue. And you forgive?"

His poor daughter. He squeezed her tight. "It'll come back. I promise."

A boy of twelve coming from the marketplace glanced at them curiously.

Pappy grinned wider. "You there! There's three pence for you if you'll run to the village at the end of that lane. Tell the husbands Lord Havan Alethaner Kristekon commands that the fatted calf be slain and a feast prepared, for my daughter was dead and is alive again. She who was lost is found."

The boy grinned. "Thank you, milord the king!" The boy raced ahead of them in the direction pointed out to him.

With his left arm still around his daughter's shoulders, Havan Alethaner turned and escorted Hosanni toward home. Good thing he could walk this route in his sleep. He could hardly take his eyes off his precious little girl.

The stains on her palla slapped him. Her bosom hadn't merely blossomed into full womanhood, his poor daughter was swollen to overflowing with milk that a very hungry baby Veritas hadn't suckled.

He glanced to the indentation on her right hand's middle finger. "Where are your husband and child?"

Wind shrieked and the traffic rambled around them with its cacophony.

Perhaps she hadn't understood him. He'd try again in English. "Where be your husband and baby?"

Her lower lip quivered. "I have none."

"Why does daughter lie? You have mark from missing wedding band on joining finger, and body of a mother. Where be your husband and baby?"

She glared. "Amen, amen, I have neither a husband nor a son!"

Tears moistened his eyes. So Lady Veritas would have an older brother when she was born. "Did you leave my grandson with my son? Why daughter come alone?"

Hosanni broke down sobbing. "Father, I have no husband. If I had a son, you would have to feed me to the dragons."

She abandoned her child in fear for her life? Did she know him so little? He spoke slowly in Diakrinthian. "Daughter, may Emi cause Hades to swallow up Pappy alive, if ever he would punish you for his own sins, when you have turned back to the path same as he."

Hosanni gasped, her eyes widening. "*Porneia*? My father?"

"I'll saddle the bull mastodon. Emi, save my grandson! But we should hurry, daughter, lest we tempt God."

His sobbing daughter ripped her palla and beat her breast. "Let me alone! I no leave a child to die. Let me alone!"

No. "You found someone besides me who would embrace a blue child?"

"Let me alone! Why think I have blue baby?"

"Daughter, I recall your tastes in men, and your English has a faint hint of an Eastern brogue." Pappy drew in a stabbing breath as they approached near to his booth. "Will you at least take me to see the baby?"

"Let me alone! Let me alone!"

"Pappy, who is this lady? She looks like us."

He tore his eyes from his poor daughter and glanced down to his four-year-old. His wife stood not far behind, with Agapan's eight-month-old baby brother in her arms, and her eyes wide and her face a pasty periwinkle.

Pappy glanced to his precious little girl.

She blinked at him, at the little brother pressing his chubby little fingers into Pappy's hand and pressing his chubby little face into Pappy's tunic. She stared at her aunt, carrying the baby.

Hosanni gaped, but then frowned, slipped into the opening stance of the dance of death, and ran screaming at her aunt.

What was she doing? She'd get herself killed. And he could only intervene this time to defend his lady.

Juris sidestepped and swept Hosanni's feet out from under her. Hosanni landed on her back on the pavement with a sickening thud. Juris leaned over Hosanni and swung an open palm at his daughter. Juris stopped just short of breaking Hosanni's nose, an injury that only dishonored the loser.

His wife straightened up and bounced their whimpering infant son on her hip, glaring at Hosanni. "You shall live with your honor, for your father's sake. Ever challenge me again, and I will show no such mercy, daughter."

At Hosanni's helpless glance, Pappy repeated his wife's words in English.

His daughter sat up and readjusted her shawl so it hid her short hair. She glared at Juris and hurled in Diakrinthian, "Thief. Fornicating with Father no make you Mother."

Now he had to step in. "You dishonor my wife." He winced. Perhaps his poor daughter had cause to assume *porneia* wrought her brothers. "Pardon, my brother and Aletheia died when you were thirteen. Juris is my wife now."

Hosanni stood, her eyes soft and mournful. She said in English, "Father, I am so sorry. Forgive me for not looking after your welfare sooner. My aunt has wickedly deceived you and taken advantage of a man's weakness. I'll re-pay your forgiveness of my sin in kind, but the path requires I hold her to account. Amen, amen, the History says that it is incest for a woman to have her sister's husband—or her husband's brother." Hosanni glared at Juris. "But you have stolen Mother's seat in the assembly as well, haven't you, Ravane?"

Juris winced. "That law no longer applies when my sister rests with our mothers, and ya be dead to us. I do my duty to my sister." She slid the arm not holding the baby through his, nudged their four-year-old forward, and said slowly, in their own tongue, "This is your brother, Agapan Alethaner."

Wide-eyed, little Agapan asked Hosanni in Diakrinthian, "Are you really my lost sister Hosanni? Why are you angry at Mammy? Please don't hate us. We love you."

His poor little boy. Pappy knelt and hugged the child. "Sissy is not really angry at Mammy. She's hurt and wants a villain to punish. Go sit in Pappy's booth while we soothe Sissy."

His four-year-old nodded and obeyed.

His nearly twenty-two-year-old trembled. Her eyes shone like an injured animal's. She said in English, "Ravane, your betrayal cuts me to the bone. I never dreamed you would dare to beguile Father into the evil Mother feared. You do not honor her in cutting off my name and calling your child by her name. If she knew of this, she would curse you for stealing her husband."

Juris spat. "So? Aletheia's dead!"

"But I'm not! You may no longer honor your elder sister, but I honor my mother. Your office will not let you get away with theft. I can and will appeal."

Juris scoffed. "To who, the aggies? They declared ya dead and invoked the law of sister marriage. Why will they now turn and tear apart our family?"

"I can appeal to the aggies' county and national councils."

"Please, think of your brothers. They be innocent babies. What they do to deserve death wished on them and their father taken away?"

"Nothing, amen, amen." Hosanni nodded. "Let the guilty woman suffer, not her children. The county aggies will be interested to hear my cause, and will grant them to me along with Father. That is a merciful penalty, given you deserve to be executed, and it's a fitting way for me to return your mercy."

"I told ya, the aggies forced us. What cause have ya against me?"

"You should've appealed to the county yourself. But you wanted to have him, though you well knew this marriage dishonors your sister. Or can you look me in the eye and say you honestly believed I was dead and that Mother would desire for her widower to marry her sister?"

Juris glanced away. Havan Alethaner grimaced. His wife still felt guilty?

"You see now, Father? Her own heart condemns her. To honor my aunt, I must call her to stop straying from the path. Only when her theft of my house ceases will the path permit me to return your mercy, as I long to, amen."

Sincerity shown in her eyes—as did fear. On top of the grief afflicting her, she was driven by a deep fear, if she accepted his remarriage, she would be condemning all three of their souls to Hades. "Daughter," he said softly, "am I correct that neither the county nor our local aggies will grant you anything unless you show yourself to be a wife and mother? If you cannot, will all then be granted to your aunt, including your own person?"

"It is so." She winced and glared at her aunt. "Ravane, I adjure you by the path of Diakrinth, return my house, or may Emi strike you!"

Juris whirled on Pappy, glaring. She spat in their tongue, "This is what you've been waiting all these years for? If I'm not mistaken, you've even sent a messenger to order a feast prepared in order to celebrate leaving me to abide as a widower in her house!"

"Pardon, my sister, but my daughter was dead. Now she is alive. How can we not rejoice over her?" Even if Hosanni was doing her best to make him wish she had stay dead. He had to convince her the attempts to "rescue" him from Juris were misguided. "Daughter, listen to me," he said in English, cupping Hosanni's face in his hands.

Hosanni drew back. "Father, I will hear you, but I am too old for that."

Pappy winced. "We be not thieves. Ya will receive your house, minus all persons, when ya present your husband or proof of him, such as his child. Until then, ya remain in our house." On second thought. "Well, ya can't dwell alone, but Irene and Korban be keeping Aletheia's house for me. Ya can take possession, if ya don't mind living with your married brother's family."

A relieved breath escaped his daughter. "Irene certainly should mind. At least I assume Korban has confessed to our childhood transgression?"

Pappy nodded. *At least she's over Korban. That's one small blessing.*

Juris squinted at his daughter. "Me ya condemn, and Irene ya forgive?"

Hosanni shook her head. "Korban was free to choose again, and there is no law against his choice, which is hardly shocking. Irene fancied him and she justly resented me for robbing her of his attentions. You, on the other hand, have stolen what you well know does not rightly belong to you."

Pappy hugged her. "Daughter, even if you be right, Juris is my wife now, and Emi hates dissolve. However ya have lost your own husband and child, I grieve your broken heart, but spreading heartbreak like the plague be no cure. Recall your curse, lest ya bring death to our house."

The baby cried.

Hosanni's gaze fell to him and a maternal longing softened her face.

Perhaps another baby could melt the ice hardening her heart. Pappy took the baby from Juris and placed the eight-month-old in his sister's arms.

She broke down sobbing, sure enough, and she headed home with them, cuddling and kissing the baby like a beggar devoured bread. Agapan resumed his usual jubilant chatter. She smiled at the child. "I will hold my peace."

BION presses the lever on the forbidden machine and a door opens stage left. He wrinkles his nose and coughs. ARGEVANE and GOD enter stage right.

BION. What is that foul smell?

GOD. Death, which you have unleashed on yourself and your wife and all your children. Because you have not heeded my voice, I will greatly multiply your sorrow in your reproduction; in pain you shall bring forth seed in the night. Your desire shall be for your wife and she shall rule over you, until the seed of Eve comes and lifts your head.

— Pauli of Denver, The Sacred History, "Creation" scene 2, lines 16-23

Chapter Twenty-Seven

A crisp autumn breeze washed over Havan Alethaner. He stopped Juris outside the assembly hall and hugged her. "Whatever the aggies want, I'm on your side, sister."

Juris trembled in his arms. "They want to take you away from me."

"But it's been over two years since Hosanni came home. She's held her peace, and no one else objected. Why would they change their minds now?"

"Now it's their babies burning with fever, not only our poor boys." Juris snuggled against him. "Honestly, brother, I haven't wanted to alarm anyone, but at the rate the plague is spreading, we'll all be on our beds with the plague before long. It's not fair. We've done everything we're supposed to. Why isn't Emi healing them? What am I missing?"

Other than consulting a witch?

Alethaner hesitated. It was awful curious. Hosanni had a keen interest in hygiene and nutrition and fighting disease, but she tried to hide it. She had to be a witch. She spent every moment beside her brothers' sickbeds, with agony dripping from her like sweat. Could she make them a magic healing potion? It would only take a few words in Hosanni's ear—how could he consider trading his daughter's eternal soul for her brothers' temporal lives? Witches dedicated their potions to idols. Any power in the brew came from demons.

No, they had their own medicine and their own god. They would continue to pray for the boys, anoint them, and minister the appropriate treatments for fever from *the Rites of Healing*.

Juris sniffled. "You're struggling with the temptation to ask Hosanni for a magic potion, too, aren't you?"

So he wasn't the only one who suspected.

Best to go back to solutions that wouldn't enslave his sons to demons as well as his daughter. "We could be more strict and not allow anyone who has even been around someone with the plague in the assembly."

Juris shuddered. "That's a thought for the future, but presently the first woman on my banned list would need to be the Ravane! And right under my name would be our entire assembly." She sighed and glanced at the assembly hall. "I guess I can't put off losing you forever."

"If you're right, they're being absurd. And I'll tell them just that."

"Amen, but do use the question mark liberally."

Alethaner nodded. He'd definitely needed that reminder. He took Juris's arm and escorted her inside the assembly. Déjà vu shot down his spine.

Elpis stood, not looking in their eyes. "The aggies elected me speaker."

Then speak.

Juris cleared her throat. "Get to the point."

"First, the aggies apologize to you and humbly acknowledge our iniquity, which is plain, for Emi's hand is against all of our houses. We must repent and offer worthy fruits, if we are to turn Emi's hand away from judgment and save our children. Ravane, consider the lives of your own children before you refuse to restore Hosanni's house in full. To compensate her for the loss of your office, return her father to her with both of his wee sons."

Juris's legs buckled.

Alethaner caught his wife in his arms. *Stay calm.* "May I speak?"

Elpis curtsied. "At your liberty, milord the king."

You'll live to regret that. "Most of you assembled today were here when I invoked a curse on you for suggesting I rape my daughter Irene. How quickly did Emi strike Lady Zoe? How promptly did the curse lift when I interceded? Why connect this current suffering, which is common to Argevane, to angry words my daughter spoke over two years ago? She too fears she caused this. She has spent six days and six nights interceding before Emi, pleading with Emi to spare all of the deathly ill children, her brothers especially."

Elpis wrinkled her nose. "Only your son Agapan is Aletheia's child. The baby belongs to Juris, although he is to become your lent grandson and your only son's nephew. Thus, both boys will remain in your house as only sons."

Men's liberation made more sense than that did. "Still, if this plague is Emi's judgment against me for choosing my brother's widow, why then has Hosanni's earnest intercession not turned aside Emi's hand?"

"Only repentance can abate Emi's wrath this time, milord."

"Why would Emi make it impossible for me to keep the path? You know the male curse. My daughter would never give me away, even if I would ever choose another bride besides my loving Juris. Pray, consider my soul, aggies, and not subject an old man to such torment. Further, were not Emi's laws intended to keep families together, not to pull them apart?"

Elpis hesitated and turned to the aggies. "Those who wish to withdraw their agreement at this time, say so."

Zoe and half the aggies answered, "So."

The other half refused to look at him.

Elpis turned back his way. Her lips pinched and her eyes narrowed. "As we are divided, we can neither censure nor compel Ravane. With great regret, we hereby suspend proceedings until further notice."

Juris sighed and hugged and kissed Havan Alethaner. He returned in kind, grinning wide. His marriage was secure. The aggies wouldn't revisit an issue they'd rendered controversial.

Wailing pierced the air and his heart. No. That couldn't be his house.

Juris ran out. He followed her trail home. "Juris!"

In the door of their home, he froze. Hosanni sat between the sickbeds. She'd removed the ribbons from the twin braids that fell to her mid-back and had torn her teal palla to the waistband of her underpants. Wailing, Hosanni clung to the motionless body of her youngest brother.

Juris snatched the three-year-old from Hosanni and shook him. "Wake up!" She released the child, wailed as loudly as her stepdaughter, and ripped her garments as deeply.

Numbness hit Havan Alethaner. No. This happened to other parents. Not to him, not to his children. This had to be a terrible nightmare.

His wife climbed upstairs.

Moments later, his clothes and Hosanni's began to rain down.

Irene and their other five daughters crowded into the kitchen, including Korban and his boys. The wailing and fabric tearing multiplied tenfold. Irene anointed the small body for burial and slipped it inside of a linen tunic that swallowed up her youngest brother.

Havan Alethaner ripped his tunic, beat his breast, and wept.

His son Agapan coughed and spat up blood.

Juris began tossing Alethaner's and Hosanni's belongings out the door.

No. He reached out to her. "Juris . . . ."

She whirled to the sobbing Hosanni and yanked her up. "Take him and anything else you believe belongs to you and go!"

No. "Juris . . . ."

His wife finally met his eyes. Death shone white in them. "I am not losing any more of my children! To your own house with you! Go!"

So grief-induced madness was taking his wife from him, too. Alethaner's lower lip quivered as he sought his voice. "As you wish, milady. I will depart. But I will always be there for you when you call."

Korban wrapped strong carpenter arms around him and whispered, "You and Hosanni can stay with us until Mother comes to her senses, Father."

His eldest son's support sapped his last ounce of strength.

Before the night ended, Irene wrapped Agapan Alethaner in a shroud.

HOSANNI MARCHED DOWN the path toward the highway. The waning aggie moon shone faintly amongst the clouds. Hosanni's hair flapped freely for her precious little boys lying so cold and stiff in the family tomb.

Her half-grown female dragonling burst onto the shadowy path. The animal tilted her head to one side. Hosanni lifted her lantern and highlighted the short, three-clawed arms signing in Draca every single thought to enter the beast's head.

Hosanni said, "I can't see as well in the dark as you do, Daisy."

The dragonling started her signing over. "Where is foolish, impulsive Mother going in dark? Brave, loyal Daisy protect sad, hurt Mother."

Impertinent, conceited Daisy was only cutting her adult teeth and not all that much protection. "You have your nerve, little girl. I wouldn't take that insult from a human child, and you think I'll take it from a dumb animal?"

"Smart, wise Daisy still ask what beautiful, forgiving Mother is doing."

Hosanni pointed. "Look, I think I see road kill!"

The dragonling narrowed her yellow eyes and sniffed.

Hosanni shivered. Being hand-raised by humans occasionally resulted in a dragonling that mimicked human body language. "Sorry. You're right.

You'd smell it long before I saw it."

A light rain sprinkled them. Hosanni sighed, lowered the lantern, went around Daisy, and continued on the dirt path. "I'm going to wake a druggist in McCall. I have to leave now, when everyone's asleep. I'm not supposed to go anywhere during the initial mourning period, let alone to buy medicine that could get me executed as a witch if I get caught administering it."

Frantic dragon arms waved beside her, indecipherable from this angle.

"Look. Those babies were my only consolation—besides you, of course. I've done everything according to the path, and now they're gone. I'm tried of watching my loved ones die senselessly." She bit her lip. "I've seen subjects die even with proper treatment, but we lose two to three out of a hundred instead of eighty to a hundred out of a hundred. I can't fix the living conditions here that turn such an ordinary epidemic into a horrific medieval plague, but I have to do something. I'll have to hide it from the others, but I should be able to slip my cousins enough medicine."

Daisy bounded beside Hosanni. Truth be told, she was going a bit over a dragon's head, a dragonling especially. But what choice did she have? Every lady, maiden, and grandchild to her aunt's name was gravely ill. Losing her cousins would be bad enough, and she'd have to return Korban and Irene to Ravane if Ravane was left desolate. And Korban's wee ones were starting to cough and ache, too. Without proper treatment, the disease taking its toll on Ravane's house might not stop until the whole village died.

No, she had to do this.

At the junction, Daisy stiffened and sniffed the air curiously. She emitted tentative hissing barks, bounded to the booth, and wiggled through the door.

Hosanni stopped a few feet away, glanced down through the opening, and gaped—her dragonling lay at the feet of a stranger. Not even Dorcas would ever have done that.

Hosanni peered at the sojourner taking shelter in the booth. By physical appearance, he would be indistinguishable in any crowd of Diakrinthian men, other than the fact his white robes looked more like an ankle-length palla than an indigo tunic. But that didn't explain why her dragonling was doing Draca's equivalent of lying prostrate before the sojourner.

She raised the lantern. The light transfigured his hair and skin from the gray of night to the reddish-brown color of a cedar's bark.

He stooped and patted her dragonling on the head. "Well done, Daisy."

What? How did he know her dragonling's name? "Daisy, come here."

Daisy glanced up at the sojourner as if asking his permission. He nodded. The dragon whined, backed out of the booth, and turned to face Hosanni. Daisy sent a longing look back at the sojourner.

Hosanni forced breath into her lungs and forced her quaking knees to hold her. "Daisy, why did you do that for a stranger?"

Daisy signed, "No stranger come. Master come. Smelling, hearing Daisy lay at Master's feet. Why is unsmelling, deaf Mother standing?"

Either Hosanni's comprehension of Draca wasn't as good as she thought, or Daisy had mistaken the sojourner for "their" pod's alpha male. The beasts were hopeless at understanding a king rightly served a queen. "Why did you tell him your name?"

Daisy squinted at her. "Master knows Daisy."

Yes, but how?

HOSANNI'S FOUR NEPHEWS and the boys' pappy clapped at her kitchen table after she and Irene finished a two-woman resurrection dance.

Korban whistled and said in English, "Mum's smoking hot, right, lads?"

Smiling, Hosanni slipped outside. Korban's bias toward his own wife was natural, but Irene would demure to Hosanni if given opportunity.

Korban ran after her, gaping. "And where are ye goin'?"

"A sojourner arrived late last night."

"Hosanni, this has to be the worst time for guests."

No quarrel there. Half the village was on their beds with the plague, and the other half was sure to join them by the end of the week. And the entire village could be dead in two weeks if they continued refusing to take modern medicine. She swallowed. "The sojourner has a skin condition that will make our country most inhospitable to him, and he's not contagious; it looks like a genetic mutation to me. So I told him that he could sleep in the hayloft."

Korban winced and turned his head.

Hosanni sighed. "Can't I mention the hayloft without you acting guilty? Brother, I've already forgiven you four times now for attempting to devour my maidenhood, and you were never responsible for my kidnapping. Now stop blaming yourself, let the past go, and get to the house of mourning."

"After you."

"Go on without me. I need to check if our guest needs anything." Hosanni kissed her brother's cheek farewell and ran off to the barn.

Please, Emi, let the sojourner be single—and willing to be bound for a whole year to a bride who has no intention of marrying him.

She swung open the barn doors, hesitated, and then called, "Milord?"

The sojourner came out and waited as she stared at him all over again. Daylight added to his mystery horrific scars piercing the roots of his hands and his feet. She'd seen such wounds before, but not on anyone who'd lived.

Hosanni's knees quaked. "Who are you? What is your name?"

The sojourner laughed in good humor. "Why do you ask after my name? Even if I gave it, you would call me Soterion."

Odd. Soterion was the Diakrinthian Greek form of a Hebrew name translated into every tongue still known to womankind. Most would use their own variant rather than what his mother called him, but his tone made it feel like he knew her. "Soterion it is then. Do you need any provisions?"

"Don't worry. I have ten thousand servants who minister to me."

He had to be a prince to have so many. But he appeared alone.

"You thought I was alone."

Was she that obvious? "Aren't you?"

"You have eyes and don't see. How is it a Ravane's daughter doesn't know the things of God? Your own History tells you that Emi will never leave you nor forsake you, Hosanni."

She hesitated. "Not those exact words, but the sentiment's there, amen."

Soterion had called her by name. She had not told him her name, or that Mother was a Ravane. Master—what had Daisy meant?

A sick husband who belonged in bed came to tend the animals, with the stiff neck of someone doing his best not to stare at Soterion's odd red-brown coloring. Hosanni and Soterion moved away from the barn, toward home and the house of mourning.

They met a horde of dragons. The young dragons of their own village had run off and returned now with dragons from the neighboring villages. Every one of them bowed down before Soterion. A chorus of hissing groans arose.

Hosanni gasped. The din in her ears was Draca's notion of singing.

She stared at Soterion the Dragonmaster. "In God's name, who are you?"

Soterion chuckled. "Ask the dragons, they will tell you who I am."

The choir's waving forelimbs signed to her, "Master. Master. Master."

She trembled. "Who is your master?"

"The Word. The Word. He made us."

Logos, the manifestation in human form of the words Emi sang in the creation song that brought everything into existence. Since Emi was Spirit, it was the hands of Logos that had formed Argevane and Bion out of the dust. Ravanes much debated the exact relationship between Logos and Emi herself, and whether likening Logos to Emi's hand violated Emi's oneness or upheld it, but certainly Logos was a most special daughter of heaven.

A most special *son* of heaven. Logos? Heart pounding, Hosanni fell to her knees, cowering as she addressed him in her native tongue. "Depart from me, for I am a sinful woman."

"Don't be afraid." A cedar hand lifted her up. Eyes filled with the glory of Heaven met hers. "I chose you before the cosmos began, and from the womb I declared you to be the most blessed of the daughters of Argevane."

Dizziness rolled over Hosanni. To be the mother of Lady Veritas? But chose her implied for marriage. She touched the ribbons on her right wrist, waiting for a bridegroom to give her a reason to braid her hair even though she was in mourning. "How can this be?"

"There is the joining of the flesh, and there is the joining of the spirit. A bridegroom after the flesh gives his bride life that perishes. The Bridegroom from Heaven gives his bride eternal life. I am the Bridegroom from Heaven."

A tingle passed through her. He spoke Diakrinthian like a native, but he pronounced *Eimi*—I am—as Emi. What did he mean to imply? "Amen, we must be joined to Emi's house and be anointed with the consecrated wine, which is the blood of the Sacrifice. But my mothers' tradition bars me from these sacraments unless a bridegroom takes my ribbon, and Ravane has whispered terrible rumors so that no mother will give me a son."

"Whom you don't want because the marriageable men are Anthon's age."

Hosanni winced. He surely also knew how tempting she found it to hope for Coyote to come and be her Meleon again. "Amen, I don't desire another bridegroom after the flesh, but I do desire to make my confession and have the wine poured over me."

Soterion turned. She looked past him and the bowing dragons. A crowd had assembled before the house of mourning, including Hosanni's household and her aunt. From their gaping mouths and bulging eyes, they had heard and seen all these mysteries. And Ravane glared at the dragons, who would kill her if she made any threatening moves toward their master.

He said to Ravane, "Why do you shut up the kingdom of Heaven to this daughter for the sake of your tradition?"

Only the wind whistling through the ponderosa pines answered.

"To fulfill the prophecy in the Gospel Song, your hearts are hardened. So you will no longer hinder her from entering in, I will take her ribbon. A year from when I depart, she will be free before you to marry whom she wishes. But when she rests with her mothers, I will come for her and take her up to Heaven. If that is acceptable to you?"

Odd, that question sounded an awful lot like sarcasm.

Ravane shrugged. "She is of age. If she accepts you, that is her liberty. But why do you, a man, and unclean with leprosy, dare to speak so to a woman?"

Korban gasped. "Mother, he's not unclean. He's a brownie."

Hosanni squinted at him. "Since when do you believe in Erini myths?"

"Since a brown-skinned man actually came to us."

Ravane glared at Korban. "He can answer for himself why he dares to speak in this manner to a woman, and we are in mourning even."

Soterion said, "Why is it that you cry out, 'Emi's hand, save our children!' when Emi's hand has given you a physician, and you bind her in chains?"

Ravane coughed. "If you were indeed a man of honor, you would know it is not the path to practice witchcraft nor to consult witches."

"Bring me herbs from the field."

A lad of seven ran and brought back white yarrow, one ingredient of the witches' brew Hosanni kept mentally concocting.

Soterion held up the flowers and asked everyone, "Who made these and gave them unto you?"

The child recited, "Emi made these. God created every herb of the field and gave them unto us."

"Amen." Soterion looked upon all assembled. "You have heard it said, 'have no part of anything offered to idols.' I tell you, but rather give God the glory, for the Cosmos is Emi's and the fullness thereof. Drink whatever the druggist sells you, asking no questions for conscience's sake, but if anyone says to you, 'This was offered to idols,' do not drink it."

Hosanni's heart beat fast. "And grow what I can myself?"

Soterion nodded.

"But will the medicine work without the incantation?"

"Who has the power to save, Time and Chance, or Emi?"

Her cheeks grew warm. "Emi."

Ravane stumbled as close to him as she could get without climbing over the bowing dragons. "If I baptize her and delegate the healing rites to her, with the liberty to minister to the sick in the name of Emi as she sees fit, will you then leave the bereaved to mourn in peace?"

"You shall be comforted."

Ravane humphed. "I will settle for stopping this accursed plague before it devours our entire village."

Chapter Twenty-Eight

Havan Alethaner sat on a stool inside his wife's carpenter shop. Korban's three potty-trained sons and the boys' seven young friends were coughing far less than they had been as they all watched and listened to Soterion's stories while he filled cabinet orders with Korban.

Sweat dampened every indigo tunic inside the overcrowded, overheated workshop, but the women would have their heads if they caught them in here wearing only their underwear.

Arching his back, Korban wiped sweat from his brow. Alethaner sighed. If his son wasn't so ashamed of the scar in his side, he would surely risk the women's ire.

Soterion pulled off his snow-white robes and laid them aside. The twelve sons of Argevane present gasped at Soterion's disfigurement. His back had been flayed to an extent that should've killed him. Korban stared at Soterion's side, who said, "At your liberty."

Korban thrust his hand upwards into Soterion's side, the same side as his own despised scar. Korban's entire hand vanished and a good chunk of his forearm as well. The wound in Soterion's side had been much deeper than the wound that had nearly killed Korban.

One of the wide-eyed boys pointed at Soterion. "You were flogged and nailed up high! And the soldiers pierced your side. To make sure you were dead. But now you're not. You're alive!"

Another child whispered, "Like the sun dies each night and is faithfully resurrected again each morning?"

Soterion nodded to the children, his eyes twinkling victoriously.

Korban shed his indigo tunic. Korban's boys imitated their father. Their friends copied them. Korban and Soterion got back to work.

The evidence before Havan Alethaner turned his world upside down and set it afire. Tears filled his eyes. No wonder Draca had come for miles to bow down and worship King Soterion. This humble builder had in truth built the entire cosmos. And he had come to redeem the entire cosmos from the grave. Alethaner missed his precious little boys, but he would see them again, amen. Juris, on the other hand . . . what if she were forever lost to him?

Soterion asked, "Who do women say that I am?"

Korban bit his lip. "Some say a man of honor, or a prophet. Some say you 'might' be a son of Heaven."

Alethaner sniffled. "And some say you're a wolf and a sorcerer, despite admitting that your teaching this morning was Veritas." Namely his Juris.

"And who do you say that I am?"

The children and Korban all glanced to Alethaner.

He swallowed. Soterion was a mystery, and the answers ringing in his heart were, well, blasphemy.

Kristos Havan Alethaner knelt before Soterion. "You are the very Logos of Emi, the Kristos of Kristos, the son of the living God. And, mysteriously, a son of Eve. And Emi's Sacrifice." He dared a glance into his maker's eyes and saw the impossible truth. "And Logos isn't merely Emi's hand, as it is said."

"Blessed are you, Havan Alethaner Kristekon, for flesh and blood has not revealed this to you, but my Father. And I and my Father are one."

Dizziness knocked Alethaner on his rear. *Here, oh Diakrinth, Emi is God. Emi is one.* He swallowed hard. Emi could've sent Logos as a conquering high queen like Agapeta. Instead, Logos had come as the Son, as the King—as a mere slave? Yet the supposedly wolfish traits he'd been taught to suppress, he'd seen in Soterion's eyes—eyes full of the glory and might of Emi.

"Amen, amen, because of your faith, I chose your house for Veritas to join. I am the path of truth that leads to eternal life. Follow me, but see that you tell no one who I am until all things are fulfilled."

They all released relieved breaths, including Alethaner. The boys would only be caned for this, but he and Korban could well be executed.

And by my own wife. Alethaner swallowed. "Master, is it against the path to want Juris back when she did not know you and is a stranger to the truth? I ache for her in my loins."

"What Emi has adhered, let no daughter dissolve. Your wife will repent of forsaking her vows in a season. Love her. Honor her as I have honored you. She could be saved through your conduct."

If only Hosanni would forgive Juris for not being Aletheia.

At a female gasp, Korban yanked his tunic back on.

Alethaner glanced to the door. Hosanni stood there staring, probably at the punishment Soterion had taken for their wrongs.

"What is going on?" Hosanni asked, covering her mouth. "We have three days left in the mourning week, and you're in here working?"

Soterion asked her, "Can the friends of the bridegroom mourn as long as the bridegroom is with them?"

Hosanni sighed. "Logos appearing is an event on par with a holiday."

The mourning week ended early whenever a major holiday fell during it. Alethaner nodded. "That was our sentiment exactly, daughter."

Hosanni's left eye twitched. "I have bad news. The epidemic is in McCall, and they're out of the imported medicine. I must go to the City of Trees."

This late in the day, she wouldn't be back until tomorrow. She'd still save the village from all dying, but his five dying stepdaughters couldn't wait another day. "Can you make them a potion with what you have?"

"Father, I'd prefer the term tea, and yes. Since our entire village has been exposed, I'll need our house and Aunt Juris's house to help distribute the teas, but I've already made up enough to last until I get back. However, it's of most benefit when administered early. The medicine I need to buy is my cousins' only hope. Others will need it, too, so it's still worth going for, even if Emi's hand doesn't allow my cousins to hang in there until my return."

Havan Alethaner glanced to Soterion and found him dressed, with tears in his eyes. He swallowed. Emi's silence in response to the healing rites had communicated a resounding no, and it wouldn't do to ask a man of honor to defy his mother—or his father. Nor could he blame Emi; if Emi healed them, the aggies would judge it a reward of Juris separating what Emi had joined together. It'd draw the village further from the true path, not closer.

But Soterion wept.

Korban swallowed. "Hosanni, please excuse me from my duty to escort you. This is not a good time for me to leave Irene and our sons."

Alethaner turned to his daughter and blinked at Hosanni's smile.

She said, "Korban, I wouldn't think of taking you away from your family, least of all at a time like this. I thought I'd offer Soterion the honor."

Soterion stepped into view. "Beloved, I am willing to offer you this honor, if your father escorts you to the City of Agapeta. I will meet you outside Lady Agnes Juristekon's villa shortly before sunset."

Hosanni frowned, scientific skepticism crossing her face.

Alethaner laughed. "Daughter, he'll be waiting for us." He rushed out to pack what he'd need for the journey.

Pray, let that villa have the grandson Hosanni bore.

THE BULL MASTODON STOOD where Hosanni had left him, on the path outside her home. She had everything packed and ready to go. Save for her escort. She patted the wooly beast's neck. "Down, Jeschuron."

Jeschuron sat down. Hosanni settled sidesaddle on the driver's pillow, right behind the beast's head. A tear rolled down her cheek. If only she was waiting for Soterion. She'd so hoped to spend tonight with her precious son. Now she'd have to simply race down and back, ignoring Father's protestations that highway travelers faced grave risk of robbery at night.

Do not tempt Emi your God, beloved.

Odd. That had to be her conscience, so why did it sound like Soterion?

Soterion stole up on her. "Have you still not yet learned that I shall never leave you nor forsake you? Amen, amen, I am with you always, even to the end of the age."

"But . . ." Hosanni sighed. Soterion was Logos. He wouldn't tell her to meet him where she'd wanted to go and bring her father if it'd bring evil. "I was wrong to give away my only son, but it'd be cruel to take him back. Would you please bless my precious son anyway?"

"I'll gladly lay hands on your son and pray over him, but your son already has been blessed beyond measure."

Hosanni frowned. "Beg your pardon?"

"You are both my bride and High Queen as prophesied. Your son Havan is the bridegroom of Veritas. He wields his mother's scepter as one of the greatest kings of your dynasty since King Phoenix reigned with his mother."

Hosanni grinned. Such a glorious prophecy. Emi would deliver Diakrinth from Romin, and she'd get her son back. Lady Charis would regard raising her king as the privilege of privileges. And none in Diakrinth was more fit to raise a king than Prince Antonio.

HAVAN ALETHANER SAT at the straw-woven table inside the empty hireling house. Hosanni had left him here while she and Soterion rushed against the dying sun to get her shopping done so she and Alethaner could head home as soon as the morning's resurrection dance ended.

But tonight he bounced on his knee his blue, slightly feverish, three-year-old grandson. His grin burst from every inch of his weary, fifty-year-old body. *She named him after me!*

The child had to be rightly Havan Hosanner Kristekon. Why else would the Juristekons leave Alethaner alone with a little boy who looked like him? Well, other than the medium purple skin, the ears, the Erini nose, and the adorable little dreadlocks. But why else would they single out this child when Lady Charis had greeted him with another dreadlocked little boy in indigo and a swaddled baby in a sling?

Little Havan sat curled up on Grandfather's lap, holding in chubby little hands an early reader about a draca named Spot. His grandson sounded out each English word. Alethaner's grin widened. Even the boy's mother couldn't read in any language until she was five.

Hosanni had chosen well for his grandson, after all. The child was so gifted. In the City of Trees, with this family, his grandson would have more opportunities to reach his full potential, to become the king his grandfather always longed to be.

Shame, though, the Juristekons hadn't taught his grandson Diakrinthian. Worse, he'd miss the boy awful. At least until the boy turned thirteen and could be lent back, to learn his true identity. Per the example of the widowed warrior queen, High Queen Agapeta, and her son King Phoenix, the boy had been Kristos Havan II, King of Diakrinth, from his very first breath.

And to think she named this great king after me!

Anthon Juristekon came in from outside. He lowered the cloth bandit's mask that had covered his mouth and nose and washed his hands at the sink.

Huh? "Why are you behaving like you're unclean? You appear to be fine."

"By Emi's hand, amen." Anthon spun and bowed. "Milord, forgive me, I've taken advantage of your lack of knowledge. My son is being treated for the epidemic. The doctor says a prior, weaker infection appears to have kept me from falling ill again now, but I may be as contagious as my son is. So we've both been cooped up here for nigh a week, under the doctor's orders."

Hmm. His host blended the way Diakrinthians spoke English with the Californian accent and hint of a brogue his daughter had brought home. "It be my pleasure to keep the boy."

"But he's contagious."

"So be my house, son."

Anthon flinched.

Why? Anthon didn't look a day past nineteen. What else did he expect a man of fifty to call him? "My daughter Hosanni be here to buy medicine. How does she know ya?"

Anthon cleared his throat. "Thank you for watching him anyway."

Little Havan announced, "Pappy, I'm reading! Shut up and listen."

Grandfather chuckled. He got spanked quite a bit for such impertinence.

Anthon frowned. "Don't encourage him."

"My apologies. He reminds me of when I was a wee one."

Anthon grunted and knelt on the pillow across from them. "Son, we will listen when you ask us right."

Little Havan snuggled closer to Grandfather. "Will you and Grandfather please listen to me read, Pappy?"

Anthon's eyebrows shot up and he recoiled. "Grandfather?"

Grandfather grinned. "The boy be awful young to grasp that he not be the only Havan in the cosmos."

The boy twisted and frowned at him. "I'm not?"

"See what I mean?" He kissed his grandson's little blue forehead. "Havan used to be my name, but I reckon ya can keep it. Looks better on ya anyhow."

Soterion and Hosanni entered. She carried a full burlap shopping bag.

Little Havan gasped, leaped up, and ran to Hosanni with his arms flung open, begging her to pick him up. "Mum!"

Havan Alethaner gaped. He'd suspected the child was gifted, but that was phenomenal. A normal child, even a bright one like Hosanni had been, would never have remembered her. What child was this? The Bridegroom of Veritas was expected to be a man as any other, with no splendor of his own.

His daughter's eyes glistened as she lifted her child up to her hip and clasped him to her breast. She cuddled her child a moment before she shot Anthon a scolding glance.

Anthon raised his hands. "Don't look at me, Mum. I've been a good boy."

Hosanni stared at the little boy clinging to her. "I must be a stranger to you, so why did you call me Mum?"

Little Havan shrugged. "I'm adopted. That means I have two Mammies and two Pappies. But my brothers only have one Mammy and one Pappy. And nobody remembers the day they were born. But I have scary dreams about the gate." A little pouty lip jutted out. "You left me."

Tears wet Hosanni's cheeks. "I had to go. I have my own house."

"Bring it here."

Soterion sent Alethaner a silent challenge.

He winced. "Daughter, why don't ya stay? I can take the medicine back."

His grandson beamed. "Please, Mum! Stay home. Please!"

Hosanni stroked and kissed her baby. "I can't, love. It's unlawful for a woman to forsake her inheritance. Besides, I am the only doctor my village trusts. People will die if I stay here."

Little Havan sniffled, tearing up. "But I miss you."

Hosanni glanced to Alethaner. She nodded. "We will have to leave early tomorrow morning, but we'll come back to visit as often as we can."

His grandson sighed. "Don't stay gone so long anymore." Little Havan turned to Soterion. "You look weird."

Anthon groaned. "Havan! Don't be rude."

Soterion smiled. "I'm a son of Adam, the twin of Argevane, amen. The daughters of Eve have brown skin, only we don't have pointed ears by nature. Cain didn't want to tell Argevane how he got his."

The child smirked at Anthon. "See, Pappy? Brownies are so real!"

Anthon glowered, looking far more like an irritated older brother than a Pappy. "Son, he's putting you on. It's a rare skin disease."

Havan Alethaner bit his lip. He could hardly wait until all things were fulfilled and he could tell them who Soterion was. Or, on second thought, until the day Lady Veritas herself sang for them all the whole glorious song.

Don't miss out!

Visit the website below and you can sign up to receive emails whenever Andrea J. Graham publishes a new book. There's no charge and no obligation.

https://books2read.com/r/B-A-EQLI-HORFB

BOOKS 2 READ

Connecting independent readers to independent writers.

Did you love *Daughter of Kristos*? Then you should read *Is There Life After Mars?*[1] by Andrea J. Graham!

On the Martian Frontier in 2084, a mystery illness threatens to kill twelve-year-old farm girl Gloria Patri Fowler Cruz. This provokes her dad, Mama's aristocrat ex-husband Peyton, to defy social class divisions that ripped him from his family. And Gloria's new, wearable medical device doesn't work without an artificial intelligence. She substitutes her entertainment AI, dressed as a digital dog, Jake. Her AI develops human qualities, thanks to magic that he believes comes from God. Gloria questions if she can trust her dad, Jake, or God. In the colony's capitol, Peyton's vice admiral father rules like a king, hates Mama's family, and will do anything to keep them out of the aristocracy. But politics is Dad's thing. Gloria would rather clobber her "bro forever," Holter Sloan. He has no time to play. He's too busy crushing on her fraternal twin!

Read more at www.christsglory.com.

1. https://books2read.com/u/3kpxAg

2. https://books2read.com/u/3kpxAg

Also by Andrea J. Graham

Argevane Series
Daughter of Kristos

Life After Mars Series
Is There Life After Mars?
Life After Venus!
Life After Mercury
Life After Paradise: Into the Web Surfer Universe

Web Surfer Series
Web Surfer ANI
Nimbus Rider
Restoring: Web Surfer 3.0
Reconciling: Web Surfer 4.0

Watch for more at www.christsglory.com.

About the Author

Andrea Graham studied creative writing and religion at Ashland University, has been envisioning fantastic worlds since age six, and has been writing science fiction novels since she was fourteen. Bear Publications released her book, *Avatars of Web Surfer,* which she wrote with three co-authors. She is the wife of author Adam Graham and edits his novels, including *Tales of the Dim Knight* and *Slime Incorporated.* Her own publishing imprint, Reignburst Books, released the Web Surfer Series and the Life After Mars Series. Find her as an author at christsglory.com and as an editor at povbootcamp.com.

Andrea and Adam live with their dog, Rocky, and their cat, Bullwinkle, in Boise, Idaho. They're adopting their first child.

Read more at www.christsglory.com.

About the Publisher

This is the personal imprint of Andrea J. Graham, who dreams of turning it into a full-service publishing company along with partners who would share her vision for a company staffed by Christians willing to go beyond the limits of the CBA while still being true to theGod whose reign is ready to burst forth in unexpected, undreamed of ways.

CPSIA information can be obtained
at www.ICGtesting.com
Printed in the USA
BVHW082048190620
581883BV00001B/68

9 781393 615729